Johnnie R. Jones

Acts

of the

Spirit-Filled

Volume 1

a novel
of the
first century

CrossHouse Publishing
2844 S. FM 549
Suite A
Rockwall, TX 75032
www.crosshousebooks.com

The Arial Narrow font used in this volume designates quotations from the
Scriptures (paraphrased by the author) and dialogue by God, Jesus, and
the Holy Spirit.

ISBN: 978-1-61315-038-2

Library of Congress: 2012955553

What others are saying about
Acts of the Spirit-Filled

"*The* Acts of the Spirit-Filled *is an excellent reading in the Scriptures. The way Johnnie Jones has clarified, personalized, and enlivened the characters and circumstances is a creative way of reading the* Book of Acts. *I highly endorse this book for all age groups.*"

—Dr. Rickey Hargrave, Secretary,
International Conference of Police Chaplains

"*Johnnie Jones is a remarkable storyteller! The pages of this novel will give a different look at the early years of Christianity as it appears in the Book of Acts. He has captured the humanity of those first believers and the power of God working in their midst. Although a fictional account, it is consistent with the history as recorded by Dr. Luke. You will be blessed through these pages . . . and challenged!*"

—Dr. Jimmy Draper, President Emeritus,
LifeWay Christian Resources

"*I think the* Acts of the Spirit-Filled *will put Acts deeper in my heart . . . I like that.*"

—Pam C.

"*Love it! Can't wait to read the rest!*"

—Marilyn G.

"*When I read this novel, I was taken back to a time and place that I'd always heard about, but had a hard time envisioning.* Acts of the Spirit-Filled *takes you on the roads of Bible times and into dramatic events that keep you wanting to read more. You won't want to put this book down as you read the events that the apostles and others experienced in this time period. Straight from the Scriptures, this novel gives a unique behind-the-scenes look as only a novel could do. Johnnie Jones writes with an accurate knowledge of the Scriptures and history while telling a story worth sharing with everyone, Christian or not."*

—Jenny M.

"Johnnie Jones is a very creative writer. He is biblically sound in his research, yet very thought provoking in his presentation. I highly recommend his novel on Acts."

—Dr. Mike Smith, President of Jacksonville College, Jacksonville, Texas

"Two thousand years separate us from the disciples' paths and the hardships they endured. In Acts of the Spirit-Filled, *Johnnie Jones retells the acts of the first-century believers in a way that challenges us today to reconsider our mission as the body of Christ. This book will remind you of the power of God and His coming Kingdom. Around the world today, there is a tsunami of sexual immorality. Our need to make disciples and plant churches is vital. If read seriously, Johnnie's book will help us stem the tides of today's spiritual storms."*

—Derek Ross, National Director, True Love Waits Philippines; www.truelovewaitsphilippines.org

"Johnnie Jones has done an excellent job of retelling the story of the first-century church and its leaders. It is told in an interesting, descriptive way that keeps you enthralled, anxious for more!"

—Lynne C.

To

Diane E. Jones

Wife

Mother

Nana

Piano Teacher

An inspiration to me and others;

A follower of our Risen Lord.

Other books by the author:

50/50 Chance to Live – An Autobiography

Transformed! – The Power of God's Presence

Metamorphosis – Changes from Within

Metamorphosis 2 – The Transforming Power of Intimacy with God

Children's Guide to Discovering Jesus – Activity Pages

Diakonos – A Word Study and Service Guide for the Deacon Ministry

P.E.D.A.L. Plan for Evangelism

Refer to "About the Author" in the back of this volume for information on his other books.

Contents

Anno
Domini
30

Circa

Prologue

"*Deus Sol Invictus; Deus Sol Invictus!*" Toward the east, Tiberius looked into the darkest hour. "Invincible god of the sun, arise and burn up the advances against my enemies!" The scribe wrote carefully as the emperor paced the floor, chanting toward the eastern horizon, awaiting the dawn of a new day. There was silence for a moment . . . then he spoke again. "There is a people whose love for the divine spurn our gods, and they spurn me!"

"O Divine One?" asked the scribe. "Who would dare spurn man's deity? Who would dare spurn your power?"

The emperor continued his easterly gaze. "They see the Unseen One as their Deity—not our gods and not me!"

The scribe returned to his quiet writing. For hours, the emperor had been awake, pacing the floor, talking—speaking many words of random thoughts.

Suddenly, over the distant, eastern range, the sun burst forth in rays of beauty. "There, scribe!" the emperor cried, as he pointed to the sun. "There is one of our gods!" He shielded his eyes as he squinted at the brilliant ball of fire.

"Yes, Divine One, there is *Sol*."

"How can these people not worship it? How can their Unseen One exceed the glory of this brilliance!?"

The scribe began to write again, but the emperor grabbed his quill and threw it to the floor. He lifted the scribe out of his chair and turned him to face the east. "Look with me, scribe; do you see beyond the sun? Is this not our supreme god!?"

The scribe feared to move his hand to shield the sun's rays. He opened his eyes, trying not to disclose his indirect stare into the blinding ball of fire. "Divine One, many of your servants remain sightless today for trying to see into *Sol*. They say everything is now unseen." He raised his hand to shield the rays from the emperor's eyes. "Divine One, do not attempt to see into it, lest it blind you as well." The emperor did not reject the scribe's motion to shade his eyes. "You must continue to see so that words of divinity may be written."

Tiberius released the scribe, who promptly picked up his writing tool, sat at his table, and gingerly dipped his quill tip into the ink. "My servants do not cherish what is written by me or the emperors before me. Augustus tried to appease these easterners with laws of moral fidelity—he even set up courts to uphold these laws. Yet these easterners ignore our rule over them. My commands do not inspire them. They abhor my edicts!"

He turned toward the scribe once again. "What have you written? Read the words to me!"

The scribe trembled. "O Divine One, these words are not ready to be repeated. Allow me time to straighten them out."

"Straighten them out?" He reached out to grab the scribe's pages, but stopped. "Straighten them out," he said again. "Straighten them out." He looked toward the east; his hand became a fist as he raised it into a beam of the sun's invasion into the room. "*Sol* has given me a word of prophecy for the easterners: 'straighten them out!'"

Near Bethany of Judea

Acts 1

A blinding light immersed the ascending figure, causing hundreds of onlookers to gasp and fall back to their knees. Only a handful of men remained standing, defying the radiant barrier. An awestruck silence overcame the crowd, that is, until a single voice cried out:

"Lord Jesus, don't leave again!"

Peter stood with his hands and arms lifted toward the light. He was a disciple of Jesus—not just any disciple, but the one who Jesus had said would "shepherd" His followers, the one who would lead and protect His followers from the ravenous wolves of mankind. But he was not ready to go it alone without his Master—without Jesus beside him!

Peter ran to a large rock and climbed on top of it to get the attention of Him one last time.

"Jesus, it's me—Peter! . . . Jesus!"

Too late—Jesus was engulfed into the brilliant cloud that continued to rise into the clear morning sky. *Where is He going?* Peter's mind began racing to the controls of the next moment (a normal response of his). *I want Him back—I need Him!*

"Master, please come back." This time he spoke in a surrendered voice—a voice that revealed the obvious: Jesus was gone. Peter shielded his eyes with his hands to stare at the bright cloud that had covered the One he had come to love.

Peter had surrendered to Jesus as the long-awaited Deliverer of Israel; He was the One of whom Moses spoke in the Sacred Writings:

"Jehovah God will raise up for you a Prophet, from the midst of your brothers, just like me; Him shall you listen to . . . and I will place My words into His mouth; and what I command, He shall speak."

Peter was convinced: *Jesus* is *that "Prophet;" I saw Him speak with Moses and Elijah! And the cloud—this same cloud!— overwhelmed us on that mountain top.* On that mountain, the brilliance of the cloud momentarily engulfed him and two other disciples: James and John, the sons of Zebedee. Back then, he thought Jesus was preparing a new camp—a staging ground to wrest Jerusalem out of the grip of a troubled Roman Empire. But just as quick as the cloud appeared, it dissipated, taking Moses and Elijah with it.

Words of Jesus began to flood Peter's mind: "Feed My sheep." . . . "Before Abraham existed, I Am." . . . "Destroy this temple and I will raise it up in three days." . . . "Lazarus! Come forth!" He thought this through: *Jesus proved Himself as the One who had power over life and, now, power over death. He is the Deliverer—the One to set our people free from the empire's control. But why leave now? Why not deliver us now?* This departure, however, was different; it was with finality.

Peter looked up toward the sky and spoke in his heart one more time: *Jesus, my Master, please return now and lead us to restore the kingdom. We cannot seize the temple grounds without Your presence and without Your power.* He slowly slid off the rock and looked up, only to see the fading remnants of the engulfing cloud.

Someone nearby broke the silence of the moment: "Why do you Galileans stand here gazing at the fading cloud? Jesus is gone; but He is coming back, just as you saw Him leave. Go now and do what He has told you to do."

Peter glanced at the two men beside him and the others, and then looked back in the direction of the cloud. *Do what He has told me?* he repeated in his mind. *Do what He has told me? Do exactly what? What do these strangers know that I don't already know? Jesus has told me so much; I can't begin to—* He stopped abruptly. The men beside him were gone! Peter looked around; others seemed equally dazed at the occurrences of the moment.

"Where are they!?" Peter shouted, turning in a circle. He ran toward several other men and pushed them aside as if someone was hiding behind them. "I can't take another disappearance! Where are they!?"

"Peter! Peter!" Another disciple, John, ran up to him, grabbed his shoulders, and looked him in the eyes. "Did you see them?"

"See who!? Where!? When!?"

"Those two men! Right here! Right now!"

Peter stared into the young lad's face. Once again, he wondered why Jesus would include himself, a seasoned fisherman, to try to keep up with the younger men whom his Master had called to be His disciples. About a month ago, John easily outran him to a grave site where Jesus had been buried—*Ah, but he was too afraid to venture in.* Peter had to smile as he remembered the empty tomb of Jesus. *That's why Jesus chose me. Someone needs to take charge of these young men and lead them until He returns.*

Peter brushed some dirt off his hands and straightened his outer garment. "Yes, I saw them. Now what did they say?"

"They were angels, Peter! They said that the Master would return again, just as He left us. So we must go back to Jerusalem and wait until the—"

"Wait?" Peter interrupted John. "I hate that word! Wait? After what the priests allowed those soldiers to do to Jesus? I say we recruit these men here, head back to the city, and take the temple away from those crucifying-hungry hypocrites! They all deserve to die." He pointed to the sky. "And I bet that same cloud will show up again and Jesus will wipe them off the face of the earth. That's what I say we should do; no more waiting!"

John was taken aback at the words he was hearing. He had been around Peter for over three years now and knew he had little patience. "Peter, please listen to me; I heard our Master specifically say that we must return and wait—'wait for the promise of the Father,' He said. Think about it: in the past forty days, He did not tell us that we would soon attack the temple, and He did not train us how to assemble an army of men. He trained us with His words, remember? It was His words that changed us. It was His words that calmed that storm on the Sea of Galilee; it was His words that pushed the temple guards back and onto the ground the night He was arrested. Peter, Jesus wants more than men's brawn; He wants their whole being—He wants their hearts."

Peter realized that, once again, his emotional reaction was premature. "John the Lover," he said. "Always speaking from the heart." Peter looked around and saw the other disciples and friends looking toward him and John. "Yes, we should gather our bags, walk back to the grand old city, and prepare for our next move." He spoke within hearing range of the other disciples. "Come on, men; it's time to move on."

While walking, Peter began to size up the crowd that remained. The 500 or so who had spent the day with Jesus were from various towns and villages, primarily in Judea. However, a mixed group from Galilee and Judea—about 120—was related to the disciples and household of Mary, Jesus' mother. Jesus had referred to the disciples as His new "apostles" for His "kingdom." Some—including Peter—had wives and children.

Nicodemus and Joseph were members of the Sanhedrin council; they believed in Jesus, but remained secret followers so as to be aware of possible plots against His life. Next were some more men, their wives and children, and Mary Magdalene, who ministered to a small group of Galilean women—outcasts—but accepted by Jesus and who always seemed to be around whenever the Master taught. (Sometimes the women interrupted the Master's teachings, bringing children and the sick to Him.)

Finally, there was Mary, the mother of Jesus, and her other children, though late in believing, yet joining now in the following. This comprised the 120 followers who were walking back to Jerusalem while the others fanned out onto the trails that led elsewhere.

"Go now, and do what He has told you to do." Peter thought this through. *I saw Him alive after the burial. I thought He was a ghost; but ghosts don't eat fish and bread, do they? No, it was Him. I saw His death scars; He is alive now, but no longer as a man . . . why? What's the purpose of His disappearance? And what's the purpose of this following? I'm the oldest of the disciples—thirty-two—so I must put a plan together. I must know what to say and do when we get back to the villa.*

"Andrew?" asked Peter, looking for his brother, who was another disciple. "Andrew, my parchment scholar?"

"Yes, my brother?" he said, with one eyebrow raised. "What are you wanting now?"

"I need your brains to help me. Find some papyri so you can write this down."

"While walking? You are beside yourself! Can't this wait until we get back to the courtyard?"

"No, no more waiting. I've got to formulate a plan, and we haven't much time."

Andrew surveyed his older brother's face, with its wiry beard and receding hairline. It had the wear and tear of a typical, sun-baked fisherman. And right now, Peter's face had that familiar look of determination which meant that there would be no deterring of his intentions. So Andrew began interrogating each among the group for some writing materials, hoping no one had any. But there were some parents with children that happened to have just what Andrew knew would satisfy his brother's wish.

After retrieving the writing materials, he returned to Peter. "Very well, what do you want me to do with this? You know I can't think, walk, and write at the same time."

Peter laughed. "Yes, that is true. You have always had difficulty chewing grain and walking at the same time." Andrew responded with a slight push. "Enough playing around. I want you to write what Jesus told us to do since He woke up from the land of the dead. What has He taught us?"

"James, John, Nathanael—the rest of you; I need your help over here," shouted Andrew. "Master Peter wants some answers to what Jesus has taught us."

"'Master'?" asked some among them.

As the other disciples drew nearer to Peter, he shot a stern look toward his brother for making such a statement. "Now, now, men; you know that I have to be ready to speak up when the time comes."

"Yes, we've noticed that trait in you, old man," said Philip, Nathanael's brother. The others laughed.

"Come now, brethren," said John. "Let's remember how Peter spoke up when we were too afraid to do so."

"Afraid!?" objected Thomas. "Who said I was afraid?"

"Oh, have you forgotten the storm on the Sea of Galilee already?" asked John. The others laughed. Thomas mumbled something under his breath.

"What is it that you want, dear friend?" asked Nathanael.

Peter spoke up. "Since the empty tomb, what has Jesus taught us to do?"

The men began to consider together as they walked, feeling that Peter, a bit pushy at times, meant well with his observations.

After stopping a few times and allowing Andrew to write, they arrived at the city gate. Peter faced the others and asked, "What do we have so far?"

John spoke up quickly: "The first thing is: Go and proclaim the good news of Jesus as the Messiah."

"Ah yes, the good news," said Peter. "This is true. Next?"

Andrew responded. "The next thing we have come up with is: Teach and train those who wish to follow the Master's cause."

"I like that, but what about baptism?"

"I was about to ask that," said Nathanael. "Don't we baptize before we teach and train?"

"You answer this first," said Andrew. "Do you see any rain clouds following us wherever we go?" Some laughed. "We baptize first, when there is available water and each person understands the cost of joining Jesus—and becoming a follower with us. However, if there is no water nearby, we teach and train those who respond to our proclamation and baptize later. Our Master's emphasis was for us to 'make disciples'."

"Agreed," interrupted Peter. "So we proclaim, baptize, and teach and train; what else have we come up with?"

"Worship Him!" John said. "We worship and adore Him as our Master, our Messiah, and our Savior."

"Then let us appoint you as our worship leader," said Peter.

"Amen, amen!" shouted the others in agreement.

"Now, what else?" asked Peter.

"Fellowship and the breaking of bread and drinking from the fruit of the vine, in remembrance of His death and life," responded Simon the Zealot.

"And keep the juice fresh and diluted so as not to intoxicate the younger followers," said Judas, son of James.

"Amen, amen," said the others.

"Who among us will take charge of our communion memorial with our Lord?" asked Peter.

"John and I have access to some used temple utensils," said James. "We'll take on that responsibility." Previously, their father was a Levite and rotated in duties in the temple.

"'We'?" asked John. "Do you have a field mouse in your garment?"

"Come now, John," said James. "This is a part of our worship and you are our new worship leader."

Peter wanted to press on. "Okay, you siblings work this out among yourselves and report back to us. What else? Is there anything missing of which Jesus instructed us?"

"Power," said Matthew, another of the apostles. "Jesus said we would have power from His Spirit to do His will."

"That's right," said Peter. "Anyone have a suggestion as to how we get this 'Spirit power'?"

"Wait!" said John.

Peter turned and faced the youthful lad. "Wait, my son?"

"Yes, Jesus specifically told us to wait in the city until the promise of His Father's Spirit comes to us. His Spirit will come and bring us power."

"How long do we wait, John?" asked Peter.

"I don't know."

"Neither do I; do any of you have a message from Jesus as to how long we wait?" There was no response. "Don't we have His teachings fresh in our minds? Shouldn't we go to the temple courtyard and begin to proclaim His message—the gospel?"

Andrew could sense his brother's drudgery of waiting. He knew how Peter hated to wait for anything. But Andrew knew

Matthew and John were correct, so how could he tell his older brother to listen to them—especially listen to John, the youngest of them all? "Peter, my brother, remember in the garden, where you cut off that man's ear?"

"What has that to do with this?"

"Listen, my brother; we all heard the Master say to wait in the city until this power comes upon us. None of us fully understand His plans to rule over the kingdom, but He just now told us not to worry about how we were to do it, but to wait until the power of His Spirit comes upon us."

Peter stood there, running his fingers through his beard and looking into the eyes of the others. Again, Andrew spoke up: "I say we let our newly appointed worship leader prepare us for some times of praying, singing of psalms, fellowshiping, and get us through the Feast of Pentecost, which ends next week."

"Amen, amen!" shouted the others.

"Yes," said Peter as he embraced Andrew. "And let's start with the food fellowship—I'm hungry!"

"Amen, amen!" they all shouted again. As they entered the city, they all walked with a sense of togetherness and purpose.

✝✝✝

Matthew pondered the turn of events as he entered the city of Jerusalem. He saw and experienced the ascension of Jesus; but, like the others, he was equally confused as to how Jesus planned to wrest the kingdom of His people from Roman rule. He knew the Romans well from his tax-collecting duties. They were a harsh breed with a strong military.

But Jesus had power like nothing he had ever witnessed before. Matthew had previously observed the power of Jesus against a host of temple soldiers: "Who are you looking for?" He asked the soldiers who came to arrest Him.

"Jesus, the Nazarene," they replied.

"I am He." But when He said that, an unseen force pushed them back and caused them all to fall down. His power was supernatural!

But now Jesus is gone; how can He continue to lead? How can this transfer of power occur? "Wait," said Jesus. "Wait until you are enveloped in power from the Holy Spirit." Surely this meant He was coming back. Surely this meant that the restoration of all Judea would soon take place through some sort of supernatural manifestation.

Matthew struggled with his newfound "job" as a proclaimer of this new "Way" into God's kingdom. *I was a tax collector; I dealt with statistics and money,* he thought. *I enjoy working alone; I'm not a proclaimer, so how can I best serve Him? What can I do to further this cause?*

Matthew thought back to his decision to leave the tax business and follow Jesus. When he looked into the eyes of Jesus, he saw hope—hope of a restoration with his family, who had disowned him because of his job. And hope of a restoration with his God. He believed Jesus when He said everything was going to be restored. And with Him nearby, nothing was impossible. Then came a startling statement from Him: "In a few days I will be turned over to the authorities, and I will be gone." And now He was.

But no sooner had Jesus left than He returned. Three days later He appeared; Jesus was back! But not as before: He appeared as in a body, but not as regular flesh and blood. He did have a body—He ate before them; but then He vanished right before their very eyes! Later, Jesus came back and taught them and revealed to them how He fulfilled all the prophecies concerning the Messiah. But why depart now? And why wait? This indeed was puzzling. Nevertheless, it was the command of the Master; now he and the others must obey.

† † †

As Philip walked with the others, his mind also raced through the encounters with Jesus since He had risen from the dead. The disciples and others went into seclusion after the crucifixion for fear of the high priest and the authorities. *But Jesus found us— He appeared before us behind locked doors! He was alive! He was real—but then, as quickly as Jesus appeared, He left again. Eight days later, He appeared again to teach Thomas not to doubt His presence and the ability to reveal Himself.*

His presence was external, but then He "breathed" on them and said, "Receive now the Holy Spirit." And just like that, His presence was felt inwardly like never before! Jesus was as real, in His Spirit, as He was previously in His flesh.

I feel Your presence, my Lord, he said silently as he walked. *You are with me—You are with us inwardly, as You were outwardly in the flesh.* Philip recalled how Jesus appeared to the group on numerous occasions, after His resurrection. He taught them how the prophets' foretelling of the current events related to the Messiah. Like never before, the words of the prophets became a present reality. The pieces of the prophetic puzzle began to fit.

But, again, why "wait"? *What is this power going to do to us that Your presence has not already done?*

Philip looked at the others; the disciples appeared to be in deep thought as well as discussing with Andrew about the main things Jesus was teaching them. "Wait until . . ." *I suppose we will soon fit some final pieces of this puzzle together.*

† † †

James observed his younger brother, John, as he was promoted to worship leader for the group. This reminded him of their father, Zebedee, a Levite, who had been active once as a worship leader for the priests at the temple. But his zeal to purify the Jewish system by dethroning the Herodian kingship brought conflict between the Herodians and the families of the current high-priestly lineage. To keep the peace—and power—the high priest demoted Zebedee to the daily affairs of preparing food for the other priests. That's what led Zebedee to move to Capernaum to become a fishing merchant—and a successful one at that.

Jesus called James and John the *Boanerges*—"Sons of Thunder"—due to their vocal dislike of the high priest's authority. Their father's zeal was passed on to them, which made them targets of the ruling authorities. James remembered several times when Jesus had to intercede to prevent the *Boanerges* from causing conflict and physical harm to those to whom He was sent to minister.

But didn't Jesus change all that? Shouldn't they use that "thunder" and speak for Jesus now? But He said, "Wait." James could hardly comprehend the waiting command. *With Jesus' spiritual presence, why couldn't the group go to the Sanhedrin council and demonstrate who Jesus actually is? And why not sit down with the high priest and his court and demonstrate how the Master's power could change everything? Besides, the family of the high priest knew Zebedee; surely the high priest would be reasonable with the sons of Zebedee and their friends?* These thoughts occupied James' mind as they walked back to the city to "wait."

†††

As she walked near the men, Mary of Magdala—also known as Mary Magdalene—listened as the apostles were describing things Jesus taught them after His resurrection. She thought back through the past month. *Jesus wasn't "teaching" me as much as He was showing me how to love Him and others. He told me how my obedience to His words was an indication of my love for Him. I love Him so much! But how can I, a single woman with a bad reputation, reveal His love to others?* She did not want to walk back to Jerusalem, but to stay where she last saw Jesus. She quickly dabbed her eyes, trying to catch her tears.

"Patience, my dear," said a voice beside her, as they walked. It was Mary, the mother of Jesus. "In time, He will reveal His plan for you."

"Do you think I can fit in with His plans?" she asked between her sobs.

Mary smiled and held her hand. "If He knows every bird that falls to the ground, I believe He knows your heart as well. You were special to Him, and I know He is going to use you in a special way. We must have faith in Him and wait for His plan to be revealed to us all. He has promised that His presence will be known by all us who love Him." Then she gently squeezed Mary's hand and ventured away from her.

My Lord, Mary Magdalene prayed, *I will wait as long as it takes . . . but please don't delay Your return.*

†††

"How long must we wait, Lord?" It was Peter's shift to offer prayers, and he was anxious to move on. A week had passed, and still there was no sign of the "promise." He looked at a few others, some kneeling and some lying on their mats, but all asking Jesus to come and bring the promise from the Father, which they understood to be the presence and power of His Spirit. "Is the 'promise' *Your* Spirit, Jesus? Will You be seen by us but not the others? Will You dictate to us our every move? Or is it the Spirit of You in someone else, as the Father did through the kings and the prophets of our forefathers?" Peter continued to pray.

"Peter, James, Matthew!" shouted John, as he leaped two steps at a time coming up to the prayer room.

"Shhh!" said Peter. "It's the Sabbath, John; don't be so loud."

John lowered his voice. "Oh, please excuse me; I'm so excited. James, our Master's brother, has returned from Bethany! He's in the courtyard, and he's brought Lazarus and his two sisters, Martha and Mary!"

Maybe Your brother is our promised spiritual leader? thought Peter, as he stood up. *Lord Jesus, please reveal this to me. I need some sort of sign that he is truly the one promised to reveal our takeover plans. I will submit to him, I promise.*

James arrived with an entourage, his face shielded by his headgear as he walked into the outer court. Peter stepped slowly down the stairway, shrouding his feelings of anxiety. A week had transpired since the abrupt departure of Jesus. Now there were only two days left before the end of the Pentecost observance.

"Wait," Peter whispered to himself. "Wait until the power to lead us comes." Peter greets James, "James, peace to you, my brother. And how was your journey?"

"Peace to you, Peter. Fine, the journey has been prosperous. And you?"

"We continue to wait, just as your brother told us."

"Yes; that is what He told us."

"So, has He spoken to you? Have you seen Him?"

"No, I'm afraid not, Peter. Oh, hello Mother; so good to see you." James stepped over toward Mary, as she approached the men. They each embraced and kissed.

"My dear son, so good to see your journey is ended and you have arrived safely."

"Nothing to worry about, woman; the excitement of an insurrection is fading, and the Romans have ceased their close scrutiny over us. It also appears that the priests have ended their watch on Lazarus and have returned to their regular duties, keeping us at a distance." John was standing next to Mary. "And you, Mother; has John seen to your needs?"

She put her arm around John. "Yes, my son, like Jesus Himself. He is so youthful and so caring. But I do miss your brother. Oh, that He would return once more; I miss Him so."

"He's coming back," said John. "He said He would come back."

"Yes, He did, John," said James. "But I'm afraid my doubts about Him may be causing the delay."

"No!" Peter raised his voice. "Don't say that! If anyone is to blame, it's me. I was the one who denied Him openly. Yet He came back to me and forgave me. Remember? He forgave me."

"But I am his brother; I should have known better."

Mary gave them both a stern look. "Stop it, both of you! Jesus has forgiven us all for our doubts and misunderstandings." Then she smiled. "Now is not the time to bring back old sins of fear and doubt. We must believe Him and wait. We must prepare for these final two days of Pentecost and continue to wait."

"I have it!" said Peter. "We're off balance! We need another!"

"Whatever do you mean?" asked James. "What is 'off balance'?"

"Twelve—Jesus chose twelve; now we're only eleven. Quickly; we must gather everyone together and choose another."

"Now what?" said Thomas, sitting at a nearby table. "Can't we just accept that this is it? We must have misunderstood His commands. Don't you agree, Matthew?"

"Hmm; I think we should listen to the old man," spoke Matthew. "Maybe he is dreaming again."

Peter ignored Matthew's verbal jab. "Matthew, Thomas—all of you listen to me. It has always been our custom to honor our forefathers with the proper representation. Jesus chose twelve of us as His disciples; now we must replace 'the traitor.'"

"Judas Iscariot?" asked Thomas.

"Please!—don't say that name in my presence!"

"Peter," said John. "Calm down or we'll have to rub more herbs on your neck."

The others began to laugh. Peter's face and neck always flushed a deep red when he got overly excited. Matthew pulled a cloth out of his tunic. "Here, now, let me wipe the sweat off your brow."

"Leave me alone! I tell you, we must select another."

"Listen, everyone," said John, "Please gather around us. Peter has a revelation."

Thomas rolled his eyes.

"Ahem," Peter cleared his throat. "Brothers and sisters, we must confront the need to honor our forefathers by selecting another follower to replace 'the traitor.' We know that he died according to the writings of our prophets, and I just now remember another writing that says we must replace him with another. I believe this may be the missing piece of the puzzle that prevents the return of our Master's Spirit. We must select another."

"Are you sure you're reading our prophets correctly?" asked Thomas.

"Yes, I'm quite sure. This verse has come to me during many a catch of fish. God always promised me replacements for those

I caught. And what He says to me about fish, I believe He says to me now about selecting another man to be one of the Twelve."

"Then why not James, our Master's brother? Or Lazarus?" asked Bartholomew.

"Well . . . well, because neither was there at the beginning of Jesus' ministry when He was baptized by John. The one who joins us must be able to testify of all that Jesus began to do and teach, from the start to the present."

"Who among us has been with us since the beginning of our Master's baptism?" asked Nathanael. After a brief survey of the attendants, two men were found who met the requirements and agreed to be selected as an apostle—one of the Twelve: Joseph Barsabas (also known as Justus) and Matthias.

No one objected to the proceedings, except John. "Peter, shouldn't we do what the Master said, and wait? Shouldn't we let Him choose the replacement just as He chose us all?"

"Wait? And how long do we wait? What if this very thing is stalling His return? Do you want to continue to delay our Master's return? I say we choose one of these men."

"And how do you propose to do that?" asked Philip, joining them from the upper chamber.

"Uh, well, we'll have them draw straws." That brought a laugh or two. "Or lots—that's right! Who has a set of lots?"

By now, the whole courtyard was filled with followers of Jesus.

Someone handed Peter a set of lots. "Step back and give me some room, will you?" said Peter, as he bent down on his knees. "Now let's pray: Jesus, our Master, you know our hearts' desires are to do Your will. We ask of You, please select the one to fill in the empty space of the one who betrayed You. Let this meet Your approval by the arrival of Your promise; and, Jesus, come back to us soon; Amen."

"In His name, Peter," said John.

"What?"

"Remember, He said to ask in His name."

"Oh; yes, so He did. In Your name, Jesus, we ask of You." Peter looked around, but no one was moving. All eyes appeared to be on him. "Okay, prepare the lots . . . Brothers, may Jesus choose between you two."

The lots were cast and the name selected was Matthias.

"My dear brother, please come and kneel before the Lord . . . Here is another, Master Jesus, who brings us to twelve. We ask of You to receive him, in Your name, amen."

"Amen, amen," responded others.

"Now let me get back to our meal," said Mary. "Come Martha, Mary; we have a lot of preparations to complete."

Supper ended with a gathering around the apostles as they broke bread together to celebrate communion with their Master. John led the group through several of the psalms and odes from the Sacred Writings. Next, Andrew read a portion of Isaiah. Then, Peter stood to share a few words of encouragement to the followers. After a few minutes, he concluded.

"Tomorrow is the final day for the Feast of Pentecost," said Peter. "Let us finish our usual prayer shift this evening and then, tomorrow, we'll all join together for a celebrated season of prayer at daybreak."

As everyone began to break up into their family groups, Perpetua, Peter's wife, and Petronilla, their daughter, approached him. "Shouldn't we be heading back home soon?" asked Perpetua.

"Abba, Father, please can we leave? I want to go home." She nestled up close to him. The feel of her long black hair and the smell of her mild perfume gave him great inner warmth and gratefulness for his dear family.

"Now is not the time to discuss our trip back to Galilee, my dear woman," he said to his wife. "Jesus wants us together for the time being. Look at me, my darling Pet." She raised her head from his lap. "Jesus has specifically told us to wait for His power to come. Remember that power, my darling? It was that same power that raised your grandmother from her sick bed."

"Ohhh," she responded slowly.

"You and your mother may have to go ahead of me; but let's talk about that after tomorrow's festivities. Now you two go and prepare for bed; I'll join you in a few minutes." As they walked away, Peter looked around the room. Lazarus was at a window looking out over the eastern sky. He walked over to him. "Lazarus, my brother; how are you feeling these days?"

Lazarus smiled. "I am blessed beyond measure. I am alive to see how Jesus plans to change the world. This is a blessing indeed."

"Well, He'd better come soon or the authorities will soon break up our gathering."

"Patience, my brother; Jesus waited four days before lifting me out of the grave. Every delay is another opportunity to trust Him more."

"I suppose you're right; but I am anxious to see Him once more . . . Good night, and sleep well."

Acts 2

*T*he morning sunrays began streaking through the sky, causing the night to quickly vanish from sight. Several men were finishing an early shift of prayers.

"Matthew, what have we not done?" asked James, the Lord's brother.

"I don't know," he replied. "Jesus said to wait for the Holy Spirit to empower us, so we continue to wait."

"Tell me again, Matthew, what did Jesus say about the Spirit?"

"He said that when the Spirit comes, He would baptize us and will be inside us to teach and warn us, and to fulfill all things. He also said the Spirit will bring to our minds the things we'll need to say at the appropriate times when we are to bear witness of Jesus; and the Spirit will empower us to witness."

James looked to the north. "He said we will be witnesses of Him in 'Samaria' . . ."

". . . 'and to the furthest extent of the world,'" added Matthew.

James continued to look north. "'. . . fulfill all things' . . . Well, I pray His blessed Spirit comes soon."

"So do I, James, because I'm fearful our gathering may soon be detected and we may encounter some difficulties."

"Difficulties? Have we not numerous difficulties already?"

Matthew put his arm on James' shoulder. "Let's remain together this day, and then we'll meet after the festivities and see if Peter and the rest are ready to make a decision."

Breakfast now over, everyone began to gather in the upper chamber. About 120 were in the large assembly room.

"This is a day of great celebration," said Peter. "Today fulfills the Feast of Weeks."

"It is the Day of the First Fruits," added John. "Let us praise God for the giving of His first fruits to us."

"Yes," said Peter. "Let us begin this hour with everyone praying together in thankfulness. Come, all of us now, and let us pray and praise our God; for this day is to be a day of praise for our deliverance from slavery to the world. And let us ask our Master to reveal Himself to us today."

"Amen, amen!" shouted the others.

In the pleasurable fragrance of the morning meal, prayers began to erupt throughout the group. Everyone was together again, in harmony, and in a unified purpose of meeting. Mary, the Lord's mother, and Mary Magdalene had gathered many of the women and the children together for a time of praise and prayer.

Peter grabbed the shoulder of John as he bent his knee and joined the lad in prayer. Peter loved to hear John pray—such simple words, and yet from a heart swelling with love and adoration for the Master.

"O God our Father, we ask for the return of Your Son, our Master," said Peter. "We need Him, O Father; please hear this prayer."

John took over, beginning to weep as he spoke, "My Lord, Jesus, I miss You so much. Your touch . . . how I long for that touch of Yours. And Your eyes . . . looking into them revealed how all things would be well. My Jesus, I love You and how I long to see You again; I miss You. Your promise, Jesus . . . how long must we wait? When will You send the power for Your kingdom's reign?"

At that moment, there was a loud noise from above—outside!—like a clap of thunder! Some of the children shrieked. The upper chamber began to resonate with the noise. It sounded like an earthquake, yet none of the walls were crumbling; in fact, nothing was shaking inside! From outside, the noise became louder, like a large sandstorm blowing in from the Arabian Desert. Yet there was an eerie calm in the room. The thunderous and roaring noise burst into radiant light above the chamber, a light just like the cloud that had received Jesus a few days ago. An enormous bolt of lightning had permeated the room, breaking into tiny rays of light. The air was electrified as many gasped and shielded their eyes from the brightness.

But the startling noise and burst of light were quickly joined by a shout: "He's here! He's here!" cried John. His Spirit has come! His Spirit has come!" John stood and began dancing in the brightness, raising his hands and crying 'Hallelujah! Hallelu-jah!' Peter looked about as he saw slivers of fire-like tongues appear from above and begin to light upon each one's head. Gradually, each began to join in the cry of praises, and some began to dance with John.

"'The God who answers by fire . . . He is God'," thought Peter. Finally, his turn came. The fire-like tongue settled onto Peter's head and began to burn through his whole body as if he had been immersed in hot coals. Peter's thoughts became overwhelmed in the brightness of this presence; soon his silence also broke as he joined in the unanimous praise.

"Hallelujah! Praise the Almighty! Hallelujah, Master, You've come again!"

For about ten minutes, the noise and the fire continued to blaze in the praise. What was unknown by them was that the noise that had begun above the upper chamber, outside, had ceased and only the praising was being heard. The sound had resonated throughout the whole city of Jerusalem—shaken by the noise, yet no damage was experienced. People ran out of their houses and the festive gatherings to see what was occurring. The reflected brightness from above the upper chamber could be seen throughout the city, very distinct from the morning sun. Then, as quickly as it appeared, the bright light faded away.

Momentarily the city became quiet once again. However, near the temple, the sound of people shouting "Hallelujah" and other praises to God was heard. Then there was another strange sound: the noise of an abundance of dialects calling for everyone to come and praise the Almighty.

"Come on, let's make sure everyone's all right," said a man from a group of Cyrenians. As they ran down the rugged street, many other festive groups began to fill the adjoining streets, running and gathering in the street by the villa, from where the light originated.

"What is this?" asked an Asian Jew. Another from Mesopotamia heard him ask but did not understand his dialect. He responded: "I hear men and women praising God in our tongue." Another group from Crete responded, confounded that each group in the street heard the praises to God, yet not understanding each other.

"This is amazing! I hear many tongues foreign to me, yet I can hear my tongue praising Almighty God," said a Parthian.

The expanding dance of praise soon spilled out of the outer courtyard, and the front street was filled with dance. The apostles had come down to the gates and were encouraging others to join in the praise. But those outside were confused and were trembling over this tremendous event.

"What could this mean?"

"Oh," said a street vendor. "This is a strange group—from Galilee, no doubt. Listen to their slang! Hah; probably full of new wine and don't even know what's going on." He began to laugh, not seeing Peter come up to his side. The man abruptly stopped laughing when he saw the gaze of Peter. It was unlike anything he had ever seen before in the eyes of a man. "Excuse me, my Lord, I didn't mean—" Peter motioned to him to hold his voice. The sliver of fire that had rested on Peter became a mental and verbal power that pressed heavily on his heart to speak.

"Men—everyone!—listen to me carefully. We are not drunk, this being way too early in the day. But we are here, standing before you, to announce that this noise has come from Almighty God—the God of our Fathers—announcing the coming of His Spirit upon His children. And we announce to you that this has occurred just as the prophet Joel said, that God would 'pour out His Spirit among His children, and they will prophesy. Yes, and the young men will see visions, and our older men will see revelations in our dreams. And God will show wonders in the heavens and reveal signs on the earth of the coming day of the Lord.'

"In fact, all who seek God through His Son, Jesus, will also receive His Spirit and will join in the proclamation of the good news of our deliverance. And whoever has ears to hear and calls upon Jesus for deliverance will be saved."

Some of the temple guards were standing nearby. "Jesus, the Nazarene?" asked one of the guards. "But didn't we crucify Him? Didn't our leaders rightly accuse Him of blasphemy? How can this be? Even if this *is* His Spirit, how could He forgive us now and deliver us from our merciless killing of Him?"

"All men are merciless, my friend," responded Peter. "But He is merciful. This same Jesus of Nazareth, whom you crucified, was foretold through King David and the Prophets that He would arise from His deathbed after three days, and that He would begin the long-awaited salvation of His chosen. You crucified Him from your evil hearts, but the good news has come from God: salvation has come to the Israelites! Jesus is our Deliverer—our long-awaited Messiah! If you continue to live under your guilt, you will perish miserably, and the judgments upon the wickedness of this world will be yours in which you will share. But if you will turn from your wicked ways and turn to Him, He will offer you a pardon for all crimes committed against Him. This is the good news of salvation, offered by Almighty God!"

"But what do we do to get His blood off our hands and the hands of our children?" asked another.

"Repent, each of you, and be baptized in the name of Jesus, the Anointed One, and you will be forgiven, and you will be reborn in your spirits, such as we. This is God's promise—oh yes, blessed Redeemer, Your Spirit has come! . . . My dear fellow Jews—men and women!—get saved from your sins and this perverse generation. Join us in our joy! Repent and receive!"

John grabbed the vendor's shoulder and looked into his eyes. "Yes, my friend, you can repent and receive Jesus as well. And then you can join in the celebration of the return of Jesus' Spirit."

The apostles, including the other men and the women who were in the upper chamber, began to draw near to various groups in the street, speaking boldly of God's salvation in everyone's dialect. What began as a confusing sound across the city now turned into one harmonious witness and praise to God for sending His Messiah—Jesus—to deliver everyone from their guilt and sin.

Since they were near the temple, everyone moved toward the steps of Solomon's Porch as Peter continued to speak to the crowd. The initial group from the upper chamber remained with various groups, taking sections of the street gatherings and motioning people into areas where the good news of Israel's Messiah could be proclaimed. Filled with His tongues of fire, they blended into the larger groups, explaining the wonderful news of Jesus of Nazareth as the Messiah. Each dialect had a Spirit-filled person, addressing the crowds with a notable glow of God's presence and power.

Peter had gotten the attention of many priests who were assembled for the final day of the Feast of Pentecost. They could not stop him—instead, they were mesmerized by the power from which he spoke. "It was David, our King, who prophesied that our Deliverer would be handed over to our leaders and that He would be killed. But, David also said that His body would not see the decomposition of a dead man, but that His Lord—our God and Father—would raise Him up. And that He did!"

"Who gave this commoner authority to speak?" asked a priest.

"How dare he speak to the people like this!" said another.

Several other priests began rousing grumblings among many of the gathered priests, especially those of the Sadducees, who did not believe in a resurrection of the dead.

But Peter, still filled with the Spirit, turned and addressed their grumblings even louder: "Listen, my brethren, this Jesus, whom you crucified, *has* risen from the dead and is responsible for what you are witnessing right now. You saw and heard of His many miracles—you even accused Him of healing some among us with the power of the devil! This same Jesus is responsible for this power you are witnessing this morning. The God of Abraham has made this Jesus, whom you crucified, both our Lord and the Christ—He is our Messiah!"

Some of the priests began covering their ears and crying out, "Blasphemy! Do not listen to this man!" However, the enormous size of the listening crowd began to invade every conceivable space outside the temple porch. This brought such fear among the priests that many retreated into the inner courtyard of the temple. Thousands of men and women were so aligned toward the temple grounds that all were hearing Peter's concluding remarks, the apostles and others assisting in various interpretations of dialect. Many were beginning to sob with conviction.

"Sirs," some cried out. "What must we do to be saved from the guilt of His death?"

"Repent," said Peter. "Repent and be baptized in the name of Jesus, as the Christ, so that your sins can be forgiven and so that times of refreshing can come into your own spirit such as you see in us today!"

By noontime, thousands of men and women had been swept into this new praise gathering, having believed in Jesus for the forgiveness of sins. The apostles formed lines near the cleansing troughs around the temple area for baptisms. Others gravitated toward the Pool of Siloam for baptisms. All who gathered to be baptized were first confessing their sins and asking Jesus to come into them as Savior and Lord. Many crippled and lame around the pool were healed as well and joined in the confession of Jesus and in the rejoicing that the Deliverer had come. Thousands were being baptized as commanded by the apostles.

"Peter, can you believe this?" asked John, as he gazed over the crowd who was baptized. "There are thousands who are turning to Jesus for salvation."

Peter looked at the crowd. "It is a miracle, John; we are witnessing the first fruits of our Lord's Pentecost."

"His promise has arrived; but with so many, what are we to do with them?"

Peter rubbed his beard for a moment. "John, tell the others to divide the crowd into groups, according to the different languages. Then have all the apostles meet with me here; we will go to each group and confirm their understanding of what they believe occurred to them today." John turned and ran through the crowd, calling out the names of the apostles.

Soon, they all assembled in the villa courtyard with Peter. "Brethren, the Spirit's power is upon us."

"Amen, amen!" they cried out.

"Together, we must go through the groups and explain to them some of the basics of salvation in the name of Jesus. These followers must understand their dependence upon one another and what the breaking of bread symbolizes. Let us be diligent in teaching everyone the truth of God's Sacred Writings and how Jesus fulfills the prophesies of the Messiah. They must understand how to continue living in the Spirit's power."

Thus, the apostles began walking through the groups, instructing them in the words of God and encouraging them to live by faith. And great awe came upon the groups because as the apostles spoke, the language barrier was not a problem. Everyone heard the apostles in their own dialect. This continued from group to group and from house to house.

Things were going well—at least from the apostles' perspective. But there was something brewing in the not-too-distant town of Bethany.

† † †

A blast of light and a rumbling sound from the northern horizon got the attention of a lone figure in Bethany. He was thinking of how to restart his mission to run the Roman government out of Judea—his homeland. But this strange appearance of light and the deep rumbling sound so early in the day broke his chain of thought. *What could it be—an earthquake?*

He continued to stroke his matted black beard. *I have seen some strange things occur in Jerusalem,* he thought to himself, *but this is most unusual!* It was the Day of Pentecost, a day of celebration for the fanatics of his religion. From his perspective, these religious bigots were simply putting on a puppet show for the Roman governors who had taken control of the territory. No one appeared to be living with purpose—or with principle. The people of his homeland had no fight left in them.

But not so with him. His mission was to besiege Jerusalem in an array of terror. Death to the Romans and their Herodian puppets! And if need be, death to any religious leader who failed to take a stand against the pagan authority! He was a zealot, and his terror was with purpose! This was the thinking of a man who had witnessed the slaughter of many of his family and neighbors. Only through his quick thinking and maneuvering was he able to save his mother, father, and younger sister. But unfortunately his two older brothers were cut down by Roman swords as they tried to defend their property in Bethany. If he had not been caught six months earlier, things would be different today.

His thinking was interrupted by a familiar voice. "Barabbas, dear," his mother spoke softly. "Barabbas—"

"Shhh," he responded as he put his fingers on her lips. "Mother, do not call me by that name. I told you that when I was put out in open display, everyone cried out my name, and now I am too well known. That name must disappear."

"What a blessing from God that you were released from prison."

"Blessing? I haven't forgotten the look on that man's face since those religious people cried out, 'Crucify Him! Crucify Him!' I tell you, Mother, He didn't say a word in His defense. But when He made eye contact with me, it was as if He was saying that this was the right thing to be happening."

"My son, there was nothing you could do to save Him under the circumstances."

"Circumstances?" Barabbas pondered that statement for a moment. "I believe there was more to Him than those people were willing to receive."

"Nevertheless, you are here now, safe from your accusers. Now you have a chance to start a fresh, new life. You have paid for your crimes—" Once again he interrupted her talk.

"Crimes!? Killing foreign soldiers and their puppets for stripping our land of its integrity? Is it a crime to stop this taxation system that steals from our labors so that Antipas can build another palace? Is it a crime to kill these men who rape our women and force them into a slave relationship that they call a marriage!?"

His mother had fear in her eyes as the rage welled up inside her once-loving and playful son. "Son, please stop thinking about the past; you have a new future now."

He stopped for a moment, and with a small piece of cloth he kept tucked inside his tunic he wiped the tears from her eyes. "I'm sorry, dear Mother, but I believe this freedom of mine is a second chance to free our people from this oppression. I must find out why Jerusalem was turned into such a mob, trying to do away with this man they called Jesus. I will return to Jerusalem and see if my old contacts can fill me in on what is going on with our people."

"I saw Him once," his mother pondered aloud, as she joined her son's gaze toward Jerusalem. "He came into town to visit some of His friends; you remember them, don't you: Martha, Lazarus, and Mary? They say Lazarus took ill and died; but this Jesus came along after Lazarus was entombed and reportedly raised him from the dead."

"Raised him from the dead? Mother, have you been tarrying in the wine cellar again?"

"Oh hush, Barab—I mean . . . oh, I don't even know what to call you."

"Inaros; call me Inaros, for that is my name."

Acts 3

"**M**y Lord Jesus," prayed Peter. "How I thank You for Your presence. I didn't realize how much greater would be the impact to have Your Spirit this close throughout the day and night. I am beginning to understand how the kingdom is to be set up inside those who will follow You. Now, instead of a couple of fishermen, or a tax gatherer or two, thousands are turning to You! And You confirm this Way—this new and living Way—by Your miraculous signs through us. This is amazing, Jesus!

"But what shall we do to keep them in the teachings of the Way? Do we release them to our Jewish leaders for instruction in the ways of the Law? Shall I go to the high priest and reason with him? Surely, with all these repentant brothers and sisters, he will listen now."

"Peter! Peter!"

Peter was startled and looked around, thinking someone was present. Then he realized the voice came from within. "Yes, Lord?"

"Do not listen to the leaders who have rebelled against Me. They must learn of the Way by faith; they must not add Me to their existent religious system. They must listen to the words that I am speaking through you and the others. They must repent and turn to our Father, through My Way. They must become obedient to My words.

"Look at their religious traditions and practices; their rituals can be accomplished and explained without My presence and power. That is why they remain dead in their trespasses and sins. The Law was their schoolmaster; but the students have rebelled against it. They have created their own law.

"You, and the others I have chosen, will disciple the men; the women will disciple other women."

"But Lord, we need the synagogues for teaching places and the porches for large proclamations. And the purification troughs—we need them for baptisms. And there are many who follow in the old ways that need to hear of the new Way."

"Peter, remember the soldiers that arrested Me and put Me on that cross?"

"Yes, my Lord."

"Did they have uniforms on?"

"Yes."

"Were they fitted to serve?"

"Yes."

"Do you think it is easy to serve in such a bulky, heavy uniform?"

"Probably not, my Lord."

"Do you think it is easy to be trained to become a warrior?"

"No."

"Neither will it be easy for you, My beloved Peter. Listen, My precious foundation builder; your mouth—that part of you that you and I both know gets you in trouble—it will become your uniform and your weapon for the battles I have planned for you."

"But Lord, I . . ."

"Silence, My friend! Listen to Me when I speak to you. What you hear, you must remember and teach them to others, and you must commit it to writing. I will give you, John, and others My words that I want you to write. My teachings must be passed along to others so that they may be trained to speak them as well."

"Others will speak for you as well?"

"Yes, My words will become the weapons for My kingdom. I strengthen and empower My words. They will be endorsed by My presence and My power. They are truth, and you will teach others to worship the Father in spirit and truth. The kingdom of God will be established by truth—words of truth. My Spirit will guide you into the purest of truth; so when you feel the presence of My Spirit within you, proclaim My truth, and write when I give you words of truth. Write it down, line by line and piece by piece. My words, combined with My Spirit, will be your weapons for My kingdom's warfare."

"Warfare? My Lord, I'm afraid I do not understand. How do we wage a war with words?"

"Not with simple words, Peter, but with truth! There is a big difference. Words have no power if they are not bathed in truth. And My truth will not be effective unless it is empowered by My Spirit.

"The world has some words of truth—words necessary for common existence. Your forefathers—My selected children—have some words of truth, but they would not wait upon Me—they would not listen to Me alone for the deep mysteries of truth. They began to blend My words with their erroneous words—truth mixed with error! This became more dangerous than the lies of the heathen."

Peter lowered his head and stared at the floor. "You mean the way of the priests, don't You? Our people—Your children—were the chosen ones to keep Your statutes . . . we were the ones selected to keep Your words—"

Jesus interrupted Peter: "To keep them pure! But they became impatient; they refused to wait upon Me. They began to add laws and practices that were not ordered by My Father. They refused the warnings of the prophets when I spoke through them. They did not wait until I endued them with words of power!

"But you, Peter, you must learn to wait until you have heard Me speak to you. I will instruct you and the others. I will empower you with My Spirit. He and I are One—and He will strengthen you for the new covenant of a new possession."

"A new covenant? A new possession?"

"Yes, My beloved one. Now you're listening! Each of you, chosen by Me, will be given assignments according to your faith and gifts. Each of you must become equipped soldiers of My testimony. My testimony is in My life, My death, and My resurrection. It will not be easy; it will be a cross that you must carry until you join Me in the place where every man's battle is consumed into eternity—an eternity of victory for My beloved followers."

"My Lord?"

"Yes, Peter?"

"You once said that I would have to be led around by others. Will I become blind? Will my eyes be put out by the enemy?"

"Enough about the future, My soldier; do not be distracted by how you feel and how you are treated. Keep your focus on My words and the power of My presence through My Spirit. I have much to say and do in the present; think on the things I have told you. Live in joy; rejoice in that your name is written in My book of life. And remember: I will never leave you nor forsake you. I will guide you into all truth.

"It's getting late; you and John go to the temple to pray. But as you go, pay close attention as to how I will redirect the gatherings toward My ways. Obey My words and serve Me in the present, and you will see and experience My glory."

"Yes, My Lord; I will obey You."

Peter had not realized that he had been praying and communing with the Lord for nearly four hours. He managed to raise himself up off his mat and blotted the moisture from his eyes. As he stretched his body, he looked at those around him; they were either praying or conversing with someone.

Thank you, Lord, for these wonderful eyes. They are Yours to use as long as I have them. Peter closed his eyes and put his fingers on them momentarily. Then he remembered His Lord's bidding. *I must find John* . . . "John? John? Where are you, my companion?"

John was in his usual corner of the upper chamber, a place where he had positioned a few pieces of furniture to provide him seclusion from distractions for his communion time with Jesus. His head appeared from under a tapestry.

"Yes, Peter, what do you want?"

"Listen, the Lord has said that we should join in the customary time of evening prayers at the temple." Peter saw him smile. "What are you smiling about?"

"My brother, I was wondering when you would get the message." The smile of his youthful comrade brought a returning smile and embrace.

"Oh, John, what an experience it is to have the presence of the living Christ at all times."

"Yes, it is . . . but, Peter, I still miss His touch—and His eyes! I want so much to draw His face on a parchment and roll it out before me every time I stop to pray. But He has said, 'No'. Why, Peter? Why?"

"Well, my brother, I think I may know why. When I was younger, my father used to discourage me from trying to find the fish by looking through the waters for them. He would say—and say it often, I'm afraid—'My son, don't look for the fish as though they were looking for you, but look at the surroundings of the lake. Look at the places where the waters are still. Let the elements of the surroundings be your guide. Do your part in preparing for a catch and let God do His part in sending them to you.'"

"Which means?" asked John.

"Which means: do not turn your attention toward an image of His face when you can entertain His presence before you. Why stare at a picture when you have Him in Spirit?"

John laughed as he circled the elder and came right up to his face, nose-to-nose. "Now I know why your father shook his head often when you tried to explain how the big ones got away. Your story doesn't make a lot of sense, but the analogy is great! Yes, I have Him! Oh what a blessing! Come now, Peter, and let's praise Him together."

"Yes—I mean, no! John, we must hurry now for the evening prayers at the temple." The two rolled up the parchment Peter had been reading and put it in a box before leaving.

The streets were busy as many devoted Jews were gathering for the evening prayers. Peter covered his head, trying to avoid being recognized, but John was much too youthful and inquisitive for any secrecy. It wasn't long before a large group was walking to the temple with them.

"Oh, Peter look! See that man there, the crippled one? Since I was a child, I can recall seeing him sitting there, asking for alms. His parents carry him there every day. Let's go talk to him."

"John, I haven't any coins for him today."

John smiled. "But don't we have something far greater than coins to offer?"

Peter stopped, eyeing his younger counterpart. John was all smiles, a face that could only garner the same expression. "Yes, my son, so we do." Peter looked upward, saying, "Lord Jesus, it is time for You to be in charge. Reveal Your presence and Your power to this beggar, who has been lame all his life. In Your name we pray, amen."

"Amen," said John.

As they neared the temple gate, called Beautiful, Peter and John began to walk deliberately toward the lame man's pallet. The beggar had grown accustomed to people walking toward him, either to rebuke him or to offer him words of encouragement. And fewer still would drop a small coin in his worn and cracked vessel. He was mechanically trained to offer a wretched face and a desperate plea for alms. But this time it would be different.

Peter stopped in front of him. "Look at us!" said Peter.

He looked up at the two men, expecting a coin—hoping for two. However, when he looked at them, his heart began to stir within him. He felt a burning sensation running down from his head into a portion of his body that had been lifeless all his life. He felt something he had not felt since his childhood days: a feeling of hope. *What does this mean?* he wondered to himself. *Almighty God, is this an answer to my old worn-out prayer for healing? Is this the day for You to deliver me?*

Peter continued: "Sir, I have no coins to offer you. But what I do have, I give to you. In the name of Jesus of Nazareth, rise up and starting walking!" Peter reached for his hand, grabbed him, and began to lift him. But as he lifted, new strength in the beggar's legs began to take over, and, immediately, for the first time in his life, he was able to stand up on his own two feet.

Amazement struck the crowd that had gathered. Many were bowing their heads to the ground, bending their knees and facing the direction of Peter and John. Still others were laughing at the skinny, old man who was speechless for the first time in anyone's recollection. But that didn't last long.

"My God and My Lord! Praise be unto You! Hallelujah! Look at me—look! I can walk, I can walk! Praise and glory be unto God!"

It was a good thing John was holding on to Peter at the time, or the healed beggar would have rolled them both onto the ground. Now the beggar felt lighter than air. He began leaping and praising God, all the while holding on to Peter for leverage. John began laughing as he pulled Peter and the beggar toward the temple gate.

"Glory to God!" the beggar shouted continually. "Glory to God!"

John managed some words over his shouts of praises. "Peter, perhaps we need to show him to the priest?"

"Perhaps? Anything to get him off me!" But deep inside, both John and Peter knew that their Master's Spirit was in control.

Thank you, My Lord, said John. *This is why You sent us here.*

They finally managed to get through the gate; all the while the beggar was screaming his head off in praises to the Almighty God. Everyone recognized his loud voice, but now his words had changed. They changed from begging for alms to shouting praises to God for a miraculous gift. The unusual noise from the beggar caused a tremendous contagion of listeners. The crowd grew larger and larger as the news spread. Peter and John had gotten as far as the temple portico, called Solomon's Porch, when the Spirit nudged their hearts to stop.

When stopped, Peter saw thousands of faces looking toward him and John, people pushing one another to see the beggar, who was still hanging on to the belt of Peter's garment, venturing further out, and nearly pulling it off! Peter's heart began to burn with that new spiritual urge to speak.

"My countrymen, my fellow Jews, why are you looking at us—fellow men as you!—as if some power or godliness was in us to heal this beggar? Listen to me: the God of Abraham and our fathers, the God who revealed Himself to us in Jesus—yes!—this same Jesus, whom you handed over to Pilate and rejected as the Messiah—it is this same Jesus, the One you had crucified instead of Barabbas, it is by Him that you witness this great miracle today. Jesus, who was raised from the dead, has been seen by hundreds of us. It is by His power and by faith in Him that this man is healed and is leaping here before you.

"But there is a reason for you to witness this healing today. What you did to Jesus, you did because of your wicked and rebellious hearts. You wanted Him—or someone like Him—to redeem you from our physical oppression. When He refused the position, you rejected His words and sought to remove Him from our presence. But by releasing a murderer in His place, you became murderers yourself by crucifying Jesus."

Some gasps and groans could be heard among the people.

"However, what you did, you did in ignorance. God foretold that Jesus would suffer and die by your hardened hearts and your cruel hands. But now He reveals a new hope through a new Way—through a living Spirit—and He is telling you now to repent and be converted, that the bloodstains of your sins may be blotted out, so that waves of refreshing may come upon you from the Almighty God, and that Jesus, Himself, may come to you, as prophesied, for the restoration of all things.

"Him you must follow, just as Moses told our forefathers that one like himself would arise from among us—*the* Prophet!—and Him we must listen to and follow, just as our forefathers followed Moses. And just like Moses, Jesus was sent to us first, that we may be a blessing to all families of the earth."

Some of the priests were listening and about ready to do whatever Peter would say. However, there were other priests who began to refuse Peter's words about Jesus. "How dare you make this Galilean carpenter equal to Moses!" said one of the priests. "Moses said nothing of the kind to make this Jesus the Prophet."

"Not only Moses," said Peter, "but all the prophets, since Samuel, have spoken of this Jesus as the Prophet. And if you choose to disobey Him, as the Scripture says, you will be far worse than this beggar was before he was healed. Listen, you who are crippled in your spirits can now join with this beggar in praising God for a restored heart and soul! Listen, your crippled hearts are far worse than lameness in your limbs; repent and turn, every one of you, from your sins, or you will meet a far worse fate than you can ever imagine!"

Acts 4

Peter and John continued to explain the meaning of Jesus' death, burial, and resurrection. Many were listening with open hearts to believe. Suddenly, through the inner temple gate, there poured out about two dozen guards with swords and spears. They pushed back the crowd around Peter and John and formed a pathway to the gate. Next, some of the priests and council members of the Sadducees' persuasion marched out to confront them.

"You Galileans!" said the temple captain. "You have disrupted the evening prayers and caused many to break our laws. Come with me for questioning." He motioned them to follow him into the inner courtyard. As Peter and John were pushed into obedience by several of the guards, the beggar and several others resisted them.

"No!" the beggar exclaimed. "Do no harm to these men, for they are prophets who are proclaiming the new Way to our God!"

"Amen, amen!" shouted others. The captain stopped, seeing he was easily outnumbered. He was about to draw his sword, when one of the priests spoke up.

"Men of Judea, hear me, please. These men have caused a disruption in our established services and must be questioned. They will get a fair hearing, and you may join us in the morning and hear the case openly. Now if several of you don't mind, please help this man release his clothing." The priest smiled as he pointed to the beggar, still clinging to Peter's belt.

"Come now, Justus," said someone who knew him. "Let go of Peter, and we'll hear his case in the morning." Justus slowly released the belt, looking intently into the eyes of the arresting priests.

"He healed me, sirs; did you hear that? He healed me!" With that statement, he reluctantly let Peter go, which signaled all others to reopen the pathway to the inner temple courtyard. Peter and John were escorted to some guest quarters for the night, under house arrest.

"Well, so much for my thoughts about influencing the priests for Jesus," said Peter.

"Don't give up yet, my brother. Did you see all those who were lining up on our side to defend us?"

"Yes; I'm understanding more and more each day the power of the words of our Father and the words of Jesus—both backed by the presence of the Spirit!"

John smiled as he leaned against a wall. "Yes, His words are like a thousand swords in our hands. Peter, do you see what is happening? Just as He promised, the presence of His Spirit is taking our testimonies and bringing about a following far greater than if we had tried to do it by force."

Peter was now lying on a straw-filled pallet. "I wonder what the rest of our brethren are doing tonight?"

"Probably praying for us . . . which reminds me, I think we had better get to praying ourselves. Who knows what they have planned for us tomorrow?" They both looked at each other and said together, "Jesus knows!" They laughed and then settled down for a long evening in fellowship with each other and with Jesus.

(Next morning) "Ah, yes, that wasn't bad prison food," said John.

Peter laughed. "This time they were nice. Next time it might not be as tasty."

"There won't be a next time for me, because I'm going to outrun you—like before, at Jesus' tomb—and get as far away from these hypocrites as I possibly can."

"John, don't be so sure about that. You know I have a way with words; I—" Peter was interrupted by John's laughter. "What!? Why are you laughing?"

"*You* have a way with words?" John laughed again. "Your words—that's why we're stuck here in this room now! I like your direct approach: 'Repent or perish!'"

"Well, the Spirit is giving me the utterance; I'm just a vessel. You know, John, I still can't believe Jesus would choose to use me after disappointing Him so. What love; what grace; what mercy He has shown to me."

"Peter, you have a strand of courage in you that I can only dream of having. Yesterday, while I was trying to take in all that was happening, you just stood up and began preaching. Jesus knew what He was saying when He called you a 'rock.'"

There was a knock on the door.

"You Galileans follow us," commanded a guard, upon entering.

Peter and John were escorted to the inner courtyard, where a seat of judgment was assembled. But this was no ordinary assemblage; everything was polished and decorated.

John whispered to Peter, "Well, my brother, it appears we have gotten someone's attention."

"Yes; you don't suppose I get to sit in that big chair there, do you?"

John responded with a muffled laugh. "If you do, give me the pleasure of fanning you with a palm branch."

They were marched out about thirty steps from the seating arrangement. "You two will stand here, and you will not directly address the high priest, unless he commands it. Any questions?"

"The high priest?" asked John.

The guard smiled. "Not only Caiaphas," he whispered, "but his father-in-law, Annas—the one who really wields the high priest's power."

John looked at Peter. "Pray and believe," whispered Peter to John. The inner courtyard doors were opened behind them as a crowd of people began making their way in along the side porches.

"Looks like your 'fans' are keeping their distance," sneered another guard.

As the crowd continued their entrance, another group of officials were escorted to their seats in the front: Jewish rulers, priests, and scribes made their way in and sat down. The scribes were brought tables that were positioned about halfway between the defendants' stand and the priestly seating. More and more of the regional priests were escorted to their seats, arranged in a semi-circle, the high priest's seating in the top middle. As they continued making their way to their seats, John took a glance behind them.

"So much for a show of force," he mumbled. "Jesus, we need You now."

"Just keep praying, my brother; keep praying." Peter closed his eyes momentarily. *O Master, Jesus. Give us Your power and Your presence to answer this group. These are the ones who turned You over to be crucified. If that is our lot, may John and I be as faithful to You as You were to our Father.*

At that moment, two trumpeters sounded, announcing an entourage approaching. An official spoke out: "The court will stand for the High Council and His Majesty, the High Priest and his court!" The trumpeters began again as servants began bringing in more chairs to seat the Sanhedrin.

John managed a small smile when Peter glanced his way. The area separating Peter and John from the priestly circle began to fill in as more and more chairs were brought in. An aisle was maintained in order for them to be viewed directly by the high priestly court.

Not all the Sanhedrin council was present. The total group of officials and their accompanists still numbered about 250 people, besides the temple servants and guards. John was aware of space between them and the spectators, who had managed to keep as far away from them as possible.

About this time Caiaphas and Annas made their entrance. Following Annas were his four sons: Eleazar, Jonathan, Theophilus, and Matthias. The jewelry and clothing brought forth a glittering spectacle of lights as the sun shone on the high priest and his court.

Peter remembered seeing Annas once, when he was a lad. His family had come to Jerusalem for a festive meeting. Peter managed to slip away from the family gathering and climb on top of the temple porch, where many commoners and curious onlookers were allowed to see the temple grounds. It was, indeed, a breath-taking sight, one he had never forgotten.

As the high priest made his way to his throne, the trumpeters stopped. He sat down and afterwards an official announced for all to be seated—all except Peter and John and the guards stationed by their sides.

"Gentlemen and guests of the court," announced Caiaphas, as he stepped forward and away from his father-in-law, who sat next to him. "We regret the short notice of this assemblage. Due to an increased uprising in our fine city of this new 'Way' to the God of our Fathers, through a carpenter's son—a Jesus of Nazareth—and not according to the traditions of our laws, I and fellow members of the council ordered these two men—from Galilee, mind you—to be arrested and arraigned, since they were bold enough yesterday to interrupt the evening prayers with some sort of a miracle."

Caiaphas made his way down the aisle to face Peter and John. "A miracle has been reported to me—one of which many of you claimed to have witnessed. And these two men have claimed responsibility for healing a beggar. But where is this healed beggar today? Why is he not standing with you?" Caiaphas moved in closer to the accused. "Was this some cheap magician's trick?"

Caiaphas swung around, staring into the crowds under the porches. "Where's the healed beggar? Is he out there among you under the porches?"

No sound was made. Caiaphas then came back to face Peter and John. "Where is he, Galileans?"

"We do not know, your Majesty," said John. "We were arrested immediately after it occurred."

"Very well," responded Caiaphas, in a much louder voice. "Does anyone know where the healed beggar lies today? Is there anyone who wishes to stand with the accused in their defense?"

He smiled as he turned to walk back to his chair. Someone from outside the gate cried out: "The beggar is here, your Majesty! He's outside the gate; the guards will not allow him and us to come in, since we are defiled."

Caiaphas stopped and turned toward the people. "Well, if he remains healed by our God, then I think the court will pronounce him clean and allow him and any others who wish to stand with the defense." Caiaphas turned toward the court. "Agreed?"

The members of the council looked among themselves nodding their heads in assent.

"Then let the beggar in," said Caiaphas, ". . . only if he can walk on his own two feet."

The guards opened the gate to the outer Gentile courtyard. For a moment no one made an attempt to walk in. Then there appeared a small, frail man with a walking stick. His legs appeared a bit bowed, and there were no sandals covering his feet. He stepped through the gate, slowly and carefully, gazing at a view he had only heard about all his life.

"I said, 'on his own two feet,' not with a crutch," stated Caiaphas. Many of the council members laughed.

John looked back at the man. "Come on, Justus," he said quietly. "You can do it. Remember yesterday?"

Justus fixed his gaze at Peter and John; next, he looked at the guard beside the gate.

"Here, my friend," he said, as he tossed his stick to the guard. "I think you may need this to herd in all the witnesses to this miracle."

Justus then straightened and began to walk confidently to the accused apostles. But he did not come in alone. Following the beggar were Jewish men who now believed in Jesus Christ through the testimony of the followers and the miraculous healing of Justus.

Caiaphas' smile turned into a look of anger and fear as he began a slow back-step toward Annas and the rest. One after another, the new followers of Jesus marched through the gate, assembling in orchestrated lines beside and behind Peter and John. Within minutes, several thousand men had assembled in support of the accused. Finally, the guards had to push the crowd back in order to close the gate. There were more men left outside the courtyard than inside.

Justus smiled as he grabbed hold of Peter's belt.

"Not again," said Peter, looking at John with a smile. "He will never let go of me now."

Caiaphas was speechless. Annas looked at him. "Stand behind me, son," he said. "I'll take it from here." Annas had been high priest long enough to know what to say in times like this. He stood and cried, "Silence in the courtyard!" The guards pounded their shields with their metal wrist bands and stood to attention. This caused a hush over the crowded courtyard. He motioned for the council to be seated.

"I see we have a witness to a miracle that you men performed in the Courtyard of the Gentiles." Annas faced Justus. "Tell me, beggar, do you know how many of our laws were broken by the performance of this miracle?"

The smile was quickly erased from Justus. He tried to speak but nothing came out. His legs began to wobble a bit, so he pressed up against Peter. Peter squatted, took his hands, and began to massage Justus' legs.

"That's one of the problems you'll find with working legs, my friend," he said, looking at Justus. "You've got to plant your feet firmly underneath them for better balance." Some of the crowd that heard Peter laughed.

"Silence in the court!" screamed Annas. "Captain of the Guard, order your men to strike the next person who finds this court amusing." Again, the guards pounded their shields and drew their swords as a hush fell across the courtyard. Justus pressed in closer to Peter, nearly hiding himself from Annas' view.

"So," Annas continued. "I see you do not know the proper procedures for a sanctified healing. And what about you two men from Galilee? Do you?" He moved slowly toward the faces of Peter and John; they said nothing. After a few moments of silence, Annas continued. "I didn't think so. Now answer me this: if you do not know the procedures for healings—those rules that have been handed down by our forefathers, since the time of Moses—tell the court then: By what name, if not Moses, and by what power do you claim as the source for this healing?"

"Stand firm and face the high priest," the Spirit said to Peter. "Look into his eyes so that I may instruct him."

Yes, my Lord. . . . "Most Honorable Annas and to the esteemed court of our fathers' faith in God, I humbly stand before you and these witnesses to the event that occurred yesterday at one of the gates of the Gentiles' courtyard. I testify openly before you that nearly all of you, at some point in times past, have observed this feeble man begging for alms at the gate. He is no actor; he is no one's favored guest, but keeps company with the stray dogs that may pass by his way." Turning to Justus, Peter pulled him from his hiding place behind him to his side. "Yet here he stands in your presence with leg muscles as stout as any of ours standing here this day. And you ask how this miracle was performed? I will tell you: This man stands in the power of the name of Jesus of Nazareth."

Some gasps were heard.

"Yes, this Jesus of Nazareth, whom you crucified, is now alive and well before all and proves His power as the Christ, the living Son of God. You, yourselves, heard Him acknowledge this, yet you rejected Him! Like a builder who rejects a stone untested, so you have rejected the chief cornerstone that God has given us to rebuild and restore His eternal temple. It is in Jesus' name that we proclaim salvation to our nation for He and He alone has demonstrated the power to heal and to save us this day."

"Silence!" cried Annas, as he turned away from the piercing eyes of Peter. Never had he heard such a response from a commoner. Now the eyes of the courtyard were focused on a poor beggar and the two men who stood by him—fishermen from Galilee. Annas stood in the front of Caiaphas, while the other counselors gathered around him as they spoke to one another.

"Who are these men?" asked a counselor.

"And where did this uneducated man get such words?" another asked.

"They are followers of that Jesus-man," said another.

Annas faced Caiaphas. "Have these Galileans removed so that we can talk."

Caiaphas pushed those around him aside as he stood up. "Remove these accused from our presence until we decide how to proceed further." Immediately, the temple guards beat their shields, turned toward the people standing around the accused, and, with their swords, began to force everyone away from Peter, John, and Justus.

"Go with them, Justus," said John. "You were not arrested with us."

"No! Let me stand with you with my new legs."

"Listen, my friend," said Peter. "You must go now and use those legs as a testimony of God's new covenant to His people."

"But what if I don't see you again? I don't want to leave the ones who healed me!"

"Look at me!" said Peter sternly. "The One who healed you is Jesus; it is by His name and by His Spirit that you walk today.

And He will use you to proclaim that same power to others who need to hear of salvation from their sins. You leave this small crowd to John and me; we'll handle this group."

Peter smiled as he helped position Justus toward the thinning crowd. "Now move along, and God be with you, my brother in Jesus." Justus slowly obeyed as he turned away and joined the others that were being cleared out of the courtyard.

"This 'small crowd'?" asked John.

"John, it is our Lord who is speaking these words."

"Yes, He spoke to me as well. It felt as if I was speaking with you—every word was permeated with power . . . power like I've never felt before, yet it is that same power that we witnessed with our Lord."

"Yes, and it's a power that these mere men have no jurisdiction over; just watch as they try to save face." Peter and John were escorted to their holding room until a decision could be reached.

"What can we do with these men?" a council member asked.

"I know this beggar; I have seen him dozens of times," said another. "All Jerusalem has heard of this miracle!"

Annas stood once again and a hush came over the council. Annas slowly walked through the crowd of men, looking at each as if he were looking for one whom he could blame for this stand-down before the community, for whom they were supposed to be the spiritual guides. He finally turned toward Caiaphas. "My son, the high priest should stand before these commoners to read their verdict. You and these assembled will threaten them to never again speak of some power in the name of that Nazarene."

Caiaphas faced the others. "This Jesus is dead! You saw Him beaten, crucified, and buried. And that will be the end of it! Do you all understand?"

"Yes, your Majesty," they responded in unison.

Annas looked at Caiaphas and his sons. "Come to me later, and we will discuss how to stop the so-called power of this name." With those words, he and his escorts left the council chambers.

"Call those fishermen back in here," said Caiaphas. In a few minutes, Peter and John arrived and stood before Caiaphas and the counselors. "You two, you broke so many of our laws yesterday, that we could not agree conclusively just how to punish you. Therefore, the council has agreed to release you and has ordered that you cease and desist from stirring up the public against the faith of our fathers by using the name of Jesus again as some phenomenal power of sorts." Caiaphas approached them to take a position of power before them. "Do I make myself clear?"

Peter and John stood as one in response. "We stand here in the court of our God, and what we hear from Him and what He orders us to say, we will declare."

Caiaphas was clearly angry now. "Listen to me, you ignorant commoners; if you ever come before me again, I will personally see that you are beaten as severely as that Jesus-man whom you blindly follow. Now get out of here before I change my mind, and let me never see your faces again."

Peter and John were turned around and escorted out of the chamber toward the outer courtyard. As they were leaving the chamber, John began singing a new song about Jesus: "Jesus is the name that releases me from the lion's mouth," he quietly sang. Peter also tried to join in the not-so-familiar lyrics. "Jesus is the name that calms the raging waters, and Jesus is the name that shall lead us home."

Outside, in the Gentiles' courtyard, many were standing with Justus. When they saw Peter and John, great shouts of joy and praise filled the streets of Jerusalem. God was worshiped as never before seen or experienced in this generation. At the villa where Peter and John resided, the crowd dispersed and allowed them to go in and visit with the other apostles and family.

"Peter! . . . John!" cried Matthew. "I thought I might never see you free again!"

"Our Lord was with us and gave us direction," responded Peter.

"Matthew, the Spirit of our Lord was there during the whole encounter!" said John excitedly. "And He gave us words to say, and His power was as great as if He were there in bodily form!"

"Come," said Matthew. "Let's report to the others; they anxiously await the good news!"

The courtyard of the complex had now become a gathering place for many friends and family members of the apostles. Peter glanced around as he saw most of the apostles visiting with others. Still others were upstairs in the official prayer vestibule, praying and worshiping their God and Savior, Jesus. Then he saw Perpetua, his wife, at a distance, helping the other women prepare for the next fellowship meal. She gave a nod as John redirected Peter's attention.

"Let's find James, our Lord's brother," said John. "I've so much to tell him."

"I think he's upstairs," Matthew responded.

As they meandered their way through the crowd, the other apostles began to migrate toward Matthew, Peter, and John. It was obvious that all wanted to see and hear of the report concerning the encounter with the high priest and council. When they reached the top of the stairs, James was there to greet them.

"Grace and peace to you both!" exclaimed James. He embraced and kissed them both. "Oh, what a wonderful day this has turned out to be!"

"Yes, my dear brother," said Peter.

"And we've got a story to tell you!" said John.

"Indeed you have, and we all need to hear this because we also have been given instructions from our Lord for the coming days."

For about an hour, Peter and John spoke to the apostles detailing all the events from yesterday to the present. At times, John could hardly contain himself as he shared of the powerful presence of the Lord.

As they ended their report, James, the Lord's half-brother, stood to speak to them all. "My brothers and sisters, this report from Peter and John confirms what each of you apostles have been reporting: that the guiding presence of our Lord—blessed Jesus—is with us through the abiding presence of His Spirit. Each of you has reported to the others how the Spirit is telling you to embark into various regions of our people to share and to demonstrate the good news of salvation through a commitment of repentance and faith toward the new Way in Jesus, who is the Anointed One—the Christ and Messiah for our deliverance."

"Through love," said John, "He set up our encounter with the council by means of us healing the beggar. Whatever we do and wherever we go, we must cover our words and deeds in the love of Jesus. That's how others will know we are His followers."

"So true, my brother," said James. "Do all things in the love of our Master, Jesus."

Peter stood up to speak. "From Jerusalem, we must scatter into the regions of our homeland, into Samaria, and on to the shores of the Great Sea, the Sea of Galilee, and beyond. And as we go, it is important that we establish communication between us all that we may be able to hear what the Spirit is saying to us and communicate His guidance to the rest. As we spread out, we must remain of one spirit under the guidance of one Lord, our beloved Jesus."

"Amen, amen!" came a resounding echo throughout the room.

"Let us now agree that this place shall become our headquarters to which all shall report," said James. "I'm sure Joseph of Arimathea will not mind it at all. Now one of you must become our headmaster, someone who can oversee all the disbursements and can delegate responsibilities to others that we may have clear and up-to-date records of who goes where, what may be needed, and what is being accomplished." James looked around. "Do any of you have a word from our Lord about this position?"

There was silence for a few moments. Finally someone spoke: "I have heard from my Lord to stay here in Jerusalem and minister to the gatherings of the tax collectors and their families," said Matthew. Murmurings could be heard as some spoke softly to each other. "But I have not got a word from my Lord to lead in such a position. I do not feel especially gifted to lead and to delegate."

"Thank you, Matthew," said James. "Anyone else?"

Again, some spoke softly to one another.

"I also have a word from my Lord to stay here in Jerusalem," spoke James, the brother of John. "I do not feel led to be the headmaster, but I will do what I can to assist in the setup of our reports."

"Ah, James," said his brother. "You were always good at reporting me to Father when I didn't do well at fishing!" That brought more than a few chuckles as John hugged his brother.

"Yes," he responded. "And had I not kept you from singing so much, we would probably have been less popular than the tax collectors! . . . Oops, my dear Matthew, please accept my apology; old habits and sayings can be hard to eradicate."

"No offense taken, my brother," Matthew responded with a smile. "Just pray that I don't slip and use some of my old language in front of you!"

Peter spoke again. "Brothers and sisters, it appears many of us have no inclination or word from our Lord to leave Jerusalem at this time. What our brother, James, has said is very important and needful. However, since no one appears to have been given a definite word to be our headmaster, I propose that those who stay in Jerusalem work this out, while the rest of you give the direction you plan to go. And let us allow our Lord's brother to coordinate our organization of elders for the fellowships to be established here in our grand city and beyond."

"Amen, amen!" came shouts throughout the assembled witnesses.

"But I am not an apostle," James responded.

"But you are acquainted with all our deliberations with our Lord. And you and your brothers have become like one of us since you have believed. I say we gather around our Lord's brothers right now and lift up our voices to the Lord and to our Father for acknowledgement that we are following the wishes of our Lord."

"Amen, amen," came the response. The room was arranged for the apostles to gather with James, Joses, Judas, and Simon. Others sprinkled themselves into the mix as many bent their knees to enter into prayer. They began to pray softly to their God and Savior. One of the apostles raised his voice to cry out to God: "O God, our sovereign Master, we appeal to You this day for divine guidance. You are the Creator of all things. And today we praise You for sparing our brothers from our so-called religious leaders. They acted like the heathen who You spoke against through Your servant, our King David, when he said, 'Why are the nations around us enraged and why do they conspire to trap us? Their kings united together to outnumber us and to fight against our belief in our Deliverer, the Anointed One.' And now our leaders—those who claim to follow the traditions of Moses!—they themselves have conspired against Your Son, Jesus, just as did Herod and Pontius Pilate. This Jesus, who You sent beforehand to do all things according to Your predetermined will, He is the One they are threatening against.

"So we cry out to You this day; to our Lord God we pray; look upon us and hear their threats to shut up our mouths. O, Abba, Father, grant us, as Your servants, to be endued with boldness to speak even louder than their threats to Your words of salvation, and confirm with healings, signs, and other wonders to show the power of the name of Your precious Son, Jesus!"

Suddenly, the place where they were praying began to shake, as it did on the Day of Pentecost—yet nothing was destroyed. But the Spirit of God filled them, and, once again, they spilled out onto the streets of the city and began to speak boldly the word of God, each according to the measure of faith given. This happened for several hours, and then they returned to the villa. It was the confirmation for which they had prayed.

At the evening fellowship meal, John worked his way over to the side of Matthew. "Matthew, I once thought that Jerusalem would be best served if all tax collectors were chained together and thrown into the sea. But now I see you and others through the eyes of Jesus. I now understand how Jesus is going to reach all types of our people."

Matthew looked at John with tears welling up in his eyes. "John, you don't know the half of it. I was despondent over life. Being scorned and rejected by my people, I saw no hope of making peace with God. But when Jesus came to me and called me out of my booth, I saw in His eyes hope. He gave me courage to walk away. But now He is leading me back to those who thought I was gone for good. John, pray that I will be bold in sharing the way to God through our Lord."

"I suspect you will do just fine; remember," said John as he poked his finger in Matthew's chest, near his heart, "Jesus is with you all the time."

"So, where is He leading you?" asked Matthew.

"Oh, for now, I think I will remain nearby until I get some age on me. Right now I have some thoughts about our Lord's message that I want to write down."

"You also? You know, I have kept tax records for a long time. I feel strangely led to help my friends connect our former covenants with the sayings of Jesus. Perhaps this will help them to see the Way more clearly."

"Grace and peace to you, my brother. May His Spirit guide our every word." With that statement John embraced Matthew and walked away to fellowship with others.

Peter and James, the Lord's half-brother, were involved in conversation with the other apostles. John stuck his nose into their deliberations.

"Now, Bartholomew," said Peter. "I want us to begin with the groups that have remained since the Feast of Pentecost. Go to the group that our Lord led you to at our initial baptism of power. Once they hear your words and observe the Spirit's power in you, they can find a synagogue or another assembly area in which you can meet. Go now and tell what things you have seen and heard from our Lord. Wait on the Lord's Spirit to speak to you and to guide you into all truth—it is essential. And send us reports!"

"Yes, my brother; you can depend on me." With that statement, Bartholomew faded into the courtyard crowd.

†††

The name, Inaros, came from an Egyptian of the fourth century B.C. He was known for his rebellion against the pharaohs. Barabbas had heard the tales of his covert missions into the cities along the Nile. This name, Inaros, would not only announce to his friends a renewed presence, but also a renewed mission: to, once and for all, drive out the Roman imperialists that lorded over Judea.

Inaros left Bethany under the evening sun, clothed with a cloak covering his Jewish tunic. Pentecost now ended meant the visitors of Jerusalem would soon retreat from the city streets and an air of normality would soon ensue. Inaros did not want the attention of visitors. He needed those whose hearts were embittered over the Roman takeover of Judea; he wanted those who hated the Herodian kingship.

On the southern end of the city, there was a brothel that Inaros sought. That was the place to find his man, Jabeth. Inside was the smell of spices and burning incense, so mixed that it was hard to tell which women bathed in which fragrance. Inaros, still hidden under his cloak, walked through the first of several women who vied for his attention. He remained focused on his mission. Among the crowd, he noticed two men who had once been at his bidding. He pushed his way between them.

"Whoa! And who is this stranger badgering in on our conversation?" blurted one of the two.

"Perhaps we should introduce ourselves?" responded the other. Both men, in harmonious coordination, pulled out curved daggers as they backed away for enough room to slash out at the intruder. Several women screamed as the crowd backed away for a fight. But before either could make a move, Inaros pulled out a pair of daggers, one in each hand, as his face became visible for the first time.

"Barabbas!?" came a chorus from the two.

"Never mention that name again," Inaros thundered as he quickly brought a dagger to each man's throat. "I am Inaros, captain of those who long for vengeance and restoration of our beloved country."

"Barab—I mean, Inaros, it's me, Jabeth."

"And don't forget me," said the other. "Sorenthasas." Both men were frozen into position, stunned by the revelation of their former leader.

Inaros put his daggers back into his cloak as quickly as he had exposed them. When it became apparent no fight was to occur, the others in the brothel began to go back to their interrupted conversations.

The two men quickly lowered their weapons as well. Jabeth was the first to continue a conversation. "You were caught, put into prison—doomed to be crucified."

"Then released by Pilate!" responded Sorenthasas. "What a turn of events! What luck!"

"Destiny," interrupted Inaros. "Destiny has visited me and has called me into a renewed contract." He backed up in order to draw both men into his vision. "Tell me, will Inaros find his comrades hungry for victory, or does fear and defeat prevail in Jerusalem?"

† † †

"This is big," said John.

"Yes, my friend," responded James, the half-brother of Jesus. "All the more reason for us to communicate with one another.

My only fear is how do our brethren survive as they go back into hostile regions?"

"What do you mean?" asked Peter.

"I'm afraid the tasks of making a living will snuff out the fire that has been lit while we have been together."

James, John's brother, appeared out of nowhere. "The Lord is providing."

"What do you mean?" asked James, the half-brother of Jesus.

"For the past few hours, many followers have been making pledges of harvest, sheep, cattle, and money from the sales of property and other possessions. It is coming in like manna out of heaven."

"Hallelujah!" exclaimed Peter. "Let's see to it that every apostle and their delegates are cared for in their small groups. And anyone who has a definite need should be counseled and receive help from God's provisions. We need Matthew's help with the distributions. Where is that man? Matthew!? Matthew!?"

Matthew was in another corner of the courtyard, speaking with a new follower, Joses, a descendant of the Levi tribe, born on the isle of Cyprus. He was so noted as an encourager that someone had renamed him Barnabas. Now Barnabas was a wealthy man and had numerous landholdings. He also managed small stables of horses, camels, and other travel animals throughout the Judean and surrounding territories. When Matthew heard that Peter and the others were calling for him, he and Barnabas went looking for their callers.

"My brothers, were you calling for me?"

"Yes, Matthew," said Peter. "We have a need for your counting abilities."

Matthew interrupted, "Before you speak further, I want to introduce you to a new follower, Barnabas." The others greeted him with the traditional embrace. Matthew continued, "Barnabas has come to me with a large sum of money from a land sale he recently made in the area."

"That's wonderful," said John. "Praise the Lord! This is exactly why Peter was calling for you."

"Yes, indeed it is wonderful news for our expanding mission," said Peter. "Thank you, Barnabas." Then turning to Matthew: "We need your help, Matthew."

James, the Lord's half-brother, jumped into the conversation. "Yes, brothers, many like yourself, Barnabas, have felt impressed by our Lord to give of their possessions to help us support the apostles as they fan out into the regions, sharing the good news."

Barnabas responded, "Brothers, I believe the Lord has spoken to my heart to give to the other brothers who need help founding a new work of the Way in different villages. May our Lord be pleased with this gift and may more come in as the Lord blesses."

Acts 5

As the news of the offerings that were gathered spread, others began giving as well. For the next few days, people gave joyfully as the Lord was instructing each family. A couple named Ananias and Sapphira, also pledged money from the sale of a piece of property.

"What do you make of this new treasury we're creating?" Ananias asked his wife, Sapphira, several days later.

"What do you mean?"

"Well, it seems to me the more you sacrifice, the more you get blessed with attention."

"I don't understand all the excitement about it," she responded. "It has been our tradition to give a portion of our possessions to the priests."

"Yes, my dear, but many are giving much more than a tithe!"

"Your point, my lord?"

"Do you remember the pledge we made to give of the sale of that piece of property just south of town?" She nodded a *yes*. "Well, the sale of the piece was much greater than I imagined. I think we should give a portion of the sale—maybe three quarters of it?—and reinvest for some additional property that we may need later on. I mean, three quarters of the amount is what I thought was the land's value to begin with."

Sapphira stopped her food preparations and sat beside her husband. "But didn't you announce before the assembly that the Lord told you to give all the proceeds to the apostles' ministry?"

"Yes, but I didn't realize the property was that valuable."

"How much are we talking about?" she asked.

"It sold for 200 denarii—fifty more than I thought. So my feeling is that we give 150 to the Lord's work and keep the other fifty for that piece of property beside our other land. The owner of that piece said he would sell it for the right price."

"My, that *is* a good amount. And if we purchase the piece beside our other lot, that will allow us to rebuild outside of the city walls. Are you sure it's the right thing to do?"

"Yes, and I'm sure the Lord will bless us for giving the 150 denarii."

"I agree," she said. "And no one has to know the full amount . . . this is great!"

"And 150 denarii is what I was hoping would be the amount anyhow. We received more so that we could purchase that other piece of property for ourselves."

The more Ananias and Sapphira talked about it, the more excited they became about getting the extra property outside the city walls.

The next morning, Ananias made his way to the courtyard of the villa where the apostles were lodging. Peter was teaching a class of followers when Ananias approached him. "Let's take a short break," said Peter, "and return back in a few minutes."

"My brother," said Ananias, "I have good news for the cause; my property sold a few days ago, and I'm here to present my pledge." With that statement, Ananias presented a large bag of silver and gold. "One hundred and fifty denarii," he stated loudly, laying the bag at Peter's feet.

"He's lying!" said the Spirit to Peter. "He has held back a portion of the sale."

"So this is the full amount of the sale?" asked Peter.

"Why, yes, my brother," he responded, but not so loudly this time. "Look, it is a large amount; why do you question me this way?"

"Because the Spirit of God tells me you are lying. You have held back a portion of the sale. Listen to me, Ananias; you have tried to deceive us, but in fact you have deceived the Holy Spirit! You didn't have to give it all to the Lord's work, but you told the assembly that He wanted you to give the full amount to the ministry. In your heart you have tried to jeopardize the work of the Lord through your deceit. Ananias, you've not only lied to us but to God Himself!"

Before Ananias could say a word in response, he fell dead that very moment. Those around the two gasped and bowed their heads. Peter motioned for several young men to come take Ananias' body away for burial.

About three hours later, Sapphira came looking for her husband, who was late for lunch. When she did not find him in the courtyard, she proceeded to request a hearing with Peter. Peter saw her coming, and, once again, the Holy Spirit spoke to his heart about her agreement with her husband.

"Your husband was here earlier," Peter said to her.

With her head bowed, she said, "Yes."

"Tell me, did that piece of property really sell for 150 denarii?"

"Yes, my lord," she responded nervously. "That was the price."

"Look at me! How could the two of you put the Lord's Spirit to the test? Look! The men who buried your husband a few hours ago are standing at the door to bury you with him." Immediately, she also fell dead before Peter. The men who had just buried Ananias were amazed when they were ordered to carry out his wife and bury her next to him.

As the news of this traveled among the followers of Jesus, many became afraid of what God was doing through his anointed servants.

"Listen to me, my brothers and sisters," said Peter. "This happened in order to keep our assembly pure and righteous before God. Liars are forbidden in God's kingdom."

Nevertheless, some who were hearing the message of Peter and the other apostles were fearful of joining them, seeing what happened to Ananias and Sapphira.

The power of the Spirit remained on Peter and the other apostles as they taught from Solomon's Porch daily. And as they preached, many men and women were turning their lives and hearts to the Way of Jesus Christ. The power of God's Spirit was so manifest in the preaching that many people brought the sick and lame along the street, believing that even the shadow of Peter was sufficient for healing—and it was! Peter spent much time at Solomon's Porch, healing others of sickness and demon possession.

†††

"Get me Caiaphas immediately!" Annas was a bit more than just anxious. "Where are my couriers!? Guards!" Immediately the thunderous sound of leather-soled footwear increased as two temple guards appeared before the former high priest. They stopped abruptly, stood at attention, and beat their breasts.

"Yes, my lord? What is your bidding?"

"Caiaphas! I need Caiaphas right away!"

"As you wish, my lord." Then they vanished as quickly as they appeared.

†††

The mid-morning air was as restless as the two in bed, one of them vying for just a few more minutes together. "Caiaphas, it's late; we must get up."

He stretched. "Isn't there some holiday today?" he responded, hoping for a glimmer of reluctance from her.

"No! Now get up!" Sharon slipped out of the bed and made her way to the water basin.

"Then allow me to declare a national holiday, today, in honor of your beauty." She gave him a glancing look. "The Olives of Sharon Festival—that's what today shall be decreed." Caiaphas sat up in the bed, proud of his creative idea.

"You should be making your way to the dinner chambers if you wish to dine with your 'Olives of Sharon.'" She walked toward the bed to help him get up. Suddenly their morning was interrupted by the sound of approaching house servants.

"My lord and madam," the head servant announced at the doorway of the bedchamber.

"It better be important," said Caiaphas.

"Annas has requested your immediate appearance in the council room."

"Oh, what is it now!? Can't he get someone else?"

"I'm sorry, my lord, but he wants you there by the sixth hour."

"Go away! Leave us alone!"

"My apologies, my lord, but his guards said they could not leave without an acknowledgement of your reply."

"Then tell the guards they can—"

"Caiaphas!" Sharon interrupted. "This is not the time or the day to ignore the wishes of the former high priest."

"You mean, your father."

"Yes, but nevertheless, we must get up and get ready for this meeting—an important meeting, I believe." Sharon knew her father, and she could read into this unscheduled appointment something very urgent—something that needed the attention of the current high priest.

"Tell the guards we will meet him at the sixth hour; now get out of here!" The chief house servant backed his way out of the chamber's doorway and was gone.

"I wonder what he is up to now?" he thought out loud.

"Darling, be patient. It won't be many more years before he weakens." She walked toward him again and began to run her fingers through his wavy black hair. Only this time she had some oil on her hands—she was preparing his hair for the day's activities. "We must look the part, my dear."

Caiaphas did not like the position of high priest with Annas still acting as the one in charge. He had hoped the crucifying of this Jesus-man would push the elder priest into retirement, but this sudden uprising of Jesus' followers seemed to invigorate him.

The quarters of the former high priest remained decorated in costly tapestries and carvings with furniture covered in silver, gold, and precious stones—just like the high priest's. Every room reflected the arrangements made with the Herodians, a peace that made life much more comfortable with the Roman governors—a peace that could not be jeopardized by the claim of another Messiah following. *This is why I'm here,* thought Caiaphas.

"Come in, come in my high priest," Annas said. "And my dear Sharon, you're as lovely as ever."

They embraced. "Father, your eyesight is as good as ever, I see."

"Oh, how I wish your mother could see you now."

"We came as quickly as we got word," interrupted Caiaphas. "We could hardly wait to see you so early in the day."

Annas eyed his son-in-law with a bit of suspicion. "I'm sure . . . What I'm about to say is for the benefit of both of you; so listen carefully." He motioned them to recline with him beside a table with fruit and wine already prepared for three. "I haven't many days left to assist you in leading our people, but I will not rest until we have made a definitive end to the following of this 'Way' of the Nazarene. The Galilean followers of this man have made a camp in our city and continue to hold unauthorized meetings on and around the temple grounds. I had hoped they would disperse after the festivities of Pentecost and especially after our previous threats, but they continue to teach the doctrines of this new Way to God."

"Then I will arrest them," replied Caiaphas.

"We did already, and it didn't work."

"I will arrest them all this time and keep them for a while. Let's see what this group can do without their leaders for a few months." Caiaphas was tired of these commoners breaking into the transition plans of the high priestly chain of command.

"And what do we charge them with?" asked Sharon. "You know the people can appeal to the Romans for a hearing."

"Yes, my darling princess," responded Annas. "And this time, we need the charges to stick! That's why I have called for the top officer of our training school and the council's court to join us tomorrow for a hearing."

"Rabban Gamaliel?"

"Yes, my son—Gamaliel. I'm sure when he sees and hears from this group, he will have an excellent and most sure way to deal with these rebels once and for all."

"Where can we find them?" Caiaphas asked.

"Every day they congregate at Solomon's Porch, teaching and testifying of the miraculous powers of this Jesus. Rumors are spreading about numerous healings from some of the leaders."

"Well then, I'll call the guards; we can arrest them for unauthorized religious ceremonies."

"Not so fast, my son. I have called for an assembly of the Sadducees—I hope you don't mind. They're due to arrive within the hour. They especially hate the testimonies of a risen Messiah and will be an asset to this process. The more we get the peoples' representatives involved, the more sympathy they will afford us."

Caiaphas realized that his father-in-law was thinking ahead of him. This made him glad and mad at the same time. He was glad a well-thought-out plan was in play, but he was angry that, once again, his scheming father-in-law was using him as a pawn. However, he decided to go along with his wishes . . . at least for now.

Downstairs, the Sadducees were assembling, mumbling and grumbling as they entered the inner courtroom. Some of them had seen the many followers of the new Way outside, listening to the teachings of the apostles. Annas allowed Caiaphas to enter the room first. The guards escorted them to the center of the tables. Inside, the pomp and circumstance was a bit less formal.

Annas spoke first. "My brethren of the court, I thank you very much for coming at such a quick notice." Caiaphas was ready to sit quietly and let Annas develop the plan. But he was surprised at his next words: "I know that you heard those Galileans at the porch as you entered the temple grounds." Outbursts of rage and cries of "Blasphemy!" filled the room. "Now, now, gentlemen, let's quiet our hearts for a time until you hear of a plan from our high priest, Caiaphas."

A hush fell over the room, quickly—too quickly for Caiaphas as he was trying to search for words. Annas looked over toward Caiaphas. "My son, tell the council what is your plan." Caiaphas stood and methodically walked to the front of the table without saying a word. For once he had this rare opportunity to see into the face of his father-in-law. He looked carefully at a weathered face that was showing signs of decay. Finally, it seemed as if both were in agreement in orchestrating the future. Now was his time to capture the moment.

"Brethren, the men teaching our people of a risen Messiah must be stopped!" It was an abrupt statement, but equally abrupt was the response.

"Amen, amen!" they cried.

"I propose that we seize all their leaders and set them before us, with our scribes and the council, tomorrow. And let us all join in a show of solidarity."

"Amen, amen!" was the response.

"I have invited our chief teacher and counselor, Rabban Gamaliel, to join us tomorrow to advise us on stopping these unauthorized meetings on our temple grounds. Together, we will quell these unorthodox gatherings with a lengthy imprisonment of them all."

"Gamaliel?" someone responded. "He's a Pharisee!"

"I know that, but he is equally anxious to stop this heresy. He knows the Law and the prophets better than anyone among us." Caiaphas did not wait for another response. "Captain of the temple, take as many of the priests and guards with you as necessary to arrest these rebel teachers immediately, then bring them to the council." With no objections voiced, the guards were dispatched to arrest the apostles.

†††

"We must remember that it is the words of our Messiah that are truth," Peter said, as he taught the multitude of followers gathered at Solomon's Porch. "But listen to me carefully; truth—to be effective—must be presented in the power of His blessed Spirit. And this Holy Spirit can only express His power through a clean vessel. So it is imperative to maintain a life that is totally yielded to the teachings of the Sacred Writings."

"But what about the traditions of our Law?" asked someone.

Peter was tired from all his teaching. "James, John, would either of you care to respond?" But before either could volunteer, there was another voice that spoke.

"The Law was written as our tutor," said Matthew as he stepped forward. "It is combined with the prophets to teach us of the steps to remaining holy before our God. But, as Peter was describing earlier, Jesus fulfilled the holy requirements of the Law and the prophets, so that means we, in turn, go to Him first. As we yield ourselves to our Lord, He delivers us from the condemnation of the Law and the prophets. Our sins are covered through the blood of Jesus' crucifixion. We are no longer bound to the Law." Matthew would have said more except that the captain of the temple, some priests, a group of the Sadducees, and a host of temple guards approached from behind them.

"Teachers of the Way," said the captain. "You have been summoned to appear before the high council to give an account of your teachings." Some rumblings and shouts began to sound from the gathering.

"Silence!" shouted the captain. "If your God is the God of our leaders and our people, you should have no problem defending yourself."

Peter stepped forward toward the people. "My fellow brothers and sisters." The motioning of his hands and his speech quieted the gathering. "What he says is true. Now go your way and remember what we've taught you. Go now and pray that we shall see you in the morning." The people began to disburse and walked away, blending into the outer crowd of curious onlookers. Peter then turned to the captain. "Is that what you were trying to say?" Peter smiled as he got even closer to him.

The captain was not expecting an easy exit. "I . . . I suppose so . . . yes, now all of you must follow us." The captain motioned to the guards as the apostles voluntarily formed two rows of six.

"Where is the council?" Matthew asked. "We are ready."

The captain drew the priests together, consulting among themselves. "I think it best we march them to the other opening so as not to draw suspicion."

"Yes," said another priest. "An indirect path to the city prison is a much better approach."

The captain turned to the guards. "Surround them and march them to the west opening, then proceed to the temporary quarters of the city prison. Feed them and allow them to rest. Make sure a guard is posted at all times throughout the remainder of their stay." The guards began to form several rows around the apostles, making it nearly impossible for any of them to see beyond the glistening armor of the guards.

"Did he say 'prison'?" asked Matthias.

"That he did," responded Peter. "That he did."

While they continued to talk among themselves, the captain of the temple began the ordered march through the outer court-yard of the Gentiles onto the western opening. *This is too easy,* thought the captain. *I can't believe my superiors are so afraid of these Galileans.*

This is too easy, Thomas thought to himself. *Lord, help us not to be afraid of these leaders.*

"Do not doubt or fear, Thomas," spoke the Lord. "I am with you all the time."

After a rather small distribution of bread and pieces of dried fish, the apostles sat together for a time of study and discussion.

"What are we discovering through this power of our Lord's Spirit?" asked Peter.

Matthew was anxious to say something. "I, for one, did not have the courage to speak before a gathering. But now, His Spirit speaks words to my heart."

"I, likewise," responded Thomas. "I was fearful of this arrest, but the Spirit told me not to doubt or be afraid."

"It's like Jesus is with us at all times," commented John.

"He is within us, and we are each fully aware of His presence," said Peter.

"The power of the Spirit is always showing Himself as we tell others of our new life in our Lord Jesus Christ," said James. The others were giving similar responses.

"Brothers," said Peter. "When Jesus told me that when I am older someone else would guide me, I did not realize that He was telling me that I'm going to get older before He returns."

"How much older can you get!?" responded Simon the Zealot. Some laughter filled the quarters.

"Hush, young lad," said Peter. "As I was about to say, this revelation to me is telling me—telling us—that we should not be sitting around waiting for His return to restore the kingdom to Israel. Rather, we must maintain contact with His Spirit and use His power to convince others to follow in the teaching and character of Jesus."

"There are thousands who have responded to our invitation to repent and to turn to Jesus for the remission of sins," stated Andrew. "I believe we must eventually divide up and create smaller gatherings in order for the Way to develop fuller."

"That leads me to another thought," Peter continued. "Observe the family leaders among those you teach. Ask Jesus for discernment, so that we may train other men to oversee the groups as they go into the Judean region."

"I have felt this as well," said James. "It is obvious that we have the same Spirit speaking to us and giving us instructions on how to further the testimony of our blessed Lord. The Spirit was not given to the orators of our priests, but to the simple-minded— we—who can make plain the good news of salvation and deliverance from the penalty of the Law."

"Keep records of what the Spirit says to each of you," said John. "There will come a day when some among us will need to write these things down so that all may hear the same message that we ourselves are hearing."

"Amen, amen," said some of the others. The discussion continued for another hour.

When everyone was through talking, John changed the subject. "Now let us retire for a time of prayer and worship." He immediately began humming a tune from the parchment of Psalms. This brought out an atmosphere of unity among the brethren. Others began to softly sing as they prepared to pray and worship together.

After about three hours of prayer and parchment readings, the apostles were finishing their worship when suddenly another man appeared in the room. It was an angel sent by the Lord. "Listen to me, you highly-favored ones. I have come to release you from this place. Only, do not run away, but go and get some rest and then return to the temple grounds in the morning. Continue to teach and proclaim the Way of the Lord. Share your testimonies of the new life that is found in the Christ."

"But won't they arrest us again?" asked Peter.

"Do not fear them, for they must see and hear of the power of the Lord. Now follow me."

The angel led them out of the prison. Each guard on duty had fallen into a deep sleep. After they had left, the angel shut and sealed the prison doors and disappeared.

"Wow," said Thomas. "I don't think I'll get any sleep tonight."

"Take note," said Peter. "Their religion put us in prison, but Jesus sets us free!"

The very next morning found the apostles at Solomon's Porch, teaching and proclaiming Jesus as the Messiah, risen from the dead. Hundreds—no, thousands!—of people were gathering in the temple courtyard, listening to the apostles. When they spoke, there was boldness and power in their speech. And the sick continued to be healed.

Meanwhile, several priests were preparing the chamber for a hearing with the apostles. The chief priest sent some guards to bring the apostles in. When they arrived at the prison, everything appeared just as it was the night before. There was only one problem: when they went inside to get the prisoners, they were gone!

"Guards!" shouted the captain.

"Yes sir?" the two guards replied.

"Were there any visitors for these men last night?"

"No sir!"

"Then where are they?"

The guards looked into the empty room with stunned surprise. The ranking guard replied, "Sir, they were here when we locked the doors, and no one was let in."

"Then you won't mind going with us to explain this to the chief priest." And with that statement, he pointed the two overnight watchmen toward the door.

✝✝✝

Three men were observing the prison from a distance. They watched as the guards stood at the door. Then a band of guards came from the direction of the temple, marching in an orderly fashion. They stopped at the prison door, awaited the opening of the outer gate, and then disappeared inside. Inaros was puzzled. "You two go up to the gate and listen in—quickly now!"

Jabeth and Sorenthasas moved quickly, trying to act normal in a situation that was anything but normal. They leaned on the bars of the gate, listening to the conversations from inside the prison. Then, as quickly as they moved toward the gate, they returned to Inaros.

"What did you hear?"

"Rather strange," responded Jabeth. "Don't you think, Soren?"

"Yes, it seems there was a break in last night, and some prisoners got away."

"What!?" cried Inaros. Then the three hushed as the guards marched out of the prison and passed through the gate. The original gate guards were now in the front of the band. The two guards in the rear were commanded to shut the outer gate, but not lock it.

"We'll be back soon enough to throw these men into their own prison," said the captain of the guards. You two in the rear wait until we return." That said, the remainder of the guards disappeared down the street, marching toward the temple.

Inaros stroked his beard as he thought through the new setting before the prison gate. *This is a sign from God,* he thought. *I must take advantage of this situation.*

"Okay, you two, go to the far side and create a diversion. I'm going in."

"Going in?" asked Sorenthasas. "You just got out a few months ago. By the gods, why are you trying to break back into—"

"Don't ask questions right now; just do as I say. Keep the guards distracted until you hear the signal. Now go!"

Jabeth looked at Sorenthasas. "Come on, Soren," said Jabeth. "We'll do our little fight scene and draw these guys into the fight."

"Okay, but if you crack my wineskin, you're going to pay!"

"Don't trouble yourself; remember, we got Inaros now to cover our drinking needs." They both looked back at Inaros as they staggered toward the prison gate, swaying onto one another as though they were highly intoxicated. It was in their favor that the new guards were not usual assignments to the prison. As the noise began, the guards were easily persuaded to go and watch the fight.

Inaros came up the side of the gated area. When Jabeth and Sorenthasas managed to get one of the guards in between them, pushing him back and forth as they tried to get at each other's tunic, Inaros made his move and walked into the prison. He continued toward the inner prison chambers, where a usual guard was posted. Fortunately, the current events were enough distraction to cause the inner guard to be away from the entrance. So, once again, Inaros walked past the inner doorway.

"Hamath? Hamath? Where are you?" Inaros heard a familiar grunt. "Hamath, come here."

Hamath eased out of his straw bed and made a few steps toward his cell door. As his eyes adjusted to the doorway light, he squinted at his caller. "Barabbas? Is that you?"

"Yes, my old friend."

"What are you doing here?"

"I'm getting you out of prison. Listen, we haven't time for talk. I have all the guards away from the door; it is time to use our method to open the cell. Quickly, we've not much time."

Hamath had a thick head of black, unkempt hair, and his body was nearly three times the size of Inaros. He didn't speak much—usually grunted—but became Inaros' right-hand man in many covert operations against the Romans.

He walked to the front corner of his cell where Inaros was waiting. Together they put their backs against the steel corner and began raising the bars into the enlarged holes at the top that Inaros had previously created by standing on the shoulders of his cellmate. They groaned and pulled, wiggling the bars back and forth until they began to disappear further into the upper clay top.

"That's it Hamath, just a little more." The cell fronts were designed to keep the door from bending or turning upward or outward. However, the steel attached to the door was heavy enough to prevent a normal man or two from budging it. Thus, it was not sealed as tightly. Several times, Inaros and Hamath had used this escape route to go to other prisoners for deals and trades. They never attempted to escape from prison due to the three guards usually assigned to the entrances. But this was different.

"There; now roll underneath—Hamath! What are you doing?" Hamath dropped his side of the steel bars. Inaros managed to put enough pressure to the side to slow down the drop.

"My pouch, I need my pouch!" Hamath walked over to the side of his straw bed, lifted one corner and pulled out the pouch of items that he used for trading. He came back to the wall and easily returned it to its escape position.

"Okay, now roll under, quickly!" Hamath slid about halfway and put his hands under the bars for support. He slowly lifted the bars until his belly and chest cleared, and then rolled out onto the floor. He continued to roll until he could get in a crouched position to get off the floor.

Inaros began to brush off the dirt and straw from his partner. "Come, big fellow; we've got to quietly walk out the door."

"Guards? Don't we have to break a few bones?"

"Not this time; just follow me—and be quiet!"

As they neared the inner door, Inaros saw that the guard was still watching the fight from a corridor window. He could hear Jabeth and Sorenthasas swearing at each other as they took turns swinging and falling. Inaros motioned for Hamath and they quietly walked past the inner doorway and up to the outer gate. They did not miss a stride as they walked out of the prison and down the street to the corner. Inaros whistled the signal. Jabeth and Sorenthasas heard it and began to push each other into the direction of the street, much to the laughter of the guards. Jabeth pulled out his dagger and made an advance toward his partner.

"This will settle it once and for all," shouted Jabeth as he lunged for his partner. Sorenthasas turned enough so that Jabeth missed him. He fell, and Sorenthasas made a run for it down the street. "Come back, you coward! Uh, which way did he go?" The guard spun him around and pointed him in the opposite direction.

"That way!" said the guard. With that statement, the guard gave him a shove as Jabeth stumbled in the opposite direction. The guards were holding their stomachs from laughing so hard; nothing had entertained them as well as this stint.

†††

"What's with the delay?" asked the chief priest. The Sanhedrin council was ready to convene, but no one was there before them. There was some commotion going on outside the chamber. "Guards, report immediately!" About a dozen guards filed into the chamber. Each one stood at attention, but no one spoke. "Well? Where are the accused?" Finally, one of the temple guards spoke.

"Your Most Holy One, when we arrived at the prison, we found everything as secure as when we left the rebels. The guards stood watch at the doors, and no visitors were allowed inside. Yet, when we went inside to the holding chamber, we found no one inside."

"What!?"

"Yes, Most Holy One; the doors were firmly secured, and here are the two guards who stood watch overnight." The two guards were pushed forward for the chief priest to interrogate. The chief priest walked toward them in silence while the priests in the chamber talked among themselves. He looked at the faces of each guard, trying to detect the possibility of a lie.

"Is this true?"

"Yes, Most Holy One," they responded together, though nervously. "The prison was secured last night, and there is no evidence of a breech in any walls."

"Do you know the penalty for allowing prisoners to escape?—don't answer that! Their punishment will be upon you!" The chief priest studied their faces, momentarily, and then turned to the captain. "Captain, what do you make of this?"

The captain of the guards stepped forward. "Sir, I am as puzzled about this as you. These men are very reliable and have nothing to gain by initiating or participating in an escape. They know the consequences . . . it's baffling."

The two were about to say more, when another guard stepped into the chamber. "Sirs!?" he shouted, as he stood at attention.

"What is so important that requires an interruption of these proceedings?" asked the chief priest.

"Your Honor, the men you had arrested and who were reported missing . . . they are all gathered at the temple courtyard and are teaching the people."

An eerie quiet filled the room. The chief priest inched his way backward as if stricken by a leg cramp. He leaned against a wall. "Then go get them now," he replied, a little more subdued. "Surely you won't lose them again, captain?"

"No, sir! I will take two dozen guards to ensure their delivery."

"Then go, and take these two with you," he said, looking at the two prison guards. "It appears I have no charges to place upon you. Go now, with your fellow guards and don't ever let this happen again; do you understand?"

"Yes, sir, Most Holy One!" And with that exchange over, they turned immediately and exited the chamber, following the other guards.

The chief priest was about to excuse himself from the chamber when the high priest and Annas walked in with Gamaliel.

"Gentlemen of the council," said Caiaphas. "Will you join me in welcoming our esteemed guest, the headmaster of the school of Hillel, and chief counselor of our court, Rabban Gamaliel."

"Amen, amen!" shouted many, as others blended in with many words of reception.

"Gamaliel has agreed to sit in on our questioning of this sect, called the Way, and help us determine the severity of their punishment.

"I'm sure this won't take long, my friend," he said to Gamaliel.

"The pleasure is mine. I have heard numerous stories about this Way sect and am curious as to what drives them to be so bold."

"Too much sun!" shouted a priest.

"And strong drink!" said another. There was plenty of laughter in response.

"Now, my friend," said Annas to Gamaliel. "Sit here next to me, and may I offer you some of Jerusalem's finest wine while we wait?" Servants began pouring small goblets of wine and setting out small bowls of various fruits and bread as the council talked with each other.

The temple guards hustled to the temple area to secure the escaped prisoners. Some of the guards were expecting some ruthless-looking rebels, trying to incite a riot. When they arrived at the steps of Solomon's Porch, they were startled to find no rousing crowd or shouts of blasphemy. Instead, there was a group of men—some standing, some sitting—quietly listening as one of them spoke out into the crowd a story of the Jesus-man. Everyone was listening to each word, soaking in everything said like the desert sand taking in a rare summer rainstorm.

The captain of the guard spoke first to the other guards: "Men, let us be as gentle as the crowd in escorting these men to the high council. I have seen this crowd respond to brute force, and they don't like us pushing these Galileans around. Do I make myself clear?"

"Yes, sir!" they exclaimed.

The loudness of the exchange caused numerous men to look their way with suspicion. "You two—prison guards—come with me, and try to remember the gentle approach." As they began walking up the porch steps, more and more men began standing up, and some of them had stones in their hands. Others had daggers and slings. The captain turned to the others. "Do not draw your swords; keep them in their sheaths," he said. The captain knew they were easily outnumbered and did not want a riot to break out.

"What do they want?!" cried one of the men. "Do they intend to crucify these men as well?" Some growling was heard through the rows and rows of the listeners. "Perhaps it is time they felt the sting of rocks and nails thrust through their hands and feet," growled another man.

"Now, now, my brothers and sisters," spoke Peter. "Do not interfere with the duty of these men. Remember, they are simply obeying orders. Rather, let us respect their position as our Lord has taught us to respect one another. This is the Way of Christ Jesus our Lord."

The entourage of guards approached the apostles. "Sirs," said the captain. "Our orders are to escort you twelve to the High Chamber. Please, sirs, for the sake of our families and for this sacred place, come without resistance."

"Yes, my friend," said Peter. "We've been expecting you."

This statement surprised the captain. "You have?"

"Yes, for you see, an angel of the Lord released us from that cramped prison room and told us to go home, get some rest, and then to come here and proclaim the good news of deliverance from our sins."

"An angel?" queried the captain. "You say an angel released you?" The two prison guards by the captain's side began to shake, becoming more fearful of the apostles.

"Sir," one of the guards said to the captain, "We heard them singing songs and weeping in prayers to our God."

"An angel," repeated the captain. He was intrigued by the response of Peter and especially his control over the crowd. "And what is this angel saying to you now?"

"Actually, the Spirit of our Master has said, 'Go and speak to the priests, and do not be afraid.' So here we are; now do you want us to line up into two lines of six?"

"Your Master's Spirit?" queried the captain further. "And what is your Master's name?"

Peter looked into the captain's eyes. "His name is Jesus—the Anointed One, the Messiah, and Deliverer." Just the mentioning of the name of Jesus caused a soreness to form inside the captain's body—a feeling of conviction, of need. The captain saw visions of his own selfishness, fears, and evil thoughts—feelings that he had previously suppressed and kept locked up in the secret chambers of his mind. Now they seemed to be unlocked, and he began to tremble.

Peter interrupted his pause. "Sir, we mustn't keep the priests waiting; let's be on our way." To the crowd he said, "Brothers and sisters, do not fear for us. But go on your way now and remember the things we taught you. We will see you again soon." Peter then turned to his comrades. "Come, my brothers, we have an appointment to keep." With that, Peter walked down the steps toward the waiting guards. The captain and the two prison guards fell in behind the apostles as they walked in an orderly fashion, two rows of six, toward the High Chamber.

After about thirty minutes, there came the familiar rapping of shields to indicate an arrival for the chamber. The chief priest announced, "Enter into the High Council chamber!" The captain of the guards came first in the procession of the apostles, the other guards forming a double semi-circle around the back of the captives. The captain stopped, snapped his heels together, and spun around to the procession. "Halt!" he cried. "Remain standing, and speak only when spoken to. Guards, position of rest!" The guards spread their legs out in an "A" shape, allowing their shields to rest on the floor beside them and leaning into a clip strapped to the outer leg, thereby providing some relief from standing alone.

The apostles were formed into a wide "V" shape, their faces clearly in view of the council. Peter, Andrew, James, and John were at the front points of the V. This was an unusual formation, but never had so many accusers been brought together such as this. Most of the apostles had their heads lowered; Peter was praying (as were the others). *My Lord,* he prayed in silence, *We need You here as never before. Give us the words and we will speak.*

"Do not fear man, My beloved friends, but speak only as instructed by Me. They will beat you in the flesh, but they cannot take the kingdom from within you. Have faith, and you will be victorious in the end."

Peter looked discreetly at the other apostles. Each heard the same message the Spirit had just delivered. There was a unity of spirit among them.

"We gave you orders not to teach our people in the name of this Jesus-man," stated the chief priest. "And yet you continue to fill all Jerusalem with this new doctrine. It's as if you are planning a riot to get revenge on those of us who called for this man's death. Do you understand the penalty for disobeying the orders of the Sanhedrin?"

Peter made a half-step toward the chief priest of the council. "Your Most Excellent One," said Peter. "If you received a direct word from our God—whether in a dream or through a prophet—would you not rather obey Him and speak His words than a thousand words of a mere man?" Peter paused as he allowed the chief priest to come near him. The priest looked into Peter's eyes, expecting to see the normal fear of a prisoner being interrogated. Instead, the eyes of Peter were as white-hot as the midday summer sun reflecting off a clear and motionless pool of water. This caused the priest to waver a bit from his courtly stance. Gamaliel sensed the fear of the chief priest.

"Sir," Peter continued. "We have heard the words of God and cannot but obey Him rather than you mere men. You murdered this Jesus by hanging Him on a cross—you crucified Him! But the God of our forefathers raised Him up to life again to make this Jesus the first-born of many, seating Him at the right hand of authority, making Him our living Leader and Deliverer. God has seated Him there to offer all our people repentance and the forgiveness of our sins. And we, who are witnesses to these things, give testimony of Israel's Deliverer who now lives in us by the power and testimony of His blessed Holy Spirit who was given to us who obey the God of our forefathers."

"Blasphemy!" was the resounding reply among the priests. "Let's show them the power of our God and take them now and stone them for blasphemy!"

"Amen, amen!" cried others. The chief priest allowed the venting of his comrades, taking note of Caiaphas, Annas, and Gamaliel's reaction. Gamaliel leaned over and whispered to the high priest; he, in turn, motioned to the chief priest.

"Silence, my brothers!" cried the chief priest. "Let the high priest respond."

"I withhold my judgment until I hear from our esteemed guest first."

Gamaliel stood up and walked onto the center of the floor, looking into the eyes of the apostles. He first studied the eyes of Peter, and then of John. He said nothing to either of them, but turned around to face the council. "May I ask that these men be put outside the chamber while I address you, my brothers?"

"Do as requested," Caiaphas said to the captain of the guards. Immediately, the apostles were marched outside the chamber.

Gamaliel walked back and forth in front of the council for a moment or two, collecting his thoughts. "Men, fellow Israelites, listen carefully to my words, for your decision as to what to do to these rebels must be thought out carefully. Let me remind you of some events of our past that we may learn from them.

"First, there was a man called Theudas, who claimed to be a somebody—a zealot no doubt. About 400 men decided to follow him in an uprising. He was killed, and not long after that his followers dispersed—nothing changed!

"After that, there arose Judas the Galilean, during the days of the census. He, likewise, drew a following—larger than the zealot! He too was killed and his followers scattered as sand in the desert wind.

"And so I recommend to you, my high council, do not rush to kill these men, making them martyrs before their followers and causing yet another uprising. Permit them to teach their heresy outside the temple courtyards, and if it be of men, their teachings will blow away in the desert winds. But if it is of God, you have no power on this earth to destroy it. For no man—or group of men—has ever taught against the doctrines of our God and survived."

With those remarks, Gamaliel walked back to his seat and remained quiet. Some of the priests began to talk among themselves. After a few moments, Caiaphas stood and all became quiet once more.

"My brothers, I think I understand what our guest is saying to us. There is a bigger picture here to which we must give thought, and that is the potential uprising we may create by the stoning of these men. Our reports are that thousands in our grand city have a sympathetic ear toward these Galilean rebels. And, to be frank with you, outside the life teachings of this Nazarene, these men have been successful in teaching the prophecies of our coming deliverer—the real Messiah.

"This Jesus the Nazarene allowed them to call Him their Messiah, the One to deliver them from bondage and to usher them into the kingdom of God. But He is dead, and already some of them have been put in bondage. Now, to save face, they say He is alive again and is leading them to . . . where?—to a new kingdom of God or to the porches of our established temple? To a new freedom from the Romans or to the same bondage as we? Don't they continue to use our porches from which to proclaim? Don't they continue to use our ceremonial water troughs to baptize?" Caiaphas turned toward Gamaliel and spoke to the others while looking at him. "I say we let them feel the rewards of their new bondage by beating them and letting them go."

The words of Gamaliel and Caiaphas pleased Annas and the council, and a low-keyed "Amen, amen," was voiced throughout the chamber.

"Guards, bring the accused back into the chamber," said the chief priest.

The apostles were brought back into the chamber in similar formation as before. They stood before the priests.

Caiaphas spoke again: "Followers of the Nazarene, take heed and listen to our verdict. You are guilty of false teaching and inciting an uprising in our grand city. We could easily have you condemned to a stoning, but to show you a side of God's mercy, we will let you go after being flogged for your teachings. Now listen to me carefully: stop teaching and speaking in the name of Jesus, lest something worse happen to you."

"Amen, amen," said the council members.

"Now lead them away for their punishment," said Caiaphas. "Captain, you are in charge of the punishing stage." With that, the high priest sat down as the captain stood up.

"Lead the rebels out into the courtyard of the Gentiles," said the captain. "Let them feel and see where their convictions are leading them."

One by one, each apostle was tied to a pole. As they were being strapped, Peter looked to his right and to his left. The beating poles were used primarily for Gentiles who tried to become acceptable to the Jewish traditions that would appease God for sins. Many times the priests would order beatings because of blemishes found on the sacrificial animals, or, perhaps, the would-be proselyte would forget a line in the old covenant sayings. The priests took pleasure in retribution. The one positive side to this was that the straps used were nothing like the ones the Romans used for severe punishment—like the ones used on the Master.

"Take courage, my brothers," said Peter. "Remember the scourging of our Lord; He did this for us. Now let us be scourged in His name."

From a distance, Peter began hearing a psalm, sung in a low key. *John,* thought Peter. *Always on cue.* Peter joined in with the others as they sang a hymn in the midst of their lashes, each grunting when he felt the whip crack across his back—forty lashes save one.

Soon, it was over. The apostles were led to the gate with their outer garments in hand. Tear streams were on nearly every face. Some helped others walk. No one complained, agreeing that they were the better off having stood before the Sanhedrin without wavering in their faith.

"They saw us as disgraceful," Peter stated. "They told us not to speak in Jesus' name, but each lash we took, in the way we took it, spoke much louder than any words."

"Amen, amen," stated the others, feeling honored to have been beaten for Jesus.

"Will this beating stop us from preaching at the temple?" asked Matthew defiantly.

"No!" said the others in unison.

"And will we keep our mouths from uttering the name of Jesus from house to house?" asked Andrew.

"Never!" replied the others.

Each apostle was more determined than ever to preach and to teach that Jesus was the Christ. And the very next day found them teaching and preaching the gospel at the temple area. From house to house, they did not cease to tell the people about Jesus.

✝✝✝

(The day before) Caiaphas watched the beatings from a distance and then returned to the high chamber. Inside, there remained only Gamaliel and Annas.

"It is finished," reported Caiaphas.

"Very well, my son," said Annas. "That should teach those rebels a lesson . . . Come sit with us for a moment. Gamaliel, tell Caiaphas what you were saying."

"Yes, I noticed a strong determination in the eyes of these Galileans. They will not disperse easily."

"So why did we not stone them while we had the chance!?" Caiaphas responded angrily. He was not in agreement with the prior decision. He would have rather killed them—be rid of them now!

"Listen, my son, he has an idea—a plan."

Gamaliel continued. "This new Way of repentance and salvation has answered the heart cry of many of our people. And so what of the so-called miracles? Miracles have occurred throughout our history. These followers of the Way continue to be sympathetic to our customs and observances. I believe if we are going to conquer them, we must do so from within their groups. We must take advantage of their using our temple area and find ways to blend the teachings of Jesus with our traditions. Not all of His sayings are bad, but when they try to teach Jesus as the Messiah, we must find ways to refute them."

"And just how do you propose we infiltrate their followings?" asked Caiaphas.

"He has a plan," stated Annas, with a smile. "And a good plan it is."

†††

Inaros reclined alone while Jabeth and Sorenthasas propped themselves at the brothel bar, telling their story of springing a man out of prison in full view of the temple guards. Other than an occasional grunt, Hamath was as quiet as Inaros. Inaros caught Hamath's eye and motioned to him. Hamath moved away from the other two and walked over to him.

"Sit with me, Hamath . . . So what do you think of Jabeth and Soren?" asked Inaros.

Hamath grunted. "Strange talk," he responded. "They speak of a ghost-man—an 'Inaros' fellow, as if he walks with us."

"Oh, that; let me explain." Inaros then told Hamath the story of his release months ago and how he had to change his name.

"Oh," responded Hamath. "Maybe they're not as crazy as I suspected. Are they good with daggers when not intoxicated?"

"Yes, very good."

"Then I say we keep them."

Inaros laughed and patted Hamath on the back. "Yes, they are keepers."

Hamath grunted. "Why did you come for me?"

"I need your help; I have been given another chance to sabotage the control efforts of the Roman imperialists. They killed my two brothers and raped my sister. They ravaged our crops and drove away our livestock. They do not deserve to stay and defile our land. They have begun to corrupt our religious leaders through the Herodian kingship. I say it is time to thwart their corroborations."

"Huh," said Hamath. "I cannot tell the good guys from the bad ones."

"That is why you have me; you, my friend, will join me in the legends of future generations as they tell stories of the zealots who brought justice back into our territory. The God of our fathers will guide us to the bad guys first, then we will be honored by the good guys."

Hamath looked toward Jabeth and Sorenthasas. "Make sure I know which ones are good and which ones are bad."

Inaros changed the subject. "Hamath, you were near those prisoners that escaped, weren't you?"

"They were placed in the large holding area near our cell."

"Tell me, who were they and why were they placed in prison?"

"They were different; they sang and prayed much to God. I liked the sounds they made; it made me feel peaceful."

"Did someone help them escape?"

"They had no visitors, but later began talking to someone else. A voice I had not recognized. I heard one say an angel was leading them—walked them straight past the guards, just as we did earlier."

"An angel?" Inaros stroked his beard a bit. "Say, did you see a bright light shining over the city a few weeks ago?"

"Bright light and loud voices. That was the beginning of crazy day number one."

"What do you mean, my friend?"

"Noises like a wind storm or an earthquake, but no movement of the cell. Voices of many men in the streets—different dialects could be heard. All seemed to be offering praise to God. Others began speaking—I heard my native tongue of the barbarians speaking of the great things that were happening because of that Man you say took your place in the beatings."

"Jesus?"

"Yes, they spoke of Him as the Son of God—God's Son, resurrected and alive."

Inaros had heard enough. "Maybe we will find this resurrected Jesus-God and ask His help in overthrowing the Roman Empire."

Hamath grunted. "We could sure use a god or two on our side."

"Come on; let's get our two heroes out of here before *they* are made into gods."

Anno
Domini
36
Circa

*A*s days turned into weeks, weeks into months, the impact of the teaching and preaching of the gospel netted a steady growth. Many followers were being added into the Jerusalem fellowship, so much so that smaller groups were being formed from within the fellowship. The apostles maintained a system of teaching, preaching, and training. However, it soon became obvious that they could not continue to oversee all of the followers in one place.

Peter, James, and John had been discussing this and decided to call for a meeting of the apostles. They met in the courtyard of the villa belonging to Joseph of Arimathea—the followers' "official" headquarters near the temple.

"Brothers," said John. "We have a problem—a good problem. We are growing fast, and there remains an important need to teach and train every follower in the Way."

James took over. "Yes, and we must now decide on several things: one is that we must divide our fellowship into smaller groups that can fit in other courtyards and homes throughout the city. There are twelve of us, so let us ask among the fellowship for places where we can send followers for further training. Maybe start with six groups? Then, let's say, about every month or so, we will come together as one body and worship together."

"This is a good idea," said Matthew.

"Did you say 'several things' need to be addressed?" asked Judas, son of James.

"Yes," answered Peter. "The other goes along with our separation. We must set aside other men who feel called to become fellow overseers—not apostles, but men who we feel safe in teaching and proclaiming in our absence."

"Shepherds," stated John. "Men who will not only instruct and proclaim, but also care for and love the sheep . . . just as Jesus instructed us."

"How do we do this?" asked Andrew.

"We must write down the teachings that we receive from the Spirit," said Matthew. "Our Master said that the Spirit will teach us all things and bring to our remembrance those things necessary for the faith. These writings, along with the Spirit's power, will keep us all together, proclaiming the same testimony of the gospel and of our Lord."

†††

"Your Excellency?" The senator was a bit annoyed as Tiberius continued his target practice.

"Yes, what is it now?" Tiberius took aim at the target and shot his arrow.

"News from the east: the Judeans are squabbling over a new leader."

He dropped his bow. "What!? I have not appointed a new prefect—this is treason!"

"Most Excellent One, it is Jesus of Nazareth; His followers say He has risen from the dead."

Tiberius remained silent momentarily. As he retrieved his bow, he thought of Agrippina the Elder and her two sons who were murdered by his prefect, Sejanus, who was recently executed. *Are the gods turning on me?* From his island resort on Capri, Tiberius felt peaceful—and safe! No senate consulate and no daily decisions about the citizens and the wars of Rome. But this Jesus-man continued to wrest his mind of complete peace and security.

A servant handed him a fresh arrow. "This Jesus is not going away, as Pontius said He would. Perhaps we should make Him a Roman god?"

"No," said the senator. "I have a better idea. We can use this event to our favor."

"How so?"

"For years, the Herodians and the high priest's family have been feuding with each other over who has control over the people. They continue to try and get Pontius to take sides. This diversion to a common enemy could be that which brings solidarity to the region."

"Peace in Judea?"

The senator smiled. "It's a slight chance, but a chance, nevertheless."

Tiberius handed his bow and arrow to the servant. "Have my scribe meet me at the observatory. I will write instructions to Pontius on how to address this with Herod Antipas; also, I will write to a family friend, Annas, just to make sure the high priest is aware of the negotiations . . . Oh, and make sure Agrippa remains in chains."

"But you educated him as a son, next to Drusus."

"Yes, and that is why he wished Drusus to take my place. He must learn the hardships of sowing the seeds of rebellion."

"Yes, your Excellency." The senator bowed and walked away; Tiberius motioned for his bow and two arrows. He quickly placed both arrows on his bow, turned, and shot them over the heads of the senator and his guards. Both arrows landed between the senator and his chariot. "Solidarity!" he shouted.

The senator, though shaken by the arrows that lay ahead of him, bowed his head. "Solidarity," he repeated.

†††

Sharon was puzzled. "You want to go see my father?"

"Yes, my love, and why not? He has done great things for us and our people."

"Wow, what are you drinking? Last week, you deplored the thought of seeing him, and now?"

"Let's just say that things have changed for the better for us. We are developing a plan for arresting the followers of the Way, which will surely improve our relations with the king. And I bet your father will finally give up his manipulations for retirement . . . retirement: doesn't that sound sweet?"

"I wouldn't hold your breath waiting on my father's decisions for anything. I've known him much longer than you and I know he's very unpredictable."

Movement from the corridors was heard; soon two house servants were at the doorway. "Yes?" asked Caiaphas. "What is it?"

"My Lord, Annas wishes you both to dine with him tonight."

"See," Caiaphas said to his wife. "I am a wizard as well; send word that we will be there."

Caiaphas and his wife were adorned in their best; he was so confident Annas would announce the plan to destroy the growing movement of the Way. Caiaphas wanted to dress the part of power so that the others would know who would be in charge of this strategy. Other members of the family were there as well, dressed more casually. Annas had several sons who were equally qualified to be high priests, but none were as cunning and crafty as Caiaphas (so he thought). The sons had about as much affection for Caiaphas as he had for them, so each maintained his turf, trying to show their best sides toward their father—or father-in-law, as was the case for Caiaphas.

Some late arrivals came in. When notified, Annas called attention to all. "Dear family and guests," he said. "It gives me great pleasure to introduce to you Rabban Gamaliel and his new assistant, Saul of Tarsus." Applause was given. "I have invited them to our gathering tonight for the purpose of some important announcements that I wish to give you after our meal; so, if you will allow my servants to do so, they will show you where your seating is and we shall enjoy a festive meal together."

After the meal ended, Annas stood up. "Friends and family, it is a great pleasure to have you here this evening. I want you to know that with the blessings of our noble king, Antipas, we have begun a plan to rid ourselves of the followers of the Way—this troublesome group that refuses to leave our temple porches where they have been spewing blasphemous heresies against our faith and traditions. With the help of our esteemed guest, Gamaliel, we have his new assistant, Saul of Tarsus—stand up, my son— who has agreed to lead a band of our best priests and guards to hunt down and arrest these rebels."

"Amen, amen!" cried some of the guests.

Saul sat down while Annas continued to talk. "Saul has been given legal permission to cleanse our lands of these disruptive meetings of the followers of the Nazarene. Even though many of them have begun house assemblies, we will track them down and arrest them—both men and women."

"Amen, amen!"

"Now while I will continue to be a close ally with Antipas, I have decided that it is time for me to relinquish my role as overseer of many of the deeds you men must perform as high priest and priests."

Sighs and some "No's!" were heard. Annas quieted the group.

"Now don't worry, because you know I will always be nearby should you need some arm twisting of the Herodian dynasty." Caiaphas could hardly stand it; he wondered why he even bothered to dress up for the occasion. "Caiaphas, please stand with me for a moment. As you know, we have been bothered by the Nazarene and His followers for some time. Antipas met with Caiaphas and me and assured us that he would back our efforts to cleanse our religion of these false messiahs and their followings. This is our moment to shine, my children."

"Amen, amen!" his sons cried in unison.

"We must not fail in our plans!" Annas continued. "So I am suggesting that our dear high priest, Caiaphas, relinquish some of his powers to you on a rotating basis."

Caiaphas was shocked. "What!?"

"Now hold on, my son; listen and you will understand this better in just a moment. As I was saying, we must not fail in recapturing our position as the mediators between our God and our Jewish brethren. We must work together to show our solidarity, bringing our customs and traditions before the people as the only way to appease God for our sins. With Gamaliel and Saul on our side, we will round up these rebels and drive them into the Great Sea.

"Jonathan, my son; please stand with us for a moment." Jonathan, although crippled in his feet since his birth, stood and smiled at Caiaphas. Caiaphas ignored him. "I've asked Jonathan to serve as high priest over the administration of the persecutions of the followers of this Nazarene. This will give sanction to the plans, while Caiaphas will continue his role as high priest over the local affairs."

"Will Antipas and Pilate go for this?" asked Theophilus, another son of Annas.

"Oh, yes; Antipas will approve of the extra care in seeing this persecution handled legally. And Pilate has other things to worry about right now. I've heard that he is being called back to Rome by Tiberius. This news makes it a crucial time for us to move in an orderly fashion."

While the mumbling increased among the guests, Caiaphas sat down; he felt flush in his face as he tried to rein in his emotions. Once again, he felt Annas undermining his role as high priest. He was speechless and was turning pinkish-red in his neck area. Sharon reached over to whisper in his ear. "Save it for another time, my dear. I will approach my father and tell him that I'm not feeling well; I will need you to assist me home." She kissed his ear and smiled at him as she stood up and made her way to her father. She knew when it was time for her husband to leave the group and be alone.

Caiaphas was in no mood to see anyone. He felt insulted—double-crossed!—last night when his father-in-law bypassed him for the recognition he deserved. He was certain that his recent encounters with Annas meant something to the old man, but, no, "Daddy Big-britches" was being his usual self. It was obvious that Caiaphas was hot under the tunic—that is, he was mad! *What can I do to get even with this egotistical, self-serving man?* he wondered. He thought for a while, then an idea came to him. *He wants peace with the Herodians? Well, I might have a say about that!* He called for his servants: "Guards!" Immediately there was a rumbling coming down the corridor.

"Yes, my lord?"

"What took you so long!?"

"My Lord, I—"

"Save it for another day! Get me a horse and one guard without a uniform on. I'm going for a little ride." The guard did not ask questions, but left as quickly as he entered. *Now let's see who has control over what!*

†††

An interruption in the meeting of the apostles occurred. Several men known to them approached.

"Yes?" asked Peter. "What is it, my brothers?"

"Dear brothers," stated Nicolas, a proselyte from the city of Antioch. "Complaints are increasing among the Greek-speaking followers. They say that the Hebrew followers are neglecting their widows in the daily distribution of food."

"Is it a language issue?" asked James.

"Well, some may think so, but how hard is it to understand that all our widows need to be equally fed? Plus, the group of widows is increasing nearly every week."

"This is as good a time as any to address this," said Peter.

"Yes, I agree," said John. "Why don't we spend the evening in prayer, fasting, and worship, then tomorrow we will address this problem before the whole congregation."

"Amen, amen," responded the others.

"Thank you, sirs," said Nicolas. "We'll see you in the morning." After that the men departed, leaving the apostles to themselves again.

"And tomorrow, we should also discuss the separating of ourselves into more groups," said Andrew.

"Yes, indeed, my brother," said Peter. "This is an awesome experience we are witnessing. Just as our Lord appointed others to go into the many towns and villages, so must we do likewise."

"The kingdom has come," said John. "Let His will be done."

"Amen, amen," said the others, and the fasting and prayers began for the rest of the evening.

On the next morning, there was a multitude of followers arriving at Solomon's Porch for the teaching and training of the apostles. Soon, they stood before the multitude. Peter stepped forward.

"My dear brothers and sisters, we have some great news to tell you this morning. Please listen with open ears and open hearts. Look around you this morning; do you see how we have outgrown the porch area? If we are going to fulfill the commands of the Master, we must divide into smaller groups so that no one is overlooked in the teachings and the care of our fellowship. There must be among us other men who feel led of our Lord who we can train as fellow elders to oversee and shepherd everyone. These men must sense an inner calling from God for this task. They must also have evidence of the transforming presence and power of God's Spirit. Pray much and seek our Lord concerning this opportunity."

James spoke next. "Several men have come signifying a potential problem in neglecting some of our widows in our daily food distribution. Due to the continuing growth of our fellowship, it is not for your benefit that we elders should stop in preparing to teach you God's word, just to serve some of you food. So we ask that you seek out from among yourselves seven Greek-speaking men whom you know are filled with God's Spirit and have wisdom. Bring them to us and let us hear their testimony, so that we may appoint them to this service. As for us, we must continually present ourselves before God, praying and discerning how best to serve His word to you in teaching, preaching, and training."

This announcement pleased all who listened. So the followers searched among themselves for seven men whom they believed were full of wisdom and the Holy Spirit. Eventually, seven men were found and were presented to the apostles. The men were Stephen (remarkable in faith and the Holy Spirit), Philip, Prochorus, Nicanor, Timon, Parmenas, and Nicolas (the proselyte from Antioch).

John spoke to them all. "My brothers, the task set before you is to see to the care of the followers as needed. All of us will have needs from time to time, but the widows and orphans among us must be cared for without any prejudices at all."

Peter spoke next. "And recognize that when you take on this ministry for our brothers and sisters, you allow your elders and apostles the necessary time for prayer and preparation to proclaim the words of our Lord. This is very important and most beneficial to the followers."

"Come now and kneel before us, that we may pray over you," said James, brother of John.

The seven came and knelt before the apostles, while the other followers gathered around them. Then the apostles placed their hands on the seven and prayed for them, commissioning each of the seven for the service ministry.

Near the end of the service, about a dozen men came to the apostles and the seven. "We've come to apologize," said one of them. "We didn't realize we were causing a rift in our assembly by showing preference to our Jewish widows and orphans."

"Please forgive us," said another of the men. For the next few minutes there were a lot of embraces and tears from all the men, including the apostles.

Peter and John stood there watching. "Only the love of Jesus could take an explosive issue and turn it into revived hearts," said John.

News of the benevolence of the followers of the Way spread throughout Jerusalem, causing many priests to send poor people to the assemblies. "We can't care for the poor," said a priest to Matthew, "but our king can expand his stables for his new horses. Greed and control are the motivators of our rulers who care less and less for the common people."

As more and more people turned to the Way, their testimony caused the words of salvation to increase in direct proportion. In fact, the testimony of the apostles and their great concern for the people caused many priests to turn to faith in Jesus.

The popularity and growth of the Way did not come without its difficulties and dangers. Stephen, one of the seven servants, was a man full of faith and had been granted exceptional power to heal many who were diseased. He was led of the Spirit to minister in the area of the Synagogue of the Freedmen. This synagogue was known as a melting pot of freethinkers, often inviting rabbis of both the modern views and the orthodox views of the Jewish traditions to voice their convictions.

A priest who had recently come to believe in Jesus as the Christ was at the meeting when Stephen was chosen and ordained a servant of the Way. He asked Stephen to speak at the Synagogue of the Freedmen. He would follow a presentation from the school of Hillel by a young Pharisee, Saul of Tarsus. No one was expected to accept the challenge, so when word was out that someone was scheduled to offer an alternate view, many freethinkers and priests crowded into the synagogue.

Stephen was walking to the Synagogue of the Freedmen for his appointment to speak. He had spent much of the preceding day in prayer and fasting. He had a burden on his heart to reason with the Jews in the synagogue. "Lord Jesus," he prayed while walking, "I only want to do Your will in presenting the truth. I come to You as an open vessel, desiring that You keep me full of Your Spirit and give me boldness to speak."

"Stephen, I have heard your prayer," said the Spirit of the Lord. "Today will be an important day for the furtherance of My name in the far reaches of the world. Do not be afraid to speak and do not be afraid of what the outcome will be. I will give you the words to say to refute the Pharisee. Only be faithful and you shall wear the crown of faith in My presence very soon."

Stephen trembled when he heard these words. He was tempted to soften his intense praying, nevertheless, he knew that Jesus had spoken to him. "Your will be done, My Lord. Let Your servant be strong in his testimony, in Your name, my Lord, I pray, amen."

Those words from his Lord were the strength given him to walk into the synagogue with a face as sharp as flint. The sounds of chatter inside were quickly dispelled as he made his way to the front. The priest who had invited him stood up to introduce Stephen.

"Men of the faith of our fathers, I have listened to some of the teachings that you are obviously aware of that concern a return of our long-awaited Messiah. Certain men of our traditions have claimed to have received a new Way to have peace with God. I have invited one such man to speak to us today. This is Stephen ben Maximus."

Stephen walked to the parchment piles and asked the attendant for a copy of Isaiah 53. When found, he carefully opened the parchment and began reading:

"To whom has My message clung? And to whom has its power been revealed? My Servant sprang up in My presence, fresh and innocent, as an unexpected plant rooted in parched soil. He appeared to us as a weed—nothing of which to be desired, so we ignored, despised, and trampled over Him, esteeming Him as an unwanted plant in our garden. He suffered frequently as we tried to rid ourselves of His presence. He longed for our attention but we did not care; we hid our faces from Him, having rejected Him.

"Because of our rejection, My Servant became sorrowful, ravaged with grief and weaknesses—all of which was ours. His lack of beauty, strength, and usefulness was due to His resemblance of us. We cursed Him and punished Him as though He was cursed and punished by God for His own sins. But it was our sins that caused Him to be pierced. It was our sins that wounded Him for our guiltiness. His beatings brought us peace and wholeness. Like sheep without a shepherd, we continued to stray and followed our own instincts, yet the Lord placed on Him all our sins."

Stephen placed the parchment back into the attendant's hands and faced the crowded synagogue. The power and presence of God's Spirit was upon him as he spoke. "I am here today to announce to you that the God of our fathers has visited us through His Servant of whom Isaiah spoke. He walked among us and told us of the Way to have peace with God and the forgiveness of sins."

"Blasphemy!" cried out one of the free thinkers, a Libertine. "Only God can forgive sins." Other grumblings came from the crowd.

"Hear me out!" spoke Stephen. "This suffering Servant was prophesied by Isaiah as one among us—one whom we would reject, yet God would choose Him to be the sacrifice for our sins."

"If He indeed walked among us," spoke one man. "Surely we Cyrenians would have identified Him—we know what suffering is."

"No more than us Alexandrians," said another. Soon, others from Cilicia and Asia Minor joined in the chorus of opposition to what Stephen had said. The priests sat on both sides of the front watching the crowds and trying to maintain some semblance of calm.

Stephen spoke up again, as he tried to regain the floor. "Let me continue, please!" he cried. "Our prophets spoke to our forefathers, telling them that a change would be made from within us—inside our hearts. Since the silence of many centuries, we have seen the law of our leaders increase so much so that no one can be expected to get right with God."

"Excuse me for interrupting." It was Saul of Tarsus speaking. "Our laws have increased because sins continue to abound. Surely you can't fault the law."

"Sir, it is not the commandments of Moses or the Laws of our Sacred Writings that I condemn; it is all the additions to the commands of our covenants that are weighing us down. The suffering Servant became the sacrifice for our sins of which the God of our fathers requires. God said He would supply the acceptable sacrifice; His Servant has come and has offered Himself as a sacrifice."

"And who is this 'suffering Servant' whom you claim has come?" asked Saul.

"It is He whom our leaders turned over to the Roman authorities to be hung on a tree: Jesus of Nazareth."

"Blasphemy!" another priest cried out. "We have heard enough of this Jesus. He was tried and condemned for speaking against Moses and our God."

"He did not speak against Moses and God," said Stephen. "It is He whom the prophets foretold, and it is He who offered Himself as a sacrifice for our sins. He was the perfect, sinless sacrifice sent by His Father—our God!"

"This is nonsense!" cried some of the priests. "We will hear no more of this; take him away!"

Before Stephen could say another word, numerous priests had grabbed Stephen, and, with the help of others, they dragged him outside the synagogue over to the side where there was an open lot.

"Stone him!" someone shouted.

"Stop!" cried the priest in charge. "We have no authority to stone this man."

"Then we'll take him before the council," said another priest. "They have authority to stop blasphemy!"

"Amen, amen!" said the men who had dragged Stephen out of the synagogue. Then they took Stephen to the court of the Sanhedrin council.

Within an hour the council convened to hear the charges against Stephen. Caiaphas was seated before the council.

"What is the charge against this man?" asked Caiaphas.

Several men came to the front. "Your majesty, this man speaks against our holy temple and the Law, saying the same things that Jesus-man said. We heard him speak blasphemous words, saying that this Jesus of Nazareth would destroy our temple. He even said He would change the customs of our faith—that which was given us by God through Moses."

"Stone him!" cried several from the audience.

Stephen lowered his head as he prayed silently, *O my Master, be my strength to the end.*

"I will never leave you or forsake you, My beloved child."

When he looked up, the Sanhedrin saw a radiant aura upon his face—just as if they were staring at an angel.

Acts 7

"Tell us now, if you wish to spare your life," said Caiaphas. "Are the accusations true?"

"Be faithful; allow Me to guide your thoughts and speech."

Stephen began to preach the gospel, starting with God's dealing with Abraham and continuing through many of the things that Moses had said concerning the deliverance of the Jewish people. Then he spoke of the tabernacle, the temporary dwelling place where man could atone for his sins. Next, he moved the message toward the temple that Solomon built.

"Solomon built God an elaborate structure—a temple with no equal," said Stephen. "Yet God had said He would not dwell in any house made by man's hands. 'Heaven is My throne,' said our

God. 'And the earth is where I rest My feet. Did I not create all the things by which you build?'

"Now listen to me, you stubborn and uncircumcised of heart. You have followed in the priestly customs of your fathers; you have opposed God's Spirit in your teachings and practices. You refuse to listen to the prophets—just as your fathers did. Which of the prophets did not your fathers condemn and even kill? They did not want to hear the words of God, so they killed the messengers. You are doing exactly as your fathers did: you're killing the messengers who are introducing you to the Righteous One. Even so today, you are guilty of betraying God and murdering His Servant, who is the Messiah; this One is greater than the angels God used to give us the Law, but you have rejected His Messiah, the Lord Jesus Christ."

That was all that the council could take, especially in the presence of the high priest. Their hearts embroiled in anger, and they lost their tempers, grinding their teeth at him like brute beasts. They joined the crowd in hurling accusations against Stephen. But the glow of God was upon him, and, being full of the Holy Spirit, he looked heavenward and saw God in His glory and the Lord Jesus, standing at the right hand of God. The roar of the crowd became as a distant sound to him as he was engulfed in the beauty of holiness.

"Look!" Stephen cried out. "The heavens have opened, and I see the Son of Man standing at God's right hand!"

The Sanhedrin cried out the more, covering their ears in protest as they rushed upon him and subdued him. "Away with the blasphemer!" cried Caiaphas. "To the Valley of Hinnom! If he wants to see heaven's portals then let's help him."

Stephen was dragged out to the city dump and tossed among the refuse, where men began stoning him. Saul of Tarsus was chosen to register all those participating in the stoning, so they laid their outer garments at his feet. Stephen looked heavenward again and saw his Lord. "Lord Jesus, receive me now!" He managed to take the position of prayer, as stones pounded his body. "My Lord, please do not take this sin of theirs as the final chance to reach them with the truth!" After saying this, he lowered his head between his knees as the stones pounded him more and more until he was covered with stones.

Acts 8

The dust began to settle as the men stopped throwing their stones and walked away. Several priests looked at the body. "He's dead," one priest said to the other.

Saul stood up and made his way to the pile of stones and the covered body. Blood was trickling off Stephen's elbow. He reached down and touched the blood with his finger; after that he blotted the blood on the papyrus and then signed the document, certifying a just punishment.

As the crowd dispersed, Joseph of Arimathea, Nicodemus, and a few followers who had come with Stephen remained behind. Joseph and Nicodemus could not walk away from this tragic scene; rather, they began pulling the rocks off of Stephen's body.

"We've been here before," said Joseph.

"Yes, regrettably so," Nicodemus responded. "This servant has followed in the steps of his Master . . . There is a cost for a close relationship with our Lord."

"Perhaps it is time for us to relinquish our dual relationships?" Others appeared with some cloths to wrap the body.

"Thank you, kind friends; now if you will, help us wrap his body for burial. We must take him to his family for proper lamentations."

✝✝✝

Word of Stephen's death reached Herod Antipas (son of Herod the Great). *Good,* he thought. *Perhaps the tension among the Jewish leaders will be vented upon others for a while.* Antipas did not care about his Jewish comrades; they were a consistent source of headaches for him and the Roman procurators of the region. The emperor had faith in the Herods' ability to keep the Judean region in check. But peace between the Romans and the Jews was at best a fragile relationship. *Maybe an uprising of my kinsmen against this new Way would help my cause.*

"Guards!" Immediately several guards appeared before him at attention. "Go to the high priest and request him to come visit me as soon as possible."

"Yes, my Lord!" They disappeared as quickly as they had appeared.

Within an hour, Annas and Caiaphas appeared before Antipas.

"Dear Herod Antipas, what ails our most holy city that you would call for me so urgently?" asked Caiaphas.

"My apologies, Most Holy One. I did not mean to alarm you. And I see you have brought the great Annas with you. Greetings, my old friend."

"And to you as well, most honorable king," responded Annas.

"I will get to the matter quickly, Caiaphas. I received news of the stoning of a blasphemer—a member of the new Way?"

"Yes, my king," said Caiaphas. "And trust me, we have a full confession, with witnesses, documentation of the cause and verdict."

"The followers of this so-called new Way have been nothing but a headache to the faith of our fathers," interjected Annas.

"I agree, and I have not called you here to question the event, but to offer you any assistance my soldiers can be to help you rein in these blasphemers."

Annas could not believe what he had just heard. He looked at Caiaphas who was equally surprised. "My king," responded Caiaphas. "I . . . I am pleased you feel this way, and I thank you for this kind offer."

"No one wants an overthrow of our religious customs at this crucial time of relations between our people and the empire. Rome needs to see our people bond together against any attempt to destabilize our region."

"I couldn't agree with you more," Annas responded. "This Way is spreading rapidly and only a united force can quell its growth."

"Then go with my blessing—and my soldiers. Find their camps, and take the male leaders captive."

Annas and Caiaphas left the king's palace elated. "We came expecting more harassment, and we leave with a blessing!" said Caiaphas.

"My son, never forget: a king's blessing always has an expectation waiting. We must be shrewd about how we go about to destroy this Way of the rebels. This uprising must not be traced back to our family."

"What do you mean? How can we not be involved if the king has given us his blessing?"

"There is another way, my son, and there is another who will restore order as well as give us the victory in which we will share."

† † †

Inaros sipped on some tea his mother had made. His mother's tea was his favorite. The evening sun was illuminating the mountain edges as it sank behind the western ridge. Hamath was outside whittling on a new dagger handle. Jabeth and Sorenthasas remained in Jerusalem, maintaining key contacts with certain informers on the Romans and the kingship of the Herods. It was important to Inaros to know the whereabouts of his primary targets.

The new conflict between the Jewish leaders and the new sect of the Way caused him to wonder if perhaps he could get some support from the leaders of the Way to overthrow the Romans' reign. He had to find out and was hoping his men in Jerusalem would get some answers.

"Hamath." The voice sounded familiar, but he couldn't tell due to the shadows creeping in. Having been sprung from prison, he couldn't be too careful.

"Who's calling?" he asked. He stood up with a dagger base in one hand and a blade in the other. Hamath's dagger blades were nearly the size of a small training sword. Usually, his size caused most enemies to run from him rather than challenge the hulk to a duel.

"It's us: Jabeth and Soren," said Jabeth. Jabeth was always careful around the giant. Hamath might look like he could be sluggish, but his size did not slow his speed when there was a challenge. "Where is Barab—I mean, Inaros?"

"Forgetting the boss's name could bring dire consequences," said Hamath. He gave a hard look at Jabeth and his sidekick as they approached.

"You won't tell him, will you?"

Hamath's serious look slowly turned into a slight smile. "I suppose not, since I'm having the same difficulty. You guys are just in time to help me with this dagger; here, you hold the blade while I push this piece onto it."

Jabeth stared at the blade and then at Hamath. "You're not suggesting I grab that blade and hold it for you?"

"You're not afraid of a small blade, are you? Maybe you and Soren could both hold it?" Hamath was not a jokester, so when he tried, it was a hard read, accompanied with awkward dialog. "Okay, maybe we should talk to the boss first." With that remark, Hamath took the blade and with his bare hand drove it into the tree trunk he sat upon. "Come inside."

Inaros was reclining at a table looking at several old maps of Jerusalem with an oil lamp. Hamath walked in with Jabeth and Sorenthasas tagging along. Inaros spoke first, without turning away from his maps. "I trust you've come here for more than just some of my mother's roasted lamb?"

"We got some good news," said Sorenthasas.

"Good news?" interrupted Jabeth. "How do you know if it's good news?"

"Let me be the judge," said Inaros.

Jabeth continued. "I made contact with one of my old friends. He said another zealot, a Simon, had joined the ranks of the followers of that Jesus fellow you spoke of."

"A disciple of Jesus? Simon, a zealot?

"Yes, and I made an arrangement for us to see him . . . tomorrow."

"Us? Tomorrow?" Inaros had now turned to his accomplices. He looked at Jabeth and Sorenthasas momentarily, wondering if it was a wise decision to let them work alone. "What if it's a trap? What if they are working together with the Romans, trying to gain some sort of favor from them?"

"Relax, Inaros," said Jabeth. "The Jews had these men put in prison the other day, and the Romans could have cared less. Besides that, my friend can be trusted."

"Meeting with a disciple of Jesus . . . a zealot . . . okay, but he must come alone and we will meet on my terms—my location. This should be very interesting. I have a few questions to ask this Simon the Zealot."

"Now what about your mother's roasted lamb?" asked Sorenthasas.

"Oh, yeah, it's out back. Now you know I wasn't expecting you, so you may have to share Hamath's portion."

A deep growling sound came from Hamath, intelligible enough for the other two to wonder if they'd get any supper.

† † †

"You want to see me, my Master?"

"Yes, Saul; do come in and take off your tunic; relax a bit, and let me pour you a refreshing drink."

"Thank you, sir." Paul had been in Gamaliel's quarters before; it was a rather small house for a man of his stature, his wife, and two children. But Gamaliel was a gentle man who never seemed to be emotionally charged in his language or his actions.

Gamaliel was fetching a cup. "I heard of your fine teachings at the Jerusalem north synagogue—the 'Synagogue of the Freedmen' they call it?"

"Yes, Master Gamaliel." He approached Saul with a cup of new wine. "Thank you, sir."

Gamaliel reclined at the table, across from Saul. "I heard also of the rebuttal given the next day."

"Not really a rebuttal, sir. This man of the new sect gave us a rather lengthy history lesson of our pilgrimage from the Egyptians to the building of Solomon's Temple. It was a bit choppy at best."

"I spoke with the high priest about it. He said the man's speech was full of blasphemy, and several witnesses made some remarkable statements about this new Way attempting to destroy the temple and our synagogues?"

"It sounded as if their leader had made some statement like that."

"And what do you make of this new Way, young Saul of Tarsus?"

Saul knew that when Gamaliel addressed one of his students by their full title, he wanted a thorough summation of the discussion. "Sir, I've only heard bits and pieces of what this Jesus, the Nazarene, taught, but when this man said that Jesus was the appointed Messiah for our people's deliverance, I knew we had a problem."

"How so?"

"Well, as I see it, this Jesus was judged for His false teachings—He's dead, and our native land is still under Roman jurisdiction. So now His followers claim His Spirit is leading them—and they call Him the Holy Spirit of the God of Abraham."

"Oh, really?"

"Yes, sir. This allows no wiggle room for the followers; it causes a conflict in both systems of belief. What I heard from this man was that our Law and our practices were completed in the crucifixion of this Jesus. To them, His sufferings were the fulfillment of our prophets, especially Isaiah. He even accused our fathers of killing the prophets who prophesied of the coming Messiah."

"That is interesting . . . I heard you kept the journal of this man's stoning?" Saul nodded his head, not sure he wanted to speak to that event. "Does this mean you approved of the verdict?"

"Sir, I felt that emotions led to the speedy verdict. I would rather there had been more discussion and evidence, but his blatant accusations toward us, and in the presence of the high priest, caused a barrage of angry responses. His words were contradictory to our laws, and I stand on the side of maintaining the traditions of our faith. So, yes, I sat in approval of the verdict."

"My son, I have listened to these men speak several times. The high priest and I sat with the high council to hear their charges. I, too, felt that emotions were driving the verdict and suggested to the council to let them go. But the report of the growth of this new Way is quite staggering, and they are spreading beyond the Judean territory. I now believe I may have made a quick judgment about leaving them alone. Their teachings do contradict ours, and I fear they may indeed overthrow our temple grounds."

"How could such a thing happen?"

"Many priests are seeing this new Way as a plausible answer to our inability to overcome the Roman suppression. Also, the Way is reported to be supplying great benevolent care to their widows and the poor. And miracles . . ."

"Miracles!?—Excuse me, sir; I should never interrupt you."

"That's okay; you, also, can feel the emotions of this troubling situation. Yes, it is reported that these men have performed many healings of the diseased. This alone has caused a great following and sympathy for their cause."

"Sir, you know as well as I that many sicknesses are due to exhaustion, loss of hope, or emotional instability."

"Yes, my son; which makes this movement much more dangerous due to the unstable times in which we live."

Saul stood up and walked slowly to a window. "I haven't thought much of our unstable times. Sir, you know I am a Roman citizen, and, although I disapprove of much of what the emperor is doing, our Roman law has brought justice and peace throughout the empire."

"Yes, I know that, and that is why the high priest and I have chosen you to be our emissary for an important duty."

Paul turned around. "Sir?"

"With your knowledge of the Law, our customs, and your Roman citizenship, you can help us rein in the spread of this sect. We need someone with intelligence to go and arrest the teachers of the Way. They need to be tried according to Jewish law. This must be done now if we are to save our customs from these false teachers. Remember, Saul, they did not get their training from any of our schools. If left unchecked, there is no telling what they will teach next."

Saul turned back to look out the window. The temple was in full view. "I trained hard to become a teacher of our Law. I have dedicated many years to master our traditions."

"Yes, my son; and you are the brightest student I've ever had. I believe the records will show that you are the youngest Pharisee of our school to be elected and seated on the Sanhedrin council."

"The council?"

"Yes, my son. I am recommending your seating as soon as your mission is complete." Gamaliel joined his side as they both looked toward the temple grounds. "I will also recommend you to become my personal assistant after we have put an end to this sect."

Saul was bombarded with emotions. *The assistant to Gamaliel?* he thought. *Would I become the next headmaster of the school of Hillel?* He had to quickly dismiss his thoughts for fear his emotions would overwhelm his ability to speak with calm. "Sir, I will need papers authorizing the capture and arrest of the blasphemers."

Gamaliel patted him on the back. "The high priest is expecting us; let us go and speak with him, my new assistant."

†††

Peter looked toward the temple as he gazed out the northern window of the headquarters. Prayers were being heard in the upper room as men, women, and a few children sought the Lord for wisdom, protection, and boldness to speak out for Jesus. He had asked John to gather the apostles together along with the brothers of Jesus: James, Joses, Simon, and Judas. He, James, and John felt an urgency in meeting due to the report of Stephen's death.

Most knew that the Synagogue of the Freedmen had established a reputation of its liberal, free-thinking views, but never had any debate ended in such a brutal attack as this meeting. The priests and Sanhedrin members that were there helped incite an uprising against the followers of the Way that had come to give Stephen support. Many ran for their lives!

The others began congregating as they waited for all to assemble. Finally, all were accounted for. "Brothers," said Peter. "This is a sad day for us as we have lost one so dear to us and so full of the Spirit of Jesus. Stephen was invited to speak, and yet, he was not protected by either Jewish or Roman law. This tragedy cries out a warning for us all. As you may have heard, supporters of Stephen had to run from the synagogue due to the mob-rule pandemonium.

"I believe our Lord has promised us eternal life in His eternal kingdom, but there is no way of determining how long any of us will live here on this earth. It is important for us to know and to teach that we must live smart among the enemies of our Lord. It is no telling what our leaders may say or do next to stop our forward movement."

"What are you saying?" asked Bartholomew.

"I believe our regular large group meetings must become a thing of the past. We must concentrate on dividing ourselves into smaller groups and maintain a low profile in our gatherings."

"How is that possible when the Holy Spirit, that our Master promised us, continues to give us boldness to speak and powers to heal people?" asked Judas, son of James. "I mean, the crowds are forming naturally."

This caused a bit of a stir among the group. Matthew spoke next. "My brothers, I, too, sense that we are about to face increasing opposition. Remember that as soon as our Master was filled with the Spirit, the devil spent forty days tempting Him. We know that Jesus is stronger than the evil one, but didn't He say we must be as cunning as the serpent? I believe we must be careful and wait for the prompting of the Spirit before we speak in the name of Jesus."

"Don't misunderstand what I'm saying," resumed Peter. "I want us to continue preaching, teaching, and healing. But we must make sure that what we do is indeed under the watchcare of our Lord.

"Now, I believe God would have us continue our Lord's vision of capturing more people of Jerusalem with the gospel. We must maintain a strong local assembly. I believe most of us will need to assemble here as a base, while we go out and check on the other assemblies that will form in Jerusalem and all Judea. So I would like to propose that we call James, our Lord's brother, as head elder of the Jerusalem church." Turning to him: "James, please come and speak your mind on this matter."

James stood and made his way to the front. "Grace and peace to us all. Brothers, for some time now, I have felt our Lord speaking to my heart to preach and teach His words here at our base headquarters, allowing you all to concentrate more on the area synagogues and house gatherings. I, too, sense an increase in persecution is coming. You will be needed more in the newer assemblies to ensure correct doctrine, polity, and perseverance.

"Now, with your approval, my brothers will assist me in maintaining a growing ministry and fellowship here. They will be fellow elders to assure all our people will be cared for properly."

Suddenly some screams were heard coming from the courtyard. Several women were at the gate talking. "Let's pause our discussion to see what is happening," said Peter.

Peter and the others arrived about the same time Mary, mother of Jesus, was handing the women a cup of water to drink.

"What's going on?" asked Peter.

"Oh, I can hardly speak!" one of them cried.

"Go on now and try," he responded.

"Oh, it was terrible! Several of our neighbors were gathering to pray and worship when there was a knock on the door. We opened the door, and several men, with soldiers, stepped into our living quarters. They somehow knew we were followers of the Way and immediately arrested our husbands and sons—all of them!" She started wailing again. "Oh no, no, no! What is happening?"

"Did you recognize any of the men?" John asked.

The other lady spoke. "One was a young priest—the other may have been a scribe. They had papers from the high priest and the king, authorizing the arrest of any illegal gatherings of those following the Way of Jesus."

Peter looked at John and his brother, James. "Go find Joseph or Nicodemus; see what they can discover." They immediately left through the front gate, heading in the direction of the temple. "Mary, thank you for seeing to their needs; brothers, I think it is time for prayer."

The men returned to their meeting room. "It appears the Spirit's burden on our hearts is preparing us for this encounter," said Matthew. "This may be a scare tactic . . . time will tell." Having said that, the men began to pray.

Within the hour, several additional reports had come in of similar house arrests. The men and boys were taken, leaving the women. John and James returned about an hour later.

"Brothers," said John. "Word is that the high priest has papers from Herod Antipas to arrest followers of the Way. And Saul of Tarsus—Stephen's recorder—is leading the search."

"What?!" shouted Thomas. "Why all of a sudden?"

"We don't know," replied James. "Nicodemus says that the high priest was requested to appear before Antipas. Annas and Caiaphas met with him and left in jubilation."

"And it gets even worse," said John.

"How could it be any worse?" asked Andrew.

"They are preparing a larger segment of the city prison to hold women and children."

"That's it," Peter said. "We must send word out to all our host contacts and warn them to flee the city immediately until this outrage is challenged by the Roman authorities."

"Roman authorities?" asked Simon (the Zealot). "If Antipas is behind this, you can bet that he's already falsely accused us of inciting unrest!"

"Shouldn't we register a complaint with Pilate?" asked James (the brother of Jesus).

"It's risky," responded Peter. "I don't think he wants to get involved, after what happened to our Lord."

"There's something else going on as well," Simon said. The room hushed as he stood up. "I didn't think much of it yesterday, but I was contacted by a former friend of mine asking for a meeting with a new leader of the zealots. I am to meet with them tonight."

"What could this mean?" asked Judas.

"I'm not sure, but I can only guess there is a growing group of dissidents who may try to take out some Roman leader—perhaps even one of the Herods."

"Is it safe?" asked John.

"A private meeting with terrorists, safe?" Simon laughed. "Let's just say that I am aware of their system of inquiry. I agreed to this because I thought I might be able to reveal to some of my former accomplices the Way of our Lord; but now, I don't know."

"Would you like some company?" asked Philip.

"Thanks, but I think these men would be suspicious if I brought a stranger with me."

"You will give us a report tomorrow?" asked Peter.

"Yes, my brothers; do not be afraid of this encounter. Remember, I was once one of them."

By the evening, more reports came in that Saul had taken men and women and placed them under arrest. The order for followers to disperse was sent out by the apostles.

Simon was known as a zealot, but he had changed. Jesus removed his anger at the injustices of the Roman authorities in Galilee and the collaborations with the Herods. He was no longer motivated by hatred. But he knew the zealots were getting more and more frustrated with the languid spirit of the Jewish leaders. But now Jesus in him caused him to understand the nature of man. What man really needed was peace inside his heart—a peace that only Christ could offer for real hope and deliverance.

O Lord, he prayed in his heart. *Make me Your instrument in this meeting.* Soon he was standing about twenty yards from a small house, the place that Simon remembered the first time he had enlisted Jabeth to the cause. He started walking again toward the house. About two houses away, another man slipped out of the darkness and began walking beside him, and then a second man.

"You still hanging out with this hoodlum, Soren?" asked Simon, without looking.

"How'd you know it was us?" Sorenthasas asked.

"I could smell you two houses away."

"Hah!" laughed Jabeth. "Same ol' wise-cracking Simon. We didn't want you to come alone down this dangerous part of Jerusalem." Jabeth was his usual prodding self.

"I bet you wanted to make sure I didn't bring backup; did I pass the entrance test?"

"Sure thing, and I hope you have your story right when you meet our new leader, because he is as serious as a rip in a wine-skin."

As they neared Jabeth's house, Simon saw what looked to him like a large animal—like a bear! He stopped. "What is that?"

Jabeth smiled. "Backup." Hamath growled at the three men. "Relax, Simon; he's one of us."

"I think he would qualify as two of us."

Jabeth made his way to the front of the three. "Hamath, I see you and the boss have already arrived." Hamath only grunted. He never was much for words, especially around strangers. He let the three pass by and followed them inside. Sitting near a table was Inaros.

"I don't believe we've met; my name is Inaros."

"And I am Simon."

"Simon, a zealot, I've been told," said Inaros.

"Yes, some reputations never leave a man even after he has had a change in life."

Inaros laughed. "Maybe you should have a complete name change."

"That would only work if I avoided certain old friends." Simon's smile, as he looked in Jabeth's direction, brought forth a return of smiles from everyone—except Hamath.

Inaros studied Simon's face. He noticed an appearance of calm, something he had not felt since a young man, before the Romans invaded Bethany. "Jabeth says you were a good operator in your early days; tell me, what changed you?"

Simon also had studied Inaros' face. He saw someone that had experienced much pain and anger. "When I ran with Jabeth in Galilee, I thought we could change our world—stop the Roman takeover and clean up our local government's corruption. Life was much simpler then. But our local Jewish authorities were just as corrupt as the Roman procurators. I discovered that there was something common among both races."

"What was that?" Inaros asked.

"Greed. With power comes the desire to have more power. Man with power is a slave to its source. If his power is fed by money, he must have more money; if it is fed by people, he must control more people. Land? The same need is there."

"Should you not stand up to those who would rob others of their basic rights to exist?"

"Oh, I would not fault a man for defending his family, his property, or basic rights for freedom. But I found out that man's basic need is to live with peace from within. You cannot bring peace to an enemy's heart unless you, yourself, promote peace before your enemies."

Jabeth interrupted. "Man, you lost me there; how do you meet your enemy with peace? Isn't that a sign of weakness?"

Simon continued. "Well, Jabeth, an enemy of peace is someone who is unsettled with who he is or where he is. He thinks he will be satisfied with having what you have by taking it from you. However, if peace ruled in his heart, he could easily come to you under peaceful terms and learn from you."

"The Romans came by force," Inaros said. "They conquered by sheer numbers; nothing peaceful about them."

"True, they took control of our region. But think for a moment: since they took over our land, have there been any raids from the Arabian deserts? Have we been attacked by the Egyptians or Assyrians or barbarians from the north? The answer is 'No.' So, in a strange way, we have had peace in our land while under Roman law."

"But we have a different law, given to us by our forefathers: God's Law! And the Romans do not know our God's Law—nor can they know it!"

"Yes and no; yes, the Romans do not know our God's Law, and no, they *can* know it."

"How is that?"

"God's Law was given due to man's rebellion to His commands. Adam and Eve lived in peace and fellowship with God until they chose to disobey Him; they were offered an alternate lifestyle through deceit and mistrust. Thus, they rebelled against God and His Law. However, God showed His mercy and grace toward them in order to teach them to trust, love, and obey Him. But the fruit of their disobedience produced a seed of rebellion in man's heart that germinated into all men—all became rebellious. This led God to create a system of laws in order for man to live in peace.

"May I sit down?" asked Simon.

"Yes, please sit here at the table."

"Thank you . . . Next, God saw the need to select a race of people so that they may become examples for all mankind. There was no favored race, but He selected our forefathers—the Hebrews. And in Abraham, He said, 'You will become a father of many nations, a father to be a blessing to all nations.' God had to keep His eye on our people to keep us in a position to be a blessing to all."

"To all our people, right?"

"No, to all nations! That is what our Sacred Writings tell us. But here is where our leaders have messed up. Somewhere along the way, our forefathers began to think that we Jews were a select group—above all others. To them, Gentiles were created to be our servants, not our equals. They saw Gentiles as creatures destined to hell, unless they become circumcised, obey our laws, and follow our customs.

"God was not pleased with this attitude of ours, so He sent prophets who proclaimed judgment on us except we repent and return to His original commands. But our ancestors killed many of the prophets and put many of them in jail. So God allowed us to be captured and placed in slavery to show us that we were not the elite, but the rebellious. And that is where we are today as a nation."

Inaros stood up and walked to a window. He was a bit on edge. "You make it sound like it's our fault and that the Romans have been sent by God to punish us. My two older brothers were simply trying to defend our property, our crops, and our livestock. The Roman soldiers just rode through the gardens and broke down our livestock barriers, killing anyone and everyone who dared to fight back!"

"This is the difficult part to comprehend, Inaros. Although God judged us as a nation, He was consistent in saying that if anyone would turn to Him, He would turn to that person. God has always said that the road back to Him was one that any man could travel on. This is what changed me.

"After hundreds of years of silence, a few years ago, God sent our people a new prophet. He was called John the Baptizer. This prophet preached repentance to our people."

"Yes, I heard of him."

"Did you meet him?"

"Afraid not; I was busy in southern Judea at the time. He may have been in prison with me a few days, but I had no contact with him."

"I met him; he not only preached repentance, but he said his repentance proclamation was to prepare the way for the Lamb of God who would take away all mankind's sins."

"A lamb?"

"Yes—but not an actual lamb. When this Lamb came, John pointed to a man and called Him the 'Lamb of God.' You see, God had prepared a sinless man to become *the* Lamb that would be sacrificed for all sins."

"A sinless man? To be sacrificed? How could this be done? That's impossible!"

"The only possible solution would be if a man came into the world without germination of sin through an earthly father. And it was done. God's Spirit overshadowed a righteous virgin, and she conceived and gave birth to a Son. This Son grew up under submission to His parents until at the right time when He came to John the Baptizer. This is the one whom John called the Lamb of God."

"Who was this man?"

"Jesus of Nazareth."

"Stop!" Inaros stood up and turned away from Simon. He could not believe what he was hearing. *Jesus of Nazareth!?* he thought. *That same man that traded places with me was the Lamb of God?* He trembled inside, but fought back any sign of weak emotions. He turned back toward Simon. "I saw that man; He was not sinless. He was turned over to the authorities for certain crimes. He was scourged for His crimes, and then they crucified Him. Are you saying He was the sinless man?"

"Yes, He was. He was falsely accused and was beaten. One of our prophets said that by His stripes we are healed. Another prophecy said that He was wounded for our transgressions. And another said that His appearance would be so marred that we would not even be attracted to Him. All we are like sheep that have been led astray, each of us turning to our own way, and God laid upon Jesus all our sins. You see, when you start reading all the prophecies about our coming Messiah, they all point to who Jesus was, what He did for us, and what our leaders did to Him."

"But He died, right?"

"Yes, for three days Jesus lay in a guarded tomb, sealed by the Roman government, and guarded by soldiers. But on the morning of the third day, He rose up out of death and became alive. An angel rolled back the sealed stone so that others could see where He had once lain."

The room became quiet as Inaros walked over to a small window. "My mother mentioned something like that to me. Did you see His tomb?"

"Yes, I was weak in the knees, but I saw it. But I saw something greater than that, Inaros—I saw Him later on, alive."

Inaros turned back to face Simon. "You saw a dead man alive?" Simon was shaking his head in the affirmative. "Was He not just a ghost or something like that?"

"No, He wasn't. I thought that perhaps we, His disciples, may be just hallucinating, but Jesus asked for something to eat, and He ate it before us. Then He spent forty days with us, teaching us and revealing the prophecies about Him—some of which I told you tonight."

"But it doesn't make sense; if He were the Messiah—our Deliverer—where is He now? Why hasn't He delivered us? Why are we still under Roman oppression!?"

"This baffled all of us—His followers. We asked Jesus one final time before He ascended into the heavens, if He was going to set up His kingdom now. He said it was not a question to be asked now, but to go into Jerusalem and wait for His Spirit to empower us to tell people of the new Way to our God through Him. You see, it's just as I was saying earlier: God has offered peace inside of us through His ultimate sacrifice, the Lamb that was slain—crucified—for our sins. Once we get our sins forgiven, we have peace with God and then we can have real peace with our fellow man."

"Wait! You mean peace with the Romans?"

"That is correct."

"I don't want peace with the Romans—I want revenge!"

"Inaros, look at me!" Inaros did, and, once again, he saw a man who indeed had peace within. *Could this be true?* he thought. Simon continued, "I once had anger in me, just like you, and, just like you, I wanted revenge. An eye for an eye! But you know what? After hurting some Romans and tearing down a few of their strongholds, I still had no peace within. Getting revenge did not settle my heart. Jesus taught us that in Him we would find a peace undiscoverable on this earth. He said the kingdom of God would be formed from within us."

"And how will you turn back the Romans?"

"Just as Jesus did to us—and to thousands of our people that are turning to Him—one heart at a time. Inaros, Jesus died for you and—"

"Don't say that! Don't you think I know!?" Inaros turned away, this time he *was* trembling.

"What do you mean? Have you been told this story?"

Inaros turned around; there was perspiration beading up on his forehead. "Now you look at me! I said earlier that I saw your Jesus, and I did! I am Barabbas! I am the man our leaders chose instead of Him! I should have died on that wretched cross instead of your Jesus." Inaros began weeping. The other men remained speechless. They had become mesmerized over the story.

✝✝✝

The order to leave Jerusalem did not have to be said twice. Families were leaving throughout the night in different directions, hoping some of their relatives would receive them. Philip, one of the seven servants, chose to leave with a group of followers departing for Samaria. He had no immediate family to stay with and no relatives in Samaria, but felt God would have him go and preach the gospel there.

The next day Philip found Jacob's well and began preaching. Interest in his message about Jesus the Messiah became very popular as many remembered Jesus Himself being at that same well. As he preached, the Holy Spirit confirmed the message preached by performing many miracles of healing among the crowd. Even evil spirits were coming out of people, screaming with loud voices. This brought great joy and happiness among the people of that city.

The town magician, Simon, heard the talk about Philip. Simon was a wizard, involved in much sorcery. The people were fascinated by his tricks, calling him a god. "Wow," some would say. "Can you believe that!?" And Simon enjoyed every bit of the attention. But when Philip started preaching the gospel and saving faith through Jesus Christ, many men and women became believers and were baptized. Simon was so amazed that he also believed and was baptized. For days he followed Philip around and hung on his every word, watching carefully how Philip performed miracles and spoke with such boldness.

In a matter of days, word returned to the apostles in Jerusalem about how the Samaritans were turning to the Lord through God's word. This announcement was so important that Peter and John were sent to Samaria to investigate. Camels were provided, compliments of Barnabas.

"Great," said Peter. "I need some fresh air."

"Don't say that too loudly," replied John. "You know what a camel can do in a hurry to mess the air up." John laughed while Peter stared at him. "A little laughter, Peter."

"Very little at that . . . Say, John, what do you make of the Samaritans receiving the gospel?"

"Well, I think Jesus was very polite to them earlier, and He did say we would become witnesses here eventually."

"Yeah, but they are Samaritans, and you know what that means?"

"I'm not sure where you're going with your questions."

"Circumcision, John, circumcision—many of the men are not circumcised."

"Oh, well, I'll do the song service, and you can do the circumcisions."

"Get serious with me for a minute, will you!?"

John laughed. "I am serious! I am not cutting no one—nothing!"

"Oh, for crying out loud, John!"

"No, I don't think it'll be us crying out loud."

"Just forget it!"

The two arrived in Samaria about mid-afternoon. Someone had pitched a large tent for Philip's meetings out by the well. Many were gathering again as the afternoon sun began to sink toward the western mountains. It wasn't long before Philip found his way out to the well and the drinking troughs for the livestock. Peter and John had tied their camels up and were enjoying a cup of refreshing water while the camels drank.

"Greetings, my brothers," said Philip. "I am so glad you came." They all embraced each other.

"We also, my brother; we also," said John.

"Come now, let's get out of the heat and into my temporary accommodations. I have so much to tell you." The men gathered inside Philip's tent and broke bread together.

"So, Philip, how do you know these folks are genuinely saved?" asked Peter.

"Well, I tell them the good news of Jesus and how they must repent and turn to Him for salvation. And most were baptized to show their sincerity. Some of them remember Jesus stopping here years ago. But they aren't sure what to do next—and I'm not sure what they should do next. That's why I'm glad you came."

"Have any shown evidence of receiving the Holy Spirit?" asked John.

"What do you mean?"

"Any language barriers removed by the Spirit?" asked Peter. "Any bold speaking of the gospel from them?"

"No, I'm afraid not, but the Holy Spirit has been performing a lot of healings to confirm the message."

"That's great!" said John.

"Do you have another meeting tonight?" asked Peter.

"Yes, we do."

"Good, perhaps tonight we'll find out what the Holy Spirit is trying to teach us about the Samaritans."

"Great," said Philip. "It's about time to start inviting people to come inside the tent."

Philip went out among the people, encouraging folks to come to the tent meeting. Some music began with some singing. Next, there were readings from the Sacred Writings. After a while, Philip stood up and introduced Peter and John. The folks acknowledged their presence and settled down to listen.

Peter spoke. "Dear ones, it is an honor to be with you again, having stopped here years ago when our Lord Jesus stopped for a drink of water. I think it took us many days to leave town. You all were such gracious hosts to us.

"Now we hear that you are listening to the preaching of our beloved friend, Philip, and many are turning to Jesus for salvation. The good news of salvation is that when you receive Jesus into your life, He comes to live in you forever. He does that through His indwelling Spirit. Now an important question has to be answered: how do you know that you have received the Holy Spirit since you believed?" The audience remained silent. "The answer is that when you receive the Holy Spirit, you will be filled with power—power to speak of salvation with boldness. Have any of you had this happen to you since you believed?" Again, the audience remained silent. "Well, may I ask that if any of you who have made an honest commitment to Jesus this week, please come to John and me now."

Dozens began walking toward them and began to kneel all around them. Nearly all in the tent moved in closer to the two. Peter looked at John. "Let's lay our hands on them, John, and pray that they may receive the Lord's Spirit." They laid their hands on a couple people. "Now I want all who wish to receive our prayer to please touch the person next to them; everyone should be touching someone else." The people did so.

Peter and John, together, began to pray for the Samaritan believers to receive the Holy Spirit. It wasn't long before the room was electrified with shouts of praises in various languages. The power of God's Spirit was evident in the tent. There was a harmonious spirit in the place and numerous people who were diseased were healed.

From the rear stood someone who did not show signs of receiving the Holy Spirit. It was Simon the magician. He stood there in awe of what was happening. Nearly everyone was shouting or praying praises to God. Some from a different part of Samaria were hearing the words of God spoken in their dialect. There was ample evidence that God's Spirit had indeed arrived and was ministering to the people in boldness and power.

Peter looked at John. "I think we can forget about the circumcision issue."

"Amen, brother, amen."

A few hours later, the service closed, and people began walking back into the nearby villages. As people were departing, Simon made his way to the front. "Sirs, I too believed, but I am amazed at tonight's outcome. I wonder, since I live here and will be here long after you men have departed, could I receive that ability to lay my hands on people so that they might receive the Holy Spirit? I'll pay you good money, if that's what it takes."

Peter could not believe what he was hearing. He looked squarely in the face of Simon. "What!? Your money and evil thinking perish with you! Do you think this is something by which you can entertain people? You can't buy God's gift, nor can you be used of God with twisted thinking. You had better change your way of thinking about God and ask the Lord's forgiveness before something worse happens to you, for I can sense that you are wrapped up in your own sins of bitterness, jealousy, and evil."

Simon was shocked at Peter's response. He could only come out with a wimpy reply: "Well, pray for me and ask the Lord not to let any of those things you just mentioned occur to me." Then he turned around and left the tent.

Peter looked at John. "I guess he didn't want to stick around and pray."

"Something's amiss in his life, Peter. Maybe he'll come back."

"Maybe."

For a couple more days, Peter and John worked with Philip in sharing the gospel with the Samaritans. Many came for miles, bringing the sick and hearing the gospel. Philip remained in the area, while Peter and John headed back toward Jerusalem, stopping at many Samaritan villages and preaching the gospel.

† † †

Philip was praying about whether to stay in Samaria or move further north toward Galilee. He could get no clear direction, so he began fasting as well. After nearly a day and a half of praying and fasting, Philip heard a word from the Lord: "Philip, pack your bags. I want you to go south, pass Jerusalem, and head toward Desert Gaza." So Philip obeyed, not knowing exactly where the Lord was leading him.

On the sandy desert road to Gaza, south of Jerusalem, a caravan of camels and chariots was traveling south. The caravan was an entourage belonging to the treasurer of the Queen of Ethiopia, Queen Candace. Her treasurer, a eunuch, was leaving Jerusalem and heading back to Ethiopia. While traveling slowly, he was reading a parchment containing the prophet Isaiah.

Philip was nearby.

"Go to that chariot and walk alongside it," said the Spirit.

Philip began to run in that direction. As he neared the chariot, he could hear the eunuch treasurer reading Isaiah.

The eunuch noticed Philip walking alongside him and stopped his horses.

"Do you understand what you are reading?" asked Philip.

The eunuch looked at the parchment and then back at Philip. "This Hebrew prophet is easier to read than to understand. I need some help; would you like to ride along and help me?"

Philip jumped aboard the chariot. "Let me see what you're reading . . . oh, this is Isaiah, a prophet of my forefathers."

"Read it for me, please?" asked the eunuch.

"He was herded like a sheep to be slaughtered;

And like a lamb to be sheared, he remained quiet.

In his humility, he was condemned unjustly,

And none of his people spoke on his behalf before he was killed."

The eunuch said to Philip, "Tell me, friend, who is the prophet speaking of: himself or someone else?"

From that question, Philip shared the gospel and how Jesus fulfilled all prophesies concerning the Messiah. As he was concluding the message, the eunuch stopped his chariot beside a sea inlet. "Look, you say those who want to follow in receiving this Jesus as Messiah should be baptized; here's some water—what prevents me from being baptized?"

"Do you understand the cost of following the Christ?"

"I do."

"Do you believe Jesus is the Messiah, the Son of God?"

"I do now."

Philip stepped down out of the chariot and proceeded to wade out into the water. He turned around, looked at the eunuch, and smiled. The eunuch understood the invitation, stepped out of the chariot, and walked into the water beside Philip. Others in the caravan, puzzled, stopped as well and watched the proceeding. Philip then took the man, lowered him under the water, and raised him up. The eunuch came up out of the water with Philip behind him.

As soon as they were out of the water, a burst of wind blew up the sand around them. When the air became clear again, Philip had disappeared—the Spirit had taken him in a whirlwind! The eunuch turned around to thank Philip, but he was gone!

"Hallelujah!" cried the eunuch. "Hallelujah; praise be to the Almighty God, for He has shown mercy and grace to all those who believe!" And from there on, the eunuch could not stop praising God and telling others of his salvation through Jesus.

When the whirlwind ended, Philip found himself in a village called Azotus. So from there, he traveled along the coastal towns and shared the gospel up to Caesarea.

✝✝✝

"Barabbas?" Simon could hardly squeak out his name.

Inaros was quivering as he tried to speak again. "I . . . I didn't know who He was; I only saw innocence in His eyes as He stood there all bloodied from the scourging. He was given an opportunity to defend Himself, but He didn't say a word in His defense. Why? If He was the Lamb of God—the Deliverer—why did He not stop His accusers?"

There was silence. Simon wondered in his heart if he should continue this discussion. *What do I say, Lord? Do I continue?*

"Continue, my child. Every man needs to be delivered."

"Sacrifices must first be slaughtered," Simon continued, "and then offered on behalf of the giver. Jesus had to die on behalf of sinners. He took your sins and mine, and became sin for us. He became a curse in our stead and hung—suspended between earth and heaven—He hung there to die. He was handed over to several men—one very wealthy—and was buried in the wealthy man's new tomb. But three days later, when some of our women went to His grave, the sealed door was open and an angel of God stood before them, telling them that Jesus had risen. They came and reported it to us and that's what I've told you already."

Jabeth, Sorenthasas, and Hamath remained quiet, waiting and wondering what Inaros was going to do. Inaros had turned away from them all and was looking out into the starlit night. There was a conflict raging inside him: one part of him wanted to dismiss this Simon fellow and forget the whole idea of trying to get insider information. Inaros knew that the more information he had the better the chances for success in his incitements. But another part of him had weakened his commitment for revenge—a revenge that he still felt justified in achieving. He turned back to Simon.

"You found your Savior and now you have peace. I, on the other hand, have not found mine; therefore, I have not found my peace. I do not expect you to show sympathy toward me and my cause, but do know that we will do our best to stay out of your way as you seek to convert the world to the Way of your Master. Only, don't be alarmed if there are a few less Romans to convert."

Simon wanted to say more, but couldn't. He was emotionally spent over the encounter. He turned around to leave.

"I'll have Jabeth and Soren to see you down to the corner."

Simon stopped and took one last look at Barabbas. "Don't bother; I know my way around these parts . . . gentlemen."

It was late when Simon returned to the headquarters, so he was surprised to see Peter walking through the courtyard.

"Simon, you've come back—in one piece, I see." He greeted the young man.

"I wasn't expecting anyone up; hope I didn't cause too much of a stir when I left?"

"Oh no, no; I'm glad that you're listening to our Lord and that He is just as involved in your life as He is in mine."

"Isn't it wonderful how our Lord speaks to us inwardly at just the right time?"

"Yes it is; now, how long are you going to keep me in suspense? Tell me how your meeting went tonight with your friends."

"Oh, Peter, you will not believe who I witnessed to tonight." Simon began telling Peter everything that happened. For about an hour, Simon rattled all the events of the evening. "Can you believe that!?"

"Umm, yes, I can believe that. When I think of how I denied my Lord . . . yes, I believe He wants to save Barabbas and anyone else who would turn to Him."

"Oh, I can only pray our Lord would get to his heart; he had so much anger inside him that it was like a wall separating him from the real world around him."

"We should remember to pray much for him."

"Yes, I will."

"Any idea who he may be targeting?"

"No, he guarded his plans very well."

"Oh, well; may our Lord be pleased to disrupt his plans to harm anyone. It's time to get some rest, Simon. Tomorrow, we'll see how our dispersion went overnight and make some additional plans. Good night, my brother."

"Good night, Peter."

✝✝✝

E arly the next day, Saul was at the prison, checking to see how many more rebels could be contained in the prison.

"There's plenty of room for them," said the chief guard. "And we'll pack them in so tight that they'll pray to their Jesus for just a cool drink of water."

"Do not treat them inhumanely," said Saul. "They will need enough strength to stand before the high priest and the council to be judged and sentenced to stoning."

"Yes, sir! Death to the heretics!" The chief guard turned away from Saul, laughing at his own statement. Saul did not laugh. He was a Pharisee who believed in a resurrection after death. He knew these captives would have no fair trial through the Sanhedrin courts. He knew Herod Antipas was delighted to have finally found something with which to satisfy the Jewish leaders' demand for some control over the protection of their local rights—especially their religious customs. The uprising of these followers of Jesus had nearly broken the peaceful atmosphere of the Sanhedrin council.

Now things were changing in the council's favor—but at the cost of many Jewish lives. This troubled Saul. Not only was he a Jew, of the tribe of Benjamin, a Pharisee, trained in the finest school of Hebrew theology and practice, but he was also a Roman citizen, and he knew Romans had personal protection from the kind of treatment these Jewish rebels were to experience.

Saul also had been brought up in Greek culture. He had studied the philosophies of the Greeks, who were very strong on the value of man's mental and physical capabilities. As a young lad, he watched many of the sports games sponsored by the Grecian culture. He knew of many Greco-Roman mythologies that steered Grecian thought. His citizenry and cultural background taught him to value the physical and mental achievements of man.

Not so with the current establishment of Jewish thought. His studies in the Scriptures taught him how far the Sanhedrin had drifted from the commands of God. Saul was an expert in the teachings of the Law and the Prophets. His natural and intellectual prowess made him a popular speaker—second to none!

But Saul was troubled from within, and he didn't understand why. He had given a successful defense of the Jewish customs at the splintered Synagogue of the Freedmen. Then came the rebuttal from Stephen. He was impressed with Stephen's ability to present Jesus as the prophesied Messiah; sure, there were some areas that he could have challenged the Hellenist, but that was not what stirred his heart. Stephen spoke with a confidence and a power that appeared from nowhere. Saul had only read of this kind of conviction and power from the prophets of the Scriptures. He had never observed it personally.

Saul had wanted to speak to Stephen after his message, if only he had not stepped over the line and began accusing the council and priests of crucifying this so-called Messiah. And since his accusations were there in the presence of many Jews, it was only natural for the members of the council and priests to rise up in immediate retribution for such statements. Saul was grateful that he was chosen to record the judgment given. Nevertheless, he thought the death penalty was pure emotion-driven—an adrenalin rush.

Stephen never lashed out at the mob who took him to a makeshift court. He had a peace in his heart that shone as bright as the noontime sun. Then his prayer to Jesus to not lay this sin upon his punishers sealed the troubling encounter for Saul. *What kind of man was this?* thought Saul. *And what kind of man was this Jesus?* He had heard the rumors about Jesus and was looking forward to debating Him. But, alas, he was too late in getting established in the Judean region. Jesus, also, had been convicted by mob-rule. *What a pity,* thought Saul. *This current quick trial and stoning could have been averted had the council only been more patient.*

Saul was not pleased with the attitude or actions of the current high priest and his family heirs. Annas' speech solidified his fears of the greed of the high priest's family. He even spoke of his displeasure to Gamaliel. Gamaliel, however, was more into the Jesus events. He convinced Saul that once the uprising of the Way was quelled, things would improve among the brethren of the council. Saul had not seen it yet, but he had a high respect for his mentor, and he respected the positions of the council and priestly system.

Now it was his responsibility to bring order back into the system of his faith. The rebels must understand that to challenge the God-established order of the priestly function and the Law, was to undermine the entire system of the Jewish faith and practice. This had to stop, and it had to stop now before it spread even further. Even if it meant the stoning of many that he had and would arrest? Yes, it was that serious if one but carried the movement to its ultimate conclusion. These rebels were congregating at the temple porches and in the local synagogues of the Jewish cities and villages. They were targeting those who already favored the traditions and faith of their forefathers, the Hebrews.

By this time, Saul had returned to his quarters, preparing to go to the high priest to obtain his regiment of priests and troops. Although he did not like their liberal trends or their morally questionable acts, he knew he must have a show of force and authority to arrest those within the confines of such a large and religious center as Jerusalem.

As he neared the temple grounds, he noticed an eerie silence from the porches. *Good,* he thought. *It's working.* Saul thought perhaps he would drop by Gamaliel's home first to give him an update of the morning quietness. It was on the way. He knocked on the door and adjusted himself a bit, wishing he had worn better outer garments. The door opened.

"Saul, my son, please do come in."

"Thank you, sir. I apologize for the unannounced visit, but I was headed over to the high priest's quarters to pick up my fellow priests and troops for today's raids."

"Yes, it's quite alright. I needed to see you anyhow. Please, recline with me for a moment."

Saul followed Gamaliel into a sitting room. "Master, as I walked into the temple area, I noticed that our rebel teachers were not in their usual places."

"Correct, the priests are excited today—but the captain of the guards is wondering what to do with his extra troops on duty." They both managed a polite laugh. "Listen, Saul, I have a proposal for you. I know you desire to sweep the entire city of Jerusalem, but I have something else I want you to consider."

"Sure, sir, but is there something wrong? Have I not been thorough enough?"

"Oh, no, no, you've been excellent. But after today, I think you will have shown the local priests and given them the courage to continue your local raids. But there is a more serious threat upon us now—one that I think needs your unique qualifications. Our sources tell us that many of the followers of the Way have scattered throughout the region. In fact, there have been reports of meetings in tents in Samaria and other regions by the rebels, bringing many people into their belief system. You, Saul, have the courage and the citizenry to go beyond Judea to put an end to this expansion of the Way."

"Sir, I feel as if I just got started here; I would like to finish the city first. I have already mapped the areas out and have notified the chief jailer of the plans."

"I understand, and that is exactly why you are needed for this greater roundup. You plan well, and you have objectives to reach your goals. That is why you are needed to contain the Way in this larger campaign. Now Annas and I have already discussed this, and he is in full agreement with the changes. Jonathan will oversee your operations here and—"

"But sir, will he be as thorough as I feel it needs to be?"

"Saul, this is the best plan for the profit of all. Look at the bigger picture with me. You can stay here and do a great job rounding up the rebels in this one—but great—city, and be known by the local priests and surrounding synagogues, or you can go out into the far reaches of our Jewish settlements, overcome this rebel infiltration, and get national recognition. And I would not be surprised if the emperor himself will take note of how we Jews handle our own rebels and, therefore, will loosen his tight grip on our blessed land."

Saul mulled this over in his analytical mind. "Sir, I will need papers for the local authorities in the areas I enter."

"We will have them ready by mid-afternoon."

"And I want my troops and me to have horses, for I intend to travel fast; plus, I want a separate supply group to follow the main route to set up camp as we ride into the towns and villages."

"I think those can be ready by the morning. Is there anything else you can think of?"

"Sir, if I'm not asking for too much, I really have enjoyed access to the parchments and books I have borrowed from the temple library; is there a possibility that I may carry some of them with me?"

"I'll speak with the high priest about this request; I'm sure he will be more than accommodating. Now, be off with you, my son. Shorten your coverage today so that you may prepare yourself for a greater experience."

"Yes, sir, I will. Thank you, again, for your confidence in me."

"The pleasure is mine; I can only imagine what this is going to do to the enrollment of our school. You'll have a lot of planning to do, when you return, on how to expand our school facilities."

Saul smiled. "Yes, sir!" Amidst all these current plans, he'd nearly forgotten his ultimate dream of becoming the head schoolmaster of the school of Hillel.

✝✝✝

"Master, there is trouble in our city; will You not come back and help us restore order?" Peter was praying alone this morning because he was uncertain as to what he would or should say. The apostles remained intact in Jerusalem, although some were staying in different quarters now. Peter had been praying about what to do next; do they split up the group further and plan regional gatherings, now that Jerusalem was being targeted? "Lord, please give me a word so that I may tell the others."

"Peter, I have heard your prayers. Remember what I told you: I will never leave you, nor forsake you."

"But Lord, do you—"

"Listen to me, My child, and do not forget My teachings. You and the others will maintain your stay here in Jerusalem for a while, but I will send you out into Judea, Samaria, and further. Soon, you will all be scattered; make sure you listen to James, My mother's son, for he will become the head elder over the assembly there."

"My Lord, what about Saul of Tarsus?"

"I know about him, and I will deal with him at the proper time. Do not let him concern you. Simon, son of Jonah, do you love Me?"

Peter remembered these words. "Yes, my Lord, You know that I love You, and I will feed Your sheep and follow You. Thank You for hearing me this morning." Peter's mind drifted for a few moments as he remembered those personal times of fellowship with his Lord. Those were most precious to him now.

"Peter, Peter!" Nathanael came running up to him. "We've a word from the Master. Come quickly!"

"Yes, my brother, I'm coming." Peter couldn't help but smile as he moved hurriedly to keep up with Nathanael. When he arrived in the meeting room, the apostles were all in conversation with each other.

John came to Peter, noticing his face of calm. "You have heard from Him as well."

"Does it show?" John embraced him. "Now let's talk some . . . gentlemen! My brothers, please, please, let's recline a bit now and discuss our Lord's plans."

Everyone settled down and reclined as Peter stood before them. "Our Lord has everything under control, as usual. As we stated the other evening, James and his brothers will take charge of feeding the flock here in Jerusalem. The Lord will speak to him and guide him in this matter. As for us, we must prepare to go into other regions—first into Judea, then Samaria, and then as far as He leads us."

"What about Saul of Tarsus?" asked Matthew.

"Our Lord is also aware of Saul of Tarsus," said Peter, "and has assured me that he will not be a problem for us at this time."

"Peter," said John. "My brother, James, has an update on the ones arrested."

"Yes, James, what have you to say?"

"My brothers, it appears that there will be some speedy trials for the followers who have been arrested. I have been informed that the council will charge them for blasphemy and for inciting an uprising—either charge could call for the death penalty."

Peter took over. "We must commit these to prayer. It seems to me that our Master is not going to prevent us from physical harm. If necessary, we must join with Him in suffering that in due time we will reap our deliverance from this earthly tent of ours."

"Amen, amen," the others responded.

"But this does not lessen the burden we should carry for those who suffer," said Peter. "And we must do all we can to fight for justice among our brothers and sisters. We must pray for one another and encourage one another to stay the course and be faithful—even unto death!"

"Amen, amen!" the others cried.

"Brothers, the Lord has told us to remain here a bit longer. This will give us time to train more men to become elders and overseers. This will allow our fellowship to disperse into smaller groups so we will not be easily detected. We must also train other men and women to serve each other in the daily cares of each fellowship.

"Now the Lord has blessed us with a good financial base, only let us use this as a continual blessing to those whom we send out and to those in need of food and shelter."

"Amen, amen," said the others.

"And now, Simon, would you come and share with the brothers of your encounter last night?"

† † †

"Let me see the cliffs again!" demanded Tiberius.

His doctor came to his bedside. "Your Excellency, you are too weak to get out of bed. Here, drink this; it will calm your nerves."

"This is poison—guards! Guards!" (No one entered the room.) "Where are my children?! They will carry me to the cliffs." (His children were dead.)

"The emperor lies ill," reported a senator to the consulate in Rome.

"What emperor?" asked another senator.

"The one who retired on the Isle of Capri," said another senator. Some murmuring was heard.

"Emperor Tiberius, he will die today . . . of his own accord or with a little help from his doctor."

"Finally! 'The Exile' will die; now, perhaps, we can get a leader again."

"He has chosen Caligula as his successor."

"Is he of the imperial lineage?"

"He is the great-grandson of Augustus and the son of Germanicus. Tiberius adopted him as well; I would say he has imperial blood running through his veins."

"He's going to need it to restore the boundaries of the empire."

"There are a lot of men now with imperial blood in their veins," said another. "They've intermarried so much, it's hard to keep track of the imperial family anymore."

Caligula sat in the emperor's receiving room. *Finally . . . now maybe I can get the respect I deserve. I will allow the consulate to continue the daily affairs of running the government, while I live out the noble traits of my great-grandfather, Augustus.*

"Guards!" Several guards opened the large doors and stood at attention. "Get word to the centurions of Judea and have them release Agrippa from his imprisonment. Restore his property and find a noble region for him to rule as a king."

Caligula stood up and looked out the eastern window. *Agrippa, my dear brother, your wish has come true. Now my wish is that you align Judea under greater Roman rule.*

† † †

Two horsemen with tunics and shielded headgear left the area just east of the temple grounds, heading south toward Bethany.

Near the outskirts of Jerusalem lay a brothel with noted sobriety. The men came near, paid a young lad to watch the horses, and went inside. After a few inquiries, a man approached them.

"I hear you're looking for some serious hirelings for a revenge stint," said the man.

"Yes," responded Caiaphas, still partially shielded by his headgear. "And it must be done with no way to trace it back to me."

"Well, my buddy and me might be interested, if you know how to pay for such a job."

"How much?"

"Ha!" the man laughed. "How much? You ask how much before you announce the target? Listen to me; you tell us who you want knocked off and we'll tell you how much, up front, and how much when the job is completed."

Caiaphas studied the man for a moment. "What if I told you it was a member of the royal bloodline of the Herodians?"

The man nearly choked on his swallow of wine. "What!? Who!?"

This time Caiaphas laughed. He motioned to his guard who stood up and revealed a portion of his guard armor to the man. Caiaphas then drew nearer to this brothel riff-raff. "Tell me, do you and your friend know of someone who can do some serious work for me?"

He stood up. "Just you wait right here for a minute while I confer with my friend." Jabeth stood up and disappeared toward the rear of the building. Caiaphas motioned to his guard. "Go check on the horses and get back in here as soon as possible." The guard dismissed himself and left the building. In a few minutes, Jabeth was back with Sorenthasas.

"Mister, we don't know who you are, but the kind of work you're looking for is going to take more than a couple of men. We have sources that we think may be interested in your proposal, but you must know that secrecy must remain on both sides."

"I wouldn't have it any other way."

"Okay, you wait in here or by the side of the building. You'll find an animal water trough and a couple benches to sit on. We'll be back in about an hour."

"Make it back in thirty minutes and the drinks are on me for the rest of the day."

Jabeth and Sorenthasas smiled as they stood up and made their way to the door. Caiaphas looked around the shoddy place. His guard came back and stood beside him. "Sit down, will you, please? And try not to act like a guard."

"Sir?"

Caiaphas reached in his tunic and tossed the guard a coin. "At least see if you can buy us a drink while we wait."

Thirty minutes passed, then an hour. Caiaphas and his guard left the building and checked on their horses that were tied by the feeding trough. Another thirty minutes passed. Caiaphas was about to mount his horse when a lonely figure stepped out from behind the building next to the brothel. "Gentlemen, I hear you may be looking for an executioner?" Caiaphas was about to command his guard to ride over the man, but then changed his mind.

"That depends on who is asking."

The man took a few steps forward. As he did, a huge hulk of a man stepped out from behind the same building with Jabeth and Sorenthasas not far behind. Caiaphas recognized the two men in the rear. The man continued to speak. "Listen, in this part of town, I do the asking. My friends tell me you are looking for some serious work, so let's begin by you answering some questions."

Caiaphas didn't speak, but continued to stand by his horse, as did his guard. He motioned to his guard and the guard immediately turned around and walked his horse out to the front corner—out of hearing range, but close enough to come to Caiaphas' aid should he need it. "I want you to attempt to assassinate Herod Antipas, and I want you to make it look as if you were hired by the high priest."

Inaros moved in a little closer to the man. "Attempt?"

"You heard right; I don't care if you succeed, but all I'm interested in is who gets the blame."

"This will require some serious coins up front for us to do such a job. Plus, we will need clothing material that will identify the attempt as from the high priest's office."

Caiaphas reached in his saddlebag and retrieved a coin pouch. He tossed it to Inaros. "This should be enough down payment; my associate will bring this much more when the job is done."

Inaros handed the bag to Hamath; he opened it and began counting the silver and gold coins. He whispered in Inaros' ear. Inaros held the bag as if he was going to throw it back to Caiaphas. "This is a third of what I require for a top-level assassination attempt." Caiaphas reached into his other saddle bag, pulled out another pouch and tossed it on the ground. Then he reached in his bag further and pulled out a headgear. He threw it to Inaros.

"Here is two-thirds of your bounty and a headgear that will tie the assassin to the high priest's office. Now do not trouble me any further. Do the job or I'll have your reputation ruined within a month's time." Caiaphas mounted his horse and turned it toward the front of the building, his guard in waiting.

Inaros did not move until the two men had disappeared from view. He turned toward Jabeth as Hamath picked up the second pouch. "Did you not recognize him?"

"Why no, boss. His face was shielded."

"That was Caiaphas, son-in-law of Annas. What if this had been a trap?" Inaros was not happy about the encounter. It was always risky to deal with a high-ranking official. The request appeared to be genuine and the less information each knew about the other, the more reliable the source becomes. Inaros tossed two coins to both Jabeth and Sorenthasas. "Go enjoy yourselves for the rest of the day, but I want you at the meeting place shortly after dark."

Inaros pondered the encounter with Caiaphas. He wanted to target a Roman official, but Antipas would be an excellent second choice. Plus Caiaphas said it did not have to be an assassination—just an attempt. But why waste all the planning and effort for an attempt? Why not send a clear message that there should be no negotiations with the Romans?

†††

Saul wasted no time in arresting more men and women of the Way. The priests and guards that accompanied him were busy shuffling back and forth from the city prison to another street where he was located.

"The fish are biting today, sir!" said one of the priests. Saul was looking at the houses ahead of him.

"I notice several boys keep coming back and forth into our view," said Saul. "Several of you trail them and see where they are going." A priest and guard sped up their walk as they kept a slight distance behind the boys. Meanwhile, Saul continued his aggressive search for followers of the Way. It was really quite easy to track them down, because the true followers would not lie about their belief in and allegiance to the Nazarene.

Soon the boys reappeared; the priest and guard followed not far behind them. This time, however, they ignored the boys and came straight to Saul. "Tell me, gentlemen?" asked Saul. "Did you find something of interest?"

"Yes, Rabbi Saul," said the priest. "I think we may have found a major gathering point of the rebels. They're not very far from the temple grounds. It is a large complex with gated entries."

"Show me."

"Yes, sir." They headed down the street to the next intersection and turned right. Within a matter of minutes they neared the complex. The outer perimeter was made of stone with an occasional opening about five feet high from the ground. The front gate was a wood and iron design that allowed the owners to preview those outside before entering.

Saul walked down to get closer, keeping on the other side of the street. This was no average resident of the city. But who was it? About that time, the two boys showed up at the door and knocked. Someone from within recognized them and let them in. "Any idea who this place belongs to?" asked Saul. The others shrugged their shoulders.

"I believe I have escorted Rabbi Nicodemus to these quarters, sir," said one of the guards.

"Hmm," said Saul. "This is interesting indeed."

"And what, young Saul, do you find so interesting about my villa?" A stately elderly man, with about six field hands, walked up behind the group. He was dressed for field work but still managed to be intimidating in his stature. Saul wondered who he might be, but it didn't take long for him to find out. "I'm Joseph of Arimathea, a member of the Sanhedrin, friend to the Pharisees, and contributor to many of the fine architecture around the temple grounds."

"Sir, I have been commissioned by the high priest and the king to round up followers of the Way of the Nazarene. I believe that there may be spies among your people who are reporting my whereabouts."

"Spies? Oh I think you are mistaken, young man. I had several of my field hands' boys keep a running tally of how many citizens of our fine city you were arresting illegally."

"Illegally?" Saul was not one to scare easily. "These so-called 'fine citizens' happen to be blaspheming our God."

"And I suppose you have personally sat down and interrogated these 'blasphemers'?"

"I don't need to; I've heard their defense."

"I know you have; I was there when one of your so-called blasphemers was dragged out of a synagogue, hastily tried by our council—without my knowing—and stoned to death! And you just happened to be the recorder. I wonder Saul, has our God turned His back on His own law about justice? Did He take back His word when He said through the prophet Jeremiah, 'I will make a new covenant with My people and My law will be put in their minds and written upon their hearts'? Is what you're doing justice? Is this God's new covenant?"

Saul paused for a moment to recollect his thoughts. "I have my orders, and I plan to fulfill them." Then, pointing at Joseph's villa, "You tell those who you may be hiding in there that I leave tomorrow to extradite followers of the Way throughout the Roman Empire. Tell them there is no city in which they can hide. They will be caught and they will be tried by the council." Saul then turned around and walked away.

"May God have mercy on your cold heart," Joseph said as he watched Saul and his entourage leave the area. "A lot of innocent blood will be on your hands, young man!" Saul continued to walk away. He must now focus on his trip, tomorrow, to Damascus. The prison was not yet full.

Peter, James, and John were in the courtyard of the villa when they saw Joseph and his men enter. While his men were washing, preparing for dinner, Joseph made his way over to the three men. "Brothers, grace and peace be yours," he said.

"And to you as well, brother," said John.

"I think you should know that I just had a brief encounter with young Saul of Tarsus outside the villa."

"Oh, my," said James.

"Does he know we are here?" asked Peter.

"I think he suspects something going on, but I wouldn't trouble yourself with him for a while. He said he was leaving town in the morning to round up other followers outside the city."

"Could this be a trick? Maybe he will come back," said James.

"No, his talk was serious about leaving town; plus, he had enough men with him now that he could have easily come in and made the arrests. So my hunch is that he saw this place as a little too much for him to take today. But I do think you may need to discuss a new meeting place to settle into. I have a few more rental places that may be of assistance to you."

"You are most kind and generous," said John as he embraced the elder man.

"Oh, don't thank me; all that I have really belongs to our mission in the Lord's work."

"We will go and speak with the others," said Peter. They turned and walked across the courtyard where most of the apostles were assembled along with the half-brothers of Jesus. All were accounted for except Simon the Zealot. "Where's Simon?" asked Peter.

"He's upstairs praying," said Matthew. "He's really burdened about Barabbas."

"And rightfully so," continued Peter. "We need to send word out to those who are dispersed that Saul of Tarsus will be heading out to who-knows-where tomorrow to make arrests and bring them back to Jerusalem for trial."

"Do you know how many are in prison now?" asked Andrew.

"This morning's estimate is thirty so far. I fear for their lives because of what happened to Stephen. We must join Simon in the upper chamber and pray, and we must pray for Saul's plans to be interrupted in a major way. Our Lord warned us that trials and tribulation await those who choose to follow Him. Let us be faithful and let us encourage all followers to be faithful and stay the course."

✝✝✝

Inaros, Hamath, Jabeth, and Sorenthasas gathered to plot the assassination of Herod Antipas. Inaros had a map of the city laid before him. "We must act soon, for the news on the streets is that Antipas may be replaced by someone else. The new emperor is making a few changes.

"Now, Antipas likes to take strolls at sunset at the perimeter walls toward the west. With the evening sun as our shield, he should be most vulnerable for an attack."

"But what about the guards?" asked Sorenthasas.

"What about them?" Inaros snapped back. "You and Jabeth will distract them until I get in the proper position and put an arrow in Antipas. That should draw the guards away from you two. You will then proceed to the hideout caves and wait until things cool down—about a month."

"A month!?" cried Jabeth. "It was only two weeks the last time."

"But last time the target was no governing ruler, you idiot!" Inaros was more irritable than usual. "Hamath will have the horses in place and a change of outer garments. He will scatter your other clothing throughout the city. Any questions?" No one responded. "Okay, tomorrow evening, about an hour before sunset, we will meet by the west-side gate. We'll walk the streets and get a feel for our setup and for your escape routes. Again, any questions?" Again, no one responded. "Okay, here's some coins; go out and enjoy yourselves, but don't be late tomorrow."

Jabeth and Sorenthasas soon disappeared. Hamath usually remained silent and followed slowly behind Inaros. However, he made a few grunts that Inaros thought peculiar. "Yes, my friend, something troubling you?"

Hamath sat near Inaros, which was a signal that Inaros knew it might take a few moments for him to speak. So he sat down as well, next to him. Finally Hamath spoke. "The man you spoke with the other night—the one who told us about the Nazarene?"

"Yes? What about him?"

"What if it's true? What if this Jesus is the Messiah?"

Inaros had little patience with Jabeth and Sorenthasas because they seemed to enjoy acting dumb. But with Hamath, talking with him was at a slower pace—and deeper level. Inaros knew that Hamath had pondered the issue deep within his soul. "I was impressed with this Simon's courage and especially his conviction. But he claims to have seen a dead man alive and that this Jesus now lived inside him, by His Spirit, to control him. I can't quite wrap my mind around such concepts."

Hamath grunted. "There are all kinds of gods out there—all are dead and have not changed the men who follow them one bit. But this fellow was a zealot; I could sense his courage and his conviction. Yet, he was changed on the inside; this man had peace. Isn't that what we are looking for?"

"But his 'love your enemy' philosophy will not drive the Romans out of our country. This Jesus-man turned His other cheek and look what it got Him—a cruel and brutal death!"

"What has our philosophy gotten us? Nations have been warring with each other for this land for centuries. There is never going to be real lasting peace until man settles this war within himself."

Inaros sat there pondering the discussion. "I long for justice in our land, free of Roman rule. We have not had real peace since the early days of King Solomon. Are not our priests commissioned to bring inner peace with God? Yet they have become as corrupt as the Romans. They no more hear from God than the rest of us. Why? Because they have lost touch with the One they claim to serve.

"I cannot lay down my weapons when the blood of my brothers has not been avenged. I have a score to settle on behalf of the dead and I will do everything in my power to drive the Romans out. That's when I will have peace in my heart."

"Will you? You've caused the death of numerous Roman soldiers—more than twice the number of your brothers. How many deaths will it take to give you peace?"

"I don't know, but not enough yet."

"Then you must follow your own destiny; however, after this job, I am going to seek out that Simon fellow and learn more about this Jesus of Nazareth."

Inaros was fearful of this line of thinking. He knew Hamath only spoke when there was a change brewing in his heart and mind. "I cannot fault a man for wanting to find lasting peace. After this, we will part ways, my friend. I will give you your portion of the treasury tonight in case things go wrong and we have to split directions."

"And if I find inner peace with Jesus, I will search you out and let you know."

"I wouldn't bother; unless, of course, you find me in a prison cell." They both stood up. "Now let's get some rest; we have some caves to fill up with supplies tomorrow."

†††

The morning sun had not crested the eastern mountain range, but Saul was up and packed for his trip. He made sure all his bags were secured on the caravan camels—especially the books and parchments. He managed to store one small book and a small parchment with a portion of Leviticus in his saddlebags. Saul was an avid reader and never allowed an idle moment for his mind.

He had already retrieved the papers from the high priest and was now ready to stop by the temple stables to collect the rest of his entourage. Saul had been given a dozen temple guards and two priests to accompany him. To make traveling easier, he decided he would head directly to Damascus first, capture the rebel leaders there, and work his way back to Jerusalem. The supply portion of the caravan would stay on the main highway and travel toward Damascus. They would meet Saul's group on the return trip.

Within the hour, they were heading out the east gate of the city wall, on the Jericho road. Saul wanted to make Damascus in three and a half days. The road to Jericho was winding and treacherous, preventing him from trying to read. Managing his horse required all his mental acumen. But he did ponder yesterday's conversation with the villa owner, Joseph of Arimathea.

Who was this council member, trying to teach me the law? I am the soon-to-be assistant to Gamaliel; I know when someone is violating our laws. But Saul knew blasphemers did not go through the usual cross-examinations before the council. If possible, they were stoned on site. This Joseph guy, however, was appealing to Roman law, which gave all their citizens equality in a trial. As a Roman, Saul knew the value of the Roman law. Justice nearly always prevailed when truth was available. Yet he knew how that many Sanhedrin councils, in years past, added many laws to God's original law, which made many situations illogical and the lives of many commoners unbearable.

A "new covenant"? How dare this man try to teach me with words from the prophet Jeremiah? "Blood of the innocent"? Again, Saul reasoned that his own intelligence and interpretation of the Law of God cleared him of any wrongdoing. *God is on my side; He will vindicate my actions.* Yet with all this reasoning in his favor, Saul continued to be troubled from within. He had always been able to see the uncertainty of a man's heart in his eyes; this had given him the confidence he needed to settle an argument. But he had never seen such confidence as that in the eyes of Stephen; this man knew what he believed, and there was power in his words. Where could confidence and power like that come from if he were a blasphemer? Saul had never encountered this before, and it unsettled him.

Once on the straighter side of the Jordan, Saul picked up the pace of the entourage and made it near the southern base of the Sea of Galilee before setting up camp the second day. Each night two fires were built: one for the troops and one for the priests. However, the other two priests felt intimidated around Saul, so he remained more to himself most of the time. But that was his preference; it gave him more time to read and to pray. *God of our fathers, hear my prayer; let me be swift in stopping those who blaspheme Your holy name. Let me have victory in making Your paths straight. Let true justice prevail.*

The third day of the journey was not as hectic as the first two. They kept to the east side of the Sea of Galilee and stopped near the north end for a fresh fish meal and some talk with the local priest in charge of the synagogue. The road to Damascus now turned toward the northeast. They traveled until the sun began to set above the western mountain range, about a half a day's journey to Damascus. Once again, Saul prayed to God: *God of our fathers, hear my prayer; let me be swift in stopping those who blaspheme Your holy name. Let me have victory in making Your paths straight. Let true justice prevail.*

On the fourth day, Damascus would be entered by noon. Saul and his entourage broke camp early because he wanted to see the priest of Damascus as soon as they arrived. It was a clear day, and as he was nearing Damascus, Saul prayed one more time: *God of our fathers, hear my prayer; let me be swift in stopping those who blaspheme Your holy name. Let me have victory in making Your paths straight. Let true justice prevail.*

Suddenly, a bright flashing bolt of lightning hit the road, just ahead of Saul. His horse jolted and reared back, throwing him off and onto the ground. Cracks of thunder pealed through the air; everyone fell off their horses. But the brightness did not end immediately. Its illumination was like the brightness of lightning. The others shielded their eyes, but Saul looked into the light, for he saw the figure of a man. He began to hear a noise—a voice from the figure: "Saul! Saul! Why are you persecuting Me!?"

Saul was trembling. "Who are you, Lord?"

"I am Jesus, whom you persecute. Don't you find it hard to pray against your conscience!?"

Saul continued to tremble and was astonished at what he was hearing. He bowed his head and closed his eyes. "My Lord, what would you have me to do now?"

"Get up, go into the city, and you will be told what to do."

The men around Saul were terrified, seeing the brightness and hearing a booming sound like a voice, but beholding no one in their sight. Then, as quickly as it came upon them, the bright light departed. The men stood up and checked their horses—except Saul. Something was wrong with him! He remained on the ground and had opened his eyes, but could see no one. "What is happening!?" he cried out.

Several guards came to his aid. "Here," one of them said. "Let us help you get up." They lifted him up onto his feet, but he refused to let go.

"I can't see! My eyes! I can't see!"

"We need to get him into town," said one of the priests. Turning to the guards, he said, "Come help me get him back on his horse."

"No—no horse!" He'd fallen off once and did not want to experience that again. So they led him by the hand into Damascus. There they left him in the guest quarters of the priest.

† † †

Simon was praying alone; he hadn't eaten since the day before. "Master," he prayed. "Will You allow Barabbas to shed more blood? Can You not save him from this hatred and anger inside him?" Simon felt that he had not been aggressive enough with Barabbas a few nights ago, so he doubled his praying effort and began to fast. So far, he had not heard from his Lord. *What if a silent answer is a "No" answer?* he wondered. "My Lord, please help me through this procedure so that I may know how to pray aright."

"Simon?" Jesus was calling.

"Yes, my Master?"

"I have heard your prayers; I will not always answer you verbally, but for this, I want you to know that Barabbas is planning to assassinate Antipas in a few days. He will be assessing the location this evening at the west gate of the city. I will allow you this encounter with him, but if he refuses you this second time, he has been warned twice and may not get another chance."

"Lord, thank you for this opportunity. Please give me the words to say that will wake him up."

"Hamath is going to need you in the days ahead. His heart is bending toward Me."

"And the other two?"

"I cannot disclose that to you at this time. Just know that I am with you always and will be using you as long as you live by faith and trust Me in the outcomes of each and every encounter. My power to deliver is not weak, but each man's sins are great obstacles to turning to Me and living by faith."

"Thank you, Lord, for hearing and answering my prayer." Simon's burden was lifted as he reflected on his quiet time with the Lord. Jesus was as real to him now as before His crucifixion;

in fact, it was even more personal since it was a one-on-one relationship.

Simon was hungry; he got up from his praying and went out to find some food. In the dining area, Simon found Peter, James, John, and Elder James (the new title for the half-brother of Jesus). "I'm hungry!"

"Well, you look peaceful," said John. "Any word about Barabbas?"

"Yes, indeed. The Lord told me I could meet him tonight at the west gate of the city and have another opportunity to speak with him."

"Will the Lord save him?" asked Peter.

"He wouldn't say, only that Barabbas would get this opportunity to hear and respond. But He did say that his bodyguard—the big guy—would be open to the gospel. So that is encouraging."

"I guess this means you won't be attending our studies tonight?" asked Elder James.

"Not sure, but it doesn't appear so."

"Do you want someone to go with you?" asked James.

"Again, I think it is best I go alone. This guy is very suspicious of any change in style or method."

"May the Lord's protection be yours tonight," said Peter.

"In fact," said John, "let's just pray over you right now." And so they did. Afterwards, Simon found some food.

✝✝✝

Inaros and Hamath walked through the side streets on the west side, testing the viewpoints from every corner and every angle, both inside and outside the wall. Next, they checked every vacant lot and every vacant house. The houses closest to the wall were too close, the next street over, however, gave Inaros the best angle. The distance would require marksmanship for a bow and arrow. Although Inaros preferred a dagger, it would be next to impossible to get that close to Antipas. Even when they wanted to get away from everyone, kings still had their bodyguards to protect them. Inaros measured the distance from several vacant housetops to the wall.

Next, he would go to the gate and wait for Jabeth and Soren-thasas. They would need an escape route as well since they would be inside the city wall, causing a distraction. Although he trusted them fully, they were sometimes careless and less than professional in their actions and escape. Inaros would help them all he could, but it would be up to them to get out of the trouble zone. This was one reason Hamath's and his hideout was not to be known by the other two.

The next project would be to spy on Antipas himself to see what his habits were when he took a stroll. His exact location on any given night would remain a mystery, but that's why Inaros charged Caiaphas extra. It would take time and money to do this right.

The time to rendezvous with the others was near, so Inaros made his way to the shadow side of the interior wall by the west gate. He and Hamath had seen a spot that was out of the normal traffic area and an earshot away from most walking trails. As they approached the area, several men were standing there. When one of the men saw them coming—especially with the size of Hamath—he quietly wandered away in the opposite direction. The other man, however didn't seem to notice the two approaching. Inaros was about to let Hamath overtake his stride to get the stranger to move on, but before he could, the stranger began stretching his hands out wide as if he were measuring the walk space between the wall and the gate shack.

"I'd say this space is probably not a good escape route for the big fellow, wouldn't you say so, Barabbas?" Simon turned around as Hamath was about to grab his shoulder. "Then again, maybe you shouldn't be seen at all, because your size is not easy to camouflage." Hamath stopped and grunted. Inaros, however, came right up into Simon's face.

"Who told you to be here!? Where are those two!?"

"It wasn't them, Barab—"

"Stop calling me that! That is no longer my name! No one else knows of this meeting tonight; what did you do? Did you get my men drunk?" Inaros was in his face, once again showing his weakness: no control of his temper.

"No, I did not get your men drunk. And I also know that Jabeth is never on time for anything, so you may as well listen to me, and I will tell you why I'm here."

Hamath grunted again, a signal to Inaros that he could be drawing too much spectator attention. Inaros backed up a few steps. Simon looked around to see if anyone else had veered into the area.

"I know of your plans," said Simon.

"You don't know anything!"

"You plan to assassinate Antipas."

For a brief moment Inaros could not respond. *How on earth could this . . . this stranger know?* "Who told you such a ridiculous story!?" *Wait'll I get my hands around Jabeth's neck!*

"For several days I have been praying and fasting over you and your men. Finally, my Lord revealed to me what your plans were. I asked Him for another chance to talk you out of it and to save your lives."

"Now I know—you got drunk with Jabeth! Ha! I should have known you would find his weak spot and try to muscle in on the deal. But I don't take to strangers that easily."

"Sir—whatever your name is—when Jabeth arrives, you will find both he and Sorenthasas to be as sober and as surprised to see me as you two were, and if you know those two at all, you can see right through their lies.

"Now both of you listen to me, and then I'll be out of your way. I asked the Lord for one more chance to tell you how to be delivered from your sins. He gave me this evening, but would not promise me or you another opportunity. Jesus is the real Messiah. He proved Himself real by healing the sick, raising the dead, and—yes—even predicting the future. He told me and the other disciples that He would be crucified, and when we said we would not desert Him, He told us that we would all run and abandon Him when He was arrested and tried. This was in order that He might fulfill all the prophesies concerning the Messiah. Everything Jesus said came true; He Himself said that He was the truth for all men."

Inaros laughed. "And what is this Jesus saying to you right now?"

Simon hesitated. "Tell him he will not succeed in his assassination." "He says you will not succeed in your assassination."

"Oh, really? And what else does He have to say?"

"Listen, He's told me more about you and your plans than He has spoken to me about anyone or anything else. Oh, yeah; He said for me not to worry about this event or you anymore after this conversation. He's given you ample evidence and ample opportunities to accept Him as the true Way. If you die in your sins, it will be your own doing, and you will be judged for rejecting Him one day."

Hamath grunted; Inaros didn't speak.

"One last thing and I'm gone: Jesus said that Hamath would search me out for the truth. Good evening, men." Simon turned to walk away.

"Stop!" said a deep voice. This time it was Hamath. "I do want to know more. How can I find you after this is over?"

"Why wait, Hamath? I didn't say you would survive this plot any more than your partner. You have this moment as an opportunity."

Hamath was not much for words, but he did think things through in cunning detail. Even though he was large and awkward, he was never the reason for getting Inaros/Barabbas in trouble. He wasn't the reason they landed in jail earlier in the year. Hamath listened carefully to every conversation and had great retention of things discussed. Now it was time for him to decide. He turned to Inaros, pulled out a pouch of coins and threw them to him.

"This is your score to settle—not mine. I choose to follow the Way of Simon's Master."

"Hamath, I need you in this matter; don't leave me now!"

"There is no peace in the plans for your future, Barabbas. I choose inner peace with God; I choose Jesus."

"You can too, Barabbas," Simon said. "You can let the politicians settle their own differences; you don't have to live a life that's wrapped up in revenge and anger."

Inaros stood there, trying to keep his cool. But he shook inside. Hamath had never deserted him before. How could he now? Why, when there was some good money to be had when this was completed? "I am not ready to change; I need more time." Inaros turned away from Simon and Hamath. Simon began walking away, with Hamath following him. Inaros waited a few moments then turned around and watched his friend of many years disappear into the shadows of the street.

A few minutes later, Jabeth and Sorenthasas appeared. Inaros was alone. Jabeth looked at Sorenthasas, and then back at Inaros. "Where's Hamath?" Inaros stood and stared at the two men. "What?" asked Jabeth. Inaros knew, in that brief exchange of words, that Simon had spoken the truth.

"Change of plans," he responded. Then he walked away.

†††

Saul would not eat. He was left alone in a house belonging to the priest of the local synagogue. He continued to rehearse the events of the day. *Jesus is the true Messiah?* Thoughts like this continued to work through his analytical mind. *I must find another follower's house; I have questions to ask.*

"Guards! Guards!" Soon a clatter was heard outside.

"Yes, my lord?"

"Get me the priest right away." The guard left, heading for the house nearby. Soon there was a returning clatter.

The priest walked in. "You request to see me?"

"Yes; actually, no, because I'm blind." The priest feared Saul, so he wasn't sure whether to take Saul's words as a joke or as sarcasm. Fortunately for him, Saul smiled. "I need to know if there is anyone nearby who is a follower of the Nazarene."

"Sir, you are in no condition to arrest anyone at this time."

"I am not going to arrest anyone; I want to speak privately with someone who is a follower of the Way."

"There is a family a few houses down—a Judas of Bethsaida—he is sympathetic to these rebels."

"Take me to his house, now, please."

"I beg of you, sir, don't go like this. You will alert the rest as to what you look like. The element of surprise will be gone!"

"I said, take me to this Judas, and I said please. Now will you do it, or shall I feel my way down this street, knocking on every door until I find this man?"

The priest stood up and guided Saul to the doorway. Saul could feel the cool air blowing on his face. "Get my horse and saddlebags: I want them with me at this visit." The priest left him in the doorway as he retrieved Saul's possessions. Soon they were walking down the street. "East or west?" Saul asked.

"East," the priest replied.

"I thought so, based on the cooler wind."

"I will bring you to the door, but don't ask me to go in."

"Quite alright; you will tell the others where I'm located?"

"Most assuredly."

Soon they were at the doorway of the house belonging to Judas. "You may leave me now; I think I can find my way back if they do not receive me."

"Yes, Rabbi Saul. Are you sure about this?"

"Go along now, and leave me be."

The priest backed away and turned toward the synagogue. Soon he was far enough away where Saul could no longer hear his steps on the pavement. He stopped to watch Saul.

Saul knocked on the wooden door. No response; he knocked again. This time an elderly gentleman came to the door. He opened the door partially. "Yes, may I help you?"

"I'm looking for Judas, a follower of the new Way."

"And who, may I ask, is seeking Judas?"

"Tell him a blind man is seeking to know more about the Way of Jesus of Nazareth."

The gentleman stood in front of him; Saul could not see the man, but sensed he was waving his hand before his face to see if it was true. Saul was unsure how his eyes looked now; all he knew was that he could not see.

"Come in." The man helped Saul into the main room and helped seat him beside a table. "May I get you something to drink?"

"No, thank you."

The man sat down near Saul. "Tell me, what do you want to know about the Way?"

"I have come from Jerusalem to do harm to the followers of the Way, but as I was nearing the city, I was blinded by the manifestation of Jesus, Himself."

The man's heart began to race. "You say you were blinded by the appearance of Jesus? And who are you?"

"I am Saul of Tarsus; I am a Pharisee. I have papers from the high priest to arrest and extradite followers of the Way back to Jerusalem for imprisonment and trial. But all that has changed since I met Jesus."

The elderly man could hardly believe what he was hearing. "Papers from the high priest? To arrest followers of the Way? Uh, may I see those papers?"

"I suppose so, since I can no longer see them." Again, this brought a smile on Saul's face. Suddenly, Saul realized he was changing the way he talked to others. "You will find them on my horse, left-side saddlebag. I do have a horse outside, correct?"

The gentleman stood up and walked to the window. "Yes, I see a horse and saddlebags. I'll be right back." When he returned, he looked at the papers described by Saul. Sure enough, they were written exactly as he said. He studied them, and then he studied Saul. "If you are who you say you are, then Judas should fear you and not welcome you at all."

"Yes, that is true, but I am no longer the same man. Jesus, the Lord, has delivered me from myself and my sins."

"You are a great man in the Jewish faith."

"No, not any longer. I am only great in my sins, but the least of all whom the Lord may choose to save."

"Then I shall no longer call you Saul, the great, instead you are Paul, the least."

"Paul? . . . Paul . . . yes, I like that. My name is now Paul; I'll have to work on this name change."

"Greetings, Paul, the least. And I am Judas; welcome to my house."

Saul/Paul spent the next three days in physical darkness, but was becoming spiritually enlightened as he prayed, fasted, and held conversations with Judas. Judas had lived in Damascus for nearly a year, but met Jesus previously in Bethsaida along the northern shoreline of the Sea of Galilee. Most of the followers of the Way in Damascus had become followers by simply obeying the words of Christ. Since the Day of Pentecost, however, new followers had returned from their pilgrimage to Jerusalem with the good news of the arrival of the Holy Spirit, who came to reside in the life of every follower.

"Jesus now speaks to our hearts from within us," Judas stated. "His Spirit resides within us and ignites His words which become the source of our light and life."

Saul sat and listened, but was constantly analyzing and constructing the ideas and explanations into a pattern that fit the covenants of the Sacred Writings. The more he heard, the more sense it produced. Fortunately, the delay in Damascus allowed Saul's caravan to arrive. Judas mentioned it to Saul, who immediately ordered a guard to retrieve his books and the parchments.

Alone, Saul remained in constant prayer to God, asking for more of the revelation of Jesus as the Messiah. He continued to fast, believing that God and God alone should fill his body with this new knowledge of the Christ. At times, he would ask Judas to read to him.

"Ananias! Ananias!" Ananias was a follower of Jesus who lived in Damascus. The Lord began to speak to him while he was praying.

"Yes, Lord?"

"Stop your praying; get up and prepare yourself to go to Straight Street and visit Saul of Tarsus who is staying at the house of Judas. He is praying right now and is having a vision of you entering the house, laying hands on him, and restoring his sight."

"Lord, I've heard a lot of people speak of this man and all the evil he is capable of doing here, as he has done in Jerusalem. Rumors are that he has papers from the high priest, granting him permission to arrest and place in prison anyone who follows You."

"Go to him, for I have chosen him to carry My name to nations, to kings, and to the people of Israel. I will show him how much suffering he must endure for My name's sake."

Ananias bowed his head one final time. "Yes, my Lord, I will obey."

Saul was in his third day of blindness and fasting. His body was craving food and drink, yet he was determined that God was going to have to rescue him from himself. As he was praying in a back room, Ananias came to the house of Judas and requested to see Saul.

Judas let him in. They knew each other from the fellowships at the assembly. Judas led him to Saul's room, and then turned around and exited.

Saul remained on his knees; he had been praying for a good while and was weak from fasting. "Who are you?"

Ananias walked over to the front of Saul. He gently touched him on his face and slowly moved his hands onto his forehead and head. "Saul, my brother, the Lord—Jesus, whom you saw along the road—has sent me to restore your sight and to be filled with the Holy Spirit."

Saul gasped as immediately things like scales fell off his eyes. He blinked and rubbed his eyes as they adjusted to the partially lit room. He could see again! Plus, he felt a surge of power in his inner being. He reached out his hand to Ananias, who assisted him up off his knees, and embraced him. Saul wept as he prayed, "Lord Jesus, through grace and mercy You have delivered me. I am Your slave to do whatever You call on me to do."

"Saul, if you mean to obey the Lord Jesus, you will be baptized as a testimony of your fellowship into the Way of Jesus, the Messiah."

"Yes, I will do whatever He has commanded."

"I believe a little food and drink is in order before we journey to the creek bank," said Judas, who happened to be at the doorway.

"And this will give me time to get a few others to come and observe," said Ananias.

Strengthened from his food, Saul was led down to a place along the creek. The water was clear and crisp, but did not cool the spirit of Saul who walked down into the water with Judas and Ananias and was baptized. "Hallelujah!" he cried.

"Amen, amen!" was the resounding response, as the three walked out from the water. The rest began to embrace them and to help warm them from the cool stream.

Hidden, but not far from the celebration, were three other men: the local priest and the two other priests who accompanied Saul from Jerusalem. "I told you Saul was up to no good," the local priest said to the others.

"This will be reported to the high priest as soon as possible," responded one of the priests.

Saul began to share his testimony with the other followers, asking questions and assisting them in correlating the words of Jesus with the old covenants of the Jewish faith. It wasn't long before he had a tremendous grasp of the Way.

On the Sabbath, Saul entered the synagogue and requested to speak. The local priest was not cooperating. "I am a Pharisee, an assistant to Rabban Gamaliel, and you dare to refuse to let me speak?"

Some of the men in the synagogue overheard the discussion. "It is our custom to let visiting rabbis speak," one of them said to the priest. "Let him have his say." The local priest was afraid to accuse Saul openly because he was unsure of Saul's new commitment to the Way. So he permitted Saul to speak.

Saul opened the parchments to Isaiah 53. Using the same format that he remembered from Stephen's message, he preached that the suffering Servant of prophesy was none other than Jesus of Nazareth, who was called the Son of God. Those who heard were astonished at his words. "We thought he had come to Damascus to rid us of those who followed this Jesus; didn't he approve the stoning of some in Jerusalem? What has happened to this man?"

Each day, Saul was able to find a group of Jews, and with great power he was able to confound them, showing from the Sacred Writings that Jesus was the Messiah. This brought confusion among the Jews in Damascus.

The local priest was infuriated over the turn of events, so he called a secret meeting of the Jewish elders. "Men, if Saul continues to speak freely of this Jesus as the Messiah, it is possible that we could lose our synagogue and our respected standing among the citizens of our fine city."

"What should we do?" asked one gentleman.

"He is guilty of the same charges that he accused others—blasphemy!—which is punishable by stoning."

"I say we take this matter into our own hands, rather than send him back to Jerusalem," said another.

"Amen, amen!" cried out the others.

"Okay," said the priest. "I will notify the governor and let him know that we have a murderer in our midst and that we plan to capture him. Since he's a stranger to these parts, the governor will appreciate our help in identifying him. We'll have Saul stoned before the governor has a chance at questioning this traitor." Everyone seemed to be in agreement. "I'll inform the gatekeepers to keep him in the city, just in case." The men dismissed and headed home . . . all but one. He lingered a bit and quietly paid Judas a visit.

Judas heard a knock on the door. "Yes, who is it?"

"It's Levi; can I come in?"

Judas opened the door. "Levi; yes, yes, do come in. My, it's been a while; what brings you by so late?"

"I just left a meeting at the synagogue; is Saul still lodging with you?"

"Yes, he is. Is something wrong?"

"Indeed, there is; please call him in."

Saul was in his room, praying and meditating. "Paul?"

"Yes, Judas, do come in."

"Paul, there's a friend of mine here who just left the synagogue. He has a message for you."

"Okay, I'll be right out." Paul put away his prayer mat, rolled up the parchment, and made his way into the living area.

"Saul, this is Levi." (Judas did not want to confuse Levi with the name change.)

"Levi, it's a pleasure to meet a friend of Judas'."

"Thank you, sir. I wish I was coming under more pleasant terms, but I have some bad news for you."

"Yes? Go on."

"There was a secret meeting tonight with the elders of the assembly. There's a plot to capture you and kill you."

"Oh, my!" said Judas.

"Yes, the priest has just left to notify the gatekeepers not to allow you to leave. Several gatekeepers were in the meeting, and they all know about you."

"And why are you telling me these things? Are you a follower of Jesus?"

"I have been listening to your discussions and I want to believe what you're saying is true, but I'm not ready to testify of him and to be baptized."

"Oh, I see; well, as I understand it, there is never a promise of a time when it will be easy for you to convert. There will always be opposition to turning your life from the old covenants to the new and living Way."

"I understand, but this meeting is not about me—it's about you and your safety. The plan is to capture you tomorrow evening after dark and to stone you out by the city dumping grounds. I happen to live along the city wall, and there is an opening in the wall next to my house. I suggest you pack your belongings, and we can let you down the wall in a large vegetable basket with a rope. Judas can ride your horse out the city gates without being stopped."

"Will they become suspicious when you return without a horse?"

"No, there's a stable outside the city. It is normal for people to leave their animals outside the city walls."

Saul looked at Judas for a moment. "I agree, Saul."

"Okay, but where do I go?"

"There's an eastern road that leads out to the northernmost part of the Arabian Desert. I have a friend out there named Jacob ben Johannes; he has heard Jesus speak and believes His message, but you may need to guide him into the fuller understanding. Ask of him as you see the sand dunes become more frequent. Tell him Judas of Damascus/Bethsaida sent you. He will see to your needs."

"Thank you. You have been so gracious to me—you and your family."

"No time for talk; Levi, you go on, and I will bring Saul over to the east side of your place by the wall opening; meet us there in about an hour's time."

"Okay." Levi left.

"Well, I suppose I should get my saddlebags packed. Oh, and I need a way to carry a few more of my books and parchments on my horse."

Judas looked at the pile. "I think I can pack about half of them. I'm afraid you'll have to leave the others here until you find a way to come back. Speak with Jacob; I'm sure he knows of some way to design a canvas or leather bag to hold more."

Saul laughed. "Indeed, I'm a tent-maker by trade, so I'm sure we'll figure something out."

Judas smiled. "Had I known that, I have a tear in my canvas tent out back." They both laughed. "You get packed, and I'll get your horse readied."

Within an hour, Saul and Judas made their way over to Levi's house and waited near the city wall. Soon Levi appeared with a ladder, a large basket, and some rope.

"Saul," said Judas. "When you get on the other side, give the rope a good tug, and we'll pull it back in. Then walk along the city wall toward the east." Judas pointed in an easterly direction. "I will be out of the city soon."

Saul nodded his head and embraced Levi. "Thank you for your help."

"It has been a real pleasure to meet you, sir, and I will speak more with Judas about my change of covenants."

"Yes, please do. I will pray for you."

Saul began climbing the ladder with Judas following with the basket. Soon he was through the wall opening and in the basket. They began lowering Saul until there was slack in the rope. In a moment or two, they felt the tug and began reeling the basket back up and through the opening. After that, Judas mounted on Saul's horse and rode off into the dark.

✝✝✝

Jabeth and Sorenthasas had not seen Inaros for two days. "Change of plans?" They wondered what that meant.

Inaros had left town for Bethany. He always returned to his hometown when things were troubling him. The evening sun had set, and he was up on the roof, looking toward Jerusalem. Simon had caused Hamath to depart from the plan. He had hoped

Hamath would come to his senses by now, but it had been five days and no sign of Hamath.

Now it was time to decide. He felt Caiaphas would be getting about to the end of his patience in a day or so. Inaros had to act soon. He kept thinking about Simon's prediction: "He says you will not succeed in your assassination." Inaros was always up to a challenge, and this was certainly his greatest challenge ever. *Can I pull this off without Hamath? Yes, I can! And my success will make Jesus a liar. Okay, God, I'm going to need your help to prove this Jesus is a false Messiah.* Inaros felt better now— now that he felt he had God on his side (so he thought).

The next day found Inaros up early as he rode his horse back into Jerusalem. He would find his partners first, and then they would revisit the west side of the outer wall near Herod's palace.

By noon, they were together again, Jabeth and Sorenthasas still not understanding what happened to Hamath, and Inaros refusing to tell. They looked for a good spot for the fighting to be staged. It had to be far enough away so that the guards would not be able to capture them easily.

Then they went outside the wall to check on vacant houses, empty lots, and some trees. A couple houses were investigated, but they were not close enough for Inaros. But there were two olive trees next to an open lot. These appeared to be just the right height and close to where the king could potentially take his evening stroll. Inaros made a few inconspicuous measuring walks to the wall so that he could practice with his bow and arrows. Finally, the three made it back to the planning house.

"Your caves have been properly stocked for thirty days— that's thirty days, remember? As soon as you hear a commotion up on the wall, you will get on your horses and leave for Bethany. Tie your horses at the same place as before, and I will gather them and take them back to my place. After the month is ended, we will meet at the brothel."

"Boss, what if you don't make it?" asked Jabeth. "How will we survive without our share of the money?"

"Have I ever let you two down before?"

"Well, uh, yes—when you got caught and put into prison. Me and Soren nearly starved!"

Inaros looked them both over and smiled. "It looks like you ate well without me. I tell you what; I will leave your portions with the bartender, and he will give it to you when you return in a month.

"Now go somewhere and rehearse your timing. I will be waiting for the lowering of the sun until it is about to drop into the western mountains. If all goes well, we'll get together in a month." He grabbed both of them by their outer shoulders, turned them around, and showed them the door. He also dropped a couple coins in their hands. "I'll see you tomorrow, two hours before sundown; now go!" The plans were complete; now it was time to implement them. But there was just enough time for a little target practice.

The next day could not advance fast enough for Inaros. By mid-afternoon, he had delivered two horses to Jabeth and Sorenthasas. Next, he rode to the west side to observe the local people and their movements. Timing was paramount to the success of his plan.

✝✝✝

Antipas longed for his daily walk. Today was a day that he needed a relaxing walk. He had heard that the new emperor might replace him. It was therapeutic to go for a stroll just prior to the supper meal. But, today, he was entertaining Pontius Pilate and his wife for supper. *Oh well,* he thought. *Perhaps I can get in a late night's stroll.*

The king and the Roman governor had renewed their friend-
ship ever since the trial of Jesus the Nazarene. Antipas was about
to go for his stroll when the chamber servants announced the arrival of the governor. *Oh, great; there goes my stroll!*

"Greetings, Governor, and greetings to your lovely wife.
What a pleasure to have you here."

"The pleasure is ours, and thank you for the invitation."

"Oh, no problem; now let me see if I can retrieve the queen
from her preparations."

"Oh, don't bother her," said Pontius. "I'm sure we three can
enjoy some talk together."

"'Talk'? Did someone say 'talk'?" It was the queen, as she
made her way toward the three. "Oh, I love to talk!"

Antipas smiled. "I can't disagree with her on that one."

She made a frown toward him. "Don't you usually go for a
walk about now?"

"Well, not with guests here; I—"

"Nonsense!" she responded. "I think all of us would enjoy
watching this beautiful day darken before we recline for a great
meal."

"No, I don't wish to bother the governor and his wife with
such a miniscule thing as watching the sun set."

"Oh, I love watching the sun set," said the governor's wife.
"Please, you men lead the way, and we will follow."

"Are you sure?" asked Antipas.

"Yes," said Pilate. "I would enjoy it as well."

"Okay, then; right this way."

Antipas and Pilate walked out of the dining area and down a
breezeway to a doorway that led them out onto a guarded section
of the city wall. The sun was barely above the distant range. A
few clouds were turning into a glorious magenta and shades of
purple.

"Oh, how beautiful!" said Pilate's wife. "I don't think I ever
saw a more beautiful sunset."

"Yes, this is a good one," replied Antipas. "I sometimes turn toward the sun and listen to the evening rustling of the trees. I once swore I heard the breaking waves of the Great Sea." Antipas stopped as though he were about to turn toward the west, but the guards were annoyed by some ruckus going on near the end of the palace perimeter where it joined the wall.

"What is it now!? Guard, go check on it, and report back to me immediately . . . Pontius, does it ever end for you?"

He laughed. "Is the emperor ever satisfied with his taxes?" They all laughed at that one.

Antipas once again turned toward the setting sun. "If just for a few minutes, I wish to cast my cares toward the setting sun, the hidden valleys, and onto the mountain peaks." He turned and stepped into a lowered section of the wall to look more closely at the ground. "Oh look, someone has left a horse out there by itself; it's a fine one too." Pilate stepped forward to see the horse. As he stepped forward, Antipas turned sideways to allow more room. As he turned, a swishing sound was heard as an arrow barely nipped the edge of Antipas' outer garment, near his neck. The arrow burst against the inner wall. The women saw it and screamed; Antipas was stunned for a moment. Pilate reached and pulled him down just as a second arrow swished by the king's head, missing him again.

"Guards! Guards!" cried Pilate. "The king! The king!" Guards came rushing to the area, first checking on Antipas, and then the others. Once they saw that everyone was okay, one of the guards took a horn and sounded an alarm signal. The signal was for the guards at the gate to shut the gate. Then the guard said, "Your Highness, where did the arrows come from?"

"I . . . I'm not sure. I was looking at a horse tied to a tree down below us."

The guard looked below as the rider and horse began to gallop away. He sounded another alarm. Several more guards came running. "Look! By those trees! The assassin is leaving!" Guards began running down the corridor and onto the street below. Their only focus was on getting outside the city wall before darkness fell. They had completely forgotten about the two drunks who were fighting at the base of the nearby stairway.

The two "drunks" walked hurriedly toward the south side of the city. They were hoping to get to the southern gate before it was closed. They could not mount their horses because of the crowd that walked against their direction. As they neared the next gate, it had already closed. In fact the horn blast was loud enough on this still evening for every gatekeeper to hear. Jabeth and Sorenthasas looked at each other and shrugged their shoulders. "I think we better go get a drink and look normal." Sorenthasas agreed.

Inaros was galloping toward the south. He missed his target. "Anathema!" he cursed. Then he remembered those haunting words: "He says you will not succeed in your assassination attempt." *He was right; does that mean that this Jesus is the real Messiah?*

✝✝✝

The Arabian Road was less traveled than others on which Saul had traveled. He wondered if he had made the right decision. As he progressed southeasterly, the lush green of the valley began to be intruded by knolls of sand, then the sand began to be intruded by pockets of green. About another hour's travel and it became impossible to find any greenery. Sand dunes were in the horizon, so Saul stopped at a community water well. While giving his horse and himself a drink, a woman showed up with several water jugs.

"Excuse me, woman, perhaps you can tell me where I might find a Jacob ben Johannes?"

"Yes, the Johannes place is a few miles in that direction." She pointed toward the sand dunes. "You will see a grove of palm trees beside his house and a watering well by the trees."

"Thank you very much, you have been most helpful." Then Saul felt something stir within him. "Say, are you Jewish?"

"My father is a Greek, but my mother is a Jew. We moved out from the Sea of Galilee area. My father did not like the smell of fish."

"And what does he do now?"

"He raises camels."

Saul smiled. "He must like the smell of a good coat."

"I guess you could say that. And you, what trade brings you to the desert?"

"I am a tent maker by trade, but I've come to study about God's new covenant."

"In the desert?"

Saul laughed. "Yes, in the desert."

"God has a new covenant?"

"Yes, have you heard of it?"

"No, but you'll have to excuse me; my mother is expecting me to bring some fresh water in for some cleaning chores."

"Yes, quite alright; perhaps I shall come by and visit later this week."

"That would be fine. We don't get many strangers out here, and father is always asking about things from the city." Saul helped her draw some fresh water, and then he mounted his horse and headed into the desert.

About an hour later, Saul began to see several treetops from a distance. The sun's heat caused the trees to appear closer than they were—or maybe his horse was slowing down due to the sand and the heat. Soon, a small house came into sight. It appeared very small, but there were several additional buildings next to it. Finally, he dismounted from his horse to offer it another drink. Several young men came out from one of the buildings. Seeing the stranger, they made a beeline in his direction.

"Greetings, stranger. Can we interest you in a fine camel to assist you when your horse gives out?" Both boys had a polite smile as they walked around the horse, rubbing it with their hands as if they were about to purchase the beast.

Saul returned the smile. "Oh, perhaps not today, but you can help me find someone."

"Sure, we know everyone around here. Who are you looking for?"

"Jacob ben Johannes."

The boys looked at each other and grinned. "That's our father! He has gone into the desert to deliver a fresh set of camels to a stranded merchant from the east."

"I wonder if he will be back in the evening?"

"He sure will; Mother is preparing food for his return. We have a younger brother and sister out in the stables making ready for his return. Please come inside, and we'll tell Mother you're here."

"Well, I . . ." The boys turned toward the house and ran as if in competition to tell their mother. ". . . I guess I'll see myself in." *Oh, to be youthful again,* he thought. Saul tied his horse to a tree by a water trough, fed it some grain, and walked toward the house.

"Here he comes, Mother!" A tall and slender woman met him at the door. "Please excuse the lack of manners for my boys. They get very excited when someone new comes by for a visit."

Saul smiled. "I can only imagine."

"They say you were asking for my husband?"

"Yes, Judas of Damascus/Bethsaida sent me; I hope you won't mind if I wait for him to return?"

"Oh no, I don't mind at all." She turned her head toward the door. "Boys! You come here at once." The two boys walked back into the front room. "Did they introduce themselves?"

Saul shook his head. "No."

"Okay, the oldest here is Jethro, the next is John, I have another boy, outside, named Joseph, and the youngest is Sarah. My name is Mariam."

"It is a pleasure to be welcomed into this fine Jewish home. My name is Sa . . . Paul, Paul of Tarsus."

"Did you say, 'Sa-Paul'?" asked John.

Paul smiled. "It sounded that way; too much sand in my mouth."

"Oh, heavens," said Mariam. "Where are our manners today? Jethro, go get some water for Master Paul. I bet your tongue is near crispy by now."

"Thank you so much. May I?" Paul pointed toward the table.

"Oh, yes, please recline. John, take his sandals, and bring a wet cloth for his feet." John sprang into action as soon as she spoke. "I pray you will allow me to return to the supper meal. I will prepare an extra place for you."

"Thank you again. Yes, that would be nice." Paul allowed John to remove his sandals and place them by the door. Next came a cool refreshing toweling of his feet. Another towel was given to wipe his face and hands. "So refreshing: thank you, young man."

"You are welcome," said John. "Master Paul, may I ask you some questions?"

"Sure, go ahead."

"Those sandals, what city did they come from?"

"John, don't trouble the man with such trivial questions," said Jethro. "I'd like to know where he got that nice-looking horse." Jethro's eyes lit up when he said that.

"They are both very good questions. It tells me that you are alert to the details of life. I will answer you both, and you can guess which city matches the right question: Jerusalem and Joppa."

"You've been to Joppa?" asked Jethro.

"Where's that?" asked John.

"It's by the Great Sea," said Jethro.

"Have you not seen the Great Sea?" asked Paul.

"We've been to Jerusalem several times," said Jethro, "but Father can never find the time to let us go to the sea . . . I want to see it someday."

"Me too!" cried John.

"Well, it is a lovely place to view, but when I get on a boat, it sometimes makes me feel sick," said Paul.

"Oh, would you tell us where you've been?" asked John. "Have you been to Egypt or Rome?" The boys forgot their initial questions.

"Boys!" interrupted their mother. "Leave Master Paul alone and go finish your chores. Your father may be home at any given time, and he will be very unhappy if you have neglected your chores."

"Oh, my!" shouted John as he sprinted for the doorway.

"Maybe Father will allow you to tell us of all your travels at supper," said Jethro, as he ran out of the room.

"Maybe he will," said Paul, as he wiped his face again.

✝✝✝

"Now who is this man?" Peter asked Simon. Peter had been out of the city a few days, checking on several assemblies of followers.

"He is Hamath, a partner of Barabbas." Peter walked around this bear of a man.

"And why is he with you?"

"Barabbas—who now calls himself Inaros—used Hamath in the plots against the Romans. They terrorized the Roman authorities. When I witnessed to Barabbas, a few days ago, Hamath made a decision to follow Jesus; he has become a follower of the Way."

"Splendid! And what became of Barabbas?"

"We don't know. The Lord told me he would not be successful in assassinating Antipas, but He did not say if Barabbas would be caught. It is not safe for Hamath to be out on the streets."

"Oh, I see." Peter smiled at the man. Hamath tried to return a smile, but his unhealthy gums and teeth made his expression look more intimidating than what was meant. "Hamath, do you speak?"

He grunted. "If necessary . . . I don't like to talk."

Peter continued to study Hamath. "Tell me, Hamath, if you partnered with Barabbas, did you murder anyone?"

Hamath grunted again, then he spoke. "I never had to. I may have hurt a few men, but never took someone's life. Barabbas would plunge his dagger in someone, while I was used as a distraction most of the time."

"Have you done prison time for your crimes?"

"Some."

"Enough?"

"Maybe."

Simon looked at Peter. "What are you thinking?"

"I know his heart may belong to Jesus, but if he has committed crimes against the authorities, he may need to go back to the authorities to get his name cleared." Peter looked at Hamath. "Sir, you must understand that when a person gives himself to Jesus, his sins are indeed covered by His blood and that person is forgiven, but it doesn't mean your crimes against the law of the land are forgiven . . . I'm afraid you must turn yourself over to the authorities to clear your name—that is, if you're uncertain."

Hamath grunted. He looked first at Peter, and then at Simon. Simon did not know what to say at first. Then he spoke to Hamath. "Hamath, the same Jesus who delivered you from the sins of your heart can see you through the sins of your flesh, and

He will never leave you nor forsake you. We must all pay for crimes we may commit. Peter is right; if you mean business with Jesus, you must face the authorities."

Hamath did not speak, but looked down at the ground.

"Do you have family?" asked Simon.

"My mother worked the streets of Jerusalem. She died when I was a lad. I am the offspring of a barbarian from the north." He then turned toward Peter. "I broke out of prison recently; I would not have heard of the message of salvation had I not been out of prison. I probably know many men who are in prison."

"They need to hear the message of Jesus as well," said Peter.

"Then they will hear it from me." He stood and looked at Peter, but he embraced Simon.

"Whoa there, big fellow; easy on the ribs, okay?" He let go of Simon, turned, and slowly walked to the front gate of the courtyard. Then he was gone.

"That was tough," said Simon.

"Yes, it was," replied Peter. "But with Jesus, every place gives its own opportunity to be a witness for the Way of salvation. I think he will do just fine in prison—especially if Saul of Tarsus returns and picks up the arresting pace." Peter changed the subject. "Have you heard any word about those who were arrested?"

"James and John and Elder James have been to the prison and the authorities, trying to seek the release of those Saul had imprisoned. Some of the first arrested were tried and stoned to death, but after Saul, the official accuser, left town there was no legal way for the others to be tried. They will be held for thirty days or until Saul returns."

"May Saul get detoured on his way back!"

"Amen, amen!"

† † †

(A few days earlier) Inaros managed to distance himself from the pursuing guards. He was nearing the location for gathering the horses of Jabeth and Sorenthasas. When he arrived, the horses were nowhere to be seen. *Okay guys,* he thought to himself. *I don't have time for delays.* He continued to circle the grove of trees, while looking in the direction of the city. Then he galloped away, heading south toward Bethany. It was nearly dark, and it wasn't safe to enter the rugged terrain area near the Dead Sea. There were caves throughout that area—places where he had visited during times when he needed to get away from people. There were other bandits in the area as well—a place where even a man such as he would not be safe traveling alone in the dark. *Hamath, where were you when I needed you most!?* He continued his ride into Bethany. *I'll stay at home tonight and leave for the caves in the morning.*

Horses were not the common mode of transportation among the Jews in Judea. Donkeys were the most favored in the rocky terrain, but many chose to walk. There was no need to travel far, and animals required a lot of care. Inaros pondered these things as he lay in bed. *I need to sell my horse . . . better yet, I'll trade him in for a donkey. It will take me longer to get to the cave, but I will blend in with the locals and be safer among the cave dwellers.* Next, his mind went to Hamath. *Hamath, why did you leave me?! Why did this Simon guy come and mess things up?*

Simon's words began to invade his mind. *God, if this Jesus was our Deliverer, why did He get caught? Didn't He have a better plan than to die?* He thought about Simon saying that Jesus had to die in order to be the perfect sacrifice for all sin for all time. *How could this be true?* This was one time he wished he had heard the readings of the Sacred Writings more often. Inaros did not like having questions unanswered. His Jewish roots had been enough for him to feel comfortable about his religion. He grew up a good boy and never got into trouble. He even considered doing some of the service tasks for the priests. Then came the Romans! And after the Roman soldiers killed his older brothers and raped his sister, he became a zealot . . . and the rest was history. Inaros continued to run things through his head until he fell asleep.

The smells of breakfast awakened Inaros. His mother was a great cook, and he often wondered why he wasn't as big as Hamath. He went out back and washed his face. His horse was there, eating some hay that apparently his father had put out. His father usually got up before the sun arose, checked on the yard animals, and then left for the sheep bin just outside the town dwellings. The shepherds took turns sleeping with the sheep to prevent thieves and wild animals from bothering them.

"Good morning, my son!" His mother kissed his bearded cheek. "I made some fresh bread and eggs for you." Inaros was not used to having such a good meal as this for breakfast.

"Thank you, mother. And where's sister?"

"Oh, she had to meet with some ladies; they are making quilts and tapestries. But I suspect they are trying to determine which men are going to court them."

"Oh." Inaros did not like to think about women for courtship purposes. He knew he could never settle down and raise a family as long as the Romans were around.

"Son, why don't you consider settling down? You know all the good girls will be taken if you keep waiting."

"I'm not interested, mother, and I'm not settling down."

She placed a bowl of eggs before him with bread wrapped in a bundle of cloth. "I don't wish to be a bother to you, but as long as you're out there trying to get justice for the loss of your brothers, you continue to leave this wound in everyone's hearts. Your father and I are not getting any younger, and we are hoping you would return home and take a lead in our family's business."

Inaros had heard this before and did not want to recite the pros and cons of his lifestyle. He could not get the sight of his fallen brothers out of his mind. He would never forget the laughter of the soldiers as they rode away. The Romans did not care for the common people. That's the way he saw things, and that is why he joined the zealots years ago.

After breakfast, Inaros embraced his mother. "Thank you, Mother. I must be going now."

"Oh, my dear son, why such a hurry? Can't you stay a little longer?"

"No, Mother, I cannot. Now, I've put some more coins in the hiding place; you and Father can use as much as needed."

"We don't need your coins—we need you!" She began to weep. Inaros embraced her for a moment. Then he kissed her forehead and walked out back to get his horse. She watched as he led his horse by the side of the house. "Goodbye, son; I love you. I will pray a prayer for you."

Mother, leave me alone! I've got other plans, he thought. He began walking down toward the stable. *I'll head down by the stables and see if I can get a trade for this animal.* His thoughts about all that was transpiring continued to run about in his mind as he walked to the stables, so much so, that the cold, stoic look of the smithy did not interrupt his thinking. "Kopas, I need a donkey; can I talk to you about a trade on this animal?" Inaros was patting his horse as he spoke.

Kopas remained cold. "I got no need for a horse, and I got no donkeys for trading."

"I don't believe that," said Inaros, as he and his horse started to walk into the large opening of the stable. He knew there were donkeys for sale nearly all the time. In fact, Kopas always complained about how much he had to feed those animals that were not being put to work by the local owners. *I bet he's got one or two in these stalls.* In the first stall on the left, he heard some rustling of hay. *Just what I thought.* He pulled back the canvas, but to his surprise, two armed Roman soldiers stepped out with their swords drawn! The next sound came from behind him— two more armed soldiers!

"Well, well," said one of them. "It looks like someone with a horse wants to trade it for an ass!" The blade of his sword was touching Inaros' chest. Then he felt another blade behind him pushing against his neck. "Doesn't sound like a fair trade to me," said the soldier behind him. Inaros remained still. "I'm thinking he might be trying to hide something," another soldier said. "Like maybe something he did and he doesn't want to get caught." The others laughed. "I wonder if he knows of a lone horseman that tried to assassinate the king and our governor last night?" Suddenly he was kicked behind his knees, dropping him to the floor. "You should have listened to the old smithy out there. You think, maybe, he was trying to warn you? Secure his hands guys; I think we have our garbage!"

†††

After the supper meal, Jacob and Paul reclined in the front room. During supper, the children had asked Paul a dozen questions. Jacob finally told them to stop.

"I apologize for the many questions my children were asking."

"That's quite alright."

"I guess we don't get them into town as often as they would like."

"They're a fine stock."

"Thank you; now, you say Judas sent you out here?"

"Yes, he did."

"Tell me more about yourself."

"I am Saul of Tarsus. I am a Pharisee and assistant to Gamaliel, the head schoolmaster of the school of Hillel. I was assigned the task of destroying the assemblies of the followers of Jesus. I began arresting His followers in Jerusalem, about a month ago. Then the high priest asked me to go to Damascus and arrest the leaders of the followers there and elsewhere as I traveled about.

"As I was nearing Damascus, a great light burst in front of me and my entourage. Within the light, I saw Jesus; He spoke to me and told me to go into Damascus and to wait for further instructions. When the light disappeared, I was blind; some of the men with me had to guide me into the city. I was placed in the guest quarters of the synagogue.

"I wanted to know more about Jesus, so I requested to visit someone nearby who was a follower of Him. That's how I came to meet Judas. Then I dreamed about another follower, named Ananias, who would come and restore my sight. He came and prayed over me and something like scales fell off my eyes. The Lord told him that I would become a witness of Christ to rulers, kings, Gentiles, and others. I began to testify at the synagogue that Jesus was the Messiah, the Son of God. That upset some of the men, so the priest had a secret meeting with the elders of the synagogue, and they decided that they were going to catch me and stone me. A man from the meeting came and told Judas and he helped me escape last night. He said you had met Jesus in Bethsaida and would allow me to come out and stay for a while until I get a word from Jesus as to what I should do next. So here I am."

Jacob sat there quiet for a moment. "So, are you a fugitive from the Roman authorities?"

"No, I'm not. I am a Roman citizen though, so it would be difficult for the Romans to arrest me without proper papers."

"What about the high priest?"

"I imagine that he is going to receive word of my new faith in the new covenant of the Way—that's what followers of Jesus are now called. Jesus claimed that He was the new Way to our

Father. So, officially, I don't know that I am a fugitive from the law of the Jewish leaders—but it is just a matter of time."

"I see, and did you say that you escaped secretly?"

"Yes, a man named Levi from the synagogue meeting slipped over to Judas' house, unnoticed, and alerted us of the plot to capture me. These men took me to an opening in the city wall and let me down in a basket to the outside of the wall. No one saw us and no one has followed me."

"Oh, please pardon my questions. I have a great responsibility with my wife and children, and I wanted to be sure your being here would not put them in harm's way."

"I can understand your situation. If you feel I should leave, I would be most grateful if I could stay the night in the stable and I will leave first thing in the morning."

"I don't think that will be necessary. I do have a hay loft above my stable which will make for you an excellent hideout until you feel the need to move on, but as for me and my house, you are welcome to stay."

"Yipee!" came a shout from around the dining doorway. The four children came in and encircled Paul. "You will stay, won't you?" asked Sarah, the daughter and the youngest.

"Children, give the man some room and a little time to think it over."

"But, Father," she responded, "he could tell us more about the Jesus-man we met at the lake."

"Yes, I can," said Paul, "and your father can tell me some things about Jesus as well."

Jacob smiled. "I can say this: I've never met a man like Him before. He healed sick people, and, one day, He fed thousands of us, from a few fish and loaves of bread. And His words . . . they were like drinking from a mountain stream."

Paul looked at the children. "It sounds as if your father has a few stories to tell me as well."

Paul awoke from the crows of a rooster alongside the stable. This reminded him of when he was a young boy in Tarsus. He loved farm animals, but his father recognized his intelligence early and decided he would send young Saul to the finest schools possible. He didn't want to leave home, but Saul soon found himself as a boarder with some relatives in Antioch. His love for reading eventually got him to excel in the languages of Greek, Arabic, and Hebrew. After a few years of basic education, he was recommended to the school of Hillel in Jerusalem. Saul became a master of the Hebrew language and the laws of the Sacred Writings. He was particularly fond of debating and speaking of the things pertaining to God.

The chatter of children brought his mind back the present. They were beginning their early morning chores before breakfast. Eggs had to be gathered, goats had to be milked, and donkeys and camels had to be fed. Paul's horse was also added to the chore list, something the children did not mind at all. It wasn't long before Paul was invited into the house for breakfast. He went inside and found a place at the table to recline. No one ate until their father spoke.

"Paul, would you be so kind as to thank our Father for the beginning of a new day?"

"Yes, thank you. Our Father, the One who has delivered us from our enemies, we thank You for another day. We thank You for these provisions that we are about to eat. I thank You for this fine family and their graciousness toward me. Grant us, this day, a measure of Your grace and mercy, and may we discover more of Your new covenant given us through the crucified One. Help me—help us all—to understand the Way of salvation through the risen Deliverer, Jesus of Nazareth. Amen."

"Amen," said the others. The meal was a welcome alternative for Paul, who had eaten very little the past week. He spoke little, as Jacob was giving the instructions for the day. The two older boys had to go to a neighbor's house several miles away for schooling this week. The children's education was rotated to numerous homes according to the skills of each family. The two younger were to help their mother around the house and to tend to the animals.

"And you are not to pester Rabbi Paul with all your questions," Jacob reminded the children. "I must journey into the desert area to meet some men for supply trades. And Paul, what are your plans?"

"Sir, if I may, I would like to journey with you to discuss an important matter at hand."

"That will be fine, but I must warn you that the winds are unpredictable and the desert sands can be a bit unpleasant. You must protect yourself and carry extra supplies, should you have to stay longer."

"I understand. I will go now and prepare, but is there a chance your wife may have some fresh bread left over?"

She beamed with delight. "Why, I will have you both eating like kings in the desert!"

Jacob smiled. "If I lingered around this house all day, I would be twice my size!" They all laughed.

In about thirty minutes, the boys were heading one way and Jacob and Paul were heading toward the southeast. Jacob was on a camel with a donkey in tow, while Paul rode his horse.

"So what's on your mind, Paul?"

"Sir, while your hospitality is just what I needed, I have a greater task than to stay around for the fellowship of your dear family. I have come out here to find out more about Jesus and His will for my life. Therefore, I have need of solitude for many hours each day; I also plan to fast many times until things are settled in my mind."

"What, then, is your wish from me and my house?"

"Just the freedom to come and go as I sense the need. Tell your wife not to expect me at mealtime. And if I do show up, tell her not to fix anything elaborate for me to eat. I want to be able to focus on Jesus; I must receive words from Him to understand my future duties of service."

"I will inform the family of your requests. You may call the hay loft your temporary home until you feel the need to go elsewhere. I will instruct the children to leave you alone. If you wish, you may follow this trail to a place where I will show you. It is a small water hole, and travelers come and go, but no one lives there. I constructed a small building to protect travelers from the sun and sand. You are welcome to spend time there as often as you feel necessary."

"Thank you, Jacob. You are a blessing to me."

"The pleasure of helping you discover more about Jesus will be mine, because I expect you to teach my family the Way of the true Messiah. We need to hear about the Way of Jesus."

"That task will become my pleasure."

"Notice our trail: it has clogs of wiry weeds. These come from the dung of animals. If caught in a sand storm, use these clogs to keep you on the trail."

"Thank you for your advice." The two continued to travel, talking on various subjects concerning the survival of a person in the desert. Jacob had many dealings with desert people. He traded numerous hides for people and received many spices for his service. He, in turn, would take the spices to Damascus and trade them for needful supplies.

When they arrived at the water hole, Jacob bid Paul a farewell and said he should be back in four or five hours. Paul took a look at the building. It was perfect for reading, praying, and resting. He tied his horse up next to an animal watering trough and put some hay down for his horse to eat. Paul then pulled out some of his parchments and began to read and to pray for a meeting with Jesus. He prayed for several hours, reading occasionally as he felt led.

Paul traveled this route for several days. Each day he would read and pray, asking the Lord Jesus to speak to him. Then the Lord spoke to Paul. At first, Paul was reluctant to ask questions. But, after a few conversations, Jesus took the lead in answering Paul's questions.

"Paul, you have mastered the Law in accordance to your intelligence and your school's instructors. But you must not rely on your intelligence or your ignorance; you must know the Law and the Prophets according to My righteousness, My standard, and My justice. Your zeal is blameless, Paul, but you must allow time to pass so that you will be able to assimilate all truth.

"You have been trying to fulfill all the Law, but you cannot, for I am the fulfillment of all the Law and the Prophets. You must learn to blend these together to see and to understand all things. I am going to teach you for many days; sit and listen carefully and write down the things that I teach you. Turn your zeal toward Me and My Word. Allow Me to use your qualities for My glory and purpose."

"My Lord, how will I write these things down out here in the desert?"

"I have given you two young men in the house of Jacob; they will take turns in writing what I reveal to you. I will use their education for My glory to be revealed. Their father will listen at times and will become a great asset to you and Me in proclaiming the truth of My words. Always look around you for the instruments I have chosen for you to use in proclaiming truth."

"Lord, may I always be pleasing to You and take advantage of all the resources You provide."

"Paul, you will suffer much for the pain you have caused in many people's lives, but do not lose heart, for I will purify you in sufferings. I will make you wholly dependent upon Me. My Spirit will empower you, and I will use you for My glory.

"Now, stay here and wait for Jacob. Then as you return to his home, tell him what I have spoken to you. He will listen, obey, and command his children to assist you. He will provide you with papyri, ink, and quills by which the boys will write."

"Yes, my Lord, I will wait and listen to You."

† † †

The apostles met regularly to compare words they each remembered hearing from their Master. Bits and pieces of the sayings of Jesus began to form into documents. They would take turns in reading the sayings of Jesus, while the others would compare what was being read with the parchments of Sacred Writings and the books of the rabbis' sayings and interpretations. They began to discover an important thread of blending.

"Concerning salvation," said Matthew, "the sayings of our Master indicate that John's preaching of repentance was a prelude to what Jesus taught about turning away from the old rituals, customs, and sin and seeking an inner transformation about His ways and teachings. The new covenant between God and man is through Jesus' blood—His sacrifice appeased our Father's requirement for righteousness to be applied over our sin nature. This application occurs through a humble surrender of one's life to our Savior's lordship.

"Baptism shows our repentance and our surrender to Him as we allow ourselves to be lowered under the water. As the water pours over us, we show our full death and burial. Then, when we are raised up from underneath the watery grave, we picture the new life in the new covenant. Baptism now marks us as a new creation in Jesus."

"Matthew?" asked John.

"Yes?"

"Remember when Jesus took a grain of wheat and buried it in the ground? He was saying something similar when He said that unless one releases the grain from his hand and buries it into the ground, it remains a seed. But when we release the seeds and bury them, they will burst forth into a fruitful harvest—some small and some large, but all supplying the resources for food and for more seed."

"This should encourage every follower to sow spiritual seeds for the harvest," said Matthias.

"Yes," said Peter. "We witnessed this in Samaria where our servant, Philip, shared the gospel and many were turning to faith in Jesus as the Messiah."

"The words of Jesus are the seeds," said Andrew. "So we must be diligent to share His words for salvation and for spiritual growth."

"Spirit seeds," said John.

Matthew spoke again. "We must also maintain refreshing fillings of His Spirit. The Spirit is the presence of Jesus—He is life and light to the Word."

"So how do we communicate this to the others?" asked Thomas.

"It is imperative that we teach these to the followers of the Way," said James. "We must spread out with the same teachings that we are collecting at these gatherings. Elder James (now pastor of Jerusalem's main assembly) will teach them here in the central fellowship. We will branch out into the smaller gatherings throughout the city."

"Others need to be called by our Lord to become teachers and preachers of His words," stated Peter. "Due to the persecution, many small house gatherings have been formed. Many who have left the city need to be visited by us."

"It is occurring," said Andrew. "I have witnessed several men who have a good grasp of the Master's words. His Spirit is speaking to them as well."

"That means we apostles must become more available to teach and train those whom our Lord is calling into the ministry," said Matthew.

"And the Spirit's baptism," said Philip. "What of His endowment of power?"

"That is a good question," said Peter. "Do any of you wish to speak on this subject?"

"That His power has been used among us evident," said Nathanael.

"True," responded Peter. "John and I witnessed His power in Samaria among the followers at Philip's tent meetings. But this is not occurring at many of the conversions that we are now witnessing in the smaller meetings. Perhaps we will get further revelation on this at a later date."

Simon the Zealot, Judas (son of James), and James the Less—all contributed in the ongoing discussions of building a foundation for the Way of salvation through the Master.

After numerous hours of discussion, Peter began to wrap things up. "Brothers, we must nourish ourselves, not only in the Word, but in our physical bodies. Let us take time to break bread together." This met everyone's approval.

"And when we finish eating," said John, "I have some new psalms and spiritual songs to teach you. Let's spend time praising our Lord together and praying especially for those imprisoned and for those whom our Lord is calling into this wonderful ministry of proclaiming the good news!"

"Amen, amen!" said the others.

† † †

Caiaphas was delighted to hear of the attempted assassination. *Money well spent,* he mused in his head. *I would love to have seen Antipas' face—and Pilate! What a double treat!* Sharon came into the reading chambers.

"My lovely dove," he said. "Should we not pay a visit to your father? I would like to hear his account of the attempted assassination of Antipas."

"Why are you being so concerned about others all of a sudden? When he suggested you share your powers you said you didn't care if you ever saw him again."

"Oh, nothing, dear; I say let bygones be bygones and let's go visit the old windbag."

She peered suspiciously into his face. "Okay, I'll see if he's available for the evening meal."

Later, at the evening meal, Annas embraced his daughter and then Caiaphas. "So good to see you both. I'm glad you came; the others are here as well. Come now and let's dine together." Although there was a drought in the land, the large, long table always had the best vegetables and fruits available.

After the meal, Annas spoke to the group in a different tone. "As you know, a few days ago, an assassination attempt was made on Herod Antipas. This unprovoked, cowardly attack was made by someone outside the city wall. A rider on a horse was seen leaving the scene. Since Pilate was visiting the king, some think he was a target as well, but there was only a sole assassin, so it does not seem logical one person would think himself able to pull off a double assassination.

"Fortunately, with Pilate there, the combination of Antipas' guards and Pilate's soldiers made for a quicker pursuit and investigation. First, the investigation: I was sent word to visit the king. At the site of the attack, a torn headgear was found, one worn by a priest. This has led Antipas to suspect someone from our Sanhedrin brethren to be a co-conspirator of this event. As you know, I have gone to great measures to try to restore our relations with the Herodians, and this discovery has single-handedly jeopardized my attempts."

Good, thought Caiaphas. *Just what I wanted to hear.*

"However," he continued. "I received word a few minutes ago that the suspected assassin has been captured, and he's not one of us, so this should help us. And I am hopeful we shall discover how this headgear came into his possession."

While the others seemed relieved, Caiaphas became more subdued than his usual boisterous self. *How could this man get caught!?* he thought. *This cannot be traced back to me!*

"I, for one, would hate to be the owner of that piece of evidence!" said Jonathan. The others laughed.

Caiaphas managed a less-than-vigorous laugh. He felt as if everyone was reading his chain of thoughts. He refused to look at his wife, the one he could usually look at to get a return consoling look.

"And where has Pilate placed this criminal?" Caiaphas was able to ask.

"Oh, I suppose in the city prison—deep inside the prison," replied Annas.

Caiaphas smiled as Annas looked his way. He still felt as if every word he spoke convicted him as the conspirator. *This man must not live long enough for the interrogation.*

† † †

Barabbas was blindfolded and placed in a deeper part of the prison, several floors below the earth's surface, he guessed. He had never been this far down into the prison. He was shackled on both his feet and hands and was chained to the wall. The room was dark with only one torch flickering, somewhere down the long corridor. It was cold and damp, and he was alone in a small cell. *Good,* he thought. *Maybe I'll rot in this dungeon and be done with it.* The only sound was a groan from someone in a distant cell.

As his eyes adjusted, he began to survey his surroundings. The adjoining cells had canvas weaved through the bars to prevent seeing into each one. The back wall, to which he was chained, was solid rock. In the rock, at the top and bottom, iron stakes were hammered into it. Beams stretched across the top of the ceiling from behind him to beyond the cell doors, across the corridor, and into the cell from across his. These provided a wedge to support the adjacent walls and bars. The rock was chiseled so that there was a long segment protruding from the rear wall that he figured would be his bed and feeding bench. There was one blanket lying on the bench. He had just enough movement area that would allow him to reach the blanket and to lie down.

He wondered about his mother and father: *Surely Kopas told them, or did they arrest him for trying to warn me? Why didn't I pick up on his warning? . . . Hamath!* Barabbas could not blame Hamath for this capture. Neither of them could have known that Pilate was visiting the king that day and hour. For once, though, he missed having Hamath around for a little solace from the cold, dark, and damp cell.

Hours passed slowly, so he thought. He wasn't sure whether it was day or night. He remembered from his previous stays that food was not brought the first day—other days were missed entirely. Barabbas tried to lie down and sleep, but every time he moved, his chains awakened him. Plus, trying to cover himself with the blanket for warmth was near impossible. Eventually, he managed and fell into a form of prison sleep—a sleep that was on and off on a cold stone bench.

Barabbas was awakened by the noise of a creaking door and some voices. He sat up, wondering if it was daytime or still night. Two soldiers stopped and unlocked his door.

"Well, if it ain't your lucky day," said a soldier. "You get to go for a little stroll in the city." They unlocked him from the wall, but left his shackles attached. Next they placed a hood over his head and tightened it around his neck. They marched him outside and placed him on the floor of a chariot. He wasn't sure where he was going, but it wouldn't be far enough. When the chariot stopped, they led him into a courtyard and sat him on a bench. He was chained to the bench and was told not to speak unless spoken to or they would stuff his mouth with a cloth.

"I need a drink of water if I'm going to speak."

"We'll see about that," said a guard. "It depends on if you're a good lad or not."

His hood was removed, but the light of day prevented him from opening his eyes for a while. Finally he began to see just a glimpse of the area. It appeared familiar. As his eyes adjusted, he began to see more. He was seated before a large porch area. There were columns lined at the top of the steps supporting a roof over the porch. In the middle there was a large seat. *I've been here before,* he thought. Then he remembered: this was the judgment seat of Pontius Pilate—this was where he was released when the Jewish leaders chose him instead of that Jesus-man!

Pilate came out from a side door of the porch. He walked over to the seat of judgment and sat there as the crime was read aloud to him. The recorder then placed the judgment papyri on a table where he sat to record notes. Pilate sat there for a few minutes, saying nothing. Finally he spoke. "What is your plea?"

Barabbas tried to speak. "Not . . . ahem . . . not guilty."

"Why was he arrested?" asked Pilate.

"He matches the description of the assassin, your Excellency," said a centurion. "He was trying to trade a fine horse in Bethany for an old donkey. He is a Jew, and Jews do not typically own such a fine animal, nor does anyone try to trade one for a donkey."

Pilate listened as he continued to study Barabbas. "Release him from his seat and bring him closer to me." The guards quickly unchained him, made him stand up, and dragged him closer to Pilate. Again, Pilate looked at his face. "Lift up his head for me." He studied him for a moment. "Don't I know you?"

Barabbas did not speak.

Guards, who is this man? Haven't we seen him here before?" Several guards began to stare at Barabbas as well.

"Your Excellency, they all look the same to me—wait a minute. Isn't he that fellow that the Jews traded for that Messiah man—that Nazarene?"

Pilate looked once more at the face of Barabbas. "By the gods! You're right! 'Give us Barabbas!' they cried. They crucified an innocent man in your place, and now look at you. You were previously accused of murder and inciting unrest. Now you're back."

Barabbas said nothing.

"Was it you who tried to kill Antipas?" Again, he said nothing. "This reminds me of that Jesus-man—'the King of the Jews,' I called Him. He would not speak in His defense, just as you, and you know what happened to Him?"

Barabbas managed to speak. "Water, please?"

Pilate smiled. "Bring me a cup of water." The empty cup was filled in front of Barabbas. Pilate took the cup and drank from it. "Aahhh, such cool refreshing water. Now, I could give you some water, but you must start talking . . . Again, I ask, did you attempt to assassinate your king?"

Barabbas did not understand why prosecutors asked such lead-in questions. "I did not . . . try to assassinate anyone. Please . . . may I have a drink of water?"

"Why did you want to sell a horse for a donkey?"

"I needed the donkey for carrying loads."

"Loads of what?" Again, Barabbas did not answer. "Let me see his hands," Pilate said to the centurion. His hands were opened in front of Pilate. "These hands are not the hands of a common laborer. Open up his fingers." Pilate inspected his hands. "Look at the calluses between those two fingers; your fingers give all indication of one who uses a bow and arrow. Do you deny that?" Again, no answer. "Take him back to his seat. Let the record show that I believe this man is indeed our would-be assassin. Take him and beat him, then send him and this record to Antipas for judgment from them. If they do not agree with me, then I want you to bring him back to me for a final verdict. If they concur, then I release my punishment of him to Antipas."

Pilate stood up. "Oh, I nearly forgot; here's the water you requested." He walked over to the front of Barabbas, grabbed his beard, and jerked his head up. "You Jews will never learn; the Roman government is too powerful for you to defeat. I should have crucified you when I had the chance." Then he took the cup and splashed the water into the face of Barabbas. Pilate turned around and walked away. "Take him to the scourging post and beat him, but keep him alive enough to show his king that we have judged him."

Barabbas worked his tongue on the hair around his lips, licking as much of the water as possible. He had been through this process before. His determination to survive got him through previous beatings. But it did not appear that there was a way out of this judgment. He was tied to a post and beaten with a whip. The whip caught his ear once, cutting a piece of it off. Blood began to coat a portion of his beard.

When the beating was over, a hood was placed back over his head, and he was dragged out to the chariot for another trip. This time he knew where he was headed.

✝✝✝

Jonathan, the high priest, alerted the council that Herod Antipas had requested their presence at the proceedings of the man who was accused of the assassination attempt. "Make sure that you attend," were his orders, "that the king may know we have nothing to hide and that we were *not* a part of this devilish plot."

Caiaphas sat in a seat, waiting for the others. *What if this man identifies me? How will I respond? I must be prepared.* He stood up and adjusted his priestly robe. *This clothing can hide anyone from the truth; plus, who will take a commoner's word against a member of the high priest's family?* He left for the council gathering at Herod's palace.

A lot of chatter was heard among the council. "What will become of us?" asked one of the priests to another.

"I don't know," said another priest. "If that assassin accuses all of us in a conspiracy plot, we may all be interrogated."

Annas and Jonathan arrived and sat in front. Caiaphas sat further behind them. Annas stood and faced the others. "Brethren—men of the council," said Annas. "I have some disheartening news to report. As you know, we sent Saul of Tarsus to Damascus to arrest the followers of the Nazarene and bring them back to our city for judgment and stoning. It has just been reported to me that he himself has become a follower of this Jesus. He claims he met Him along the road during a freak electrical storm."

"Oh, my," were some of the comments—others even cursed.

"The local priest had planned to arrest him and stone him for blasphemy, but he escaped the city during the night. That's unfortunate. I will send messengers throughout Judea and surrounding regions to alert those in charge of our synagogues. If any of you are interested in covering a portion of the region, please inform me after we are dismissed from today's hearing."

"Attention," said the guard. "The accused has arrived, and the proceedings are about to begin. Please follow your high priest as I seat you in the judgment hall." Jonathan stood and walked toward the doorway. Caiaphas allowed several of his brothers-in-law to go ahead of him. Most of the council was present, which gave Caiaphas hope that he would not be noticed by the man on trial.

The council sat to the left front, facing the middle of the hall. The king's court sat to the right with the king's judgment throne in front middle. Two tables were positioned near the front center with a single stone seat in the middle, just ahead of the tables. Everyone, except the accused and the king, were in their positions and seated. Near the rear, on one side, a door opened and six guards marched in, in formation. A lone prisoner followed, who was followed by six more guards. The procession was slow, but deliberate. As the front guards marched beyond the stone seat, they turned and faced the accused, who was forced to stop. The rear guards stopped behind him and stood at attention. Then four of the guards—two in front and two in the rear—seated the prisoner and chained him to four hooks at the base of the stone seat. Once secured, they rejoined their ranks, and all but two proceeded to backtrack to a standing area on both sides of the hall. The two remained behind the prisoner.

When all the soldiers were in position, the chief guard called attention to the arriving king. Antipas made his way in to be seated in front center. He called for the reading of the records.

"Attention to all in attendance. A male by the name Barabbas is seated in the judgment seat, accused of the attempted assassination of our blessed King, Herod Antipas, with potential harm to the king's guests: his wife and Roman Governor Pontius Pilate and his wife. Two arrows were shot at the king: one nipping his outer garment, near his neck, and the other just missing his head. Governor Pilate is commended as having, perhaps, saved the king from devastating harm from the second arrow.

"Let the record show that Governor Pilate sat in the Roman Chair of Judgment this same day and has ruled his judgment, that this Barabbas is indeed the one who carried out this devilish crime against the peacekeeper and protector of our land. The prisoner was scourged as a sign to this court of the governor's ruling."

The recorder sat down at one of the tables. The king looked at Barabbas. "Chief guard," he said, "would you tell one of the house servants to come in here and wipe this trail of blood off my floor?" He then turned his attention to another man seated at the other table. "Advocate for the accused, how does the accused plead?"

"Not guilty, your Majesty."

"Don't they all?" The king smiled, as controlled laughter spread throughout the hall. "What evidence do we have that would tie this man to the crime?"

Another man at the recorder's table stood. "Your Majesty, Barabbas is a well-known criminal. He was previously imprisoned for murder and inciting unrest among our people through the terroristic plots of the group known as the Zealots. By the providence of our God, he was released in favor over another criminal, Jesus of Nazareth."

"Really?" asked the king. He leaned forward as if to study Barabbas more closely.

"Yes, your Majesty, this is the same Barabbas."

"Tell me more."

"Your Majesty, the accused was chased from the outer walls of the city toward the south/southeast in the direction of Bethany. He was lost in the chase. Again, by the providence of God, Governor Pilate's soldiers were assigned to several local towns, including Bethany, and stayed overnight in hiding. The following morning, the accused was caught as he tried to trade his horse for a donkey at the local stable."

"A fine riding horse for a donkey?"

"Yes, your Majesty."

"Why on earth would someone want to trade a horse for a donkey? Were there many horses in the stable?"

"No, your Majesty, just a few old donkeys. The community is a farming and shepherding community, neither of which is conducive to the needs of a fine riding horse."

"Thank you for presenting the evidence. Now, let us hear from his advocate for his defense."

"Thank you, your Majesty. The accused has not been identified by anyone in this hall as the would-be assassin. Also, a priestly headgear was found at the scene of the crime. Plus, there is no law against trading a horse for a more suitable farming animal."

"Thank you, advocate; you may be seated. Is there any additional evidence or witnesses you wish to bring before this court?"

"No, your Majesty."

"The prosecutor may now speak."

"Thank you, your Majesty. Governor Pilate personally examined the accuser's hands and found conclusive evidence of calluses that are naturally created from the use of a bow and arrow. Also, the accused has no one who will stand up as an alibi to his whereabouts during the time of the crime."

"Advocate, do you wish to respond?"

"Yes, your Majesty. This man is an outdoorsman, and many outdoorsmen use bows and arrows for hunting. And, dare I say, it is likely that many of us in this hall do not want certain others to know where we are on any given night." Subdued laughter was heard.

"Well, I suppose you are correct. Is there anyone else who wishes to speak in behalf of the accused?" Several moments of silence passed. "Then, as the victim of this crime, allow me to ask a few questions. First of all, Barabbas, did you attempt this assassination on your own or were you paid?"

Barabbas did not respond at first. Then he managed a couple words: "Water, please?"

Antipas paused for a moment. "Sure, give the man a drink so that he may speak." Water was brought to him, and he drank profusely until the cup was taken from him. "Now, can you answer the question?"

Barabbas coughed a little and then cleared his throat. "I was paid to make the *attempt*, your Majesty. If I had wanted to assassinate you, you would not be here today to judge me."

"Perhaps you are correct, but that is not the question being asked. Who paid you to assassinate me?"

"I cannot disclose that information, your Majesty."

"And why, may I ask?"

"Because he still owes me money for the job." Laughter broke out in the hall but quickly ceased when they saw the king was not laughing.

Antipas opened a small canvas bag by his side and pulled out a piece of a headgear. "This was found in the tree where the assassination attempt occurred. To whom does it belong?"

Barabbas looked to his left toward the Sanhedrin council and then slowly back toward the king. Caiaphas did not make eye contact. Barabbas remained quiet.

"Okay, so you won't speak. Then I shall continue. I saw the horse on which the assassin was riding; I saw it quite clearly. It was from a beautiful stock . . . Guards!" The back door of the hall was opened; a horse was brought in and led down to the front of the king. Barabbas pretended not to be moved by his treasured friend of many months. "Is this the horse belonging to the accused?"

"Yes, your Majesty," said the guard.

"Ah, such a nice horse indeed." The king stood up and stepped down from his seat. He made his way around the horse, patting it occasionally. He then went to the front of Barabbas and spoke to him. "You may not want to speak, but your horse speaks loudly against you! Take the horse away!" The horse was led back outside the hall. "Let the record show that I recognize this horse as the horse of the would-be assassin!"

Chatter broke out in the hall. The chief guard cried out, "Silence in the hall!" All the guards stood at attention and rapped their wrist bracelets against their shields. Silence was restored immediately.

Antipas went back to his seat. "I ask the accused one more time: who paid you to assassinate me?" Barabbas said nothing. Antipas turned toward the advocate. "Do you have anything else to say on behalf of the accused?"

"Yes, your Majesty: as a fellow Jew, I ask for you to show mercy on his misguided soul."

Antipas stood again and faced his court representatives. "You have heard the evidence; what verdict would you render?"

"Guilty!" was the resounding cry throughout the group.

He then turned toward the Sanhedrin council. "And you, leaders of the Law of our God, what verdict would you render?"

The council members conferred among themselves and relayed the message to the high priest. Jonathan stood up. "Your Majesty, we find the accused guilty as charged."

Antipas returned to the front middle, facing Barabbas, but speaking loudly. "Is there anyone who wishes to speak further concerning this case?" He looked out among those behind the tables, then to his right, and then to his left. There was no one who wanted to speak. He walked back to the seat of judgment.

"Let the record show that, for the accused named Barabbas, the verdict is guilty of the crime of attempted assassination of the king. This crime is punishable by stoning to death." Some subdued whispering was heard, scattered throughout the hall. "His punishment will be delayed, however, until the guards can try to beat out of him the name of the one who apparently assisted in this crime.

"Also, there is still the unanswered question about the partial headgear found at the scene of the crime." Antipas stood and faced the Sanhedrin. "Let us pray that none of you had motives to try to remove me. The headgear may have been a diversion;

perhaps within a few days, or a few beatings, the criminal's tongue will be loosened."

Caiaphas felt somewhat relieved. He must now decide whether to leave Barabbas alone or to have him strangled in the prison. Numerous guards would welcome a pouch of coins for the "accidental" death of a prisoner due to his attempt to escape. But it was also risky to pay guards for a prison killing.

"This case is closed until more information can be extracted or until the public stoning occurs. The recorder will send a copy of our verdict to the governor for his seal of approval. Chief guard, have him beaten again before he leaves and set up daily scourges to loosen his tongue."

The chariot slowly made its way back to the prison. Several dogs were following its trail of blood. One dog got a little too close and a guard kicked it—it yelped and ran away. "Just as soon give him to the dogs as putting him back in here and messing up the place," said the guard. The chariot stopped in front of the prison gates. He reached into the chariot and untied the bloodied hands of Barabbas. "Hey, come give me a hand and help me drag him in," he shouted to the other guard.

"C'mon man, I just had my gear shined up for the court hearings. Can't we just dump him out and let the prison guards take it over?"

"Our orders are to get him inside the prison gates; then he's all theirs."

"Let me find some cloths to handle him." Together, they managed to drag Barabbas off the chariot and let him roll onto the ground. His body was badly beaten, and he appeared semi-conscious. His hand clasps remained unchained from the beating post at Herod's palace. Each guard grabbed a wrist and dragged him to the gates. "Hey! Open up! We got company for you."

"Ugh! What is that!?"

"It's Barabbas; don't you recognize him? He's had lunch with the governor and a mid-afternoon snack with Antipas." The guards laughed.

The prison guard opened the gates. "I'm glad he didn't stay for dinner." The other two got him inside the gates and dropped him onto the ground. Then they turned to walk out. "Whoa there, guys, you ain't leaving him here!"

"You watch!" They smiled as they walked out and proceeded to get on the chariot. "We gotta go clean this mess up here . . . so long!" And with a pop of the reins, they disappeared down the street.

The guard locked the gates and went back to the prison entrance. "Hey, Saberth, will you give me a hand?" No response. *Now where is that man?* "Saberth!" He continued to walk down the prison corridor. "Saberth!"

"He's in the dungeon," said a prisoner nearby. "I can carry that man inside for you."

The guard stopped, scratched his head, and looked at the prisoner. "I suppose you could, but how can I trust you?"

"Keep my hands and feet chained. I will bring him into my cell till he's strong enough to walk to his own."

The guard pulled out his sword. "Stand back to the rear of the cell." When he did, the guard unlocked the cell door. "Now *slowly* move out and toward the prisoner, and remember, I know how to use this sword." The prisoner obliged and began to walk out of his cell. He was much taller than the guard and about twice as wide. He walked slowly toward the beaten and mangled body that lay on the ground. As he bent over, he grunted, then, having squatted down, he raised himself up while scooping the body into his arms. He turned around and slowly walked back to his cell. Once inside the cell, the guard shut the door and locked it. "You're pretty handy to have around; glad you turned yourself in, Hamath."

Hamath grunted.

"I will bring you a basin of water and some cloths to clean him up. He will have other meetings with the guards."

Hamath checked Barabbas for a pulse; it was weak, but still there. He laid him on the rear bench and put a blanket on him. Soon the guard was there with the basin of water and cloths. Hamath began to wipe the dirt from the wounds on his badly beaten back. Barabbas never flinched or groaned; he was in a state of shock.

✝✝✝

Paul did not eat much in the mornings. For days, he had developed a schedule that allowed him several hours of prayer and worship to God before the children got out for their pre-breakfast chores. He had the older boys come to him, when their schedules allowed, and write down the things the Spirit of Jesus was teaching him. They enjoyed working with Paul, especially when he would stop and answer their questions about the writings. This also helped Paul to explain the words on a level that the common person could read and understand.

Sometimes Paul would walk east toward the desert; he would hide himself behind a sand dune and speak with the Spirit for hours, frequently missing lunch and dinner. Jacob would sometimes go out and find Paul and bring him some meat, bread, and water. This continued for months.

One day, while worshiping, the Spirit spoke: "Paul! Paul!"

"Yes, my Lord?"

"I want you to go back into Damascus and proclaim the new covenant to those who will hear."

"But won't they try to kill me?"

"I will confuse their plots, but you must learn to express My words in such a way that many others will respond to My bidding to come to Me and be saved from their sins. Now go!"

"Yes, Lord, as you wish." Paul wasted no time, but saddled and loaded his horse for the two-hour journey to Damascus. When he arrived, he went straight to the synagogue and, outside, began to discuss the new covenant as compared to the old. He was very meticulous in explaining the old covenant through the lens of the new covenant, refuting any and all objections through the power of the words of Jesus, accompanied by His Spirit. He proclaimed Jesus as the Messiah and that, as Messiah, He was none less than the Son of God. Paul did this, two and three days a week, two or three weeks each month. In Damascus, many were becoming followers of the Way; some became disciples of Paul.

Although Paul was eager to share the message of the gospel, he longed for more time to spend with Christ in the desert. He asked the Spirit for more clarification of the new covenant.

"Paul, in your thinking, you see the Law as physical; that is okay in the Old Covenant. But you must stop your focus on the physical in the New Covenant. The Jews do this; they remain in a state of anger and frustration over the rule of the Romans. They continue to seek a physical Messiah who will establish them in a peaceful, physical promised land. They refuse to see this in Me. In Me are peace, love, and joy. I am what they seek, yet they refuse Me and rebel against My new nature as Spirit. I am deliverance; I am faith; I am peace, love, joy, and all characteristics that bring harmony among mankind. You must not hide these from them; they must see these traits in you—in your flesh—as genuine, as from above.

"Do not fear the consequences of living in My likeness before all men. Even in death, show yourself alive! Death is no end; death is just the beginning—it is fulfillment. Do not seek it as a treasure; it will seek you at the proper time. What natural man does not understand he will try to conquer to rule or destroy. I will be with you; abide in Me and whatever happens to you is in My permissive will. Only, rejoice! Let the peace of God rule in you."

Paul had these words written as soon as possible. Although he did not fully understand all that the Spirit told him, he knew enough to trust in His presence. He understood that the Kingdom of God was now active on earth through the lives of those followers who were in daily communion with God, in Christ, through the Holy Spirit. He also knew that these words of the Spirit needed to be kept for future copying.

†††

"What this time?" asked Pontius Pilate to the messenger from Rome.

"My Lord, the emperor has requested you return with us to Rome immediately."

"He does? Then I will make arrangements to leave in a few days."

"My Lord, my orders are to accompany you."

"Then accompany me, but for now, get out of my sight until I'm ready."

The soldier in charge was not sure what to do. "Guards!" cried Pilate. Six guards appeared. "Show these men and their fellows the barracks; make sure they are entertained and that they are to remain there until I'm ready to depart with them."

The two soldiers were a part of eight who came to escort Pilate, but the other six were further down the corridor from them. "As you wish, my Lord," replied the soldier in charge. "We will camp outside the city walls for several days, but then we must leave."

Pilate ignored them as they yielded to the coercion of Pilate's guards. As soon as they were out of hearing distance, he called for his chief servant. The servant was soon before him, bowing. "Yes, my Lord?"

"Bring my wife to me immediately. Tell her it's urgent."

Procula Claudia stopped her usual observation of the educational instruction given to her son, Pilo, and followed the servants to Pontius. As soon as she entered the library, Pontius ordered the servants out of the room.

"My dear," she said, "what troubles you so?"

"Tiberius calls for me."

She joined in her husband's nervous look. "The emperor?"

"He sent eight soldiers to escort me . . . that can only mean bad news."

Procula walked over to him and put her arm on his shoulder. "What are we going to do?"

"I have several guards who are loyal to me; I can have them smuggle us out of the city during the night."

"But to where? And what about Pilo? You know his limp has not improved."

"Listen to me, woman! The emperor is old and is clinging on to any power he can find. He suspects anyone who exerts any bold leadership in a region of the empire."

"The Samaritans," she whispered aloud.

"Yes, it has been reported to him of my annihilation of that uprising. I tell you, he is up to no good. We must gather our belongings and prepare to leave during the night. I have made friends among the rulers of the Parthians; we will seek asylum there."

"Yes, my love; I will pack our things, and Pilo's servant will come with us."

"Why the servant?"

"If someone must carry him on foot, we must have the servant."

"Then go! Stay in the bedroom until I send for you."

Procula made her way back to her son's room. The teacher was gathering her things and speaking with Pilo's servant.

"Oh, there you are," she said. "Are you ready for my report?"

"Not today—I'm not feeling well." Procula turned to the servant. "Please show her out to the gate and return to me." He bowed his head and politely escorted the teacher out of the room.

"Mother!" cried Pilo. "Listen to what I've learned about our world today!" He picked up a few maps on the floor and proceeded to show her the Roman territories.

"My darling son," she said. "I have a better idea on how to show you the things on your map. We are going to take a trip across our land."

Pilo's eyes lit up. "Really!? Wow! How exciting!" Then his face began to sadden.

"What's wrong, my dear?"

"Father . . . will he have to stay behind and watch over the people?"

"No, not this time. He has spoken of a place far to the east that he wants to show us first."

"This is wonderful! I must go and tell my friends!"

"Oh no, no, my dear; we must keep this a secret or your father may have to stay behind. He says we must sneak out if he is going with us . . . no one must know."

Pilo's servant reentered the room. "What about Pantego?"

"I will speak to him; now I want you to find three or four of your favorite playthings and put them on Father and Mother's bed."

Pilo fell asleep in his mother's lap as they waited in his parent's bedroom. It was near midnight when Pontius arrived with two of the house guards. When he saw his son asleep, he quietly put his finger to his lips. "Let him sleep," he whispered. He then motioned for Pantego, who gently put the boy in his arms. The guards grabbed the bags on the bed and began to walk out of the room. "Follow them," he said to Procula.

Outside, the group mounted on their horses and carefully began their trek toward the eastern city gates. The night air was crisp and only a few sounds of barking dogs broke the eerie quiet of the night.

"Will the guards at the gates be a problem?" Procula asked Pontius.

"I sent word to them that a small group was leaving tonight and to let them pass. They should oblige."

When they neared the gates, one of the house guards galloped ahead to notify the gate tenders. The gates began to slowly open, revealing a huge midnight sky of stars. *Pilo would love this sight,* thought Procula. They began to pass through the gates, when suddenly a squadron of twenty soldiers appeared from nowhere and encircled them, with their swords and spears glistening in the moonlit sky.

Several of the horses reared up and snorted; Pantego held on to Pilo.

Pontius uncovered his head. "What is the meaning of this!? I am the governor of this region; let me pass now!"

One of the soldiers who came to Pilate earlier in the day appeared. "My Lord, by the orders of Emperor Tiberius, you are under arrest. You will remain in my camp tonight; tomorrow we will return to Rome. If you cooperate, your family and these attendants may return to their quarters under house arrest until I send word back that we have arrived safely in Rome. After that, they will be escorted to Rome to join you." He then turned to Procula. "And trust me, I will have soldiers camped at every gate until then."

†††

Simon the Zealot could not shake his burden to pray for Barabbas. The Lord had not said that he could not pray for him, or that it was a waste of time. So he continued to do so. He had heard through Nicodemus that Barabbas was back in jail and had been condemned to die, but his stoning was delayed as the authorities would try to beat more information out of him.

"Lord, don't let my connections with him cause undue persecution against Your followers. I pray that You will intervene in his life before it is too late. Let deliverance of his soul bring the peace he has been searching for in his heart." Simon prayed daily for Barabbas, that the evil one would not get the final victory in his life.

✝✝✝

Barabbas tried to move his body again. His eyes had been swollen for days, and he had difficulty opening them. Each day, he was dragged to a post and whipped. He tried to move again, but the tenderness of multiple wounds only gave him pain that could only be comforted by useless groaning. Nevertheless, he moved. When he did, he heard the sound of dripping water and sounds of what sounded like a water stream. Soon, a damp cloth was gently rubbed on parts of his body from where the pain emanated. "Aaugh!" he groaned. *Who is with me?* he wondered. *And why is he treating me with kindness?* He tried to move again.

"Be careful moving; you have many scabs and open wounds yet to be healed," the voice said.

The voice sounded familiar. Barabbas wanted to speak, but his mind was not yet ready for a conversation. "Drink," was all he could say. Soon he felt water trickling into his mouth. He opened it to allow the cool water to enter in. He swallowed hard and choked a bit on the drink. He spoke slowly. "Who are you? Where am I?"

"I am Hamath, your friend, and you are in my cell."

"Hamath? . . . Your cell?" He tried to think this through but could not understand how Hamath got caught and put back into prison. "Lift me up."

"It's going to hurt."

"Aaughh!" Pain shot through his body as the flesh pulled against the healing scabs and open wounds. Barabbas tried to use his eyes again. As he peeked through his matted eyes, his blurred vision caught images of a familiar scene. He turned his head to look further. "I think I've been here before."

"It's our old cell," said Hamath. "It's been reinforced with more bars, plus top and bottom plates to help prevent escapes."

Barabbas began to feel dizzy. "Lay me back down, please." Hamath obliged and carefully helped his friend lie straight on the bench. Barabbas began to feel stable again. "How long have I been in here?"

"This is the middle of the fourth day."

"I'm hungry." Hamath reached for a small folded canvas and unwrapped it. He pulled out some dried camel strips.

"Here, try to suck on these." He handed him several strips of meat. Barabbas managed to wiggle a piece into his mouth. As he gnawed on the strip, it began to soften and he began to chew it. One piece was quickly consumed—then another piece disappeared into his mouth. Next, Hamath handed him a piece of bread. This also was consumed quickly, then came some more water. He managed to sip some while lying down. This was enough for now.

"Any word on my schedule?"

"Word is that as soon as you are physically able, you will be interrogated by the chief guard."

"Guess I better allow for a slow recovery."

"They send a report on you each evening to the high priest. The recorder hasn't paid us a visit today."

"What time is it?"

"Lunch was served about an hour ago."

Barabbas used his hands and arms as he sat himself up again. "Aaugh! Curse the Romans!"

"The Jewish authorities beat you like this."

"Then curse the Jewish authorities!" He tried to stand up, but his wounds were still too tender. "Pilate is the cause for my missing Antipas with those arrows. Antipas moved to give him a better view of my horse. Then the stunned king was an easy target for the next arrow, but Pilate pulled him down . . . Aaugh!" Hamath reached for another camel strip and piece of bread. He handed it to Barabbas. "Why are you in here? I thought you joined those Jesus followers."

"I did join them, but I found out that Jesus was living truth. And living truth meant that I had to live in that truth. To be truthful, I had to get things right in my past. That included my serving time in prison for breaking out of prison."

"You turned yourself in?"

"That I did; the guard nearly wet his tunic when he saw me at the door."

"Did Simon tell you to do this?"

"Not exactly; when I surrendered my life over to the Nazarene, I began to feel different inside. That peace that Simon spoke of flooded inside me. For the first time in my adult life, I experienced real joy and peace inside me. I became transformed from within. Conviction of sin became the normal occurrence from within. I began to realize that in order to live a life that pleased the God of our fathers, I had to be truthful and live in truth and peace."

"Has your mind changed now that you're in here staring at rock walls and iron bars?"

"No, this is where I'm supposed to be. I am happy on the inside now."

"But you're useless in here; there's nothing productive to do in here."

"Yes, there is. There are other followers in here due to some priest named Saul. He arrested a bunch of followers of Jesus. Some were even stoned simply for believing on Jesus as the Messiah. I have been able to meet with them on occasion and we have sung psalms and prayed for one another. I even made a guard or two listen to the gospel of deliverance. So, things have been busy for me in here."

Barabbas sat there in silence for a while. He was recalling the words of Simon and his offer for him to find that inner peace: *He says you will fail in your assassination attempt . . . He said Hamath would search me out for the truth . . . He's told me more about you and your plans than He has spoken to me about any-one or anything else.* Those were the words of Simon.

Hamath spoke again. "Everything Simon told us has come true. And his Jesus has become my Jesus. His peace is now my peace. I have witnessed groups of poorly dressed and poorly fed followers come in here with a peace and joy that surpasses all understanding."

"You're making me want to become a follower."

Hamath grunted. "I know you, Barabbas; you have much anger embedded in your heart . . . only a miracle will change you." Hamath stood up and faced Barabbas; he had the biggest smile Barabbas had ever seen on a man. "But you know what? I prayed that Jesus would give me the chance to tell you the things I have just spoken to you. Four days ago, when I heard of the as-sassination attempt, I thought I would never see you again . . . now look who's in my cell!"

"And you are talking more now." Barabbas tried to smile.

"One thing else I prayed: I prayed that if I got this chance to tell you about how Jesus changed my life, that somehow, some way, you also would open your heart to the truth and let His truth set you free—free on the inside."

"I'm condemned to die by both Roman and Jewish courts; there is no freedom left for me."

"You're thinking just like a Jew—everything physical, every-thing according to the flesh."

"I *am* a Jew."

"So was Jesus, yet he told Pilate that His kingdom was not of this world."

"Who told you that?"

"The leaders of the followers of Jesus—and they're Jews too! Peace with God comes only from the inside out; Jesus said He was the way, the truth, and the life. And because Jesus became the final sacrifice for all sin for all time, no one comes to our God except through Him."

"Jesus said that?"

"Yes, He did."

"So, all that the priests are now doing is vain?"

"I think you can answer that for yourself."

Barabbas tried to lie down again. Hamath helped him get comfortable. "I need to rest."

Hamath walked to the front of the cell. He turned back to his friend. "I don't say much, but when I speak, it is based on much thought. What I've said to you is the truth. But you hearing it will not change you one bit; you must repent of your evil ways and ask Jesus to deliver you from yourself. Otherwise you will experience a greater pain than what man can lash upon you. There is an eternal judgment that will come from God upon those who reject Him and His offer of deliverance through His Son."

"Jesus is the Son of God?" Barabbas closed his eyes completely. *Jesus is peace . . . Jesus is truth . . . Jesus is deliverance . . .* He faded off into sleep.

† † †

Peter was happy to see his wife and daughter. They had traveled to Jerusalem to check on the work of the followers of the Way. "My, how you've grown!" exclaimed Peter as he tried to lift Petronilla up. "Whoa, Perpie, what are you feeding her?"

She smiled. "Me? My mother is feeding her honey and bread after each meal."

"Oh, Father, I've missed you so! When are you coming back home?"

"Yes," said his wife, "we have missed you."

"I'm afraid my work here is not finished. In fact, we have decided it is best we work from out of Jerusalem. We are planning some regional trips to check on the region's groups of followers and to see how they are progressing. And we must train other men for the work of ministry at each town and village."

"But what of our home and the fishing business?"

"Oh, I wouldn't worry about that; our Lord has made great provisions for us here. In fact, I believe our Lord would have us stay together for now. I want you and Pet to travel with me for a while and help me visit the new followers."

"Oh Father, I would love to see the pyramids in Egypt!"

"Now hold on, my Pet. I never said anything about Egypt. We need to start in Judea first, and then Samaria. Then maybe, someday, the Lord will send us south of the border."

"Really!? Oh thanks, Father. I love you!" She gave her father a big hug, while Perpetua had this "question mark" look on her face.

"Now I did say 'maybe,'" he reminded them both. "Why don't you two go and find the other ladies; I bet they're anxious to see you both and to hear of the news from Galilee." As they left him, Peter made his way to the upper chamber, where many of the apostles were gathered. "Simon, any news from the prison?"

"No, but I'm going there to visit Hamath this afternoon. Care to go with me?"

"Oh, I think I've seen enough prison walls for a lifetime already—plus, my wife and daughter have arrived and I want to spend some time with them. Why not take Matthew or Elder

James with you? He could visit with some of the followers while you talk with Hamath."

"That's a great idea; thanks."

Peter walked over to Elder James. "And how is my pastor today?"

"Doing well, and how is my apostle today?" They both laughed. "Peter, the teaching and training continues to grow and improve. Our benevolence in the city is very orderly, thanks to our men-servants and women-servants."

"That's encouraging."

"Yes, it is, and their service has allowed me to pray and study more. Visiting our membership is very important, so I thank our Lord for His gifts to our fellowships."

"Our Master is looking after us all. How blessed we are to be chosen by Him to spread His word throughout our land . . . Say, before I forget, my wife and daughter are in town and I was wondering if perhaps you—or a group—could go to the prison with Simon and visit with the followers?"

"Sure, that'll be a good opportunity to pray with them and encourage them."

"Great! I'm going to spend some family time with Perpie and Pet."

By the time Simon was ready to go to the prison, Elder James had gathered about a dozen men to go with him. Also, Mary (Jesus' mother), Mary Magdalene, and several other women decided it would be good to go see the women in prison as well. As they gathered in the courtyard, John stopped them all.

"Let's pray for a prosperous visit before we leave." They bowed their heads as John led the prayer. "Our Lord Jesus, as we go into the place of physical bondage, may we set the captives free in their hearts. Will You grant us freedom to speak and Your power to heal broken hearts and fearful minds? And if there is a need for physical healings, give us guidance to do so. In Your name we pray, amen."

"Amen, amen," said the others, and off they went to the prison.

The prison guard was bored. His shift was just getting started, yet he wanted to leave. *This place is giving me the creeps,* he thought. *Why don't they send these low-life criminals to the quarries or to do some clean-up details in the Valley of Hinnom?* He was about to go into the prison corridors when he heard a commotion outside the prison. He stood up and saw a large group of men and women standing at the gates. *Now what?* He walked up to them. "Yes?"

"We wish to come in and visit the prisoners," said Simon.

"You do, eh? Well, I . . . ." He was about to deny them entrance, when a sudden fear entered his heart and mind. He had never sensed such a power of weakness before. It so rattled him that he decided it was best to let these folks come in after all. He immediately unlocked the doors and let them come in. "I . . . I must get a count from you . . . don't want any extras to leave with you," he said with a smile.

"Thank you, and we'll try not to leave anyone behind as well," said Matthew. "Could you lead us to the followers of the Way? We'd like to gather with them for a time of fellowship and prayer."

"Sure, I was about to go in there and check on them." The guard immediately felt better as he helped the group inside the prison. As they walked down the corridor, prisoners began coming to the front of their cells to speak with the group. Simon was looking at the prisoners, but did not see Hamath. Then, on the right, he peered into an empty cell—or so it seemed. Simon looked in and saw Hamath with another prisoner.

"Guard?"

"Yes?"

"Please let me into this cell. I wish to speak to the prisoners."

"Oh, you don't want to go in there; these men are vicious and will tear you apart!"

Simon looked at him; once again, fear welled up inside the guard. "I will let you in, but beware, for I cannot save you from them." The guard unlocked the cell door and swung it open. Simon motioned for Matthias, James the Less, and Judas son of James to come with him.

"Hamath, how are you, my brother? Do you remember Matthias, James the Less, and Judas?"

Hamath smiled. "Yes, I remember. It is a welcome sight to see you all. You fill this place with great warmth."

Simon looked at the limp body lying on the bench. "And who is this?"

"It's Barabbas; he's not doing well."

Simon felt a surge of emotions in his body. *Barabbas!? Lord I didn't know.* "What is wrong?"

"They beat him daily for his attempted assassination; they're waiting for him to heal so they can beat him again until he gives them the information they want."

"What information?"

"They want to know who paid him to attempt the assassination. They want to know who gave him the priestly headgear. After they get this information or until they tire of beating him, they plan to stone him to death."

"When will this happen?"

"I don't know, but I don't think he will last much longer."

"Wake him up, Hamath."

Hamath carefully grabbed his shoulder. "Barabbas, wake up." He shook him a little. "Wake up; you have a visitor."

"Huh? What?" Barabbas moved his head a bit.

"I said 'Wake up; you have a visitor.'"

He moved his arm slowly toward his face to rub his eyes. "Aaugh!" The torn flesh remained tender on his face. Hamath grabbed a wet cloth and put it in Barabbas' hand. He slowly dabbed his eyes. "Who's here?"

"This is Simon; remember me?"

His breathing was shallow with a gurgling sound deep within. "Yeah . . . I remember you . . . what do you want?"

"Do you want to be healed?"

"What?"

"I said, 'Do you want to be healed?'"

Barabbas struggled through each response. "No . . . They are waiting for me . . . to get well so they can . . . beat me again."

"Jesus is offering you spiritual healing to deliver you from judgment."

"Is He going to . . . deliver me from . . . my appointment . . . with death?"

"No, that was not His doing, so you will have to accept your penalty. But, He is offering you eternal life if you will but admit you are a sinner and will turn from your sin and receive Him into your life."

"Life? . . . You call this life? . . . I have no life . . . I gambled and I lost . . . There is no life . . . left for me."

"Barabbas, listen; there is eternal life after this physical life. I saw Jesus alive after His crucifixion—after His burial. If you die in your sins, real judgment begins—real pain begins."

"I think Hamath . . . has already told me this . . . I don't understand why Jesus is going . . . through all this trouble . . . to save a bitter, battered . . . murderous person like me."

"Because He loves you, He is offering you salvation from your embittered, battered, murderous self."

Barabbas hesitated. "Love . . . now that's a word I haven't heard . . . in a long time . . . How can I expect . . . love from someone . . . for whom I've done nothing? . . . How can Jesus love me? . . . Look at me! . . . I am done with living! . . . There is nothing to offer Him! . . . Let me die!" He tried to turn away. "Aaughh!"

Simon ignored his screams. "God so loved you, Barabbas, that He gives you this opportunity to receive eternal life, through Jesus; you don't have to perish and be sent to hell to be in torment."

Barabbas dabbed his eyes again. He sobbed. Hamath put his hand gently on his shoulder. "Jesus took my pain away from the inside, Barabbas. That's what He offers you, and when you die physically, you will die with peace in your heart."

"Hamath, my friend . . . you have been with me . . . since all this anger . . . was first formed . . . I don't fault you for leaving me . . . I deserve this . . . but you don't! . . . You never killed anyone."

"But I've made a few wish they were dead, and I was there holding the horses for us both as you fulfilled your murderous plots. This prison is exactly what I deserve. But Jesus has come into my life now, and I have purpose in living—right here in this prison. And what Jesus has done for me, He will do for you."

"How, Hamath? . . . How can I be delivered . . . from this hatred . . . and bitterness inside me?"

Hamath turned to Simon. "Simon?"

"The blood of Jesus covers all sins committed in the body. God forgives sin, not based on whether you deserve forgiveness, but based on the shed blood of His Son, Jesus. To receive it, you must turn and look to Him for it. As Moses held up that brass serpent, all those bitten by the poisonous snakes simply had to look upon it to be healed. None of them deserved it, but each one who looked was saved."

"What must I do . . . to be saved?"

"Believe on the Lord Jesus, and you will be saved."

Barabbas bent over on his side on the bench. There was silence momentarily. Then he spoke. "God of my fathers . . . I have been trying to rid our land . . . of these foreigners, . . . but they kept coming . . . I am hurt . . . I am spent . . . I don't care if You heal this flesh, . . . but I do want eternal healing . . . I do want to be delivered . . . I saw Your Son, Jesus, . . . when He suffered . . . a just man for us sinners . . . I now understand, and I . . . I now turn from my sins . . . and turn to You . . . for deliverance . . . Deliver me in Jesus, . . . I ask . . . I join my friend Hamath . . . in believing You to heal me . . . from within . . . I believe in the words . . . of Your servant . . . Simon . . . Oh, God . . . save me in Jesus!"

"Aaughhh!" Barabbas screamed out and then he became limp on his side. His energy was spent. His body seemed as if it would cease to exist at any moment. His breathing became shallower than before and now out of rhythm.

Hamath looked at Simon. "He's not going to make it." Hamath held Barabbas' hand, and with his other hand, took a wet cloth and wiped his forehead.

Simon took a few steps toward Barabbas' body. He placed his hands on his head. Matthias, James, and Judas moved in closer and put their hands on Simon's shoulder. "Lord Jesus, we have heard his prayer, asking You to save him. Please show us a sign of his salvation. In Your name, I pray."

Simon took his hands off his head and stepped back. Hamath stood up beside Simon and the others. As they looked at Barabbas, a radiating light covered his body, from head to toe. His body began to straighten on the bench. The mangled flesh on his arms, legs, and face began to heal over. His back arched momentarily and then straightened. All his flesh was restored as if he had never been beaten. Then the radiance faded into the darkness of the cell . . . Barabbas stopped breathing.

The group in the cell stood there in silence . . . watching . . . waiting. But Barabbas remained motionless.

"Lord, thank You for his eternal healing," said Simon.

"Amen, amen," said the others.

✝✝✝

"I am nursing a viper in Rome's bosom," Tiberius once said. *"I am educating a Phaethon who will mishandle the fiery sun-chariot and scorch the whole world."* Caligula smiled as he thought of this description given to him by the aging Tiberius. *"A viper,"* Tiberius? *"A roaring lion"* would have been a better description.

"Guards!" cried Caligula.

Several guards appeared. "Yes, O Divine One?"

"Do we have some fresh prisoners?"

"O Divine One, you slaughtered over 160,000 in last week's celebrations. There are perhaps a few hundred remaining."

"Then let's have a circus tomorrow, and let them dance and box for us. See to it that they have no clothing." Caligula walked over to the western window. He could see the sea's inlet from a distance. "Oh, and see to it that all the ships in Puteoli are aligned, two-by-two, lengthwise, and tied together. I want them to reach the Baiae."

"But that's nearly three miles! Why, Divine One?"

"Someone once said that the chance of me becoming emperor would be easier than for someone to ride a horse dry shod across the Gulf of Baiae . . . I plan to ride a horse to Baiae soon." He turned to the guard. "Make sure there is enough dirt on board for the horses."

The guards dismissed themselves as the emperor looked out across the hills of the imperial city. *Let's see if the gods can top this!*

† † †

Acts 9:26

P aul was ready to return to Jerusalem. The Lord had told him to confer with Peter. He was not afraid to return, for he knew he could trust in the words of his Lord. Paul had lost a few pounds since his days in Jerusalem, plus he now had a full beard and was no longer wearing any priestly garments. Jacob had sewn him some leather sandals that strapped around his legs to the bottom of his knees. Jacob had also fixed him a leather belt that contained several pouches for parchments and writing materials—things he found very handy when he was alone in the desert receiving words from Jesus. In return, Paul repaired Jacob's camping tent, making it waterproof again. Jacob's family was sad to see him leave, but received great comfort in knowing Jesus better and receiving Him in their whole family.

The ride into Jerusalem was much different than when he left. Saul the Conqueror, was now Paul the Least. The more time he spent with Jesus, the more he realized how much human nature could cloud the reality of the spirit world. "Grace" was a new word in Paul's vocabulary, and "mercy" was as close to grace as any spiritual thought. Yes, Paul had learned a lot in the desert sand dunes. But it was time to communicate with the brethren; it was time to unite his calling with the calling of the apostles.

Paul remembered the villa not far from the temple grounds. He remembered the discussion with Joseph of Arimathea who challenged him on the street. At that encounter, he marveled that any Jew would dare challenge a rabbi, but now he realized how much greater a spiritual man Joseph was than he himself. Paul smiled as he thought about his previous life as a self-centered, egotistical, power-hungry Pharisee. *"Assistant of the Head*

Schoolmaster of the School of Hillel"? Wow! If the Sanhedrin would only hear him now.

Before reaching the villa, Paul dismounted from his horse and began to walk the final street. He watched the street vendors doing their usual tricks of trying to get a sale from a passerby. He was constantly being approached by young children asking for a coin or item of value that they could trade for something to their liking. He stopped near the closed gate of the villa and waited . . . After about an hour, he saw a man heading toward the gate. He appeared as a man of well-fashioned upbringing—not poorly dressed as most on the street. The man knocked at the gate. This was Paul's opportunity.

"Excuse me, sir?" Paul approached him.

"Yes? How may I help you?"

"My name is Paul; I am from out of town, and I am looking for some followers of the Way and one of their leaders named Peter. I do hope you may be able to help me?"

The man looked at Paul and then spoke with someone through a small door window. "One moment, Paul, and I will speak with you." The man stepped inside the villa gate and closed it behind him. In a few minutes he came back out, but with him were several men; one was of slender to medium build, but the other was built like a bear—the size of two men! They came out on the street to where Paul was standing, brushing some of the road dust off his horse.

"Paul, my name is Barnabas; these men are my friends. Before we help you, can you tell us why you are seeking followers of the Way?"

Paul put his horse brush away. "Yes, I am a follower of Jesus. I was converted near the city of Damascus. I have spent some time studying the things of the Messiah, but He has spoken to me and told me to return to Jerusalem to meet with a man called Peter and to share my story." Paul stopped speaking. He felt he had given enough information that would either allow him entrance into the villa or to be denied entrance and sent away.

Barnabas spoke softly to the others and then turned back to Paul. "I think we may be able to help you." Barnabas reached out his hand to clasp Paul's. Paul obliged, hoping it was the right response. "Please follow me." The men started to go inside the gate, but stopped when they noticed that Paul was not following them.

"My horse could sure use a rest with some water and hay."

Barnabas looked at the others. "Hamath and I will take him around back; we'll catch up with you and the others soon." Then, looking at Paul: "Bring your horse and follow us."

As they were dismantling the saddle and bags from Paul's horse, Barnabas noticed the parchments, books, and writing materials. "It looks as if you may be well-versed in the Sacred Writings?"

Paul smiled. "My parchments and books give me away . . . I am a former rabbi and a Pharisee."

Barnabas stopped and looked at Paul more closely. "Where did you say you were from?"

"I was recently in Damascus, but I'm from Tarsus."

"Would you happen to know of a rabbi named Saul of Tarsus?"

Paul knew he had to speak the truth, but he had to get Barnabas and Hamath to listen to his story. "Yes, I know him quite well. He was commissioned to destroy the group of which I am now a part. He put many of the followers in prison here in this city. Then he got permission by the high priest to go to Damascus and arrest any leaders of the followers in that region. But something happened to Saul on his way into that town. It was at noon, on a clear day, that a great light shone from the heavens and caused him and his entourage to fall from their horses. The others saw the light, and some claimed to have heard an unintelligible sound—but this Saul heard a voice coming from within the great light: 'Saul, Saul, why are you persecuting Me?' Saul looked into the great light and saw a figure of a man. 'Who are you, Lord?' he asked. The Lord replied, 'I am Jesus, whom you persecute. Don't you find it hard to pray against your conscience!?' Saul was astonished at what he was hearing, for indeed his conscience had been bothering him ever since the stoning of Stephen. On his knees, he bowed his head and asked, 'My Lord, what would You have me to do now?' And He said, 'Get up; go into the city and you will be told what to do.'"

Barnabas interrupted. "Are you saying that the one who persecuted us is now one of us?"

"Please allow me to finish the story and you will understand it better."

"Well, let's sit down first, and then you may continue."

Hamath continued to care for the horse nearby as Paul and Barnabas sat on some straw. Paul continued his story. "The light disappeared, but Saul was blinded by it. The others led him by the hand into the city, where he lodged three days without sight. Then the Lord spoke to a follower of the Way, an Ananias, and told him to go lay hands on Saul and he would receive his sight. Ananias also had a word from the Lord to tell Saul. 'I have chosen him to carry My name to nations, to kings, and to the people of Israel. I will show him how much suffering he must endure for My name's sake.' Ananias obeyed the Lord and went to Saul and healed him of his blindness.

"Saul immediately proclaimed in the Damascus synagogue that Jesus was indeed the Messiah, the Son of God. He began to show the Jews there how Jesus fulfilled the prophecies of the long-awaited Messiah and called on them to repent and seek the Lord for deliverance from their sins. Many believed in Jesus, but the local priest incited the men of the synagogue to capture him and stone him. However, several of the men who believed Saul's message was genuine smuggled him out of the city.

"After that, Saul met with the Lord out in the desert area east of Damascus for about three years. During that time, Saul was taught many things by the Spirit concerning law and grace. God, in His grace and mercy, stopped Saul from further persecutions of the Way and made him a witness of Jesus in Damascus. It is now believed that he is being sought by the high priest in order to arrest him and to put him to death."

"And how did you come to know of this conversion of Saul?" asked Barnabas.

"Once it was revealed that the Jews and the government officials of King Aretas were seeking to capture and kill Saul, a follower of that fine city recommended that he have his name changed, and so he did. Saul of Tarsus is now known as Paul— Paul of Tarsus . . . so here I speak before you, this hour, to testify of how Jesus met with me and changed my life."

The atmosphere in the stable became an eerie quiet. Paul was not sure what these two men thought, but he knew he had come to Jerusalem under the direction of the Spirit of Christ.

Barnabas was the first to speak. "Is it possible for the one who is responsible for the stoning of our brethren to become one of us?"

"God is my witness," said Paul. "What I did to the brethren, I did in ignorance."

Hamath grunted. "If Jesus can deliver and forgive Barabbas and me, He can save anyone."

"Yes, He can, Hamath," said Barnabas. "Yes, He can. So this explains why Saul did not return with captives and why the house-to-house arrests ceased." Barnabas sat there for a moment, studying the face of Paul. "And you say you have seen the Lord?"

"Yes, He appeared to me on the road to Damascus, and He has appeared to me in numerous visions in the desert to tell me things about His fulfillment of the Law and the Prophets. It has been a humbling experience to learn how far we rabbis have veered from the truth as He intended."

Barnabas stood up. "This is truly an amazing turn of events," he said. "Saul—or Paul—I think it best that you share your testimony again, after our evening meal, to the disciples and women present. This word needs to spread from first-person accounts and not from us two men only. Many of the women here belong to the families of the other apostles who are out on regional assignments. It will be important for them to hear this from their families when they return."

"That will be fine with me, but I do have a request."

"Yes?"

"Is there a place where I may bathe and rest until the evening meal?"

"Why of course! My apologies for having to talk with you privately, but we have enemies all about us. Listen, Hamath here will finish up with your horse; allow me to show you around."

"Thank you," said Paul.

Paul was ready to clean up, having traveled for nearly six days from Arabia. Barnabas led him down along the porches. "Please allow me to show you where the men's bathing area is located. After that, it will be several hours before our dinner meal. You may rest awhile, if the children will let you. Come now, and I will show you where everything is located."

Barnabas turned and walked away from the stable area and entered through the rear of the villa. Paul had to pick up his walking speed to keep up with the energetic Barnabas. The bath houses were below street level: one for the men and another for the women. The women had rooms on the upper level, while the men were on ground level—for protection. There were couples and family dwellings around the corner on both levels. This was truly a magnificent villa for such a group as this.

After he cleaned himself up, Paul was shown a room for him to rest awhile. He was grateful for the hospitality of such people; it made him feel a bit nauseous knowing how he formerly treated some of their friends—perhaps even family members. "Oh, my Lord, please make me a humble and acceptable servant in this place, I pray in Your blessed name, amen." Paul then closed his eyes and put his trust in the One who led him back to this villa.

Two lads began to push on Paul. He opened his eyes and then smiled. "Sir," they said in harmony. "Dinner is ready; please come now." And off they ran. Paul was amazed at how innocent and trusting were children. He had forgotten his childhood until Jesus invaded his life. Now it was like reliving as a child again. He arose, straightened himself up, and walked toward the dining area. He was greeted cordially by some and was soon placed in a reclining position beside Barnabas. The table was a parade to the senses, chock full of fresh vegetables, certain meats, and seasonal fruits.

"Before we begin," said Elder James, "let us bow in humble appreciation for such a meal as this. God of our fathers and of our Lord Jesus the Christ, we thank You for supplying our needs this hour. We pray for the prisoners and the poor and the misguided. We pray for our guest, Paul of Tarsus, who will share his testimony after our fine dinner. Bless the hands who prepared this wonderful meal, and we bless You for our salvation. In Jesus' name we pray, amen."

"Amen, amen," the others said.

"Amen," said Paul. And the eating began with much talk and laughter.

Barnabas kept Paul engaged in the discussions going on nearby. In about thirty minutes or so, everyone seemed to be either getting up or spreading out from the table. The children were making their way into the courtyard to play while the women were busy putting leftover food in carrying baskets.

Paul observed the women's project. "What are they doing?" he asked Barnabas.

"After each group meal, many of the followers go out to certain areas of the city to distribute the food to those in need. This one act of kindness has brought many people to a belief in the Way of our Master."

"Wow."

"Yes, it is putting feet to the acts of Jesus. He was careful to feed the hungry, and, just as He promised, if we share our fortunes, the blessings come back to us."

"And have the assemblies grown in our city?" asked Paul.

"Yes, into the thousands. There are house assemblies all over the city; we cannot keep up with the new growth. The apostles stay busy visiting the assemblies in the city and throughout Judea. They spend a lot of time witnessing, teaching, and ordaining new elders."

"And is that Peter?" Paul asked, pointing to Elder James.

"No, that is Elder James; he is our lead pastor of the Jerusalem fellowship. Peter should arrive soon."

Paul felt very comfortable with Barnabas. He was a friendly man and seemed positive about everything and everyone.

At that moment, Peter arrived. He made his way into the dining area and sat down for a meal.

"Come," said Barnabas to Paul. "Allow me to introduce you to him."

"Okay, but please allow me to break the news to him as to who I used to be."

"Oh, yes, certainly."

It was announced that there would be a meeting with Paul in the upper chamber and that the men and women who wished to hear a word from the guest should gather now. About thirty men and about a dozen women began to assemble, while others prepared their children for evening stories from the Sacred Writings before bedtime. In John's absence, Barnabas led the group in a few psalms of praise. Peter read a passage of Scripture. Then

Elder James stood and spoke. "Brothers and sisters, in lieu of an exposition on the sayings of our Lord, I would like for our guest, Paul of Tarsus, to come now and give us his testimony."

Paul made his way to the front. He turned and looked out into the crowd. "Grace and peace to you, my brothers and sisters. I consider this an honor to be able to share of my experience in meeting our Lord Jesus. As I mentioned to some of the men earlier, my encounter with Jesus comes through my knowing Saul of Tarsus, a rabbi of great harm to the followers of the Way . . ." Paul continued—as Saul—to tell of how he met Jesus and how Jesus had sent him back to Jerusalem. "Once it was revealed that the Jews and the government officials, under King Aretas, were seeking to capture and kill Saul, a follower of that fine city recommended that he have his name changed, and so he did. Saul of Tarsus is now known as Paul—Paul of Tarsus." Some gasped. "So here I stand before you this hour to testify of how Jesus met with me and changed my life."

Talk began among all those in the meeting. Some of the followers did not trust him. "Can he who was sent out by the high priest to jail us now be one of us?" Others wanted Peter or Elder James to speak.

Barnabas spoke first. "Brothers and sisters, we have heard a truly remarkable testimony tonight. Saul of Tarsus, who is now Paul, has given a detailed testimony of his encounter with and surrender to our Lord Jesus. Before any further judgment is cast upon his testimony, I would like to say that he has previously met with Hamath and me; we have heard his testimony and have not been warned by the Holy Spirit of any deceit in his words."

Peter stood up next. He walked over to Paul. "How do we know that this is not a trap? Can we trust the one who has imprisoned some of our brothers and sisters?"

Barnabas stood up. "It has been nearly three years since Saul troubled our fellowships. This explains everything that has happened during his absence—no further arrests and no report of his journeys in the regions."

"Then let us hear him speak in the local synagogues and see if, indeed, a great miracle has occurred. One or two of us will be with him, at all times, to listen and to confirm that his gospel of Jesus is the same as ours. So until you hear otherwise, let us commit to pray for his new ministry that is about to occur. If no one else has a word from our Lord concerning this, we will dismiss in prayer . . ." No one spoke. "Barnabas, would you lead our prayer?"

"God of our fathers, You are a gracious and merciful God. You have provided us with deliverance from our sins. We are grateful for our Lord Jesus and the presence of the Holy Spirit. Now we call on Your Spirit to give us a discerning heart on the testimony of Saul who is now called Paul. May You reveal Your will in this matter and give him a confirming voice as he preaches the gospel, in the name of our precious Savior, amen."

"Amen, amen," said the others. As they dismissed, Peter called out to Mary, "Mary, please come here." Turning to Paul, "Paul, this is Mary, the mother of our Lord."

Paul did not know what to say. He bowed his head and kissed her hand. "Never, in a million years, would I have thought that I would meet the mother of our Messiah."

"It is always a blessing to meet those of His who are answering the call to spread the good news of salvation. Do not be afraid; He will be with you always."

Barnabas walked over to Peter, Paul, and Mary. "I will show our guest back to his room."

The next morning, Saul awakened to the crow of a rooster. He rubbed his eyes. *Thank you, Lord, for a good restful night,* he prayed to himself. *I pray You will guide our hearts in a harmonious way today. Don't let me be a wedge in this fellowship, but an asset as we continue to tell others about the Way of salvation.*

He rose up, dressed appropriately, and made his way to the back of the villa. There was a gate, unchained, that led to the stables. He walked over to them to check on his horse. Hamath and Barnabas were already there, feeding and watering the animals. There was a younger boy who was gathering hen eggs from the nests. Paul smiled as the boy ran past him and through the gate.

"Good morning, Paul," Barnabas said. "Did you sleep well?"

"Yes, my friend, very well indeed. Now, are you an apostle?"

"No, I'm not one of them, but I did meet Jesus a few times in the Galilee area."

"And Hamath?" Hamath looked their way and managed a partial smile.

"He's not an apostle either, but came to know Jesus later on. Hamath doesn't speak very much, but when he does, it is worth listening to. I think he has a gift of discernment."

"That is such a needed gift among the assemblies."

"Yes, I agree."

"Uh, has he spoken about me?"

"No, not yet." Barnabas smiled. "So I guess you're okay so far."

"May I ask about last night's meeting?"

"Sure, no one has spoken against you, so, like I said, I guess you're okay so far."

"Oh, that's good. Thank you, Barnabas; may our Lord bless you with His peace and grace today."

"And thank you for that fine testimony last night; I sat there drinking from every word you said. Our Lord is genuinely at work among us."

"Yes, He is," said Paul. "Yes, He is . . . Say, would you and Hamath like to go with me to a synagogue today?"

"I can't speak for Hamath, but, sure, I'd like to go hear you preach. How about it, Hamath?" Hamath grunted and then smiled. "I take that as a 'yes!'" After breakfast, the three of them left the villa.

Peter and Elder James were in the upper chamber praying for the other apostles who were out in the Judea, Samaria, and Galilee regions, checking on numerous assemblies. The assemblies were growing, and there was peace as the fear of the Lord and the comfort of the Spirit were being manifested among them.

It was nearing lunch time; Peter and James had stopped praying and were discussing Paul's itinerary. "He wants to preach in different synagogues," said Peter.

"It's risky," said Elder James, "even though he is well-suited for such a ministry. But we are experiencing peace among the assemblies." At that moment, there was a pounding at the front gates. Someone ran out to look through the window, and then the gate was opened. Barnabas, Paul, and Hamath came in rather hurriedly and shut the gates.

"Let's see what's going on," Peter said. They went downstairs and walked over toward them. Paul and Barnabas were a bit shaken, but Hamath seemed to be at ease. "What did you do to them, Hamath? Take them down to your old hangout?"

Hamath smiled. "Paul preached, and some did not like him." Paul sat there for a moment, catching his breath.

"Where did you preach this morning?" Peter asked Paul.

"The Synagogue of Freedmen, where I first met Stephen."

"Oh, my," said Elder James. "You must have bumped a hornet's nest over there."

"They sure didn't ask me to return. There was a group of Hellenists there who was highly offended at my presentation."

"They cried out, 'Stone him! Stone him!'" said Hamath. "But I wouldn't let them."

"Hamath took us through some different streets and businesses to prevent anyone following us."

"Uh-huh," said Peter. "Just as I suspected—your old hangouts."

Hamath smiled. "I knew they wouldn't follow us through there."

"I think it best that you take it easy in going to the synagogues of Jerusalem," Peter said to Paul.

"Perhaps tomorrow will be a better day." Paul then went to his room and rested for a while.

At the evening prayer time, Paul joined a few others for prayer at the temple. He kept his head covered to avoid being recognized. While praying, Paul had a vision; he saw the Lord speaking to him, saying, "It isn't safe for you to remain in Jerusalem; leave as quickly as possible."

"Paul, Paul." Several men were shaking him. "It's time to go."

When they returned to the villa, the men began to go in different directions, but Paul found Peter and spoke to him. "May I spend some private time with you?"

Peter thought for a moment. "How much time do you need?"

"A month would be nice."

Peter looked at him. "A month?" Peter mulled the request over in his mind. "Paul, I'm a married man with a child; how about a couple of weeks?"

Paul gave an "okay" nod. "There are a number of things the Lord spoke to me about that I want to share with you. Also, you know a lot of things about Jesus and what He taught that would interest me."

"So when do you want to talk?"

"The Lord has told me to leave Jerusalem as quickly as possible; is there a place outside the region that we could visit?"

"What!? You just arrived!"

"The Lord said it wasn't safe for me to be here, and I don't want to hinder the ministry the followers are performing now."

Peter thought for a moment. "How about a little mission trip? I have felt the Lord telling me to go toward the sea and trek northward toward Caesarea for some unfinished business."

Paul thought for a moment. "I do know that area very well, and from there, I can go back to Tarsus and visit my family and some friends. They need to hear about Jesus, and I'm sure they have heard a lot about me."

"And you need to leave Jerusalem for a while," said Peter. "Okay, we'll leave at daybreak and spend a couple of weeks of conversation time."

✝ ✝ ✝

"What have I done!? Guards!"

Sharon walked over, grabbed a soft white cloth and moistened it. She slowly wiped the head of her father. "It's okay, Father," she said. "There's no one here to harm you."

"First it was Agrippa, then Antipas, and now Agrippa again! What has happened!?"

She reached for a cup and carefully put its edge to his lips. "Sip this, father; it will soothe your nerves."

Caiaphas walked in as she put her finger to her lips to keep him from disturbing Annas. He reclined at a nearby table, watching his wife try to comfort a man who, in the past, would even betray his children if it would get him political gain. Caiaphas smiled. *Finally, the old windbag has met his match; he must now deal with death and the devil, and neither one will let him win.* Caiaphas once wanted Annas dead—out of the way of his high priestly dreams. He grew weary of the ploys and plots of his father-in-law.

But Annas got out of favor with the Sanhedrin council. He had made Jonathan the sole high priest, demoting Caiaphas completely. But Jonathan had a speech impediment and was crippled.

The council felt the high priest must be able to carry the ceremonial utensils and sacrifices by himself, but Jonathan could not do so. Annas tried to help him, but was getting too old to carry things himself. The council had had enough of Annas and his manipulations, so they appealed to the emperor.

As soon as Caligula received this information, he immediately deposed Jonathan and instead assigned the position of high priest to Theophilus, another son of Annas. Furthermore, the emperor ordered Annas to leave the high priest assignments alone. This frustrated Annas, which caused more frustration and bitterness among his sons. Annas was no longer in control.

Emperor Caligula not only took over the assignments of the high priest, he also freed Herod Agrippa from house arrest and gave him back all his previous possessions and political positions. This caused Annas to suddenly become ill.

Caiaphas smiled again. When Sharon looked over at him, he pulled out his knife and with the blunt edge of the blade ran it across his neck while holding out his tongue. Next, he turned the knife around and, with a gesture and a devilish smile, offered the instrument to her. She looked sternly at her husband and rolled her eyes as she continued to cool the fever in Annas' head.

All this mess stands on his shoulders, thought Caiaphas. *He will die with no possessions, no position, and probably without any of his sons close by. Only his daughter will be with him when he passes into the realm of the dead.*

†††

"I want a temple to be built," said Caligula.

"Where, Divine One?" asked the chief of his affairs. "And for which god?"

"Someplace where the people are friendly toward our gods . . . Miletus of Asia sounds like a good place, wouldn't you agree?"

"O Divine One, Miletus has a temple dedicated to Apollo."

"So they do—a large one, I might add. Too large for any other god than myself; I will take its clay and cover it with precious metals and the finest of marble and gemstones."

"For you, Divine One?"

"Of course! You remember Vitellius, that exiled king from Syria, how he fell at my feet and worshiped me? I want my personal temple. Ephesus worships Diana (Latin for Artemis), Pergamum worships Augustus, and Smyrna worships Tiberius."

"And who will be its caretaker?"

"I will be its priest . . . and my horse will be my colleague. Go now and inform the senate of my plans and that I will speak to them of this matter tomorrow."

✝✝✝

As soon as they cleared the western gate of the city of Jerusalem, Paul wanted to know all about the life and ministry of Jesus from Peter's perspective. Paul also wanted Peter to hear of the words he had received from Jesus while he was in the desert. Hours turned into days as they compared revelations each had received from the Master.

What they both discovered was that the new covenant was not only the fulfillment of the old covenants, but was God's last covenant to man. What the old covenants failed to achieve, the new one accomplished. The old covenants failed in bringing man into an eternal relationship with God.

The failure of man's high priest was replaced by an eternal High Priest after the order of Melchizedek. This allowed the putting away of sins to be complete and, therefore, eternal through the shed blood of Jesus, the Lord and the Christ.

"Were you in Jerusalem when the earth shook and the veil of the temple was torn from top to bottom?" Peter asked Paul.

"No, I was in Caesarea—but I heard about it. I marveled that the quake was not felt in Caesarea."

"This signified that God accepted the death of Jesus as the sacrifice for all sins for all time. Man will no longer go to God through an earthly priest for the forgiveness of sins. God is now accessible to all men through Jesus."

Paul shared with Peter how the new covenant was the new testament of how God put His law into the hearts of man. This was the theme of the Master's plan for all to understand and experience. God was transferring Himself from an external Spirit of which to be fearful, to an internal Spirit with whom to live on a continual basis.

Together, these two men made the trip to the coast one of great impact for the unifying of the kingdom of God. They were able to make it to Lydda in four days—longer than usual, because several times they had to stop and talk and even wrote things down as the Spirit impressed them.

"Paul, I want to introduce to you several of the elders of the house assemblies in the area."

"That's great; perhaps I can go and speak at the synagogue in town as well."

"I don't think that is a wise decision at this time, Paul. Remember, you asked for a month of my time, and I'm giving you a couple of weeks. We should focus our attention on who Jesus is, the message of the gospel, and how we are proclaiming that message."

When they arrived at an elder's house, Peter was barely able to introduce Paul when the elder spoke of a man who had fallen off a cliff about eight years ago and was still paralyzed. This man had become a follower of the Way. Peter recognized the urge of the Spirit from within him and sought out this man. When Peter found him (his name was Aeneas), he was lying on a cot. Paul observed how Peter handled this need.

"Aeneas," said Peter. "Our Lord Jesus Christ makes you well right now. Now get up and put away your cot." Aeneas was immediately healed, got up, picked up his cot, and put it away. The elders bowed their heads and worshiped God. Paul stood there in awe of the presence and power of the Son of God through the vessels of a yielded man.

News of this healing brought many to the house where Peter and Paul were planning to stay the night. They decided to stay a few extra days and proclaim the gospel to the people. Many were saved at Lydda and others were delivered of their diseases.

During much of the time, however, Paul and Peter continued to share how Jesus was now working through the apostles. They learned much from each other.

"What do you consider as the signs of an apostle?" Paul asked Peter.

"I think an apostle must be someone who has seen our Lord and has been selected by Him for the ministry. I also believe He promised to protect them from poisons and that they would possess certain gifts for the ministry, such as power to proclaim, discernment, physical healings, and the ability to cast out demons."

Paul thought through this list. "I believe our Lord has called me to witness to peoples of many nations—even kings. I may be an apostle, but I have not had a need to heal people or cast out evil spirits."

"There are plenty of days ahead to confirm your position."

"How do you know if you should heal someone?

"In my experience, I have either heard the Lord direct me to someone or, as with Aeneas, I feel a surge of power within me. It is initiated by the Spirit of our Lord Himself."

"Why?"

"'Why'?"

"I mean, why does He heal some and not others?"

"That is a question I cannot answer. Only our Lord knows the 'why' of select healings.

"When Jesus was on earth, many people followed us from town to town seeking to benefit from the miracles Jesus performed. He did heal many, but He also was wearied by those expecting a miracle at every meeting. Jesus wanted people to believe in Him as the One to deliver them from their sins and not for the miracles He performed."

Now it was Peter's turn to ask a few questions. "Paul? You say you saw our Lord in the brightness of the light on the Damascus road; how did you know it was really Jesus?"

"Well, He said He was Jesus, and He said something that only someone who could have read my mind would know. He said, 'It's hard for you to pray against your conscience.' I was under conviction in my heart that Stephen knew more spiritual truth than I did. I kept praying to God to help me defeat the thoughts of Jesus, but my conscience continued to bother me. When He said that, I knew I was dealing with Jesus as the Son of God. Only God could have heard that prayer and only His Son could have been there beside Him to hear it."

"This blending of God as Father, Son, and Spirit . . . I need help comprehending it, Paul. It seems so mysterious."

"Yes, it is a mystery, but it continues to be revealed to me that they have different functions, even though they are one and the same God. You are a son, a husband, and a father—different functions, yet one person."

Peter reflected on another event. "Jesus once told a Samaritan woman that God is Spirit, and they that worship Him must worship Him in Spirit and in truth. Jesus also identified Himself as truth, and many times He allowed people to bow before Him in worship."

"It appears that the personification of God as an angel in our history may have sometimes been the person of Christ. This has always puzzled me in my rabbinical studies—until now. God became a man . . . but a man without human sin."

"Mary conceived Jesus as a virgin. She said an angel told her that the Holy Spirit would overwhelm her and she would be with child of the Spirit of God."

"Oh, I do hope I may return to Jerusalem again and spend some time talking with her. I have so many questions to ask."

Peter laughed. "I hope you don't ask her for a month! She's a very busy woman. She treats every follower of Jesus as one of her very own children. She is constantly traveling throughout the region, checking on every house assembly, making sure all needs are being met. And her faith in her Son meeting those needs is very strong. We are so blessed to have her ministry."

Fifteen days of travel and they were still in Lydda. But Peter was in no hurry because he wanted to check on the followers throughout the Valley of Sharon where Philip had done much ministry.

On the other hand, Paul was anxious to ride on to Caesarea to board a ship for Tarsus.

"Well, I think we've picked each other's brain enough for a while," said Peter. "Why don't you press on to Caesarea and catch a ship."

"I think you're right. I feel in my heart that I need to put more distance between me and Jerusalem for a while."

"I agree, but let's have some prayer time together before we part." And pray they did. Afterwards, they embraced and split up. Peter then returned to the house in Lydda.

Later that day, several men came to Peter from Joppa. "Sir, we have been sent by many disciples of the Way to get you to come with haste to Joppa, for one of our beloved women who is mighty in deeds for the Lord, has taken ill and has died."

Peter immediately left with the men. When he neared the house, several followers of the Way recognized him and came running up to him. "Peter! We need you inside immediately!"

Peter immediately recognized the crippled beggar he and John healed at the temple gate. "And blessings to you, Justus. And how are those legs doing?"

Justus smiled. "Strong as ever! . . . Peter, this is my brother-in-law, David. I told him that if anyone could heal my sister, Peter could!"

Peter wanted to correct him as to who really does the healing, but the urgency he saw in their faces made him move on into the house quickly. As they entered, there were some women wailing, both downstairs and upstairs in the bedroom.

"Hurry, Peter," said Justus. "Upstairs!" They went up to her room, the rest of the women following. The women were widows whom Justus' sister, Tabitha (her Greek name was Dorcas), had ministered to by sewing them many pieces of linen and clothing. In fact, the women were gathering around Peter showing him the fine pieces of clothing Tabitha had made them.

Peter made his way closer to the bed. He looked at her lifeless body. The women had bathed her for burial. He looked at the sorrow in David and Justus' eyes.

"Get these women out of here, please," Peter said to Justus.

The women stopped their wailing and stared at Peter for his rudeness. "Okay, ladies, you heard the man. Now go downstairs and stay put until we call you back up." Justus began herding the women down the steps. When he turned around, David was leaving the room as well and shut the door.

"What's going on?" asked Justus.

"He said for you and me to stay with the womenfolk and to keep them busy while he prayed."

"Well, what's with that!? I want to see what he does."

David grabbed Justus' arm. "Do you trust him?"

"I certainly do! Look at this new pair of legs!"

"Then let's do as he says. Come help me entertain these widows."

"Uh, they make me nervous!"

Peter knelt beside the bed and placed his head between his knees, praying, "My Master and Lord, Jesus. Once again I beseech Your wisdom in this matter of healing this woman. She has done much good for the community of those who need help. I ask that You heal her that she may bring glory to Your name and that salvation may come to many because of her testimony. My Lord, be glorified in this place." Peter continued to pray over and over again that Jesus would heal this woman and that she would be used mightily to bring salvation to this city.

"Peter! I have heard your prayer. Now stand up and tell Tabitha to rise."

Peter stood to his feet and, facing her, said, "Tabitha, wake up!" Tabitha's eyes opened immediately, and she saw Peter. She rose up, putting her feet to the side of the bed. Peter took her hand and helped her stand. "Tabitha, someone downstairs needs to see you. Now put on your shoes and let's go downstairs."

She looked around. "Why are all these garments of mine scattered all over my bed and the room?"

"Why don't we let the women downstairs answer that question. Come with me to the doorway for a moment." Peter opened the door and walked out onto the ledge holding Tabitha's hand. When David saw her, he leaped to his feet and ran for her. Justus saw her and started leaping and praising the Lord. The women were astonished; some had become followers of the Way, but others were not committed until they saw with their own eyes this miracle standing before them.

"We washed her dead body," one of the uncommitted said. "Now I come to her Healer to be cleansed of my sins." And many more became followers of the Way, seeing the miracle and believing in the testimony of Peter about Jesus, the Christ.

While preaching in the city, Peter resided with Simon, a tanner. Devout Jews never touched a dead animal for fear of becoming defiled. But Simon's widowed mother had insisted he stay with them and share with her son about the Way of salvation. Peter was careful how he mingled with the items and the people in Simon's house and his workshop. But he stayed there for a long time, preaching the gospel in the region.

† † †

"When will he die?"

"Soon."

"Can you be more precise?"

"It is contingent."

The centurion hit him in the jaw. "This is not a riddle!" Apollonius lowered his head and spit out some blood. "You're wasting my time," said the centurion, "or you're stalling, hoping to save some more time for yourself?"

"The emperor will die soon, and that is all I have to say."

(At the emperor's quarters.) "Did he say more?"

"No, Divine One," replied Senator Demarkus. "He has been beaten and drugged . . . Shall we proceed with the execution?"

Caligula lay in his bed in silence for a couple of minutes. Then he stood up and walked to his window facing the east. Each minute of silence seemed to last for an eternity . . . "Tiberius once said that *Sol* gave him a word of prophecy for those troublesome Jews: 'Straighten them out' was the prophecy. This soothsayer from Egypt is the same as his neighboring Jews—stubborn!" He turned to Demarkus. "Let's wear him down some more. I will permit Tiberius' prophecy to trump this soothsayer's meaningless words. Bring some Egyptian slaves before him; let him watch them being beaten and killed before his face. Kill at least one a day until his prophesies are more specific. That should straighten him out."

"As you wish, Divine One." Demarkus slowly exited from the room. As he walked out into the corridor, he was joined by his guards. They stopped in the courtyard. "It is time to stop this madness," he said to his chief guard. "Let the Egyptian proceed with his plan."

"When, your Excellency?"

"Tonight."

The morning stillness was broken by a scream from the emperor's quarters. A house maiden had discovered the emperor's lifeless body in his blood-stained bedding. The Egyptian house servant stood nearby to clean up the bed, after the body was removed. *The prophet spoke the truth,* he thought. *Now he will be released.*

Anno
Domini
40
Circa

The further away from Jerusalem, the less tension was felt between the Jews and the Romans. In fact, there were God-fearing Romans sprinkled throughout the Middle East. Cornelius, a centurion of the Italian Regiment, worshiped God. He was stationed in Caesarea because of the growing unrest in Judea. He and members of his family believed in the God of the Jews and prayed to Him regularly. Cornelius also had a reputation for his generosity to those in need.

One afternoon, during his regular prayer time, he saw, in a vision, an angel that spoke to him. "Cornelius!"

Cornelius rubbed his eyes to make sure he wasn't dreaming—he wasn't! He began to tremble. "Yes, my lord?"

"I am a messenger sent from God; your prayers and your generosity to the needy have ascended into heaven for a memorial before Him. Now send some men to Joppa and ask for a man named Peter. He is staying in a house by the seashore with Simon the tanner. This Peter will tell you what you must do."

When the angel departed, Cornelius rubbed his eyes again. He could not believe what had just happened. Quickly, he called several of his servants and a trusted soldier among those who waited on him and told them of the vision. "This angel told me to send some men to Joppa to find a man by the name of Peter . . . Quickly! I want you men to go to Joppa, today, and find him!"

The next day, about noon, Peter headed to the housetop of Simon to pray. This was his usual habit for a time of prayer. But, while praying, he became very hungry. *I wonder if Simon's wife is preparing a meal.* He stood up and walked back downstairs to

Simon's tanning room. Dead animal carcasses were lying everywhere—disgusting!

"Hello, Peter," said Simon. "What can I get for you?"

"Ugh! These animals are off limits to us Jews . . . now I know why!" Peter put a cloth to his nose and mouth. "I was about to ask for a meal; I skipped this morning's breakfast to have some time with my Lord. But now I'm unsure I can eat anything."

"Don't you worry about a thing; I said I would keep you as long as is necessary. You go back to your affairs, and I'll help the women put together something for you."

Peter made his way back upstairs, wondering if he had already defiled himself by walking around the tanner's workshop or lying on the straw-filled canvas bedding that was provided him. He lay there, waiting . . . However, while waiting, Peter had a vision from God. He saw a massive sheet come down from heaven, bound at all four corners. Now, when it was placed before him, all kinds of four-footed animals, wild beasts, creeping things, and wild birds were in this sheet.

Next, he heard a voice from heaven say, "Peter, you're hungry; kill and eat!"

"No way, my Lord! You know I have never eaten anything from these common and unclean creatures."

"Listen, what God has made clean you must never call common or unclean!"

This vision occurred three times and each time the sheet was returned into heaven. After the third time, Peter sat up and tried to figure out what all this meant. While he was thinking this over, the three men sent by Cornelius arrived at Simon's house and stood at his front gate.

They knocked on the wooden gate support. Simon saw them from a window; he put down his skinning knife and walked to the front entrance. "Yes? May I help you?"

"Sir, we're looking for a man called Peter; is he lodging with you?"

Simon observed the three men for a moment. "He's in and out; remain here and I'll see if he's in."

While the exchange was occurring at the gate, the Spirit interrupted Peter's ponderings. "Peter, there are three men at the gate seeking an audience with you. Go down now and speak with them, for I have sent them. Do not question them, but do what they ask of you."

As Simon was about to reenter his house, Peter met him at the door. "Peter, these men—"

"Yes, I know they seek me," Peter interrupted. "Allow them to come in and I will speak with them."

Simon turned around, scratched his head, and made his way back to the gate to let the men enter. They met Peter at the front entryway. "I am Peter; what can I do for you?"

The men bowed. "Sir, we serve a centurion in Caesarea named Cornelius. He is a righteous man who fears the God of the Jews and has been very beneficial to the Jews in his area. A few days ago, he was visited by an angel who told him to come seek for you and ask you to come to his house and have a word with him."

Peter mulled this over in his head for a moment. "I will do as you have requested. But come in now and rest a bit. I want to send for some other men to travel with me. Please lodge with me here tonight and in the morning we will get a fresh start for the journey to Caesarea."

"As you wish."

"Simon, please show these men where they can care for their animals and themselves."

"Come, follow me, and I'll show you the stable." Simon took them back out to the front and led the men around the side of his house to his stable.

†††

Cornelius was anxiously awaiting the entourage from Joppa. Runners finally sighted the men returning, so Cornelius went out and gathered as many friends and family as he could find. By the time Peter and his company arrived, the house was full. As Peter walked toward the house, Cornelius came up to him and fell at his feet to worship him.

"Stop," said Peter. "Stand up, Cornelius, for I am a man, just as you." When he stood up, Peter noticed something familiar about him. "Have we met before?"

"Maybe. While stationed in Capernaum, I sought your Master to heal my servant. He graciously turned aside and healed him. I have never forgotten that act of Jesus."

"Yes, I remember now. Jesus blessed you for your great faith. And your servant?"

"He remains well; he and his family are still with me. I was transferred to Caesarea several years ago."

He brought Peter into the large house. Inside, Peter saw many adults and young people. Children were playing nearby. Things looked different inside Cornelius' house; in fact, this was the first time Peter had ever been in a Roman Gentile's house. Although it was beautifully decorated, Peter still felt uncomfortable with this assignment. *Why, Lord?* he thought. *Why are You telling me to come to the Gentiles?* Things remained quiet. Peter looked out into the entryway and saw his Jewish brethren standing there. He motioned for them to come inside as well. Although they were reluctant, he managed to get the Joppa brethren in the doorway.

Peter made sure the men from Joppa heard his statements as plainly as everyone else. Turning to Cornelius and his gathering, he spoke. "You all should know how awkward this is that we Jews have come inside this house, for it is against our law to enter into the dwellings of people outside our race. However, a few days ago, God spoke to me—three times!—teaching me not to call any man common or unclean. So I did not turn down your request to come. Here I am; what is it that you wish to know?"

"I have been fasting for four days," said Cornelius. "A few days ago, while praying, a man appeared to me in radiant clothing and spoke to me, saying, 'Cornelius, your prayers and your generosity to the needy have ascended into heaven for a memorial before God. Now send some men to Joppa and ask for a man named Peter. He is staying in a house by the seashore with Simon, the tanner. This Peter will tell you what you must do.' This is why I sent for you, and you have honored me by coming before us. Therefore, we all stand before God to hear what He has to say to us through you."

Peter immediately felt the power of the Lord's presence to speak. "I fully understand now that God has set up this meeting to show that, with Him, there are no prejudices among men, but in every nation, whoever fears God and works righteousness can come to Him and be accepted by Him."

Peter continued to share the gospel of Jesus Christ to the household of Cornelius. In detail, he taught them how Jesus died for all men's sins and that He rose from the dead three days later. "This is the gospel—the good news—that we proclaim. And this same Jesus will return to judge both the living and the dead. This is what our prophets foretold, and, in the name of Jesus, those who believe in Him will be saved from their sins."

While Peter continued to preach, suddenly the Holy Spirit came upon those who were hearing the Word. The presence of the Spirit was confirmed by the understanding of the language of the Gentiles by the followers who came with Peter. They were astonished as they heard Cornelius and his gathering speak another language magnifying God.

Peter was amazed and turned to his brethren. "Can we forbid baptism to these Gentiles, since they have received the same Holy Spirit just as we?" The other followers just stood there in awe and wonderment, afraid to say anything lest it disrupt the pure power of the Holy Spirit.

Peter told the household of Cornelius that they should obey the Lord who just saved them by being baptized in Jesus' name. This they did gladly; afterwards, they asked Peter to stay a few days to teach them more. The brethren from Joppa returned home while Peter lodged with Cornelius for about a week. Cornelius also introduced him to the servant whom Jesus had healed. It was a wonderful experience to see and speak with people who had encountered Jesus.

Acts 11

*F*rom Joppa, the news of the Gentiles receiving the Holy Spirit reached the apostles and followers throughout Judea. The news was quite astonishing—so much so, that they eagerly awaited the return of Peter for a full disclosure.

When Peter stopped in Joppa on his return trip, he heard that the news had reached Jerusalem. "Please gather the six men who went with me to Caesarea to the Gentile's house. I need them to go with me to Jerusalem."

The men met with Peter for fellowship and discussion. "Brothers, what you and I witnessed in Cornelius' house was the fulfillment of the vision I received at Simon's house. I was not prepared for this breakthrough of the Way to enter into other nations. And you know, many of our Jewish brethren will object to this encounter. That's why it is necessary that you join me in this report so that all Jewish followers of Jesus understand and accept what the Lord has begun to do in the Gentile world." They listened, and then they prayed together. Afterwards, they decided it was best they travel with the apostle to Jerusalem.

The trip into Jerusalem was a bit more subdued than when Peter had previously left with Paul. When they arrived at the villa headquarters, everyone was glad to see him again.

"Grace and peace to you my brother," said Elder James as he embraced Peter. "And who are these men who travel with you?"

"Grace and peace to you. These men are fellow followers of the Way; they were here on that great Day of Pentecost when our Lord energized us to speak to many Jewish brethren. When they heard and saw the power of the Holy Spirit, they became followers of our Master, returned to Joppa, and began a warm and growing fellowship of followers in that town. They also accompanied me to Caesarea to witness the outpouring of the Lord's Spirit upon the first Gentile converts in that fine city."

"Peter! Peter!" John shouted, as he ran down the steps from the upper chamber, embraced his friend, and spun him around.

"Whoa, you young rascal, you! You're making me dizzy."

"I thought maybe you retired down by the seashore and started fishing again." John was always a warm sight to see, and so full of life and the glow of God upon him.

"No, my friend, I'm afraid there is no such thing as 'retirement' in our Lord's work."

"Did Elder James tell you about the great meeting we have planned for you and the wonderful report you'll be giving us?"

James smiled. "I was just about to tell him, but we were still chatting—"

"We have a meeting? Oh . . . that's fine. In fact, I am anxious to share what our Lord is doing in other regions—and these men have come to help me with my report."

"Yes, of course," responded James. "But I'm sure you will want to tidy up and refresh yourselves. John, please show these men our guest quarters and where we will meet for supper before our meeting."

John escorted the six men across the courtyard, talking to them all, while Peter and James walked toward Peter's living quarters. "Oh, to be that young again," James said.

Peter nodded in agreement. "Yes, when I go to heaven, I want to be that very age—that is, if we can choose."

The supper meal was delicious; Peter had missed the local delicacies of his Jewish diet. The Gentiles ate very differently than that to which he was accustomed, but, nevertheless, he ate with Cornelius for about a week, believing that God had broken down certain eating regulations established in the Sacred Writings.

After the meal, everyone reassembled in the villa courtyard, including the elders and converted priests of the city. The news of the Gentile conversions had reached Jerusalem, which made this report an important meeting for Peter.

Elder James called the meeting into order, asking John to pray for the meeting. "Master—our Messiah—Jesus, we pause for a time of instruction from You and Your servant, our beloved Peter. Give him Your words to speak to our hearts this day, I pray in Your holy name, amen."

"Amen, amen," the others responded.

Peter stood before the crowded courtyard. "Brothers and sisters, I am happy to address those who call themselves followers of the Way. I and these brethren from Joppa were privileged to see our blessed Spirit work among the Gentiles in Caesarea—"

A priest interrupted Peter: "We heard that you went into the house of an uncircumcised Roman centurion and ate with him and his family!"

"You have defiled yourself!" another priest shouted.

"Brothers, brothers," spoke James. "This report is not from some foreign person. Let us hear the full report, and then we can make our comments known."

"As I was saying . . ." Peter then gave a detailed report of his vision from Jesus, three times, and how He had declared all animals clean. Next, he spoke on how the Spirit had told him about the three men from Caesarea coming to Joppa, requesting that he come back with them to Caesarea to visit their master. "We entered that man's house—yes, a Roman centurion who feared our God—and he told us of an angel sent from God that visited him, *in his house*, and told him to find me. That's when the centurion asked me to speak.

"I felt an inner surge of the Spirit's presence as I began to speak. Based on the vision I received, I told him and his household that the God of our fathers was now revealing His salvation to all nations. Those of any nationality who showed evidence of turning to Him and did works of righteousness God would accept.

"I said that when Jesus is proclaimed and received as Master of anyone's life, peace would come to inhabit that person's inner life. Also, that word of peace and deliverance—which began at John the Baptizer's preaching of repentance—was revealed at the anointing of Jesus of Nazareth with the Holy Spirit and with power. Jesus demonstrated His anointing when He went about our land in empowerment of the Spirit, doing deeds of righteousness, healing many people, and delivering many people from the power of the evil one, God being with Him in presence and in power.

"Next, I said that we followers—especially the apostles—witnessed firsthand what Jesus did among us, especially how He was crucified, but then, God raised Him from the dead three days later and showed Him alive to hundreds of people, making special visitations to the apostles. What Jesus revealed to us after His resurrection, He commanded us to go in this same power and preach and to proclaim Jesus, not only as our Messiah, but as the Judge of the living and the dead.

"I also said that this same Jesus is the One who was prophesied to our forefathers through the prophets, that through His name, anyone who commits to follow Him will receive remission of sins.

"Brothers, I gave them the gospel in detail and would have continued to speak, except that I was interrupted by the baptism of God's Spirit—the Spirit of the living Christ—which came upon this Gentile household such as it did to us Jews when we were in the upper chamber, praying on the Day of Pentecost. We saw it occur, fully evidenced by the utterance of numerous dialects of the Gentiles present, which we all understood in our language what they were saying. And they were glorifying our God and our Savior, Jesus Christ. This reminded me of something our Lord said to us, how that 'John truly baptized with water, but you would be baptized with the Holy Spirit and fire.' Now if these uncircumcised Gentiles received the same Holy Spirit as we did, who am I to contend with our God? Would you have forbidden God to act in grace and mercy?"

Peter stopped speaking, allowing anyone else to respond. Little by little, praises to God were being voiced by the crowd. The priests who had objected withheld their criticisms.

"This means that God has truly granted repentance and salvation to eternal life to the Gentiles," remarked Elder James.

✝✝✝

Paul arrived in Tarsus when the sun was setting. He viewed the old sites of his boyhood days where walks northward toward the mountains made him think of faraway places he dreamed he would visit. Those dreamy walks were shortened by the determination of a father who observed his son's remarkable ability to comprehend and express things all around him. So he was sent off to Jerusalem to the school of Hillel to study the customs and the language of the Hebrews.

Paul made his way closer to his father's home, half excited to see his family and half filled with anxiety, wondering if somehow news of his conversion had reached his homeland. Perhaps one of his two sisters—one lived in Jerusalem—had told his father and mother of his conversion to the Way of the Nazarene? Would he be received by his father and mother?

But he was home now and Jesus was as real as anything he had seen or been taught in Jerusalem. He could not be silent about his new life in Jesus; however, he would not push his new name before the family.

Slowly, he unlocked the front gate and approached the front door. Although he knocked on the door gently, it sounded like a bell tower. He could not turn back now. The door opened, and there stood his mother. She had aged some since he last saw her, but the new wrinkles on her face quickly smoothed into nothingness as she smiled and embraced her son.

"Oh, Saul, my prayers have been answered; you've come home."

"Hello Mother; it's so good to see you again. You look so well."

She laughed. "Are you saying that I've put on some weight?"

He smiled. "No, Mother, you always look so perfect—my perfect mother . . . And Father?"

"Oh, he went to a meeting at the synagogue. You know he has to put in his two-coins worth on anything different they want to do down there."

"What's going on down there?"

"The usual: how much to spend on the writing utensils, new parchment purchases, the priest's allotments on the assets brought in this harvest—just the usual synagogue discussions. The place could use a woman's touch, but they won't let us women say or do a thing to freshen it up."

He smiled. "I'll try not to tell Father."

"But let's not talk about us—tell me what is going on in Jerusalem? And where have you been? We've heard about a lot of unrest stirring in the grand city over the followers of that Jesus-man from Nazareth."

Paul did not want to tell his story until both his mother and father were together. "I've got some things to tell you about this Jesus, but I want to wait until Father arrives. I've been on a ship a few days and would really appreciate a bath and change of clothing, if you don't mind."

"Well, I haven't seen you for over four years, so I guess I can wait a little longer. I'll heat you some bath water and see if I can find some of your old clothes to wear. Oh, I bet you're hungry too; my, my, where's my mind!?"

The bath was so soothing. Traveling always added a disgusting weight and odor to the body—especially traveling by ship. The salt spray and sun reflection off the water made the body feel like camel's leather. His mother had brought him a change of clothing, and he had just finished dressing when he heard his mother greet his father.

His father came to him. "Saul, my son!" They embraced.

"Father, so glad to see you again." His father was a slender man, but tall—taller than he was. But his black hair and facial features reminded him of the many priests of the Sanhedrin council—a true Jew of the tribe of Benjamin.

"I have longed to see you for several years. I have heard many things concerning your travels to Damascus. Please, let us break bread together, and you can tell me all about it."

"Yes, Father, I told Mother that I wanted to speak to you both concerning my travels."

"Ha! I'm surprised she let you bathe. Come now and let us dine for a while. Dear woman, would you join us for some bread and wine?"

His mother met them at the table; she had already set out some dishes for fruit, bread, and wine for the occasion. "Wow," said his father. "You should come home more often."

"Perhaps I will."

"Now tell me, I've heard some rumors of you causing some trouble in Damascus. I would not believe in such gossip-talk because I know you better than that. So give me an update and tell me exactly what you've been doing."

Paul stopped nibbling at a piece of fruit and took a small sip of drink. "Father, do you recall the history lessons of the prophets of old and how that God spoke to them directly? And many times, the prophets spoke against the established practices of our leaders."

"Yes, and some lost their lives over what they said as well."

"That is true, and that is why I would never go against our leaders unless God Himself had spoken to me." Paul did not wait for a response. "Three years ago, I gave a detailed speech of the Law of our fathers in a rather liberal synagogue in Jerusalem. This synagogue asked if anyone wished to speak against my presentation. It was announced that a man who was a follower of Jesus of Nazareth would give his presentation the following day. I was interested in what he would say; in fact, many priests came to hear his speech.

"It was an okay speech, but nothing to write home about. However, he accused our leaders to their faces that they crucified the Messiah when they crucified this Jesus. He said that Jesus had risen from the dead and was now alive."

His father shifted his body some and refilled his glass. "Really? I've heard this report before."

"And I judged it as nonsense. But this Stephen was taken before the high priest and the Sanhedrin. Again, he accused them of crucifying the Messiah. They cried out to stone him on the spot for blasphemy. Everything happened so fast that before I knew it we were at the Valley of Hinnom where I was elected the recorder of the event and witnessed his stoning. I think this was the straw that broke the camel's back, because the next day I was approached by Rabban Gamaliel and the high priest to start a campaign to round up the followers of the Way—"

"The Way?" asked his father.

"Yes, the followers of Jesus were explaining his death, burial, and resurrection as the new Way to have one's sins forgiven and to have peace with God and eternal life in heaven."

"Oh, I see."

"I began a local search party and arrested many followers in Jerusalem and had them put into prison. I was so successful that the high priest wanted me to go to Damascus because he had heard that many followers of the Way had migrated there. I was given papers to arrest these people and to bring them back to Jerusalem for trial."

So far, Paul's father and mother were enthralled over the experiences he had gone through in Jerusalem. He could see the pride of his parents as he presented his story. But what would they do in the next part? *My Lord,* he prayed to himself. *Give me the words and the strength to get through this part.*

"On the third day of travel, as I was nearing the city of Damascus, a great light appeared before me and my riders. It was midday and it was clear; nevertheless, this light was brighter than the sun. We all fell off our horses. But as I was shielding my eyes, behold, a voice began to speak out of the light. I looked and saw the figure of a man inside the light. And the voice spoke to me saying, 'Saul, Saul! Why are you persecuting me?' I lowered my head and said, 'Who are you, Lord?' Then he said, 'I am Jesus, whom you are persecuting'—"

His father interrupted. "What!? You say you saw and heard this Jesus speak to you out of a bright light!?"

"Father, it is the truth. It was midday and no storm clouds whatsoever."

His father held out his hand. "Stop; say no more!" Paul did not speak. His mother looked on as if she had seen a ghost. His father stood up. "Stand with me, Saul . . . now look straight into my eyes and tell me again: Did you really see this, or maybe the sun had burned on your body too much? Maybe this was a hallucination of some sort. Look at me, son, and tell me again what you saw."

Paul knew that his father wanted to give him a possible way out of this on-the-road revelation of which he had just spoken. He also knew his father could become unpredictable when he was angry. "Father, I spoke to this figure, and He was Jesus! I am as certain of this conversation with Him as I am of this conversation with you."

"Oh, you are? Well *this conversation* is now ended. Speak to me no more in this house about this Nazarene; I have heard enough! All the rumors I have been dismissing are true. You have rebelled against your family and your countrymen. You have rebelled against your faith and the God of your fathers."

"I thought that same way, Father, until I met Jesus."

"Stop it! I said speak no more of that name in this house. You will gather your belongings and get out of my house immediately! You are dead to me, do you understand? Now get out before I send word to the priest and elders and have you arrested and returned to Jerusalem in chains!"

Paul knew his father, so he spoke no further. His mother held her head down, trying to keep her sobbing from bursting into a river of tears and wailings. He quietly picked up his soiled garments and canvas bags and walked out the front door, into the dark night, devastated . . . and alone.

†††

The rugged terrain of Cilicia, against the beautiful mountains of the north and west, made for an excellent hideaway for someone who wanted to be left alone. And that was the life of Paul for the next ten years. His trade in tent-making allowed him to blend in with those who made their living off the trade routes to Antioch, Lystra, and Derbe. Paul was able to rent a room and managed to stay out of sight of the local priests. He did, however, speak to the Gentiles, using many dialects unknown to him, to tell them about Jesus. And he saw many come to follow the ways of the Master.

However, his main goal was to spend many hours in prayer and fasting in order for him to solidify his calling as a follower of Jesus. Frequently, Paul would go up into the mountains and find a cave to sit in and pray for hours—sometimes, he stayed in a cave for days on end. On numerous occasions, the Spirit of Jesus would speak to him and tell him many things that he needed to write down. Since his blindness, however, his vision was not very good. So, when he had gathered a small group of disciples, he asked several of them to write things down that the Lord had revealed to him.

Paul missed his family. He prayed often for them to come to know the truth. It was painful for him to be near his parents, yet unable to visit them. One day, while praying, Jesus spoke to Paul.

"Paul?"

"Yes, my Lord?"

The voice of the Lord was gentle. "Paul, I have heard your prayers for your family. It is not for you to know, at this time, if your father ever breaks away from his pride in order to be saved. Understand that a man is wrapped tightly in his self-image—so tightly, it is near impossible for him to be delivered."

"But Master, I miss them; can't You make my father see You as You did to me?"

"I can do anything, but that is not what's at stake here. You searched Me out to destroy My people. What you did, you did in ignorance, but your father has much pride in who he is and what he has accomplished in the name of the customs and traditions of the Law of the Pharisees. He had heard of Me several times before you arrived and has refused to open his heart toward Me. Your mother is still searching for the truth. Continue to abide in Me, Paul, and I will give you a family of disciples that you cannot count."

"Yes, my Lord. I will continue to speak in Your name and give testimony of Your mighty deeds. And I will stay here and wait upon You until You tell me to go elsewhere."

† † †

"Have things settled down in Judea?" asked Emperor Claudius.

Senator Demarkus responded. "The leaders of the people have settled down since the order of Caligula was disposed. His image at the temple was more than the leaders would allow."

"What about the high priest, Kantheras? Is he cooperating?"

"Yes, he is busy pleasing the opposing priests of the Pharisees. I think they were in shock that a Sadducee was placed over them as high priest."

The emperor laughed. "I can't get over their volatile religion. Why don't they give up on this unseen deity that they worship and follow me as their deity?"

"They seek a Jewish king to rule them."

"Then give the regions of Judea and Galilee to Agrippa and let him be their king. Give him authority to manage their religious leaders for a while. But keep a tight rein on him; make sure he knows I expect a peaceful, tax-paying territory."

Demarkus and the senate delegation dismissed themselves and left the emperor. Claudius walked over to the eastern window of his quarters. *I need peace in Judea.* His thoughts were on re-assigning more soldiers to the northern territory where a large battle of the Britons was occurring. But Judea was a different kind of battle. It was not brute strength with which the Jews fought. *These people will turn on each other for their beliefs in how to approach their God . . . so strange.*

✝ ✝ ✝

The gospel continued to spread throughout the Roman Empire. Barnabas was excited to hear of the growth of the Way in his homeland of Cyprus. The scattering of followers from Jerusalem, which started with the stoning of Stephen and the arrests by Saul of Tarsus, had actually turned out for the good of the assemblies. For a decade—as far as Phoenicia, Cyprus, and Cyrene—the word of salvation was proclaimed to the Jews. But even greater, many Gentiles were now turning to the Lord.

It was this news, when it reached Jerusalem, which gave Barnabas the assignment to go into these regions and confirm the work. This he did, with great excitement, for he was concerned that the mission to the other nationalities was being neglected by those in Judea.

When Barnabas reached Antioch, he found his contacts and heard of the great things which the Lord was doing in the local assemblies. Barnabas was invited to speak at a gathering on his first night in Antioch. He was always ready to give a word of encouragement to the followers. And that night he encouraged them to follow Jesus in a spirit of unity with one purpose of heart—that is, to add many more followers into the Lord's assembly. Barnabas did a great work in Antioch, being full of the Holy Spirit.

One evening, in a local meeting, Barnabas listened to testimonies of several of the followers. They each spoke of a man near Tarsus that was doing a great work among the Gentiles, and that they had come to believe in Jesus through this man's witness.

After the service was ended, Barnabas approached them. "I was blessed to hear of your faith in Christ, but tell me, who was the man in Tarsus to whom you made reference?"

"His name was Paul," said one of them.

"I thought so. And can you tell me how I might find him in Tarsus?" They gave him the location of a new assembly of followers just north of the city, meeting in a house.

The next day, Barnabas set out to travel to Tarsus. It was about a two-day's journey, but it passed quickly for him. He found the assembly just as it was about to begin a worship time. Barnabas sat in the back. The service began with several readings of Scripture and prayer. Next, there was music from several stringed instruments, which led into mass singing of a psalm. Occasionally, a prayer or a testimony was offered by someone. After about thirty or forty minutes of singing and testimonies, an elder stood up and invited Paul to speak.

Barnabas took note that Paul was much slimmer than when he first came to the Jerusalem villa. His color looked well, and, other than the eye patch, Paul looked better than ever. He preached an excellent message on Jesus as the Son of God.

After a couple hours, the meeting began to close. Paul looked for someone to dismiss them in prayer. That's when he recognized Barnabas. "Barnabas, my dear friend, I am pleased to see you. Would you be so kind as to dismiss this meeting in prayer?" Barnabas did so with great joy. After the prayer, Paul came to him and they embraced.

"Oh, what a sight for these poor eyes of mine!" said Paul. "One of them anyhow!" They both laughed.

"No, it's the other way around: What a joy to see you again!" They embraced again.

"What business brings you to Tarsus?"

"You, my friend. Several of your disciples gave testimony of your work here, so I had to come and see you."

"Oh, they did? I beg people not to mention my name because of the Jews who seek to destroy me."

"They didn't mention your name. After I heard them speak of the mighty work here, I approached them. They felt comfortable giving me your name. So, what's with the eye patch and what have you been doing all these years?"

"Since the blindness I received in Damascus, my eyes have never been the same. I have some ointment on one of them; this patch gives the ointment time to heal.

"But, Barnabas, the Lord has been gracious to me. I have sewn a few tents here and there, and I have camped out in a few caves in the mountains. Plus, our Lord has sent me into Syria and Cilicia to give testimony to some people who have since started new assemblies in their regions."

"Some Gentiles were in the mix, I presume?"

"Some? How about mostly Gentiles. Although I have visited the synagogues, the news of me has not allowed me the freedom to debate my people like I used to."

"I see."

"But I am not complaining; my greatest experiences have been my quiet times with our Lord. He continues to teach me so much in the Sacred Writings. I thought I knew some things, but I really know so little. Enough of me now; tell me, how is the work in Judea and Jerusalem?"

"Things have settled down, now that 'Saul of Tarsus' has moved on." They laughed. "Also, the change of emperors has caused enough squabbles among the council and the priests that they no longer have a solid front against the followers at this time. Also, Herod Agrippa's influence has grown; so far, he has not been a factor."

"It sounds as if things are going well," responded Paul.

"Not in Jerusalem, spiritually speaking."

"Oh, really?"

"Yes, since the dispersion, it appears the Holy Spirit is moving the headquarters of the Way to Antioch."

"Antioch of Syria?"

"Yes, I was sent to Antioch because of the news of many Gentiles coming to know and follow our Lord. When I heard the testimonies of your ministries, I knew I had to come and get you."

"Get me? Now, Barnabas, I'm trying to stay away from Judea as long as possible."

"I understand, but you must come to Antioch and help give the assemblies there some depth. The elders need teaching and training."

"My heart and my burden are in planting new assemblies where there are none. Barnabas, I want to go where no one else has gone."

"And I would love to go with you—someday. But Antioch has become ablaze with the glory of our Lord's presence. You must come and help me give the local elders some instruction. We can still go house to house and lead people to Jesus."

That got Paul's attention. "Let us spend some of this evening in prayer, and, unless the Lord says no, we will leave soon."

(A week later) Antioch was a major trade city. Many people of many nations came there to do business. Paul had visited the city a few times, on his travels through Syria, but never intended to stay and search out any followers. Barnabas took him to an elder of one of the assemblies; he, in turn, took the two throughout the city, showing them where a number of house assemblies were gathering. Occasionally, a follower met them on the street and thanked Paul for sharing the gospel with him previously.

Paul became more excited about staying as the day went on. That evening, there was a meeting planned at the main assembly. The elder asked Paul to speak. He agreed, but asked that he be able to go somewhere and refresh himself before the meeting.

"I already have a place for the both of you," replied the elder.

"How did you know we were coming?"

The elder looked at him. "How did you know to come?" They stared at each other momentarily.

Paul then smiled. "I suppose the Lord has been here for some time."

"Yes, He has, Paul," said Barnabas.

Barnabas and Paul remained busy in Antioch, preaching and teaching the followers of the Way. Paul had been given much from the Lord with which to teach and train the elders. The fellowships in Antioch grew in size and were strong in the Spirit. The Gentile influence and population was so great that Paul hardly ever thought about the dangers of a local priest or group of Jews hindering him. The fact was that in Antioch there was a blend of nationalities in every fellowship.

Although Paul taught in the local fellowships, his greatest joy was to take a group of disciples house to house to train them how to share the gospel for themselves. The power and presence of Christ was so obvious in their witnessing that the followers in Antioch became known as "Christians" (Christ-followers).

Living along the coastlands, it was hardly noticeable that there was a drought going on further inland. Its seriousness was not weighed in until a traveling prophet-evangelist from Jerusalem named Agabus came into the city and, in the power of the Spirit, showed how bad it was going to be in Judea and surrounding regions. (This great drought occurred during the days of Emperor Claudius.)

News of the drought circulated throughout the fellowships in Antioch. The elders of the fellowships began to encourage all to give a relief offering for the fellowships in Judea. This was received by all, and so the offering was gathered for several weeks. Then it was determined that the offering should be delivered to the Judean elders by Barnabas and Paul.

Acts 12:1-2

(One day earlier) "Has James returned?" John was anxious to see his big brother.

"No, I haven't seen him," replied Peter. "You might want to check the upper chamber."

"He's not up there," said Philip. "I just came from there. Try the dining area."

John walked across the courtyard toward the dining area. As he was approaching, he heard that familiar laugh—the one only James could produce. "My brother!" shouted John as he approached James and several other men. They had been together for most of the afternoon, sharing the gospel with the families of numerous priests.

"John, you should have been there tonight; there were a dozen or more men and women of the priest's servants, each listening to the good news of deliverance."

"My brother, I wish to speak with you in private."

"Oh, sure—pardon us, will you?" James asked the others. The sons of Zebedee walked away to a different area of the courtyard. "What is on your mind, little brother?"

"James, I feel we need to move on from the priestly quarters; I sense in my heart a need for us to head for other regions."

"I know that day is coming, but the needs are so great among the leaders' families. Listen, tonight several men made commitments to become followers of Jesus. The atmosphere was charged with excitement!"

"James, it's dangerous for us to stay in one place; we need to move on."

"I tell you what, let me commit it to prayer, and we will discuss this further tomorrow night . . . agreed?"

John could read his brother better than any man and knew when it was his final answer. "Okay, tomorrow, and I will pray with you on this matter. Just be safe, you hear?"

James smiled. "Hey, it's me." He then turned away from John and joined the men with whom he was talking.

"Tomorrow," said one of the men, "we will see an even greater response." Both men agreed to meet James at the servants' quarters near the end of the day.

† † †

"So this is the kingdom I inherited!?" Herod Agrippa I was staring at the shriveled fruit and dried vegetables on his table. He was angry that his servants could find no fresh food for his dinner guests.

"I will not serve guests with this poor excuse of food!"

"But your Majesty, we cannot control the weather," said the head chef. "We've looked throughout Judea and can find no better." The chef began trembling as the king walked toward him.

"Then go beyond Judea! Go into the northern mountains or go to Egypt—go wherever you must go, but GO!"

"But your Majesty, fruits and vegetables won't stay fresh from that distance—we've already tried."

"Guards!" Several soldiers came into the dining area. "Take this poor excuse of a cook and show him the prison where he can enjoy this kind of food." The guards grabbed the chef and removed him from the room.

"Housemaster!?" Quickly, another man entered the room. "Yes, your Majesty?"

"Send couriers throughout the city and the regions, and find me someone who can bring life back into this food. I want no excuses; do you understand?"

The housemaster bowed as he exited the room. Agrippa could not believe that a drought had strangled the land for years now. *I have carried on the traditional sacrifices on behalf of our forefathers' God, and this is how He repays me?* He continued to think of how things were when his grandfather was king. Herod the Great provided the finest of dinners in the country and rivaled any spread throughout the empire.

"Guards!" Again, several soldiers appeared. "Get me the high priest; tell him it is urgent!"

†††

"I said I would look into it!" Simon Kantheras ben Boethus was impatient with the council's continual bickering over the less-than-desired meat rationings for the priests and their families. The drought was affecting all levels of the Judean populace. This meant that the sacrificial animals were thinner and older—tougher meat on which to chew!

He stormed out of the council chambers and retreated to his quarters. He promised a new era among the Sanhedrin—one of cooperation and stability. But the drought was not helping his promise.

The Pharisees remained contrary because of their loss of control of the high priesthood. They wanted the family of Annas to maintain control, but Agrippa was given charge by the emperor to appoint the high priest, and he was ready for a fresh start.

Had things changed for the better since the appointment of Kantheras? Hardly; the drought continued to be blamed on the religious leaders and their inability to get relief for the region. The temple treasury was at a record low, and the animals offered to the priests were hardly without blemishes. But it was all they had.

Kantheras was home now, removing his dress clothing. The "war of words" meeting was over. Relationships and tempers thinned among the Sanhedrin. He was never quite sure he would survive another day without an uprising against him. *Can anything worse happen?* he wondered.

"Most noble Lord?" It was Kantheras' chief priest. "Yes? What is it?"

"The king, Herod Agrippa, requests your presence immediately—he says it is urgent."

Oh, why did I even think this!? "Yes, send me some helpers to come suit me; oh, and you will join me for this meeting."

In less than an hour, the high priest and his entourage entered Herod's palace. Usually, when the high priest was called by the king, there were favors to be exchanged, but this time things were different. The guests were shown into the dining area where Agrippa reclined.

It was customary for even the king to stand and exchange bows to the high priest, but Agrippa made no effort to stand. Kantheras stood near the far end of the table as the king finally looked in his direction.

"High Priest, look at this table," said Agrippa without a smile. "I see nothing but death lying before the king and his guests." Several servants were waving palm branches, trying to keep the flies off the spread. Kantheras surveyed the food. It was as edible as any he had seen lately, but, of course, no fruit or vegetable was as attractive as the days gone by.

"Your Majesty, shall I offer a blessing upon this for your own safety and health?"

The king looked at him in silence for a moment. He then burst out in an eerie laugh. "You think I sent for you so that you may pray for my health? Ha!" He stood up and began to walk toward the high priest. "My kingdom is starving, I cannot have guests from other regions to dine with me, and you priests have done nothing to get our God to favor us! I appointed you as high priest and is this what I get in return!?"

The high priest knew the shrewdness of the Herods and that they craved blood for the consequences of unfavorable situations. A diversion was needed. "Your Majesty, perhaps our God would favor us more kindly if the king addressed the rebellion occurring in his kingdom."

The king moved in closer to him. "What are you talking about? I know of no such rebellion."

"Your Majesty, for years, there has been a following of a man—Jesus of Nazareth—that has grown in popularity among our people. We have tried, several times, to weaken and destroy this rebellion against our traditions, but they continue to grow."

"And why can't you stop them?"

"I have enough guards for the temple grounds, but not enough to chase through the city and countryside for rebels."

"And you blame these rebels for our drought?"

Kantheras nodded. "As soon as Antipas withdrew his support for our cause, this drought came upon us! Help us now, and we will see the favor of God upon our land once again." It was a calculated risk for Kantheras to turn the tables back onto the king, but his statement was needed to divert the king's rage to a common enemy.

The king backed away from him. "I see, and what is your recommendation?"

"Send your soldiers to harass their fellowships. Plant spies in their meetings. Arrest their leaders."

The king thought momentarily . . . "I'll do that—and more!" He walked away from the high priest and gulped down some wine. "Our God requires a sacrifice to appease sin, does He not?" The high priest nodded. "So, I will find one among their leaders and do something to get the rebels' attention *and* to appease our God."

This caused the wheels to turn in the high priest's mind. "There is one of them who has befriended some of the priests' families, a son of a former priest—James ben Zebedee—who continues to show kindness and teaches the beliefs of this new Way."

"And you know the whereabouts of this man?"

"Some of my servants can find out where they meet."

"Then take four of my guards with your servants and bring this man to me immediately!"

Kantheras bowed. "Yes, your Majesty; as you wish."

†††

James was up early the next morning in prayer. "My Lord, I wish to speak to you about this great need among our priestly leaders." He remembered his brother's concern and request to change his location. The drought had stricken all the land and everyone was sensing a spirit of desperateness in the air.

"Lord Jesus, let me be effective in reaching the priests and their families. Let these servants be an inroad to the priests. Let the priests have open hearts today, I pray." James continued to pray for several hours before going to the dining area for breakfast.

When he approached the dining area, several of the apostles, Elder James, and Hamath were eating. "I trust you saved a bite for me?" he asked as he put his arm on Hamath's shoulder.

Hamath grunted and managed a semi-smile, with a few pieces of egg hanging on his lower lip. "There is bread, eggs, and juice left—if you hurry!" Hamath never ate more than he should, but he did eat more than most men.

"Always good to know you will save a portion for the needy—and I am needy!" James reclined beside him and blessed the Lord for his friends and the food.

"So what was John so anxious to see you about last night?" asked Peter.

James chased down a large bite of breakfast with some juice. "Oh, he wants me to pray about moving to a different region."

"Oh, I see. And . . . ?"

"And I said I would pray about it, and I have been praying much of the morning for wisdom in this change of venue."

"He's concerned about the priests, isn't he?"

"Yes, but I am seeing some intense interest in numerous servants about following the Way of our Master. I believe I am at a turning point in reaching some additional priests."

"Maybe so, James, but do remember your little brother has your interests in mind as well; plus, he has a very discerning spirit on these matters."

"I understand . . . Peter, it's been over ten years now since our Lord departed; why haven't we seen more of the city converted to the Way?"

Peter was quick to reply. "The Spirit is leaving this city, James. Remember when Jesus stopped and wept over Jerusalem? He said this city will become desolate. I think the Spirit is leaving here, and perhaps it is time we do the same."

"Now you're sounding more like my brother." They laughed. James was not ready to give up on his mission to the priests. He grew up around some of their families. "I will be meeting late this evening for another testimony service, and I promise to continue to pray about moving on."

"Do that, my brother, and I will join you and John in this prayer . . . Well, I must be gone; I've an appointment with an elder that James, John, and I are training on the east side of the city."

"Did I hear my name?" Elder James spoke as he turned in Peter's direction.

"Yes, and it's time for us to pray and head further east. Let's find John and be about the Lord's business."

That left James and Hamath. "Hamath, do you have anything going on later today? I was wondering if you might want to accompany me to the priests' servants' quarters?"

"Maybe; Philip and I are looking for feed for the animals. Very hard to feed animals under the current drought."

"I understand. Well, if you are finished, I plan to leave here before the usual evening mealtime. I like to get to the servants' quarters as they are finishing up the meal chores. And sometimes they save me a special leftover treat."

Hamath managed a smile. "I will try to join you."

James left the table and returned to the upper chamber. He saw Elder James, John, and Peter huddled in prayer. He quietly made his way past the praying men and found a secluded spot.

"My Lord Jesus, I continue to pray for your harvest to be great today. Let me be used of you to reach many of the priests and their households." James continued to pray for several hours. Then he heard a voice.

"James, My faithful friend," the Lord said.

James bowed even lower. "Yes, my Lord?"

"Are you willing to drink the cup that I drank?"

James remembered this statement; Jesus had asked it before when his mother had asked Jesus if he and John could rule on the immediate sides of Jesus in heaven. This was before the Lord had been beaten and crucified. James spoke softly. "Yes, my Master, I am willing."

"And are you willing to be baptized with My baptism?"

Again James was slow to respond, but he was sure that he would do whatever was necessary to win the lost priests. "Yes, my Lord, I am willing."

"Indeed you are, My friend—My dearly loved one. Be strong and faithful to the end and you will judge the nations with Me."

"But Lord, should I move on with John?" The Lord's voice began to fade away as James heard once more, "Be strong and faithful to the end . . ." James sat up and reviewed in his mind the things that he, John, and Peter, as disciples, had spoken about with Jesus. They tried to fathom the depths of the Lord's words, but they often discovered that when Jesus spoke, He spoke from an eternal perspective—a perspective that they could not see nor perceive until later on. What Jesus was teaching them, early on, was to remain faithful to His words to the end and to focus on the bigger picture of the plans of the Father.

"My Lord, forgive me for being so selfish and short-sighted; I will follow You to the end . . . regardless."

"Have you seen James?" asked Hamath, as he neared the dining area. Some of the ladies shook their heads, "No." Hamath grunted. He had decided to come in from the fields early to be available to go with James. He knew an approximate area where the priests and their quarters were located, but was not sure where the meetings took place. As he was turning away, a lady handed him a small cloth—it was Mary, the mother of Jesus.

"Take this, my child," she said to Hamath. "A small parcel of bread can feed many hearts of resistance."

Hamath smiled and could only respond with a grunt. He was always amazed at the peace that was in the face of his Lord's mother. He walked toward the front gates and turned toward the temple grounds.

Many priests had special provisions given them by the people, and the high priest kept the elder priests in nearby quarters for the daily maintenance of the temple and the offering of the sacrifices. The area was sprinkled with temple guards—some that knew of Hamath and some that did not. Those who knew him knew that he had served his time as one who helped other zealots commit crimes of terror. The others, however, viewed him with suspicion and maintained an alert position around him. Therefore, Hamath steered clear of the temple area as much as possible.

Now, he was heading in that dreaded direction again. He did not carry a dagger anymore; however, his size continued to demand a certain amount of respect wherever he went. As he neared the temple, he turned to go down a side street that he remembered from a previous trip he and Barabbas had taken. It led toward the priests' quarters, and, if you turned to the left just before the quarters, you would be heading for the city prison grounds.

Hamath could not hide his size, but he had learned how to drive out the movements and stares around him; however, the noise ahead alerted him. Several people were running in his direction. They were quiet but determined to get off the street as quickly as possible. He knew they were afraid because no one stopped to warn him; he grabbed the arm of the next runner and lifted him off the ground.

"Please let me go!"

"What are you running from?"

"Soldiers—four heavily armed soldiers and some priests broke up our meeting with a leader of the Nazarene."

"What was his name?"

"Please, let me go!"

"His name?" Hamath squeezed the man's arm a bit harder.

"James—his name was James; they arrested him by order of Herod!"

Hamath dropped the man who quickly darted into the evening shadows of the approaching night. He grunted.

†††

(Thirty minutes earlier) "If He was the Messiah, why didn't He present Himself to our leaders and show Himself as the Deliverer? Why didn't He do signs and wonders before them to convince them?" These were some of the questions being asked to James as he taught several households of the priests.

"He did many signs and wonders throughout Judea and Galilee," he responded. "Many priests and scribes followed us from all regions, and they saw what Jesus did, but they did not like what He said."

"What do you mean?" asked a priest.

"He demanded a surrender of one's heart and soul to His ways, but the religious leaders were not willing to let go of the traditions—traditions that go far beyond the scope and intent of Moses and the Prophets. Go back into the Sacred Writings and read them carefully. Listen to the prophets calling for a sacrifice of obedience—obedience to God's words."

"Jesus of Nazareth is our Deliverer?" asked the priest, more to himself than others. "The prophets said our Messiah would come from the City of David, not Galilee."

"Jesus was born in Bethlehem, but moved later to Nazareth. But Herod wanted Him dead, so an angel of God sent His parents to Egypt. Later they returned and resettled in Nazareth because the danger from the Herodian family continued to exist." While

James continued to teach, the two priests quietly disappeared through the rear entryway.

"Be faithful to the end . . ." James heard the Lord whisper to him again.

James sensed a surge of spiritual power. "Listen to me now; the danger is still among us who believe. The Herodians and the religious leaders this very day are corroborating together to destroy the Way of deliverance—of salvation—of any who commit their lives to the Christ. They are so blind to what is happening around them in this city that they will lose everything in which they place their hope in order to keep their status. They—"

Suddenly the door burst open with a loud bang. Several children who had dozed off screamed. Temple soldiers brandished their swords. "Don't anyone try to leave this room!" But the back exit was not guarded; therefore, numerous listeners escaped from the house. James and several others stood before the soldiers.

"These men are passersby; you don't need them. I am the one you are looking for." James looked steadfastly into the eye of the captain of the soldiers. The captain felt a sudden fear in his heart—a fear he felt once before when dealing with these followers of the Nazarene.

"Leave them here," the captain told the others. "This man will do." They tied ropes around James' hands and waist, and then they tied a rope to the other rope in order to pull him. They brought him outside. The priest who had been inside the house with him—the one asking many questions—stood there with several other priests. The captain approached him. "Is this one of their leaders?"

"It is," the priest replied.

"Fine, you come with us."

The priest obliged and walked alongside of James. He looked at James, thinking he would see terror on his face. Instead, there was an aura of peace and confidence. This caused the priest to think about his own dissatisfaction with the high priest and the

Herodian family. He felt emptiness in his heart and genuinely wanted what James possessed—peace with God.

The clanging of the temple guards always annoyed Agrippa. They seemed to be louder when they had accomplished the king's wish. As they noisily entered, a few of the servants scurried out of the king's view, like mice that had been discovered by a stalking cat. James was marched before the king's judgment seat. Numerous guards and priests joined in the gathering.

Agrippa thought it beneath his title to interrogate this man. James, on the other hand, faced the king. As a boy, he remembered playing in the courtyard with some of the Herodian children. The Zebedees were a part of the priestly team that visited the king's palace often.

"Do you see any food on my table?" Agrippa asked as he pointed to a side table. James said nothing. "The answer is obvious, don't you agree? I have asked the high priest if there is a reason for this dreadful drought. It seems that the more this Way of the Nazarene grows in followers, the greater our drought has become . . . are you hungry?"

"I am nourished by doing the will of God," James replied.

Agrippa stood up, walked over to James, and slapped his face. Kantheras appeared at the same time and received the attention of the gathering. Agrippa turned toward the high priest and spoke—much louder this time. "And I intend to appease our angry God by offering him a sacrifice—a living sacrifice!"

Kantheras glanced at James and then back to the king. He gave the king a nod. This signal gave Agrippa the approval he was looking for. "Guards, take him to the post of scourging—but don't tie him to it. Take a sponge and some water and clean him up for the ceremony."

James was led out the side door with a throng of guards. The king stared at the high priest and the few priests who remained. "You want to be rid of these followers of the Nazarene?"

"Yes, we do," replied Kantheras.

"Then follow me, and I will show you what it takes to stop an uprising." Agrippa turned for the side door where James previously walked through. Outside, James was stripped of his outer garments. Then the soldiers began throwing water-filled sponges at James and laughing. "Stop toying with the sacrifice!" the king shouted. "Lay him down on the table and tie him securely."

James began to leave the presence of the gathering and felt less pain as the soldiers readied him for whatever they planned to do. He thought he could hear his Master again . . . yes, it *was* Him! And there his Master stood, unseen by the others, as the Lord gently wiped some of the dripping water from his head.

"My baptism is your coronation into glory, My beloved." James smiled as the lesser king looked on.

"Who wishes to offer the sacrifice to our God?" asked Agrippa, as he motioned for a soldier to pull over to him his sword cabinet. The soldier obliged and opened the cabinet door, revealing several large-bladed swords. Agrippa inspected each one and carefully pulled out the largest in the cabinet. He walked over to Kantheras to offer the sword to him—he refused it.

"No one better than the king himself should have this honor before the Most High God," said Kantheras.

The king turned to the soldier. "Heat the blade!" He faced the high priest once again. Without looking, he gave another command: "Sponge with water!" A guard brought it to him. Agrippa then gave it to the high priest. "Wash my hands." Kantheras began a ceremonial incantation as he recited a cleansing ritual for a sacrifice. "Wash my head and my feet!" The high priest continued to circle the king, immersing him in the ceremonial cleansing.

James continued to smile and began talking to his Master. The priest, who had earlier questioned him and identified him before the guards, looked at James; his head had been turned toward the priests. Again, he saw the peace that he wanted!

"My beloved," said Jesus to James. "You see that priest, the one in whose house you gave a testimony?"

James moved his head a little. "Yes, my Lord, I see him."

"He will soon join us and will become a catalyst for many priests to follow Me."

"Really?" James tried to see him more clearly.

"Your baptism in death will bring forth more fruit than you ever imagined possible. Your faithfulness to be all and to give all, to the end, speaks louder than any ritual he has ever witnessed. He now believes My words—My words that you have spoken to him."

Agrippa turned away from the high priest and took the sword and raised it high above his head as he walked around the staging table upon which the sacrifice laid. The sword's blade had an amber-red glow. He stopped at the backside of James, facing the priests. He methodically lowered the sword to the neck of James. Then he raised it high again and—

"Stop!" cried out the believing priest. "I also believe in Jesus, that He is the Son of God!"

The king lowered the sword. "You do?"

"Yes, I am renouncing my claim to my life—I now belong to Jesus, and I have been delivered from my sins." The priests around him began to curse him and to push him out of their ranks. Before he knew it, he was standing alone, facing James. "Yes, my brother," he spoke to James. "I believe." They both began to smile. "Forgive me for participating in your arrest."

James thought for a moment. "'Unless you release your seeds and bury them into the soil, they remain as seeds'—Jesus taught us that. When you release your life into His, you are buried with Him in His death that, just like Him, you will be raised to spring forth into real life."

Agrippa had heard enough. "So, if you wish to be like him . . . then join him. Lay with him."

The priest looked at James and then looked at Agrippa. He smiled at the king and began to move toward James. He slowly raised himself up on the table and lay back-to-back against him, adjusting his neck to be at the same location as James'. The soldiers tied both men together.

Agrippa turned to a guard. "Reheat the edge, quickly!"

"His love," said James, "removes all fear."

"Yes," said the priest. "I now know His perfect peace."

In a matter of minutes, the sword was reheated, sharpened, and given back to the king. This time, he made no fanfare; he quickly came to the table, raised his sword, and repeatedly hacked away until the heads of both men were severed. The area became silent.

Agrippa raised the head of James above his own. "This is how you appease an angry God!"

The quietness of the event was slowly and softly broken when a priest began to say, "Amen, amen." The phrase was repeated over and over until many of those standing with the high priest chanted it loudly: "AMEN, AMEN! . . . AMEN, AMEN!" During the frenzied chanting, no one noticed a large figure of a man, looking over a distant wall, observing for a moment the glory of God shining on a sacrificial table.

Pronunciation Key for Some Characters

Inaros – In-NAH-rus

Jabeth – JAY-beth

Sorenthasas – So-ren-THAY-sas

Soren – So-ren

Hamath – HAY-muth

Perpetua – Per-pa-TU-ah

Petronilla – Pet-tra-NEE-ah

Procula – PRO-cu-la

Pilo – PEE-low

✝✝✝

Bibliography

The Scriptures used in this series are paraphrased by the author; any similarity with any copyrighted editions of Scriptures is purely incidental. The author has consulted the following works:

Baker, Simon. *Ancient Rome – The Rise and Fall of an Empire* (Croydon: BBC Books, an imprint of Ebury Publishing, 2006)

Complete Word Study New Testament with Parallel Greek, by Spiros Zodhiates, ed. (Chattanooga: AMG Publishers, 1992)

Chronological Bible, Edward Reese, ed. (Nashville: Regal Publishers, 1977)

Interlinear Bible, Greek / English, Volume IV, New Testament, Jay P. Green, Sr., ed. (Hendrickson Publishers, 1985)

Jones, Timothy Paul. *Bible Time Line* (Torrance: Rose Publishing, Inc. 2001)

Liberty Annotated Study Bible, King James Version, Jerry Falwell, ed. (Lynchburg: Liberty University, 1988)

New King James Version (Nashville: Thomas Nelson, Inc., 1982)

Sterling, John. *An Atlas Illustrating the Acts of the Apostles and the Epistles* (London: George Philip & Son Ltd., 1954)

About the Author

Johnnie R. Jones was saved in Hawaii in 1971. He was licensed to preach in 1974 and ordained in 1976. He has pastored churches in Virginia, Alaska, and Texas. He is a graduate of Tunstall High School, Dry Fork, Virginia; Dallas Baptist University, Dallas, Texas; and Southwestern Baptist Theological Seminary, Fort Worth, Texas. After high school, Johnnie served four years in the U.S. Air Force.

Johnnie has written articles for the *Southern Baptist Texan* and has written numerous articles for several daily newspapers. He is chief editor and publicist for SYD Publications, McKinney, Texas. He has authored four books and numerous booklets.

Johnnie is currently founder and revivalist of His Abounding Grace Ministries, Inc., McKinney, Texas. This is volume one of a series of novels based on the first century A.D.

Contact Information

His Abounding Grace Ministries, Inc.
(501c3 nonprofit)
3101 Woodson Drive
McKinney, TX 75070

Phone: 214-544-5920
Website: www.HisAboundingGrace.org
Email: jj@HisAboundingGrace.org

About the Acts Novel Series

There is no literary work greater than the Holy Bible. Whether you read in the Hebrew Bible (called the Old Testament by Christians) or the New Testament, you will find a God who consistently works among people to bring holy living, justice, and peace. Specifically, in the New Testament you will find the Creator God presenting a solution to mankind's fundamental need of deliverance from its sin nature—that part of mankind that is egotistically self-serving.

In *Acts of the Spirit-Filled*, you will experience the passion, drama, and results of first-century people who choose between good and evil. You will discover how God provided them with a solution to their basic need of deliverance. The timing and scenes of *Acts of the Spirit-Filled* are from the Book of Acts of the New Testament. If you have read this particular book in your Bible, you know there are many gaps surrounding many of the events that occur. For the most part, we have to use our imaginations as to what led to certain events, trips, and crises of the early followers.

Acts of the Spirit-Filled fills in many of the gaps in the Book of Acts with fictional dialog, narration, and historical events that allow the reader to experience the emotions and drama of the New Testament characters who participated in the birth of the church.

There are multiple novels being prepared for publishing in the series of *Acts of the Spirit-Filled.*

Other books by this Author

50/50 Chance to Live

SECOND EDTION

© 2009; 2012; 350 pages

100+ pictures

From Virginia to Texas to Hawaii and Alaska follow the tracks of one man's trail that slipped through the grips of death five times, while touching the lives of thousands.

Order online at: www.HisAboundingGrace.org

"Here is the story of a man and his family who have walked through difficulties as severe as anyone can face . . ."
–Dr. Paige Patterson, President,
Southwestern Baptist Theological Seminary

". . . an outstanding journal of one man's triumph over seemingly impossible circumstances. It is a must-read!"
–Dr. Jimmy Draper, President Emeritus,
LifeWay Christian Resources

Transformed!

The Power of God's Presence

Solid, biblically-based principles for spiritual growth!

There's more to a marriage than the wedding day! And there's more to the Christian life than the first day of salvation! Discover the beauty of a transformed life in Jesus Christ. It's called the "new and living way" of reaching your potential through an intimate, maturing relationship with Him.

Children's Guide to Discovering Jesus

Interactive pages filled with puzzles, pictures, and Bible verses that a parent, children's leader, or elementary to middle school children can use to help them discover what it means to become a Christian. Covers baptism and Christian growth as well.

8½ x 11 – 10 activity pages

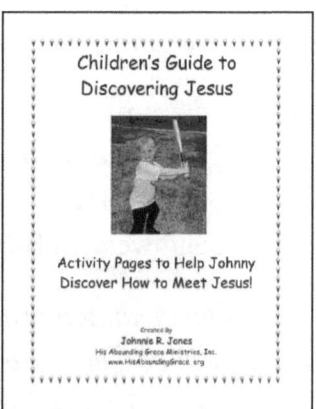

Diakonos – Deacon
A Word Study and Service Guide for the
Deacon Ministry

For individual or group study, seeking the biblical foundation for a servant-based ministry

8½ x 11 – 50 pages

διακονοσ

Diakonos

A Word Study
and
Service Guide
for the
Deacon Ministry

For Individual or Group Study
for Pastors, Deacons, & Anyone
Seeking Biblical Foundations
for Ministry

by
Johnnie R. Jones

One Reader Comments: *"Wow! It is rich with information. I wish every church would make it required reading for all deacons."*

P.E.D.A.L. Plan for Evangelism

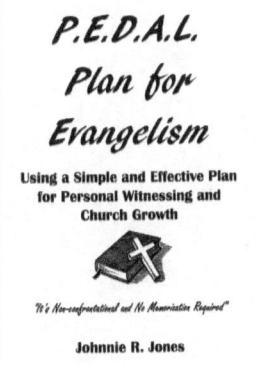

P.E.D.A.L.
Plan for
Evangelism

Using a Simple and Effective Plan for Personal Witnessing and Church Growth

"It's Non-confrontational and No Memorization Required"

Johnnie R. Jones

Be a Powerful Witness . . .
in Personal Prayers.

It's non-confrontational and no memorization required!

Online Orders: **www.HisAboundingGrace.org**;

Acts of the Spirit-Filled is also available in paperback and eBook editions at **www.crosshousebooks.com**.

Qty.	Title

____ TRANSFORMED! *The Power of God's Presence*
© 2010 - Comes with NEW Study Guide!
Price per book: $14.95*

____ 50/50 CHANCE TO LIVE *In the Grips of Death*
© 2009; 2012 SECOND EDITION
Price per book: $19.95*

____ CHILDREN'S GUIDE TO DISCOVERING JESUS –
Activity Pages
© 2010
Price per booklet: $4.95*

____ DIAKONOS – *Deacon Word Study and Service Guide*
© 2005, 2009
Price per booklet: $9.95*

____ **P.E.D.A.L.** PLAN FOR EVANGELISM
© 2012
Price per booklet: $2.95*

____ Acts of the Spirit-Filled: *A Novel of the First Century*
© 2013.
Also available at crosshousebooks.com in paperback
and eBook formats; pbk: $19.95*

*Prices are subject to change. Texas residents, please add 8.25%
sales tax. Price includes standard shipping charges in the U.S.*

Order at: www.HisAboundingGrace.org

*All orders in the U.S. will be shipped U. S. Postal Service, unless otherwise
requested. Additional shipping charges may be added for other locations or
methods of shipping.* Contact: **jj@HisAboundingGrace.org**